Untruly Yours
101 Lies

Untruly Yours
101 Lies

Subhadip Chakraborty

Srishti
PUBLISHERS & DISTRIBUTORS

SRISHTI PUBLISHERS & DISTRIBUTORS
N-16, C. R. Park
New Delhi 110 019
editorial@srishtipublishers.com

First published by
Srishti Publishers & Distributors in 2014

Typeset by Eshu Graphic

PROLOGUE

I stood there silently, my posture calm, the tormented soul suppressed. My eyes were a bit puffy though I could blame it on my insomnia,

At moments I would feel dizzy and sigh silently. It was all so invisible and indistinguishable from my usual personality that only my heart could register it.

So, was it really possible?

Was love really so strong that it could break any person, no matter how tough he would project himself to be?

That it could completely wash away the definition of one's existence and prove every step of his life a mistake?

Love and life were so confused that they were always infused together, members of the same string, pull one, the other house comes down. But hey, that was never the story of a shrewd, smart and bad bloke.

Damn! How could it end up being mine?

People besides me were crying, mourning, aghast and broken.

They would take out their handkerchiefs every now and then and wipe away their sorrows, they could do it.

I was stuck, as if petrified, as if all my responses had gone numb. That was so not me. I tried to cry, at least for the sake of my heart but my tears had frozen in the cold cruel wind. I was helpless and for the first time, felt my head waver.

Oh, get a grip, dude, I thought to myself. I repeated the statement for a count to infinity and then they opened the coffin.

My lips twitched and I felt my heart turning into a block of iron. The priest started the last prayer. The requiem had begun and my story had ended.

Katie lay there, silent, the life gone out of her eyes. Hail the sarcasm of life, the girl who talked the most was so silent today that it made the Sunday morning ominous. I saw Katie's Mom run towards her, hug her and yelp in indelible pain, I saw General uncle fall to his knees as others hurried to hold him. And then, I saw her. Oh, Katie.

I need to leave ... can't take it anymore ...

But then I see ... I discover the last lie...

VOLUME 1

Port Blair Diaries

LIE 001

They say that every substance in this universe has logic, a reason, a master plan that guides it, pretty scientific, huh?! I mean, the scientists and the mathematicians were so crazy that they could even define small and indivisible a substance like atoms, they had explanations like the "butterfly effect" and "theory of everything" that would take you hours to figure out the math behind it.

So, the point here is that there's this origin to everything somewhere, even to me, or to be precise, my lies.

Aakash was born early on Thursday, a rainy August morning, 13th, 1987.

But this incident dates back three years from then.

Scene 1:

It starts off with the dull background of a Government office. It's the Ministry of Finance and you could see people dozing off on their tables, yawning, flexing their muscles, glum, bored to death.

The tubelight is constantly flickering, with every sign of passing out any moment, and the walls could collapse any time now.

At table 4, a thin, frail bespectacled guy is seated. His hair is long and cut in the 1970s style.

He is all sweaty and solving arithmetic calculations with titanic concentration. Nothing in the world can distract this young, stereotype, hard working employee from his goals ... wait a minute, did I say 'nothing'?

Enter the young lady in the blue jacket. Her hair is silky, with a fragrance of lilies, her complexion sparkling gold with a slight blush on her dimple face. Her posture is timid and benevolent and when she walks, she carries herself with a grace that is bewitching. She's the girl whom James Blunt would've gladly dedicated his '*You're beautiful*' song with delight and gratitude.

She walks up to the bespectacled guy at table 4, "Excuse me."

Now, this employee is so awestruck he spills ink all over his worksheets.

"Oh, my God, I'm terribly sorry," she cries.

"No, don't be," the panicky employee manages with a voice so serene, the birds outside start humming in unison.

"Umm ... let me help you with these," she says picking the papers up along with the guy.

"So," stammers the guy trying to strike a conversation, "You wanted to enquire something, did you?"

He could feel all thirty pairs of eyes of his colleagues staring at him, engrossed and highly entertained.

"Yeah," the charismatic princess speaks slowly, "Umm ... can you please guide me to the manager's office? I am here for an interview".

"Ah, it would be a pleasure," says the employee as he gulps down some ink from the open bottle accidentally mistaking it for water. He coughs and she is all worried; she takes out her handkerchief and wipes ink from his lips. There are giggles and hooting. Now that's a great working day out here!

"Oh, heavens," the guy is embarrassed as hell, "take the stairs and the first right."

He manages to clean his face while going to the washroom.

There's applause and more hooting as she disappears up the aisle and the guy down the washroom.

✶ ✶ ✶

He finds her waiting for the bus the next day. The princess looks upset and the employee, determined. He prays in the usual way: "Oh, God ... help me this time, I'll be indebted to you for life."

Then swiftly he walks up to her.

Scene 2:

"Err ... hello there, ma'am. Do you recognise me?"

She is taken by surprise, there's a hint of recognition which gives way to a million dollar smile.

"Why, of course, you are the guy who drank ink!" She has a sense of humour. The employee goes all topsy-turvy.

"Yeah, the very same." he gives a kinda cute smile, the one that girls adore and think, "aww, how sweet!!"

"So", he continues, "Did you get the job?"

"Oh! That ...," the woman becomes sad, "...no, I didn't".

I swear to God the guy's 'heart-break' had a sound to it, like that of shattering glass!

"Anyways, I really needed it." She gives a sad smile.

"Oh! I'm so sorry to know that." the guy is crestfallen.

"I just wish somebody could help me get another chance." The woman sighs. "Just someone who could help."

"I'm the one."

Really?! You filmy cowboy!

That's what even the employee thought after he had said it.

"Really?" The woman looked so hopeful, you could see her cheeks going red with a fresh dose of blood.

"Err ... umm ... you know ... maybe, ... yeah," the guy couldn't let her sweetheart be disappointed, so he made the first mistake ...

The origin of it all.

See, here's where it started.

HE LIED.

"Yeah, you know what, why don't we meet tomorrow at the Café, at East Street and we'll discuss your chances," the guy made it all up.

"Do you really think I still have a chance?" the girl almost pleaded.

No ... there was no vacancy.

"Yes, absolutely," the guy uttered.

"See, I've a lot of connections. I'll see what I can do for you."

He had no connection, only love-connection!

"Great!" she jumped in happiness and almost hugged our liar-hero.

"Okay then," she managed, blushing.

"Yup, okay," he said, his heart skipping a beat.
"Um ... by the way, I didn't catch your name."
"Oh. It's **Radhika**. And you are?"
Rajesh Khanna.
"**Anshuman**."

✳ ✳ ✳ Character Analysis ✳ ✳ ✳

Mr Anshuman Roy is my dad.
Late Mrs Radhika Roy, my mom.
and I ... well, I am the result of the 1st lie, I'm Aakash.

P.S. *For the record, my mom never got the job. But my dad did get his soulmate.*

LIE 002

I t was raining cats and dogs on the first day of school.

Now, Dad could be very strict but he was one lousy guy at parenting.

"Dad, got school today."

Dad was sleeping on his chair in his study, his head bent over the table, his papers scattered beneath the study lamp. He sat upright with a start.

"Oh, yeah," he said completely dazed. "Yeah, I ... err ... forgot that!" He gave a sulky look.

"Great work, dad," I faked an applause.

"Don't give me that look now." He stood up switching the lamp off and arranging those sheets he always worked on.

"Let's see," he said commandingly, "Go finish your morning ablutions, I'll pack you something for lunch ... and umm...," he scratched his mustache which was growing longer by the hour, "have some cereals for breakfast."

Yeah, I'll probably skip breakfast, I decided while going for a hot shower.

As expected, we got late.

The school bus driver honked like mad before getting off the bus and coming personally to our door.

He did that for the next four years.

Now, let me tell you my geographical location in detail. I lived in Port Blair, the Capital of Andaman and Nicobar islands. It's an amazing place. As a child, I would marvel at that place, filled with beaches and forests and countryside locales, the place is awesome.

My house was a small bungalow at the foot of the hill. That part of the country was called "Jungli Ghaat".

Now yeah, this is quite embarrassing, I mean for heaven's sake "Jungli Ghaat"? What kinda name is that?

Alright, here goes the explanation. Now Port Blair is a holiday paradise for the foreigners and it was also the biggest prison during the British administration. They called it "kaala pani" or "the black waters".

So, most of the names out here had an English origin which actually got dubbed into Hindi. Thereby 'the forest lane'

became 'Jungli ghaat', 'love square' became 'prem nagar', and 'church road' became, 'ram nagar' .

My first school was Kendriya Vidyalaya. It was an old British construction, spread over seventy acres of land; and on every windy night, students would bet that the west wing would surely collapse. Our class was in the west wing. I won't go into the description of the plaster and the paint, make a wild guess!

So, let's go back a little to the driver knocking or literally slapping the door, my dad going out and explaining to him the various uses of the door-bell and I hurriedly running down the stairs zipping my bag, tying the shoe laces and then wearing the rain coat before setting out into the open world!

The island looked exotic, trust me! I mean, there was fog everywhere and although it rained like hell, you could see the moist foliage, the drenched tarry roads and the hint of the ocean far on the horizon.

The bus was jampacked with students my age, some older. They had so many expressions that I would rather skip that part, too. Beside me, a fat obese kinda cheese-bag was seated. And, dear God, he really took half of my seat leaving me almost to sit on the window pane. There were a hundred curious eyes that stared at me but in my oblivion I avoided them. That's me. I have always been like that, as if emitting a negative vibe or something. No soul dared ask me even my name except the fatty extrovert, "Hi, I'm Pritish," he gave an affable smile and extended his hand.

"And, I'm not interested." Remember the negative-vibe thing. See, I wasn't wrong. My response took him by such shock, I swear, to God I could see his eyes welling up.

"Okay… err … on second thought, I'm Aakash and err … nice to meet you, Pritish," I made an attempt at a vague smile.

That did cheer up the fatty, but he didn't dare say a word again throughout the ride.

Well, my dark image was evident in the class, too. I was one of those guys who sat alone on the very first day of school. Students sat gossiping, some crying out loudly, some frightened as if they were left in the wild, and some cheerful like they just got the Filmfare award. Everyone existed somewhere or the other but I disappeared into the crowd. Gave me reason to think, to observe, to crack my own jokes. The only big problem throughout the first few hours of school was my tummy! Yeah, remember that idiotic idea of skipping breakfast? Well, it didn't work out that great for me. As recess approached, my tummy started making such weird noises that even teachers stared at me.

So, when the bell rang, it was a relief for me which, well, soon turned into a nightmare. Thanks to my dad, he had forgotten to pack my lunch. I was gonna die of hunger right on the first day of school! Now, I really panicked. People all around me had started devouring their 3 course meal and it was killing me, the hunger!

I felt my eyes going moist but hey, Aakash never cried, not even as a kid. I sat quietly trying to concentrate on the rain and then noticed it. Someone else was sad today. Someone else had no friends and to add insult to the injury, he was being made fun of. I craned my head and saw the helpless kid, of all the people in the world, it was the fatty chubby bloke, Pritish sobbing hideously as others mocked at him calling him names such as "motu" and "fatso". Poor guy! I tried to ignore the shocking situ   ation but then something drew my attention. It was a statement by a scum bag of a kid, directed at Pritish. He said, "I bet fatso brought a trunk full of food".

Now that was tempting, sumptuously tempting.

I was bewitched and the liar in me was aroused for the first time. The rest as they say is history.

"Mind if I sit beside you," I say to Pritish.

"Really?" He is bewildered, "Well, okay.".

"Hey, I saw what happened in here. Those guys are bad. Don't listen to them." I consoled.

It was my first lie.

"They called me fatso," the chubby-baby cried.

"Oh, they're just jealous of your looks. They think you're gonna impress the girls."

"They think that?"

"Oh they so do. And, I bet you haven't even brought a trunk full of tiffin."

Pritish shrugged, "Actually, I kinda did."

I felt happiness overwhelming me.

"Oh, that's a problem with quite a simple solution," I said with unfathomable expertise.

"What's that?" Pritish was all hopeful now.

"You just need to share it."

"Share it? With them?"

No you duffer.

"No, not them. No. Someone good," I looked around as if looking for the right person.

I could see my lie had worked and I was not gonna die hungry. All I had to do was wait.

"Well, why don't I share it with ... err ... you and maybe, you could be my best friend?"

P.S. *lies are good but they come with high price, sometimes heavy ones.*

So my first day at school was not a story of how lazy my Dad gets, nor about how rainy the day was nor was it about how mean I was as a kid, it was the story of " how I met my best friend."

Lie 003

Top 5 embarrassing situations of my life:

Number 5: I got chased by a crazy dog all around my school campus while the assembly was on, so the students could enjoy the funny scene and yes! The dog bit me, too.

Number 4: I tripped on the microphone wires while giving a speech on Independence Day. I was talking about rebellion and the setbacks and then well, I ended up setting an example myself. The thought still hurts.

Number 3: The scene where I got confused with the word "lakdi" i.e., wood and "ladki" i.e., girl, throughout a skit. I kept saying the wrong word at the wrong place of the likes of: the "ladki" is made by cutting trees, and the "ladki" is used for setting fire!

Number 2: I was fired on the what-could've-been-the-best-day of my life. It's humiliating now that I think of it!

✶ ✶ ✶ NUMBER ONE ✶ ✶ ✶

I was in the fourth standard. It was the time when students started linking their names to girls.

They would talk about "their first love" (wannabe Romeos and Juliets) and a guy named Vicky who had proposed to a girl named Natasha and got beaten up later by our class teacher, had become a hotshot celebrity.

Every boy had his heart for someone, not me.

You remember me being the loner! Well, by now I had made some friends but only one of them was a girl and to be frank she was my friend

11

just because I needed her English notes. She went to Sujata ma'am for tuitions and Sujata ma'am was the one who'd set the question paper...So, you see the connection.

Well, so the day my friends pressurised me for a name, the only one I could score was — "Anisha", the girl with the English notes. She was a nice girl for the record and as for the first girl I had talked to, she was really innocent and benevolent, so unlike Aakash, the mean spoilt brat.

I had taken a promise individually from each of my friends that there would be no further talk about my relationship with Anisha (which didn't even exist!), but you know, those naughty little misfits; they would resort to every possible treachery to create an incitement.

The next thing, you know, someone had written "Aakash + Anisha" on our blackboard.

Every time Anisha entered the class, students would shout out my name along with hers.

Now, I never paid attention to rumours and controversies. For me, things worked out fine. However, Anisha had stopped playing with me in the recess but she'd always lent her notes to me and so I had a fictional girlfriend, ready guide for exams and I was famous, too.

UNTIL THE SAD DAY OF RAKSHA-BANDHAN.

The day my so-called 'girlfriend' walks up to me in front of a shocked audience and out of her bag pops up a tiny Rakhi.

"Oh, dear Lord ...What is that?" I'm terrified.

"It's for you, my brother." Anisha mumbles. There is wild laughter and jokes, students singing special "rakshabandhan" songs all around in chorus and I stand there like a lame, tied up goat as Anisha slowly ties the band.

I sigh, I'm embarrassed but hey, I'm not gonna give it away like this... Aakash always wins, even if there's a bit of cheating involved.

Later that day, the wounded animal, i.e. me is being followed by paparazzi everywhere with queries of what just happened??

And, do I have an answer or what!

"So, Aakash, Why'd Anisha tie that rakhi to you if you were her boyfriend?" a dud asks. There is another round of giggles.

"Oh that." I give a vicious smile that silences everyone, "You guys noticed that, huh?"

Everyone nods in a confused state.

"The plan did work then." I give another of my fake smiles. Everyone's curious now. The liar in me is getting stronger.

"What's the plan?" There is obvious curiosity.

"Can't tell yah!" I try to walk away but as I had presumed, I'm blocked by the mob.

"You answer the question, Mr. smarty pants," a strange looking weirdo, obviously in some other section, asks.

"Alright then, here it goes." I give a surrendering sigh as I start with my version, the lie.

"Remember all the crap you guys have been up to for the last 3 months since word got out about our relationship?"

Everyone nods in rapt attention.

"Well, evidently Anisha was upset about the fiasco and we worked out a plan of tying a FRIENDSHIP BAND on raksha bandhan, we're still friends."

I immediately put my hand over my mouth and whispered in quite an audible tone, "Lord! I shouldn't have said this."

I sprint away as if I have spilled out top-secret docs.

I can hear appreciation and respect for our plan. I'm the new rockstar now, make way ....

"You really think that's what happened? You can get away with that stinking lie of yours?" The air out of me is blown away.

Someone has punched me all of a sudden on my face right in the middle of the corridor. I trip and fall. Somehow I raise my head, shock and outrage all over it!

That strange looking weirdo from the other section is standing in front of me.

He flexes his knuckles and then bam, another punch! There is chaos everywhere, students fleeing in a rampage.

I feel a milk tooth break.

I shiver, "Who the hell are you?"

"I'm Aditya but hey what's in a name!" the villain smiles mercilessly, "I'm the brother of the girl you just humiliated in public, Anisha's my sister."

I see him walk away before the blackout.

"And yeah," he mocks, "Happy raksha bandhan!"

P.S: *I hate lame brothers. I mean why in the world does every pretty girl have a filthy athletic brother?*

This might be the story of my first public embarrassment but more than that it's the story of the first enemy I made ... Aditya!

LIE 004

PRESENT DAY

I sit at the Chhatrapati Shivaji International Airport blogging. My plane is scheduled to depart at 2:30 am for Los Angeles. That leaves me with an hour and a half to wait for the security checkup.

"Came a bit early, didn't you?", *a stranger sits beside me, a tall young guy, his complexion brown, face unshaven, blue eyes.*

"Yeah, I … ," *I'm confused* "Have we met before?"

"Aakash Roy, the topper," *the stranger smiled talking to himself, then he turned to me and said,* "They used to say you've an eidetic memory."

Pritish used to say that, I remembered.

"I've definitely seen you somewhere." *I rack my brains. A screen saver has popped up in my laptop screen where I had been writing before.*

Blue eyes, curly hair, oh, good Lord!

"Kabir … man!" *I almost hug the guy,* "Whoa, long time … no see, man! How're you?"

"Well, not that great you know … but hey, you look dashing … how's life for the success seeker?"

"Unsuccessful," *I gave a hollow smile.*

"So, what's up with you … you look … err …".

"Sick." *Kabir helps,* "I'm sick Aakash. But let's not go into that for now." *I'm quite curious but let the question float in the air.*

"So, how did you recognise me in there? I mean how many years has it been now?", *I'm astonished.*

"Nine years. Yup." *Kabir nods. I gape at him.*

"I saw your name on the boarding pass. I was behind you in the queue. We're on the same flight."

"Hey, that's awesome, man. So, let's catch up." I'm extremely excited, "What do you do for a living kabir?"

"Oh ... I was a teacher for this government college at Port Blair. You see, never made it out of that place, I couldn't afford it." Kabir sighed, then gave a sad smile. "It was like my personal cell."

"Hey, don't say that, dude. We loved that place. And lemme tell you," I said in the know-it-all style, "It's crazy out there in the world." I shrugged, "all boring and kinda messy."

"Is it?, Kabir meant it more as a statement than a question.

"Hey, remember Anisha?"

I shrugged, "How can I forget her! My first fictional girlfriend and then, first sister!" I winked. Kabir gave a disgusted expression, then said, "She got married."

"Really? To whom?" I was surprised.

"Vicky."

"Oh, heavens...no", I laughed out loud, "Man oh, man!"

Kabir had changed so much, I observed. He looked kinda lost, ill and there was this vibe in him that smelled of sadness. I couldn't take it. We shared two minutes of utter silence.

Then I tried to break it, "Hey Kabir, tell me something."

Kabir looked up.

"What happened to your dream of becoming a writer?"

Kabir looked stunned, "jeez!! how do you know that?"

"Hey, no worries, I just remember you saying it out aloud once, when Goldie sir asked us our aims in 3rd Standard."

Kabir looked at me, impressed, "You really have an eidetic memory, don't you Aakash?"

I laughed, "So what happened to it? Published any novels yet?"

"Aah, that," Kabir sighs, "I just kind of lost interest."

"Why?," I'm disheartened.

Kabir chortles, "I'll put it this way. Have you read about 'The butterfly effect' Aakash?"

"Yeah... I saw the movie once. Aston Kutcher."

"Yup that one ... it's a theory, it says 'events like even the flapping of its wings by a butterfly in some place like say, Africa can lead to tiny climatic changes that would ultimately result in tornadoes in Los Angeles'. Getting my point?"

"Well, I know that you're really good at science, you're a professor after all, but sorry, I don't get your point." I gave him a blank expression.

"Okay ... I'll try again. You might remember the Story Writing competition we once had in our school?"

My heart skipped a beat.

I nodded in silence.

"Yeah so ... that was the first time I had written down my favourite story on paper and submitted it. I was certain that I would win. I was definite about it, Aakash." Kabir is all sand papery now. He was sharing something very close to his heart.

"So?" I stammered. Kabir had gone silent. "You know the rest, Aakash. Put the pieces together."

I did know the rest.

"So, you're telling me that just because you lost a bloody competition, you gave up your dream." I felt anger boiling through my nerves.

"I gave up my hope, Aakash. I keep giving it up. Like this time."

"What do you mean?" I said hysterically.

"I'm dying, Aakash. I'm going to Los Angeles for treatment but I know it a lost cause." He grew quiet again.

But my mind was zooming in and out of focus.

✴ ✴ ✴ TWELVE YEARS AGO ✴ ✴ ✴

It was a sunny morning. I had written down my first story that dealt with aliens and such weird stuff. I was sure I was gonna win. I had never lost much till then, you see.

At 10.30 am we had to submit our self written stories at the school auditorium.

I left at 9 am. I had to go to Kabir's place first.

He had called me up in the night and said he had fever. He asked me for a favour.

Kabir lived at a one bhk house with his mom. They were poor but Kabir was the most talented guy in our class. He was the best in the literary field and my sole competitor.

At 9.30 am, I reached his house. Kabir was waiting at the door, a piece of parchment neatly folded under his palm. He gave it to me and smiled in gratitude.

"My pleasure," I replied to his expression, "and get well soon, Kabir."

"Oh! Yeah, I will. I'm so gonna win this time, Aakash. I can promise you that. The title of my story is Tribute."

His faith came as a shocker but I got a grip on myself.

"Yeah, I hope you do."

It's gonna be me, you stupid sicko. I thought to myself as I trotted towards the school, but something had snapped in me.

✶ ✶ ✶ PRESENT DAY ✶ ✶ ✶

"Wasn't it you, Aakash?" Kabir broke my train of thoughts.

"What?" I almost panicked.

"You won that competition, didn't you?"

I kept quiet.

"You were always better, Aakash, I should've known, the loser I am."

"Don't say that, Kabir. You lost because … ." I stammered. My throat had gone dry.

I could tell Kabir was looking at me now in earnest.

"You lost because I cheated, Kabir."

"What … how ?", Kabir was bewildered.

"I swapped the names," I sighed, "I changed our names and submitted your story as mine, that's why I won. It wasn't your fault."

Kabir looked shattered.

"I'm sorry, Kabir. I never meant anything bad. You shouldn't give up on youself, Kabir. You were always the better person."

A tear trickled down Kabir's eye. Then, he walked away.

But before that he told me something I would never forget.

He had said, "I should've known, Aakash, I remember your aim, too, do you?"

"Yes." I replied, "My aim was to win, always."

"You know what, I pity you, Aakash. I see a loser in you. But know this, I ain't. I'm not gonna give up now, ever. Now that you're the winner, Aakash, why don't you write a story for me? Write all your lies down. How many are there huh? 40 –50?"

"It's more than that." I whisper.

"Well, see, you're already thinking." And with that Kabir walked away, "you betrayer."

"I get that." I smile sadly.

P.S. I never switched Kabir's story. He just lost.

I lied to him now, because I didn't want him to lose the greatest battle of his life.

For once, I wanted to be the butterfly, flap my wings and make him live.

Lie 005

Now, well, this story is a lot of things to other people. For Pritish, it was the first time he really broke the code and went on a rampage. For Vicky, it was that part where he met the friends of his life.

For Nikhil, it was the day the band came into picture.

For Kabir, it was the day that ruined his childhood.

And, for me and Aditya, let's find out.

But first let me tell you how the story actually started.

(The story behind the story!)

Lie 005:

Rumour has it that Kendriya Vidyalaya was built beside an old cemetery where prisoners of the 1857 war were buried. Students said that the place was haunted and there have been cases of kids getting possessed.

Well, I thought it was an old wives' tale.

Even our class teacher Sona Kumar sir (we called him 'goldie') had the same opinion. "There is nothing out there kids, it's all a bunch of lies. KV denies it", he'd say.

I was always the kid who dared to visit all the deserted places in the huge campus, covered in thick moss and old shrubs, the old monolithic structures behind our west wing building.

And frankly, those places were prohibited. You never knew when a light wind blew by them, and the next moment, the entire collage of stones would come down. Well, that'd make the cemetery part true then.

So, this is the incident of the day before the school closed for Diwali vacation.

We four of section A, Pritish, Nikhil (Niks), Kabir and I were playing hide and seek. I loved that game!

It was then that Aditya and his group of suckers showed up. They had that filthy slimy smile plastered on to their faces like they were the Kings of Timbaktoo.

"Hey, smarty pants, got the guts to play? I dare you." Aditya gave a mischievous smile.

"Err ... I don't like his tone." Pritish whispered in my ear.

"Stop being a killjoy fatso." Niks chided, "Let's see what these dumbos got in them."

I pondered for a moment.

"Oh, c'mon, Aakash, it ain't that hard a decision, is it? Is the topper of section A afraid of the one in section B? "

"Yeah, right", I made a face, "Now tell me, what the catch is?"

"Smart ass huh?" Aditya chuckled, his yellow teeth protruded, "Well, here's the condition, whoever loses has to stay here at the campus for an entire night."

Pritish shivered, "Ohhh, man, I told you I didn't like his tone." I gave him a stern look to shut up.

"Wait, there's more to it," Aditya chided, "you will have to stay here for the entire night, on Diwali!"

"Ohh....c'mon you scumbag!" Niks was outraged.

"You gotta be kidding." Kabir gave a shrill laugh. Fear was evident in there.

I kept quiet. I hated Aditya.

Aditya and his group of four jerks which included Vicky, guffawed. Made me sick.

"You giving up then Aakash, Mr. topper?" Aditya teased.

"Who said anything about giving up? Aand puhleez ...," I said, disgusted, "we have a difference of 10 percent in aggregate, you loser!"

Aditya scowled and clenched his fists.

"Think again, Aakash", Kabir said. There was seriousness in his voice, "You don't want to ruin diwali, do you?"

"No, that's why we're going to play and win, you in or out?" I fired the question at all three of my friends.

They nodded, confused. They couldn't just back out on me.

And so, the game started.

We had to hide while Aditya and group were to hunt us down.

Okay, now, I'll tell you the sad part! My gang, sucked in hide and seek!

I mean, Pritish was so fat, no bush could hide him. Kabir was always lost in imagination. God knows what! He might be standing right at the centre of a conspicuous ground considering it his hideout and Niks was pretty much a show off, which was not good for this game, not good at all!

That left it up to me to get the job done. I worked out the maths. Simple enough, I just knew the place where I could stay secure for the next half an hour of recess without getting caught and being a deadlock.

It was an old monolithic structure at the complete end of our campus. It was deserted, ominous and looked haunted.

My perfect hideout!

It might've been fifteen minutes, I don't remember now, when I saw Aditya searching the bushes near the structure. I was stooping behind an old statue of Mary, I guess. I was shocked by Aditya's searching capabilities!

Now, Kendriya Vidyalaya was situated high up on a hill, most of the places in Port Blair were. A huge slope lay behind the campus that went straight down to the deep blue sea. That meant, if you crossed the fences, skidded off the slope and went overboard, you were gone for sure.

I had to run, I had to get off, I needed to get away from Aditya's search perimeter *asap*. I looked at the fence to the slope behind. A sprint, a jump, a slip and soon enough I was skidding off through sands going down the slope. Oops, that wasn't one of my best ideas.

I was slipping and falling and getting scratched but the greater worry lay below … I could see the ocean now. I had to brake. I tried in earnest to hold on to something, maybe a stone, an uprooted branch, something!

Everything was a blur of a vision, as I somersaulted like a rolling stone, ready to crash.

And, there it was, my hands touched something to cling onto and I grabbed it as my chest hit the brick and my breath was knocked out.

I was in pain, there were cuts and bruises and I couldn't feel my legs.

I sat upright after some agonising moments over the stone hedge that saved me, and looked at the part I was clutching onto. Dear God! It was a huge cross.

I freaked out. I looked at the stone hedge properly and now I could see engravings over it.

A grave had just saved me!

I looked around; there were hundreds of them all around the part where the slope had ended. It was a beach, full of graves. It was the cemetery!

The sea had been hiding it all along. I could see it now due to the low tide.

The revelation settled in slowly. The rumuors were true after all.

Next thing, you know, I was running up the slope. I had to tell my friends the freaky story of the lie, Goldie had proclaimed.

I jumped over the fence, ran straight to the ground and saw the seven guys staring at me, three in shock, four in utter delight.

"You just won't believe what I saw." I said with excruciating excitement.

"Let me make a wild guess." Niks bursted out in anger, "you saw us spending Diwali night at this freaking campus getting dead!"

I tried to process the sudden outrage.

"What … I … ?", and then it struck me, "oh … bloody hell, the game!"

"That you just lost." Vicky sing-songed and danced like a maniac.

"There there, Aakash, you really gave me chills for a second there, I thought I'll never find you, but the fool you are," Aditya was laughing now, "you show up, precisely two minutes before the recess ended."

I had hands over my head. How could have I been so stupid! I had lost the game.

Pritish was in tears now. Kabir looked worried and Niks just appeared psycho.

"I'm sorry guys, I just … " I felt disoriented and shocked. My bruises had started to show.

I heard the bell ring in the distance, saw students walking away from the playground. Pritish was asking me whether ghosts exist and Niks was kicking the sands off the ground, but I was somewhere else.

You can still go to that campus some day, take a stroll on the prohibited beach and you'll just be stupefied by the hundreds of graves lying there. I don't know whether of the revolutionaries or the Englishmen but I do know that on a full moon night, in the low tides, that beach is the place for thrills.

But hey this ain't the end of this story; it's just the start of the most eventful night of our lives.

"I really don't want to spend Diwali night at a haunted place," Pritish sobbed as he steered his car through the race track of Autobahn. He was playing Need for Speed 5.

"You've been saying it for the last six hours. I mean you might be on the same track, crashing, but I really need to solve this numerical." I burst out.

"I hate you." Pritish cursed.

"That won't be a problem", I tried to concentrate.

Two minutes of silence.

"How are you going to get us out of our houses on Diwali? Our parents won't allow us." Pritish enquired, breaking the silence.

"I'll tell them you guys are invited to my place. I'll disconnect my phone line for the night and tell dad I'm headed to your place."

That way we're going to be all out there in the night.

"You're such a liar." Pritish swore.

"Yeah, I know." I smirked.

Three minutes of silence.

"What happens if we don't do it?"

"That's a bad question, reframe."

"What happens if we accept defeat?"

"Reframe."

"Why're you taking it personally, Aakash?"

"Because more than anything, it's a personal issue, Pritish. I can't let Aditya win again."

"They say there's a cemetery in there somewhere. What if it's true?"

"It's a lie," I lied.

I had not told anyone about my earlier expedition to the graveyard yet. I knew that if I told them the truth, everyone would walk out from the dare.

Pritish sighed, then resumed his game, "Hope others agree with you on this."

All three of them did.

P.S. *I had a way with words.*

LIE 006

✶ ✶ ✶ DIWALI ✶ ✶ ✶

"We have a guest here." Niks said viciously.

I look at the familiar, thin, white face of Vicky. The show off. He'd be involved in every single controversy of our school and Goldie took pleasure humiliating that guy.

"Why're you here?", I pointed at him.

"Well, Aditya didn't trust you guys with the dare, so he sent me to check on you ... "

"And, the dog ran after the bone." Niks commented.

Kabir, Pritish and I burst out laughing.

"Well then, welcome comrade, hope you have a bad time." Kabir wished.

All Vicky could do was make faces. I could see that he was totally out of place. Poor chap. Gonna have a rough time tonight.

"Alright guys, check your watches, it's quarter to eleven, we leave now." And so, we went bidding farewell to the festival of lights. Rockets and crackers dazzled all around the island. A lot of People had called it a day and were retiring to bed. Everyone was happy. Except the five of us.

We reached the campus at nearly five past eleven on our cycles. A cold breeze swept off the coast. Gave me goose bumps.

"So, here we are ... ", I said trying to kill the ominous silence that had started to ring in my ears.

"Looks unreal man!" Kabir said, his blue eyes scanning the dark huge school building, "Five minutes back, it was all candles and lights and crackers and look at this place. It's pitch black here!"

"Schools suck." Pritish shrugged.

"The guards are on the eastern corridors, so we'd better avoid that part." Vicky added.

"Okay." I started to think of a safe haven.

"Hey, guys, why don't we go beneath that huge banyan tree where we meet at lunch? We can stretch our legs there and maybe, take a nap." I suggested.

"You freaking insane!" Niks almost shouted, his voice reverberating off the west wing walls.

"Shh ...," Kabir warned.

"Dude everyone knows banyan trees are haunted."

"Ohhh, c'mon now, a sacred tree is haunted! Trust me whoever told you that lied. My Dad told me it's the safest refuge. Take it from me, banyan trees are the safest."

Banyan trees are haunted. Never ever go near them in the night.

Niks poke-marked face had utter confusion written all over it ...

"So, it's the banyan tree then." Kabir concluded.

✲ ✲ ✲ 1 hour later ✲ ✲ ✲

"Damn the mosquitoes", I felt sore and irritated ,"Pritish, pass me the bottle."

I looked at Pritish and then stared at him. He looked shaken.

"Hey, you, okay man?!" Niks nudged him, "Man, you're all cold."

"I wanna go home." Pritish sobs in a sandpapery voice.

"Hey, don't do this to me now", I am frustrated.

"If the poor fellow wants to go home, just let him. Accept defeat." Vicky smirked.

"Shut up before I slap you red and white." I warned Vicky and then looked at Pritish, "c'mon, dude, don't get scared, it's okay. We're all here, see. We gonna make it. Don't give up now."

"Have I told you about the new call of duty game I've bought?" Niks tried to distract Pritish, "I can give it to you if you want ... "

I see colour coming back in Pritish's face. Then, he whispered, "I just don't like the way those aerial roots spring down from that tree. It's spooky, dude!"

"Hey, first thing tomorrow morning, we're gonna bring down this tree," Vicky chortled.

"Thanks, Vicky", Pritish looked at him gratefully. So did I.

✱ ✱ ✱ 2 hours later ✱ ✱ ✱

My fluorescent watch showed two o'clock. Apart from some howling and barking dogs which was really scary, I've to admit everything else was quite ordinary.

"Hey, I think I should write a poem on fear", Kabir is far away again, "See, my dad is really ill and we're always frightened about what is going to happen to him. The uncertainty, the darkness of it all, the not knowing, that's fear!"

"Hey, I'm sorry about your father, Kabir. Hope he gets well soon." Pritish looked sad.

Kabir nodded appreciatively.

"Well, I can put some music into your poetry, and we can make it into a song." Niks looked hopeful.

"Hey you play music? Which instrument?", Vicky asked excited.

"Don't talk to me, you duffer", Niks was still pissed at Vicky, "Aren't you with that bossy Aditya because of Anisha? His sister? You like her, don't you?"

Vicky blushed. He looked embarrassed.

"Hey, give the guy a break, dude," I commanded, "Niks, why don't you just answer the question Vicky asked."

"Guitar", Niks grunted quietly.

"I can sing well." Vicky spoke softly.

"Wow, we got our lead vocalist. Yipee! I've a band now!" Niks went sarcastic.

I was savouring the comments when it happened.

All of a sudden, all the streetlights went out. It went pitch black and we could not even make out the faces of each other.

"What the…," I heard Pritish scream.

"Shhh shhh …,", I cried, "you'd get us caught. Relax."

"Hey, what just happened?" I heard the terrified voice of Vicky.

"It's probably a blackout." I was trying my best not to panic.

"Hey look at the road. What's that?" Niks spoke.

I wish he hadn't said it.

Far in the distance, on the road to the old monolithic structures, a figure had appeared out of nowhere. It was visible under the light of the stars.

The figure sauntered towards us at a brisk pace.

I was frozen to the ground, my eyes, fixed, unblinking at the creature, speeding towards us. It had a huge hood on and a pouch hung from its shoulder.

It was a six-foot-something and it was now some thirty metres from us.

" Run…," I tried to speak but the words couldn't escape my mouth.

I could hear Pritish sobbing vehemently, I could feel the other three guys shivering and I could smell a strange fear gripping us. My legs had gone numb and I couldn't move.

The creature stopped ten feet away from us then ransacked through its pouch. Out came a metallic object. It aimed it right at me.

Good bye guys. I could see it coming.

And then, a beam flashed over my eyes and I squinted, my nervous system prepped up for a breakdown.

"What the hell are you doing here?", the creature's frightening voice commands.

I am shocked.

"Didn't you hear me?" the old heavy voice sends goose bumps down my spine.

"Er … we're going right now. Forgive us." I hear Vicky speak. I can't even open my mouth, "Don't kill us please."

"Go right now." the heavy voice booms again. Another fresh beam of light blinds me, "Before I make you vanish."

And off we went. All five of us. We were sprinting, falling, crying, but fleeing away.

"Greetings from the magician," the voice booms from the distance.

We ran two and a half kilometres that night, at killer speed. Even fatso Pritish accomplished the task.

Then, we lay on the road, gasping for breath.

"What was that?" Kabir squeaked.

"Ghost." Pritish replied, his voice still shaky.

"Aakash?"

I lay down on the road, my eyes on the stars, my heart trumpeting.

"I don't know," I answered, earnestly, "let's get back to our homes. We'll collect our cycles tomorrow."

I got slapped so hard that it bled. My dad and the parents of all four kids were waiting for us at the door. My dad was frenzied.

I deserved that slap.

For I had commited a sin, my very first one.

Someone had died that night.

Kabir was not with his father in his last moments. The man had a massive heart attack. And, Kabir's mom was left alone with her only son participating in some stupid "prove to the world" freak show.

This is the story that shattered my childhood the most. Left footprints, it did.

It's the story of how Kabir got scarred for life, of how Pritish had his first adventure, of how Vicky was introduced to the group.

But that day also brought in an unknown stranger. More about that later.

For now. "Greetings from the magician!"

LIE 007

It happens.

That one night, when you can't sleep, someone else is awake, too.

You trot to your balcony and let the cool breeze soothen your senses. Then, you look down at the empty highway, trying to find a friend.

She's doing the same, out there in some other part of the world, some other continent; maybe, amidst the oceans.

You grab your keys, tiptoe to your parking and then, with a low rumble of your car, you take a drive across the empty roads. You smile, and you cry, you hum and you look out for the shooting stars to tell her that you're there for her.

And, as faded and distant that unknown relationship might seem, you have that strange presence felt all over. And, all you ask for, all you want to do with your life is to look into her eyes, share a comfortable silence and tell her ...

✶ ✶ ✶ This is that story ✶ ✶ ✶

I was in standard 7, when I won a silver medal for a national level painting competition. They called me to Delhi to collect the prize.

They funded my travel expenses and my stay over there. It was the Lion's Club.

The programme was held on a Sunday at The InterContinental Eros Hotel. Students from all over the country selected for various competitions were to be felicitated and the five star hotel was thicky crowded. I remember standing by the huge archway of the magnificent garden of the hotel, staring at the vibrant fountain for hours. I had no one to talk to, just the place to see. It was a one day affair, so I couldn't even roam around Delhi much. I pretty much roamed around the huge multi-storeyed complex instead, watched teenagers like me gossiping, playing and having a blast. I was happy, too. This place had a familiar feeling; I don't know what it was.

5:00 pm.

I was one of the earliest. The auditorium where the show was to be held was empty except the organiser's team. I could see them ransacking through stuff, laying the tables, checking the mikes, rehearsing the scripts.

I took a seat at the balcony, top right corner, took out my cell phone and dialled my Dad. The phone rang for a couple of rings and then went to the answering machine.

There was a beep, and I struggled for words.

"Hey ... umm ... Dad", I scratched my brow trying to say something, "I just called to say I'm fine. Call you later. Bye." Calling dad was a bad idea.

I took out my I-pod, played the switchfoot album. The song "dare you to move" kept me preoccupied, as I ransacked my bag, and took out my favourite book, Catcher in the Rye.

My eyes went down to the girl sitting below the balcony, curly hair, pink shiny jacket, black cowboy boots. She sat with her back to me, I couldn't make out her face. She was the only audience out there except me. I cocked my head to make out her face. Then, I observed she was reading something.

A red hard-back, I instantly knew the name. It was "Catcher in the Rye".

I tried to make out the chapter she was reading. So, I craned my head above and then, all of a sudden, she turns.

Her eyes meet mine. Brown, big, round, surprised eyes. They move from my eyes, linger at the copy of the book in my hands, then rise up to my eyes again, stay there for like an infinity. We are spellbound, beholding each other. And then, she blinks away, rises from her seat, her sharp face is expressionless, as strands of hair play on her cheek. And, she walks away.

I am still sitting there, my neck craned, my responses gone haywire, my pupils dilated, looking at the exit.

What the hell just happened there, Aakash? I thought. I had never experienced it before. Something euphoric, something like a fresh breath of air, ecstatic. It won't make sense, the sudden expectations. Logic seemed without reasons. My heart was beating like drum rolls. Her beautiful face was like a dream that kept on replaying. I tried to calm myself down. "Count ... 10, 9, 8, ... relax."

I stood straight, then slapped myself hard on the face. "Ouch!"

I saw a manager of the arrangement's committee stare at me and give a 'what-is-wrong-with-this-kid?!' look. He just didn't know.

I looked around the empty auditorium desperately, still empty, she wasn't there. I looked down back at the empty seat she had been previously occupying. I ran down the pavilion to her seat. Then I walked on to it, and *yes!*..a small blue cellphone is lying there.

I pick it up promptly, dial a number and make a miss call.

"Err ... that's mine," a soft voice jolts me like a 440volt shock.

I turn around, and voila, there she is, two feet from me, her eyes on the cellphone in my hand. I am stupefied, again. The neurons in my brain have short-circuited and bloody hell, she's asking me something now. I don't hear what she says. She is worried now and she points at the phone with her index finger, then points back at her, trying the sign-language.

"Ohhh ... the phone", I come back to life, "yeah ... sorry ... I was just ...", I stammered ,"you know ..." *c'mon Aakash, for heaven's sake*, "gonna search for you."

"Search for me?" she asks, slowly pushing away the hair that had slipped out of her ponytail.

"I mean ... err ... you know ... to give the phone."

"Oh ...," she nods "Okay then ... umm well, thanks and bye" and she starts walking away.

"Hey, stop!"

Oh no ... why did I say that! shit Aakash! Think ...

She stops midtrack, then turns "yes?"

"um ...", I'm blank again, "err ... nice shoes ..."

She's taken aback for a second, and then she smiles, "My mom gifted them to me on my birthday."

"Ohh ...," I managed.

"Thanks anyway ... see yah."

"Yeah ... I really hope so."

And, she's gone again.

8:30 pm

The programme has been on for an hour now and it's boring.

Filled with monotonous long speeches, I could see even the host yawn at backstage.

I'm tired. I've been looking all around, looking for the last three hours, looking for the girl in the black cowboy boots.

Damn! I should've asked her for a cup of coffee or something. I was in a hotel for god's sake!

That's when they call my name. I run down the aisle, ascend up the stage and collect the silver medal, shake hands with some president or chairman of the Lion's Club, face the audience, say thanks and then walk off through the backstage. I could hear the host explaining why I had stood second.

"That young boy had drawn a brilliant sketch", he says, "Of a lady waiting at the balcony staring down the road, he named it 'the wait'."

People applaud.

I smile.

"We had decided to award him the gold, but the strange coincidence", the guy continues as I start heading for the exit, "Someone else sketched a very similar painting and we went for a tie. The other competitor had drawn a girl looking 'out her balcony at the moon' and she had named it 'atonement'. It is she who has won the prize."

I closed the door and went outside.

I could still hear slow sounds of applause and the announcement of the winner.

"Katie Thomas."

Later

I wait for her at the archway the whole night. I look for her in the gardens. I stroll around through the dining spaces and then even go to the roof at the 51st floor in search of her.

But like every other sad story, she's just not there.

I leave for Calcutta the next day. I've my flight to Port Blair from there.

I'm at the Hazrat Nizamuddin railway station. The train has arrived and is gonna leave in five minutes. I've kept my luggage inside and am buying a magazine from the book stall.

"*Ek ladki ko dekha toh aisa laga,*" the track is playing on the radio by the stall at full volume.

My phone rings.

Unknown number.

✷ ✷ ✷ 209.

I board the train, stand at the door and answer the call.

"hello ..."

"hi."

I'm numb again. I go all topsy turvy.

"Who's this?"

"You know my name, make a guess."

"The girl in the cowboy boots", I smile, nervous and hyper, ventilating.

"Bingo! But hey, why did you save your number on my cell?", she asks.

"So that I could talk to you again", I pause, then sigh, "tell you that ... err ... you know"

There is silence. Just the track "*ek ladki ko dekha toh*" buzzing in the background.

"Do you know the guy who shot down John Lennon was found at the murder site reading the book *Catcher in the Rye?*" she suddenly asks.

"No ... I just ... it's my favourite novel", I say softly.

"Mine, too", she whispers.

The train has started to move but I can still hear the song.

The realisation dawns.

"Hey, where are you?" I almost squeak, looking out of the door at the platform and then I see her. Pink jacket, curly hair, brown eyes and that million dollar smile.

"Bye, Aakash, have a safe journey, your drawing was better than mine, you deserved to win, not me."

"Hey, how do you know my name? Wait a minute you stood first?"

She's silent.

"Katie?"

"No … bond … James Bond," she smiles and winks and then hangs up, but the phone is still in my ear, my eyes at the trailing platform fading away.

That was the first time I had felt good after losing a competition to someone.

That was the day I came to know that "love at first sight" happens.

It just happens.

Present day

I still have her number on my phone, she won't just answer anymore ⋆ ⋆ ⋆ 209.

LIE 008

Well, you remember Anshuman, the bespectacled frail athletic honest government employee or maybe, Radhika, the lady in the blue jacket?

No?

Hint: They're my Mom and Dad.

Now here's what happened next or what my uncle proudly told me about my dad's 'love story' over a cup of coffee.

See, my dad was like a devoted fan of Rajesh Khanna and Dharmendra and all other such romantic heroes, so when my dad fell in love, he fell 'the filmy style'.

There were a pile of love letters involved, teddy bears for gifts and roses, roses! A lot of 'em, my grandpa had this huge garden of roses and he loved it with his life before one night someone stole off the entire lawn, not a single flower left, some plants even uprooted!

The burglar even took away the white and black roses! My grandpa was admitted to the hospital for that episode and dad never revealed the name of the thief.

Dad had it all planned, a small house at Salt Lake City, a red Maruti 800, a pet dog whom he was gonna name "Dharam!"(he respected the actor a lot! No pun intended!) aAnd of course, Radhika, the love of his life ...

Dad was good with the plans; he just had not done the math. Radhika was a millionaire's only daughter, lived literally in a castle, with servants, one Chevrolet, had a lot of price tags attached and she owned a Labrador named 'Bond'.

There were economic differences, status issues and the arranged marriage concept, too!

But see, love is when you like the Back Street Boys over Metallica, when you're up allnight because reality is better than dreams and love does make you go blind. Dad got a pair of deaf ears too, so did my Mom.

The movie "Bobby" had just hit the screen and mom–dad were the burning examples of the rebellious young generation, passionate lovers. What followed next was Radhika getting slapped by her dad, running up the stairs to the bedroom, shutting her door and crying while some anonymous servant would knock incessantly at the door pleading with her to open it, talk about melodrama!

On my father's side of the tale, grandpa would explain to him how the whole world would deny the 'poor' rights to have a good life and how the middle class and the rich people had their differences, then there was the "kasam part" where the parents would ask their young love birds to swear that they would never see each other and if it were to happen it would take place over their dead bodies. Cliché.

What followed was the broken hearted phase. My dad had turned into Devdas. He would ask for soda on the rocks at bars!

My mom was like the unconsolable Kindergarten girl whose teddy bear had just got crushed by a car!

They didn't meet for three months and they thought the love was lost.

It was the eve before Christmas and "Aradhana" had just premiered. My dad went for it alone. First day first show, Liberty talkies, Chittaranjan Avenue, Calcutta. He bought some salted pop corn, got his favourite seat on the top right corner of the balcony, went and sat ready for Rajesh Khanna to make an appeerence. However, it was Radhika who stole the show. She had booked the seat next to dad unknowingly. All alone, she came and sat beside dad, both oblivious of each other's presence, drowned in solitude until the second frame where Rajesh Khanna sings *"Mere sapno ki Rani"* to impress her lady love Sharmila Tagore and Dad and Mom both started crying. All of a sudden their eyes met, then there was a pause, a minute of surprise and extreme happiness and then, there were tears of joy! My dad looked at what he had been missing for such a long time, appreciated the silky curls of Radhika's brown hair, her cute dimples, and mom beheld her dream, her hero, the innocent government geek who had made her crazy and then avoiding Rajesh Khanna for the first time in his life, my Dad kissed Radhika, a long lingering kiss, then wiped her tears and they held hands throughout the movie, both just blessed by destiny.

Two days later, my dad packed all his bags, took all important docs, made some important calls, finalized a deal and took a cab to the railway station even before grandma and grandpa had got up.

He took the metro to Shakespeare Colony, and then took another taxi to Salt Lake City and then, getting down at Central Park, he waited. At nine thirty, Radhika emerged with her bags and Labrador. Dad used to tell me she looked the prettiest that day, as if she was an angel.

They sprinted towards each other (pick a scene from any Hindi movie) then hugged and laughed and kissed and ... fled.

They ran away, from the world of inhibitions and boundaries.

They got married the next day. My dad had managed to buy a small flat at Salt Lake City from a housing loan and they moved in, the young carefree lovers.

It was right on the first day that mom understood she would have to live in a 1bhk for the next couple of years before some miracle happened. And yet, she was optimistic. It was right that day, my dad understood he had to cook for himself, find a new job and buy a car, too. And, yet he was happy.

And, bereft of the truth and money, they held hands and promised each other, "We'll make it work".

They lied.

LIE 009

I was a music addict since birth. As a kid, I would listen to Mohammad Rafi and Kishore Kumar and listen to dad hum his favourite tunes. Dad had this really old PC, Celeron, he called it "The Dharam Veer" where he would have folders of antique expired Hindi songs. I mean, as a kid, I loved all those classics, but as I grew up, things got repetitive and I grew sick of listening to the same old songs.

This was the time of 'Summer of 69' and 'Escape'. I remember I heard those songs at Pritish's house. Pritish used to download such awesome western songs and videos, I swear they blew my mind off.

Well, so, this is where it started. My love for music, its that story.

"Aakash, you ought to get a PC, man." Nick told me over lunch.

We were sitting under the old banyan tree at Kendriya Vidyalaya having sandwiches. I raised an eyebrow.

"Why?" I queried.

"You know, it would be awesome, dude." Nick cheered up, "I mean, then we could jam at your place and prepare for the Foundation day show."

Alright, here's what I missed. Now, Nick was this guitarist, I mean, he played decent guitar for his age and so was quite famous and Vicky had been taking drum lessons. Last we heard about that, it was about wooing some girl Vicky had developed his latest crush on.

And, there were rumours that I could sing well. So Goldie Sir asked us to perform on the Foundation Day. Nick was the new rockstar in town overnight; Vicky was showing off like he was the next John Elton or something and me? I practically sulked because I sucked at singing. I knew we were going down, that we were amateurs, so I wasn't enthusiastic at all. Although the event was like two months away, Nick was pretty worked up about jamming sessions and rehearsals.

So, that brings us back to the current proposition.

"We could install microphones and listen to songs at your place and practise." Vicky supported Nick, "you see the point?" he made it obvious.

"I don't know ..." I looked up confused at Pritish.

Now, Pritish had been quiet about the whole affair. He had not been selected. He was left alone and somewhere he felt bad about it, like our group had been fragmented and while we were the heads, he was some tail or something like that, I don't know!

"Yeah, they're right, bro." Pritish looked pensive (which was so not him!)

"You could play some games, too, then." He said over a bite of his thick cheesy meal, getting back to normal.

"See, the problem is dad won't agree." I deduced, "I mean, imagine asking dad for a brand new PC just because of some silly perform ...", I paused abruptly looking at the faces of Vicky and Nick which showed signs of getting offended, "I meant err ... for some 'good 'and 'great' but a 'normal' school performance." I managed somehow.

"Yeah, but...," Vicky tried hard to stand up to the debate, "See, we can't arrange a PC now. I mean I just started drum classes and I also have to buy gifts and stuff for my girl friend, you know." at which all the rest of us scoffed.

"I mean, I can't ask my parents, it's like a bait for them to slap me!", he cut it short.

"And even I just got my brand new electric guitar, so no hopes on my sides, too, dude." Nick shrugged.

"I guess that leaves me." I sighed.

"And, you don't have to tell Mr Roy the real reason." Vicky said with a corny wink, "I mean you're always good at lying, you could suggest to him that you need it for your school assignments."

"Dad won't agree guys, I reckon the most he would do is give me his outdated Celeron, 'The Dharam Veer,' I shrugged, "lies like those don't work, they never do."

"Can't we do this without the PC?" I asked again.

"No!", they shouted in unison.

There was a momentary silence as we had our lunch grim-faced.

"Alright, here's a solution guys." Pritish suddenly announced and it did come as a surprise.

"What we're gonna do," Pritish said in an over-confident whim, "is eliminate the options."

"Err... what's that supposed to mean?" I scratched my head, confused.

"It means, gentlemen," now Pritish was getting all futuristically crazy, "That we're gonna screw Aakash's dad's computer."

At this I burst out laughing, so did the others...

"For crying out loud, Pritish, was that even an idea? I mean, what's that supposed to mean, we're gonna go there in my dad's study and break his PC into pieces? You gonna get us killed."

"Nay, fellow warrior, fear not." Pritish had lost his head, "I have a better solution, we gonna infect your dad's computer."

Alright, here's the deal, in the next two minutes, Pritish uttered some words that I had never heard before, maybe b'cos I never had a PC, or maybe b'cos I was still a kid, or maybe, what I thought at that time was that Pritish was a computer genius. (well, that turned out wrong though!)

"We're gonna infect your dad's PC with a 'virus' called 'Trojan Horse' and then add some 'malwares' and 'worms', you know I had this 'pen drive' once that got infected with such stuff and I never used it again because it was 'beyond repair'. He gave a huge laugh.

The three of us looked at each other, out of explanations.

"Er ... I have a question." I stuttered, perplexed, "What's a virus? and is it living, like real?"

"What's a pen drive, dude?" Vicky asked.

"And, what's that horse stuff you said?" Nick was clueless.

Two days later

At dad's study.

THE MASTER PLAN

1) As per the plan, I had already asked dad for a computer specifying that I was having problems with my hypothetical fake assignments and projects at school.

Dad had promised to allow me to use his old PC whenever I was in need, at which I had presented a fake smile of gratitude and left.

2) Now, there's another part to the story.

Remember, Aditya? He and his family had recently moved to our neighbourhood and Aditya would visit my dad every Sunday to learn computer and stuff. I hated the entire ordeal and stayed away from the whole settlement. Now was the time to use this opportunity to implement my plan.

3) We entered Dad's study (Me, Pritish and Nick, while Vicky watched the door) around one hour before Aditya and dad would meet for the computer classes. We booted the old Celeron 'Dharam Veer'. A yellow screen popped up with a faint tune of Windows 98. We inserted Pritish's infected pen drive and there, the virus was right in my dad's PC now. Soon enough the PC was gonna crash.

4) We were going to frame Aditya, because Aditya would always get CDs and stuff with him that he would play on the PC. We wanted the scene to look like it was all Aditya's fault.

However, here comes the setback.

5) As soon as the virus comes into play, a software pops up on our dad's screen. It's called 'THE NORTON ANTIVIRUS'.

It points out that the PC is infected and then quarantines the 'trojan horse' and reports that the PC is safe again. Thanks to our negligible knowledge, we are rendered speechless as we watch the whole affair.

"What the hell happened?" I whispered in shock.

"What's an antivirus, dude?" Pritish spoke, stunned.

"Oh, you moron!" I wanted to punch Pritish though I too didn't have a clue about this NORTON thing.

"What do we do now?" Pritish was already stepping back towards the door.

I was frustrated, I wanted a new PC, P-4 or something. And, I needed it now.

6) "Here's what we gonna do." I growled and pushed the CPU and monitor right to the edge of the table.

"One small touch, and this goes down." I whispered vindictively and cursed the PC, "you're as good as dead."

"You're gonna get us killed." Pritish said in a panicky voice.

I grinned devilishly, "I'm gonna get us a new PC."

We left.

7) It happened exactly an hour later. I heard the PC crash to the floor, heard it shatter and heard my dad's scream of rage. I heard him slapping Aditya, saw the poor chap fleeing the scene.

That was how our Celeron died, "Dharam Veer" was wrecked at last...

* * *

I got my brand new Pentium 4, a week later. My plan was successful and dad also complained about the entire episode to Aditya's parents. For all I knew, Aditya was in deep shit.

P.S.: My new PC never had all those old classics and today when I look at it, it hurts. You see, my dad lost his best friend the day "Dharam Veer" died. And, a liar won again.

Lie 010

"Revenge is best served cold"
— Marie Joseph

***

March 22, 2001, Monday 9:45 pm

"Hey dude, check out my new geometry box, it's the new Superman series." Pritish shouted with joy as he entered my room. I was busy with my plans.

"Not now, Pritish, I ain't interested, I got some evil stuff to do." I was jotting down some formulae.

"Hey man, I'm really sorry about what happened at recess today. That guy is a jerk. We'll beat him up some day." Pritish tried to console me.

"If we had to beat him, it should've been today." I whispered, "It's too late for that now."

* * *

I didn't have a lot of enemies or rivals for that matter during my cool school days. However, the last man standing would always pose a threat, in my case, it was Aditya. And, God bless that moron, he was even in my section now.

He would always ruin every good time and mess up the nightmares. And, I hated him.

45

So, after the 'Dharam Veer' episode, Aditya didn't show up at school for a week. It was like spring. Classes would resume without any irritating disturbance from the trouble maker, the bully, Aditya. There wouldn't be annoying jokes, egoistic clashes and I kind of felt that our school was gradually becoming the kingdom of heaven where I could see angels in white cloaks, their fingers raised making peace signs and I felt happy, contented until the day Aditya resurfaced, this time at his worst.

He looked depressed, infuriated and whenever he looked into my eyes from the last bench, his eyes would ignite with wrath and that did kinda freak me out. Now, I knew that bad times had enveloped Aditya's life lately since dad had complained to his parents about his breaking up my PC (which of course was my part of the crime) and as far as I knew, Aditya's parents did pay some money, too, for the losses. Guess, that explained the red scars on Aditya's right cheek!

I tried my best to avoid the bloke's foul mood but not for long.

✹ ✹ ✹

March 29, 2001, Monday 8:45 am.

Exam was to start in fifteen minutes. As far as roll numbers were concerned, I knew exactly where Aditya's seat was.

I saw his pouch lying on the bench. He was nowhere to be seen. I tiptoed to his seat. I opened his pouch which was designed with animated superheroes and right at the bottom, I kept the piece of paper with the formulae.

Then, I tiptoed back to my seat and never once looked back. Goldie entered the class ten minutes later.

✹ ✹ ✹

March 22, 2001, Monday11:45 am

We had a massive canteen at K.V. and at recess, it would be like completely filled, with no room even for a needle. There would be frenzied waiters who would stand behind counters and keep on collecting coupons and distributing food items randomly. So, if you stood at the counter amongst another hundred guys and girls all jumbled together with your open hand extended at the counter, sometimes you could get lucky and a samosa or burger for free!

It happened to me that day. I got lucky and had a sandwich for free but as I turned to savour it, I faced the person I least expected.

Aditya stood in front of me, his porky face twitched into a frown.

"That's my order." he roared.

That grabbed the attention of onlookers and every pair of eyes settled on me now. I couldn't accept the truth, that was shameful, so I did what I was best at.

"Sorry dude, finders, keepers." I tried to walk away swiftly, but he grabbed my wrist.

"Not that easy, topper." Aditya growled, "You stole it, now you're gonna give it back to me."

I lost my nerves but I continued, "I don't know what you're talking about, buddy." I lied swiftly again faking a calm smile, " but you can have the snack if you're that hungry or desperate." I handed the jerk my plate, "Here you go, do lemme know if you need monetary help, too."

At this, I heard other students break into bouts of laughter. I had won again, so I turned for the exit in my playful attitude.

Then came the flying sandwich, which crashed directly into my face.

"You and your dad are nothing but petty thieves, you scumbags." that was the last thing I heard before I felt my eyes moisten over the insult.

***

March 29, Monday 9:20 am

"What is this?" I heard Goldie Sir scream at a back bencher, "You brought cheats, how dare you?" I heard the sound of a brutal slap.

Mission accomplished.

Revenge taken.

Aditya's suspended now, for this term. He would be disqualified for this paper and I felt a cold relief.

"But I swear it's not mine, Sir."

It was Pritish's voice and my hands went cold.

His voice took the breath out of me. I looked back in panic and I was stunned. I had miscalculated the seating arrangement.

God damn it! I had misplaced the cheat in Pritish's pouch, mistaken it for Aditya's seat.

And, there stood Pritish, clueless, in deep shit just because of his best friend's idiotic vendetta.

"I don't have a clue how it got here, I swear Sir, I'm not a cheater." Another slap.

"Shut up, you know what, you're getting suspended." Goldie yelled like a madman, "Look at your guts, you disgraceful dud."

I saw Pritish break into tears, I watched Aditya casually writing his answers on the exam sheet, his lips twisted into a smile and I saw other fellow students look at my best friend with scowls over their faces. I felt anger wash away my fears and then I had to do it.

"No Sir, it's not him." I shouted from my seat rising up.

All eyes on me (I always felt like a stupid attention seeker!)

Goldie's furious eye balls were almost breaking loose of his eye lids. He looked like the devil ready to cut my throat, "What do you mean, Aakash?"

"I mean that." I shivered with fear as I told the lie.

"It's Aditya's."

I heard the entire class gasp, watched the smile on Aditya's face fade away into a contorting confusion as he looked up at me, petrified.

"What are you trying to say?", Goldie went numb and perplexed.

The same happened to the rest of the class, Pritish included.

"Yes Sir, it's Aditya's cheats, I saw him with them. I don't know how it got into Pritish's pouch, but let me tell you, Pritish has been set up. It's Aditya's cheats."

"He's lying Sir", Aditya squeaked, "he's framing me".

Goldie was going berserk now.

"I'm being honest, Sir. Why would I lie to you, Sir? I'm the class monitor for heaven's sake, I'm telling the truth, I promise." I had my fingers crossed.

Goldie looked at my humble (or so it seemed) face, then at the sheepish face of Pritish, pleading for innocence, then his eyes turned in Aditya's direction. Aditya's porky, demonic face ruined his chances.

"You know what, Aakash." Goldie said at last, "I trust you and I'm thankful to you that you saved an innocent fellow's exam."

"Thank you, Sir." I had no hint of guilt.

"Aditya, I want you in my office, now." Goldie stalked out.

There was momentary silence as the entire class tried to comprehend the chain of events.

Aditya rose up from his seat, his expressions haywire, then he walked up to me and said only one word, "Why?"

I saw his eyes well up. For the first time there was fear rather than stubborness in them.

"Because, I always win." I heard my ego speak.

✳✳✳

March 29, 12:00 noon

"YOU NEVER SAID THAT ANIMATED POUCH WAS YOURS, STUPID."

I cursed Pritish right after the exam.

"I showed it to you the day I bought it, remember?" Pritish explained.

"But, hey." suddenly he paused, "wait a minute, why do you ask that?"

"Nothing, forget it." I suddenly realised my slip of the tongue.

"Oh man!" I saw Pritish do the maths, his eyes widen, and then he stuttered, "You did that? You placed those cheats? Why?"

He was bewildered.

"It wasn't for you." I started walking away.

"Oh, so, this is what happened, you got Aditya falsely accused. You took revenge, didn't you? You planted that cheat." Pritish was outraged now.

I kept quiet as I packed my bag.

"You're such a bloody liar." He cursed.

"Don't say that." I retorted, "Just saved you, didn't I?"

"Oh, did you?" Pritish mocked in frustration, "You betrayor, you got me into trouble, then saved me and destroyed another guy's exam."

"Don't over-sell it, fatso." I said loathingly. I could feel the monster in me speak up in self defense.

"I'm ashamed even to call you my friend. Our friendship is over." and with that Pritish stalked out.

I stood there, frozen, anger gripping my soul.

P.S.: *Lies make you real bad, like me!*

LIE 011

"*Our friendship is over ...*"
I see Pritish walk away, and as he turns the corner, I see the hatred, the disgust he feels over his 'once best friend', the guy who never called him fatso, who loved him even over his flaws and who really appreciated his skill at some video games. Today, he has no place for the liar, today after the liar took the courage to defend him against a suspension, the liar who saved him from a term of humiliation, all he has in return, is hatred.

I know I can be bad sometimes from another perspective, but that's okay, right? I mean, even I don't like the 'over-confident-Nick' when he is advising others about what they should do in spare time, when he insults others saying they got no future in music as if he is some Sinatra or somebody!

I don't like Vicky when he's staring at girls as if he has seen that species for the first time! And I absotulely hate Pritish's irregular eating habits, the guy literally could do some good with exercise and diet control programme, but hey, I don't complain.

I respect people for their own decisions, and I don't stop them from screwing up their lives. It's their private territory we're talking about, who're we to advice them, we got our own problems!

Well, but that didn't work out too well for Pritish. Soon after he came to know about 'how-I-trapped-Aditya-and -got-him-failed', kaboom! he just decided to ditch his best friend. Suddenly, he had this dawning of self-realization and the justice league cartoon characters were in sudden action, and then the stupid fatso leaves me.

And so, here I was, handling the after effects. Dad had gone out of town, for some official work. These were golden times when I'd normally call up Pritish and ask him to stay over. We'd stay up late, have popcorn, watch movies in my new PC, play NFS-7 and have a great time.

But with the 'no Pritish' era, I had to rely on my other friends, so I called to check on them, for the night. We made plans to rehearse our foundation show presentation. They came prepared with a guitar and a drum set and soon there was havoc! I mean, at first I thought that Vicky could really play those drums but soon I realised, that all he kept doing was hitting a stick on wood. There was no rhythm, no music, for crying out loud, it was even worse than the tunes the tribes make in the jungles of Timbaktoo!

To worsen the situation, Vicky would keep stupefying Nick with his tales of how he flirted with all the beautiful girls of our school, only we knew that half of those girls never even knew who this Vicky the 'so-called playboy' was. Vicky was engaged talking about all his inherited property and how they had farm houses in every corner of the country. It all looked like an irritating lie at that point, but around three years down the lane, Vicky's fortune did materialise (hey, that's another story!).

Two and a half hours of torment later,

Nick was busy playing '*Tum toh thehre pardesi*!' on his guitar, I mean, how lame is that!

"You know, Aakash," Nick tells me in a matter-of -factly tone, "I think if we can change the tune to c-minor here, we can get an all new remix version of '*tum toh thehre pardesi*', how's that?"

"Dude, we're not playing for a leaky bar, it's the Foundation Day of our school." I said, irritated.

"I mean, there would be kids our age, and they would've gathered for fun, you know what I mean?" I looked at them trying to make sense, "We should give them peppy and rock, not some rhetoric sad bolly song!"

Vicky and Nick looked at me as if I had stabbed them with a dagger or something far brutal.

"That's really mean, Aakash", Vicky pipes in, "did you even hear how nicely we were playing the song, all we'll have to do is change the lyrics or something, so that nobody can make out it's a copy!" .

"Exactly." Nick was hopeful again. I shrugged.

"We can change the lyrics to something like "HUM TOH THEHRE COOL KV, HUMSE KYA TAKRAOGE." Vicky spilled.

"Wow, that's good, dude." Nick winked.

"THAT"S GOOD!" I almost yelled "THAT FREAKING THING'S GOOD?"

It caught them off guard and both of them stepped back nervously.

"What kinda line is that, Vicky, have you lost it completely? I mean, are we making some sadistic torturous spoof song?" I was literally shouting now.

"Look, I don't care that you guys know to play only one crappy song, and I don't even care that you can't play it well, all that matters to me is some peace of mind, so get the hell out of here!"

They both looked at me, flabbergasted.

They rose from their seats quietly and started packing their stuff. I could see Vicky's cheeks had turned red and Nick was avoiding my gaze.

"Okay, look guys, I didn't mean that." I tried to make it up to them.

"Hey, you don't have to do that, we get it." Nick said in a sand-papery voice.

"You don't like our company, you're a topper and you're smarty pants, we get it."

"Hey guys, why're you accusing me? You know I..."

"Let's go, Nick" Vicky stormed out, his drum set dangling in his hand. Nick looked at me one last time as if it were a farewell scene and then he too disappeared.

I sighed, my heart had turned steel and I felt choked. What had gotten into me?

✶✶✶

Things had turned gloomy in around here. I had lost all my friends and my small tiny bubble world had burst.

And, that's when I flunked for the first time and repeated the track record twice more.

I remember, it was a mathematics class test and I got 0/10, silly mistakes in each one of the sums, our maths professor Deshpande Sir, called me in his cabin personally to give that paper.

"What's wrong, Aakash, you used to be good at this?" he said with a tone of disappointment.

"I don't know, sir," I lied.

"You know son, you do, it's all in your mind," he said watching me closely.

My expressions remained composed, I couldn't show him tears, I was too proud for that.

"Aakash, you know mistakes are the best things that can happen to a person, don't be ashamed of them."

I looked up at Deshpande Sir and I could see a hint of kindness and benevolence in his old eyes, "Remember, Aakash, you never lost your focus, you just forgot to use it, start from the beginning again and figure out where you went wrong."

Five minutes later, I was walking down the hallway to the canteen, trying to figure it all out and then, it all made sense.

We always have the answers; we just can't accept the facts.

Truth is just never spicy enough.

LIE 012

It was just like my first day at school all over again. No friends to talk to, no games to play, just the solitude which suddenly felt overrated. I would skip past the entire class, sitting firm and rigid in my bench, no turning my head back to talk to Pritish, no high-fiving Vicky and no Nick jokes anymore. There was no Aditya to fight with and I was surprised to see that I missed the clashes, on second thoughts, *maybe, I was losing my mind.*

It happened one day before my dad was to return from his trip. Right after school was over, I knew I had a lot of time to kill. I mean, there was no one waiting for me at home and I felt too bored to get back to the monotony of my place, so I took a detour. I biked through the edges of jungli ghaat (hope you remember my explanation for this weird name!), then I sloped down through the small hill beside the airport road, and soon I was zigzagging through a small clay road, cutting through small bushes. My cycle kept hitting bumps and it seemed anytime we would have a giant fall. Even though all I could see were forests in front of me, I had this gut feeling, that something lay right behind these woodlands, some deserted place and as I made chivalric cuts through the forest lanes, I could feel it coming, after some more bushes, shrubs, a terrain filled with coconut trees I finally skidded to a halt!

I was around five miles from my school in a completely new haven.

The zephyr took my breath away. I stood, one foot in deep golden yellow sands, my eyes squinting in the scorching sun, facing the most blissful sight of my life; I stood on a huge deserted beach, and looked at infinite stretches of deep ultramarine sea that blurred into the horizon.

The beach was massive, an arc of around two kilometres, all sparkling with hot sand and sea shells. The waves clashed vehemently with the shore. There were no other islands in sight and it was vast expanses of never-ending blue.

However, this story revolves around something else, it's about what I discovered on that sea beach that maps this story.

It was an old, abandoned and broken ship. It was wood crafted, with a narrow hull and two masts. Its two main sails were large and smaller sails were installed at the bow and stern. The ship had a large bowl. It was anchored around 400 metres from the beach where the waters were quite deep.

I gaped at the sight! This was surreal. A solitary deserted beach in the middle of nowhere with no sign of human existence and an antique old ship with no crew, only barrels and wood and mast! I was thrilled.

I returned home at twilight. I felt euphoric. I knew this was going to be a secret that I'd preserve, and I also had the feeling that I'd go there every day starting from the next one.

✳ ✳ ✳

Dad got home the next day, and I had no time to waste after school. I was also enrolled into this stupid tuition centre where they taught maths and made us memorise tables up to 25.

So, this left me with no spare time, until, of course, I made some out of thin air, and that's exactly what I did.

The plan was to skip the last period every day and spent that hour at my favourite place experimenting. But it had its shortcoming. Luckily, we had different subjects in the last class every day. And, it was utilised for checking assignments. Anybody who failed to submit their home assignments were thrown out of the class, and somehow, that's exactly what I wanted.

So, I started lying. Every day, I would hide my bag in the canteen in the second last period, then tiptoe back to the class, wait for the submission obstacle to start, and as soon as the teacher would inquire about the defaulters who had not completed their assignments, my hand would fly up. It shocked the teachers at first, after all, the topper had started showing his grey colours and I knew complaints were supposed to follow, so I made my **back-up** plan, too. Right when I would be shooed out of the class, I'd quietly disappear into the canteen, grab my bag, then go to the staff room, submit the **copy of my home work** at the respective teacher's table and then saunter away for my adventure visit to the sea beach.

***

14th June, 2001

It had been a month since the plan had been initiated and things were still manageable except some regular slaps and canes.

I remember that day even now. I sat, legs crossed, my drawing book wide open, as I sketched the ship. By now, I had a lot of theories for its existence, the most controversial being a hypothesis that stated it to be a "PIRATE SHIP"!

I mean, think about it. Port Blair is a very secluded island, once it hosted British decks and colonies and so the possibility of an old pirate ship was irrefutable! The unrealistic part of the whole hypothesis though was my curiosity about ransacking the ship and discovering a hidden chest filled with treasures! Yeah, I know it sounds silly and stupid, but I was a kid with a curiosity and a lot of imagination.

This immense curiosity had been egging me on far too long and every day for the whole of last week, I kept swimming around 100–200 metres near the coast, then getting frightened by the giant waves and doubling back. On 14th of June, I finally made it to the ship!

***

13th June, 2001

The phone rings impatiently. Dad answers.

"Hello, Anshuman Roy here."

"Hello Mr Roy, this is Sona Kumar, Aakash's class teacher."

"Oh, hello Sir, how're you?"

"Well, I'm fine, I err ... actually needed to talk to you about some things."

"Oh", dad is worried now, "Go on please."

"It's related to your son, Aakash, we've had complaints."

✶✶✶

LIE 013

13th June, 2001

"What did he do?" My dad is shocked at what he hears next.

Sona Kumar explains "I mean, it started a month ago. Your son has been getting punished on a regular basis due to incompletion of his home assignments."

"What?", dad retorts, "Are you sure, Sir? I've seen him doing his studies without fail. There must have been some mistake."

"Yes, I am coming to that," Sona Kumar clears his throat, "See, that's the problem. I mean, he gets thrown out of the class everyday and the next minute he walks up to the teacher's room and submits his assignment neatly done with no errors."

"What are you trying to say, why'd he do that?" Dad is speechless.

"Well, that exactly is the cause of my concern." Sir explains, " and unfortunately even I don't have an answer. Your son is quite intelligent but looks like he has something else cooking up."

"So, you think if I talked to him, I could make him confess the cause of his actions?"

"That's exactly what I am trying to say," Sona Kumar verified.

My dad shrugged.

"It's not that easy, Sir." he said after an instant. "My son might be smart and intelligent in science and maths. He might be dumb and bad at sports. But one thing, he's the best at." Dad grimaced as he completed his sentence "It's his lies. He can fool anybody. Make them trust him."

"Lies?" Sona Kumar is stupefied. "Aakash makes up stories, too? I always thought he was a very honest kid."

59

"My point exactly." dad smiles sadly to himself.

✳ ✳ ✳

14th June, 2001

The waters swallowed me once and again as giant waves would form, but after around 300 metres, the surface waves had subsided and I could feel the massive water body haunting me. I gathered up all my courage and stroked through. I needed to get into that ship for my investigation. It was high time that the wrecked ship be brought back to life. I knew there might be nothing in there worth prying but the curious heart would just not see reason.

Finally, I reached the ship. Now, somehow I had to climb up, but there seemed to be a problem! It was like a two–storey building with no stairs to get to the rooftop! I circled around across the entire edges for ten minutes before finding a rope ladder finally that hung from one edge of the ship!

I sighed with relief. Finally, I made it to the ship and let me tell you this, all the risk and danger involved felt like worth it, I mean the place (the deck), was filled with antique weird stuff. There were empty barrels, huge canisters, old trunks and a pile of empty wine bottles. So, indeed, it felt like a true pirate ship. I could see the huge sails tied with heavy ropes, the white colours faded and moist. For split seconds I felt like cutting off the ropes and let it snake through the brisk wind. Every step I took in any direction, the wooden deck would make cracking sounds as if they were gonna twist apart. So, I advanced warily towards a ransacked cabin which was dimly lit. All of a sudden, there was a scream!

It was dreadful and I shivered. I looked wildly at all sides trying to find the source of the scream, but no more sounds! Silence enveloped me. I was chilled to the bone. Something was very wrong.

I stepped forward, my heart rate accelerating. The wooden floor cracked some more. 'Careful now', I mused as I raised my leg for the next step.

It came from behind me. A scream so wild, it made me sprint for cover. There was a deafening noise of rattling wood. One fatal step, next,

I felt the wooden deck collapse, and there I was, free falling under gravity, down twenty feet, right into black dark waters.

The fall was unexpected and horrifying. I swerved below the deep blue ocean before I could actually try for survival.

Picture this, I'm trapped right there, at the base of a broken ship, totally isolated from all sides by the hull, and it's very dark, I can't even figure out where I am. I panicked, my hands thrashing water on all sides, trying desperately to find a support, anything to cling to. I had to find it fast; I could feel the current now, trying to drag me to hell. And then the next mistake. I gasped for breath, while I was still five metres below the water level. Next thing you know, my lungs were filled with salt water and my throat cried out for air. My instincts went haywire spontaneously and all my brain could register anymore was fear and a dying urge for oxygen.

I tried to shout but couldn't breathe, I was dying and the sense of shock was indelibly frightening.

Slowly, I feel my panic subside; it's all like a blur in slow motion. I feel my brain going numb, a peace dragging a white canvas over my eyes. I see static and then all I can feel is a pull, something that separates your soul from the body, something that frees your existence and then, when you least expect it, I feel ... pain. The hit jolts me upside down and suddenly my neurons register a quench as I take a breath ...

LIE 014

14th May, 1989

It's the day that the mom dad story ended.

***

"*Life's got a lot of surprises*", Uncle used to say, "*And, they're what make us live.*"

But what about those tiny scratches of sadness that destroy the masterpiece?

The scars of the moon, life has its flaws, too.

I was born on an early Thursday rainy August morning, 13th, 1987.

Dad says it was the happiest day of their lives.

They celebrated, my dad filled mom's hospital bed with bouquets of roses, lilies, orchids and hundreds more but even then, he says my mom won the competition. She was the most beautiful thing in the world, more vibrant and fresh than those flowers, prettier than Marilyn Monroe.

The expenses increased with my birth, mom still didn't have a job and dad would be tense half the time; He was not the old Rajesh Khanna anymore. He had turned into something more like Manoj Kumar, sad, pessimistic, hands over his face!

And so, the masterpiece got stale, there would be heated arguments, fights and crying and sobbing. And, things got worse when mom offered dad help through her parents. Dad got hyper and he questioned mom's love.

Two years passed by and 1989 started. However, life got stuck in the same old lane. My dad tried every possibility, he wanted to fix up every broken bond, and would be out there fighting with the world all the while.

So, one fine day, mom got a call from her parents. Her dad had fallen ill, he was very sick and wanted to see his beautiful princess.

She went away at once, stayed with her parents for a week and after her dad got a little better, she returned. But you could tell, something inside her had snapped.

We never got to know what it was.

Dad asked for reasons, for explanations but he was unanswered. He could not make his beloved smile anymore. Things were changing, they were moving fast and dad could not stop them from falling apart. He had to get it all back, desperately. And, somewhere he knew he himself was to be blamed. So, one day when he got an offer from his office, something that promised him more salary, increments and maybe, a good life in the years to come, he accepted it, without second thoughts.

That night, mom and dad had a big argument.

"We can't go to Port Blair, it's some out of the way island in another part of the world! Oh, Anshuman, why did you take that transfer?" my mom lamented.

"This is the best shot I got Radhika, you know we're going broke and life's just getting wasted, I can't handle all this anymore." dad tried to explain.

"You could've asked me once before you made the decision, Anshuman, I mean, my life's also concerned. I could've asked dad for help." she abruptly stopped.

"Oh, so is this what it's all about." now dad turned cold, "So, are you saying you will have problems to live without your rich parents? That you don't care about your son anymore? I mean, you don't even have a job, do you remember that? What's keeping you here then?" dad crossed a line.

Mom was humiliated. "How mean can you get?" she felt fresh tears trickle down her cheek, "I didn't get the job because you made a fake promise remember, you lied. That's what got me stuck."

They went quiet as mom sobbed.

"See, I know that I can't gift you a life full of luxuries and pots of money, that I won't be able to buy you diamond rings or take you out to those countries we saw in silver screen together, but that's how life is Radhika, it's real."

"All I wanted was some love Anshuman, all I wanted was the old you, but that's not how life is I guess." mom whispered between broken sobs.

"Yeah, I've changed, the old impracticality is dead and don't worry, you'll get used to this Anshuman too", dad walked out.

The next day, mom left to spend the last few days with her parents, before our departure to Port Blair.

She promised dad she would meet him at the airport on the day they were supposed to leave for Port Blair. Dad and I made it to the airport at 7:30, an hour before the flight.

We waited the next hour.

I was some two years old when I last saw mom. She never came to the airport. She left us that day.

She was tired of her mediocre married life, she was tired of the fights, she was tired of the wedding that promised happiness and so, she walked out on us.

She broke dad's heart that day. She lied to him.

***

14th June, 2001

They say your entire life flashes before your eyes when you die.

Strange thing, the only thing that flashed before me when the world faded was my mom. I had seen her so many winters back that I didn't even remember her face, but right in those final moments after the incident in the pirate ship, I saw her, standing right before me, at the door. I saw her smile, saw those dimples that had made my dad go topsy–turvy once again and I felt her embrace, that warm happy feeling.

Life's full of surprises. They make us live ...

LIE 015

I open my eyes to blurring halogen lights, I see needles stuck to my arms, oxygen mask attached to my face, people in white medical suits rushing me down an alley and it blacks out.

I gain momentary consciousness again, try to breathe but it strains, I cry, and then amidst tears, I see them. I see my dad, his face serene; I can't make out what he says. Then I see her, standing there right behind the operation theatre window, beside dad, I see her tears, I can almost hear her silent prayers, it wipes off my trepidation and the valium comes into play.

"Mom," my lips form the words and I fade into nothingness once more.

***

How long have I been here? I can't make out the ambience. I'm in a small well-lit glass cabin, covered with olive green curtains, it's quiet out here, I can only make out the small whirring noise of an a.c. machine behind.

There's also a periodic beep. It's coming from a strange machine on the table on my right, which is displaying graphs of some analogue figures.

I try to sit up, and there's a sudden heaviness in my head. I stoop with the buzz in my ears.

"It's the drugs", a stranger's voice breaks the silence.

The voice is notably familiar.

I look up in his direction. A middle-aged heavy man, with a thick braid, French-cut moustache and green sparkling eyes, sits on a couch on the side. His eyes are focussed on mine, there's a mysterious glance in them that makes you aware of some divine wisdom.

I massage my scalp as I rest my head back on the pillow.

"Who're you?" I try to ask, and am immediately shocked with a fresh dose of pain down my throat. The labour moists my eyes.

"You should try silence, it'll help." the heavy voice is back into play, "And hello, I'm your guardian angel."

I look back at the man with bewilderment.

The man gives me a heavenly look as I notice his shiny starry colourful apparel. I can suddenly feel goosebumps as I try to make some sense.

"I'm just kidding ... oh boy, look at your face." the man breaks into a fit of laughter. I try to place that voice in my mind, I've heard it before.

"Okay, enough of my bad jokes, hello Aakash, lemme formally introduce myself, I'm Paritosh Sarkar."

"And", he stops me as I open my lips again, "In case you're wondering why I am here, well then, let me tell you, I'm the one who got you out of that black hole."

It hits me like a bloody memory. The pirate ship, the black waters, the drowning, the scream.

"And, no need to thank me," the man continues on his own, "I did what I had to do, not that I didn't try to stop you twice, for heaven's sake didn't you hear my screams!"

"It was you!!!" I screech through my battered voice as fresh ache strikes back.

"Yes, monsieur, it was I who saved you from this debacle." The man stands up, with a lordly air and there's a hint of joyful glee in his expressions.

"Boy, you should've looked at yourself when I first got you out of the mess, you seemed lifeless."

Your screams got me into that lifeless situation, I curse in my mind.

"Anyways, now that you're awake, I should go alert your dad and others."

I'm suddenly expectant. Did he say *others.* I can suddenly feel adrenaline rush through my veins.

As he starts walking off, I speak somehow, "Hey what's with those fancy clothes of yours?"

The bloke stops mid-way, turns and then approaches me with a swift stride, his overcoat swishing.

"You see, for people like us," he whispers in a nearly inaudible voice as I strain my ears, "there's a dress code."

Then, he raises his right hand which is empty, moves it in a blur, and out of that empty hand pops out a blue lotus.

"Whoa," I'm astounded as Paritosh hands me the lotus, then smiles in his majestic way, "It might come as a surprise, but I've started feeling like I really am your guardian angel, saved you twice."

I'm confused. The guy walks to the door, then booms in his heavy voice, "Greetings from the magician", and in the next wink of an eye, he's gone.

Greetings from the magician, suddenly I'm back to the old banyan tree on Diwali, and I remember the stranger in a cloak, who had flashed the torch in our eyes and ordered us to leave. I rack my brains. Now, I knew the ghost, the magician. I'm struck by the coincidence.

The door opens, and I see my dad enter. He reminds me suddenly of the Rajesh Khanna of 'Anand', where the actor is playful and happy and at the same time there's a tinge of sadness in his eyes.

"For a moment you scared the shit out of me, son." Dad sighed as he stroked my hair.

But I'm not listening to him, my eyes are on the door, I can see shadows on the glass, somebody else is approaching

Mom. I wait for her to enter. My heartbeat accelerates.

I've waited for this moment forever.

Then, the door opens, and to my astonishment, unexpected guests arrive. Pritish, Vicky and Nikhil stand right in front of me, their faces filled with impeccable excitement. They come and hug me and the expression freaks me.

"Yeah ... err ... okay." I try to set myself free of the sudden gesture.

"Hey", Pritish says patting my back.

"Hey." I reply in my ruptured voice. There's a moment of uncomfortable silence, then my dad clears his throat.

"I think I should give you guys a minute for some quick boy's talk." Dad walks away.

"Guys, I'm really sorry for what I did." I apologize without wasting a moment. I know it's my last shot.

"Hey, it's okay man! Cheer up!", Nick smiles at me, "You're always our friend, you've always been." Pritish and Vicky nod, "As long as you tell us the entire story ..."

"That does cheer me up." I start to giggle, maybe it's the drugs again.

"Alright, let's catch up,..," Vicky is all mushy.

"Okay then, here's what you missed."

✷✷✷

It's twilight. Doctors have stated that I'll have to be under observation for one more day.

Dad enters my ward with a plate of fruit salad. Then, he places it over the table, kisses my forehead and starts to leave.

"Hey, dad," I say calmly. Dad turns back.

"I saw mom." I can see dad's eyes widen, "I saw her in my dream." Dad remains expressionless.

There's a moment of curiosity as I wait for a reply, anything.

"Was she here?" I can hear my voice break.

Dad is quiet for two seconds, then he shrugs.

"No." He whispers and closes the door.

P.S.: *It took me two years to realise dad lied that day.*

LIE 016

The Cellular Jail! Also known as the *Kala Pani,* it is what represents the Port Blair that the British had built.

Now, the history of this prison is grave, pathetic. It is not a jail anymore, technically.

During the revolutions, thousands of prisoners were exiled for life to this dark prison. They were hanged, tortured and their fate was sealed.

The building had seven wings, at the centre of which a central tower served as the fulcrum and was used by guards to keep watch on the inmates. The wings radiated from the tower in straight lines, much like the spokes of a wheel. A large bell was kept in the tower to raise the alarm in any eventuality. The entire architecture was a masterpiece.

So, after my legendary (stupid, idiotic, cliché and depressing according to others) adventure of how-I-nearly-got-drowned, something new had developed inside me. Somehow I had developed a fear, of seas and waters, it was more like hydrophobia, And man! I really cringed at even the thought of the oceans. And see, that was the problem, I was on a landmass covered with oceans on all sides! Hence my dad had this sudden change of mind, and he felt that I could really do with some sightseeing. So there I was, along with my dad visiting places. However, the effort was in vain. Somehow I had started to become a real grown up coward, and I hated it.

It was a Saturday evening and I was strolling down the corridors of the Cellular Jail, watching out for the execution chambers. It was then, that I saw him again, Paritosh Sorkar, the magician, sitting at the corner of the huge prison, showing off magic tricks to a bunch of small kids.

The man's way of displaying his talents had a flair that was so innate that it would compel you to cherish the magic tricks he pulled off. He had this whimsical attitude and this casual enigma that made him an impressive character. The magician performed around five tricks, each flavoured with such fluent presentation, that you could savour the whole affair. I applauded after he made a dove vanish into thin air.

"Alright fellas, the show's over for tonight, five rupees each, kindly." He forwarded his black magic hat to everyone in turns, and we paid the money. When he noticed me, his extraordinary smile was back into play, "Oh, great heavens, look who we have here with us tonight, it's Robinson Crusoe!", he broke into his explicit fits of laughter. I couldn't help noticing the effort he made to carry off his convivial image.

"Wow, you really did pull off some great stuff today. That was fab," I said making a fake applause after the kids had left and Paritosh had started packing.

"Thank you, lad." he smiled back, "I'm really glad to see you in perfect shape again. I was wondering that you'd gradually turn up in my search to know the story of how I escaped you twice."

"Yeah, about that, I guess I know. But I would leave it at that. Consider you to be my guardian angel. Don't wanna know the truth, you see", I pointed out, "I like magic more. Lies in perfection they're. Has a power to heal your soul."

"Good God", Paritosh's eyes sparkled, "you have a philosopher in you," he winked.

I stayed quiet.

"But you know something, Aakash, magic isn't just lies. It's the moment of true happiness in them. And, it's not the lies, it's not the sleight of hand that makes a show remarkable, it's the happiness that heals."

I stared at the humble bloke, "Why is it then, you can't hide your sadness?"

Paritosh went quiet. He looked at me with astounded amusement, "I don't ... err."

"You know, I'm quite small and all those things, but I am really good at recognising a person with issues." I commented, smirking.

"Oh, boy, you're really something, aren't you?" Paritosh scratched his brow, "I'm sorry, but I can't deny the fact that you're quite right and yeah, I'm a bad actor", he simpered.

"What is the reason that a guardian angel is troubled with such a simple matter as life?" I humoured.

The magician chuckled, "The same old most common thing in the world, thin green pieces of paper." He showed me the five rupee notes. "Got a daughter, Aakash." Paritosh lifted his bag and we trotted out, "Need to get her married, you know the same old story."

I didn't have anything to say to the sorcerer. He couldn't hide his grief.

"Hey, I've an idea." I said after a while as we approached the gate, "Why don't you perform in our school on Foundation Day, it'd be great to have you there."

"I don't know, Aakash." Paritosh shrugged, "I really get nervous before a big audience, it's quite hard to carry off my 'lies' in a crowd." he winked at me.

"No, c'mon it'd be great, and I'll introduce you to my friends also. You can tell them the story of how you saved me twice and all." I tried to encourage him.

The guy beamed, "I'll think about it."

I *start to part ways, when the bloke calls out my name. I turn back at him and he's standing there, ten feet away from me, his silhouette dazzling with an aura,* "Always remember, Aakash, that your heart is pure and it can't be shrouded; it'll continuously beat away with rebellion, and even if you're a liar or a betrayer, you always have a second chance. We are all escapists, but we should always remember our way back home when we have nowhere else to hide."

"I'll remember that." *I promise him, pensive.*

"Yeah, you do that. Helps me every time I face my conscience." *He smiles and leaves,* "Magic is lies in perfection".

P.S.: *Happiness is a lie. You just need to deceive your heart with it.*

LIE 017

The scribbling noise is the most audible thing in the atmosphere. There's a vibe of nervousness floating around. I look at Pritish, he has this expression of utmost concentration, every muscle in his temple is twitching and the effort has brought drops of perspiration on his face drastically. I break into silent giggles just by watching Pritish think!

I concentrate on my paper, the sheet is full. I've written down all the answers and revised it twice. No probability of mistakes. I feel satisfied. Five minutes for the exam to end. I smirk, I'm good.

***

"How was the last paper?" Dad asks as I set off.

"Great, dad." I give him a wide grin, stopping on my tracks.

"Nice, err ... where are you headed?"

"Dad, you forgot? We have a picnic today, mid-terms just ended, so we gonna go out, have some fun."

"Oh yes, I remember." dad beamed, "It's just that I had to talk to you about something."

I looked at him with rapt attention, "I'm all ears."

He opened his mouth, thought for a moment, closed it and then shrugged, "You know what I think." he said in a sheepish way, "I think it can wait. We'll talk when you return."

"Is it something I should worry about?", I'm curious.

"Naah", dad pops out the newspaper, "It's nothing important." He lies.

"Fine." I sprinted away, oblivious of what dad had in store.

Pritish, Vicky and Nicks are standing outside, from the look of it, they're super-excited.

"Alright guys, what's the plan??" I'm welling with anticipation.

"Carbines cove, the entire class will be there. We're so going to have a blast." Vicky shouts loud enough for the entire neighbourhood to know.

"The ocean," I hesitate, my fear triggering.

"Dude, trust me, you're going to be fine." Pritish persuades, "I'll keep you busy with my review of the new halo game."

Okay now, carbines cove, it's a popular beach at Port Blair. It has all these coral views and a garden filled with thousands of coconut trees. It's sensational.

We reach the place at 1:30 in the afternoon. The place is all crowded and filled with classmates, kin and foes. I even spot Goldie Sir amidst the congregation. He is sporting a flannel shirt playing with his kids. He looks at us and waves at us to join him. Soon we're having a gala time. Running off to the shore, playing football and cards, having samosas and the adrak wali chai, it's just brilliant. Later, we set out on boats with bases made of heavy glass, to check out the corals and mangroves. After an hour or two of aggressive fun, we're tired and my friends are all diving into the water while I sit under the sun, enjoying the breeze. The hydrophobia is still there tying my wings.

"Hey, Aakash." the familiar voice comes as a surprise.

"Anisha, oh wow." I'm taken aback, "It's such a pleasure. How've you been?"

She sits beside me on the sand, her eyes on the ocean, "I'm fine, have been hearing about your wild adventures."

"Gee, I'm famous", I wink at her.

"Yeah you've been quite some star. Though beware of my brother. He really isn't taking the publicity in a positive way."

"Aditya, yes of course." I smirk smugly.

"You know what, I just saw a small alligator in the coconut garden." Anisha is all worked up.

"It might've been a chameleon." both of us burst out laughing.

"So, you don't talk to me anymore now. Why's that? Have you gotten over your first girl friend?" she looks at me now, and I stare back at her. Amidst the playful expressions, I spot a vague expression of sadness.

"I err..." I think then shrug, "...have eventually run out of excuses."

"You don't need to have one. It's okay." She grows quiet and oblivious.

"You know when I first met you Anisha," I mumble, "all I wanted was a bit of help in English. Competition and all." I sigh.

She's listening attentively, I can tell, so I went on.

"But later when I got you into all those stupid controversies, it really took me one good punch right on my face to understand the fact that when you first met me, all you needed was a good friend. You were so innocent and faithful to me, that I couldn't stand it. I guess that's why I walked out of our friendship. I was tired of lying, you know. "

"Then, why're you telling me this now?" Anisha is curious.

"A sip of the truth." I face her now.

Her eyes meet mine, and somewhere I know our friendship hasn't died through the test of time.

"You might've killed it today." She understands me as she replies, "but you proved your mettle. You deserve my friendship, I think", she's making a fake pondering expression.

"Yeah, sure." I stick my tongue out, and the next minute we're fighting and playing.

Later that evening, as we return, Pritish is done with his tale of the best video games of all time, Vicky is day dreaming about his special yet-to-be-girlfriend. Rumour has it, that he spotted her in the beach again, and she was really looking pretty. Nicks is humming 'Hotel California' by eagles.

And, all I can think about is Anisha. She had done it today. She broke into my mind and got the truth out of me and I was feeling so light and happy, it felt amazing. There was a sudden change approaching, I could feel it.

✱✱✱

"Aakash, you awake?", dad enters my room. He looks real serious and apparently I'm worried now.

"What happened, dad?"

"Okay, here it goes." dad fires away, "I don't know how to tell you this."

"What do you mean?" I'm confused.

Dad scratches his scalp, and then he looks right into my tense face.

"We're leaving, Aakash."

LIE 018

7th September, 2001

This is the story of our Foundation Day. These are the last few memories I have of my days at Port Blair. I was to leave this place in the next seven days. Dad had got his transfer order, and we were moving back to our native land, Calcutta. But to me, Port Blair was my real home. This was the place where my entire life was, this was the place that I cherished, and it had my friends, without whom I couldn't contemplate my future. Now, can you believe it, for the last eight years, I have met my friend Pritish every day, even if sometimes we talk, sometimes we would hurt each other, sometimes we were bored of each other's presence, but I was used to him. He was part of my daily routine. He had to happen, like sunrise, like heart beats and life was incomplete without him.

I was real quiet about the whole matter of my departure. I mean, I never liked goodbyes and those sad songs and stuff. So, I couldn't gather up the courage to declare the news to my friends as of yet. So, the Foundation day was like the last thing that we were all gonna do together. It was really important for me, and even a week before, we were out of ideas for our performance.

Vicky and Nick suggested that we should go with *Summer of 69*, or *Yaaron dosti* by K.K.

But I didn't want that. I wanted something new, something that was ours, that had our name and our memories attached to it, something that we would treasure in the days to come.

That was the day "ENVY" came into picture! Envy was the name of our first band (or so we referred to it). 'Envy' came from the letters "ANV", the initials of our names, Aakash, Nicks and Vicky (A.N.V.).

Though envy does refer to a negative vibe, but I cherished the name a lot. It was like our personal "Metallica".

"So, now that we have our own band, we need to have an original song for it", I thought out loud.

"Not even remixes are allowed, are they?" Vicky asked.

"No, only creativity." I said with pride.

"Okay then, where do we start, lyrics, music or genres?", Nick queried opening his guitar case and taking out his black pluto semi-acoustic.

Now, that came as a bummer. Even I didn't know how to compose songs. I mean, all we ever talked were about dreams, about how our band might be, what'd be our icon and all those extra affairs, but we were no expert musicians! How then?

"Okay, let's start with a concept", I envisioned.

"It should be about happiness and love", Vicky was all perked up.

"Um...that's a good one, you know Vicky I was thinking on the lines of a song, that's about a person who has the happiness of his life, who has great love, awesome friends but then, who has to leave it all away, and go, escape from paradise."

"I don't get it, when somebody has all the happiness in the world, why does he need to leave it? why has he got to lock himself up in some "cocoon"? quit living?" Vicky is confused.

"Cos he doesn't have a choice," I mumbled, pensive.

"That's pretty messed up. I mean, we always have a second option." Nick said tuning his guitar.

It took me 97 lies, before I understood his statement, the other option. But that's another story. Now, back to the present context.

"Yeah, I know it's pretty difficult, but hey, that's how songs are." I smiled at him.

"Alright what's the lyrics gonna be?" Vicky took out a pen.

"I don't know yet."

And so, we started with our first song. It took us the entire night to figure out the lyrics, the music wasn't still in rhythm, but we kept going on. It was like Nikhil would first compose a tune, which had right ingredients, like nostalgia and a hint of sadness. Then, we would rhyme it with words, with lines of a poem, that was based on the concept we had in mind.

Our first song was "*jo thi dil ki khushi*". It was all about the place I called home. It's my favourite composition till date. The most subtle, honest and simple lyrics I ever penned.

***

Five minutes to our performance...

It's mayhem out there. There's a huge audience, lights, teachers, expectations. Nick is having problems with the guitar, it's not properly tuned. Vicky isn't sure he remembers the beats or not, and I, well, I was hyper-ventilating, as usual. See, singing in front of people was never my cup of tea, I felt it was embarrassing, silly and juvenile. I always liked seclusion, estrangement, but okay, this was not the time for such solitary thoughts. I tried to get my head back on the show. I could see the enthusiasm in the crowd. They had all gone berserk! They howled, booed, jumped and danced like frenzied maniacs and man! they were really counting on us.

"Okay, guys, you ready to roll?" the host points at us in the backstage, as he walks off to the podium, "guys and girls." he announces...

I look at Vicky and Nick, they look back, there are butterflies in my stomach, We tap, wish each other luck and then walk towards the stage. I see Pritish at the front row with popcorn and samosas, his face beaming. *Breathe, I say to myself, breathe now.* I feel the pump of adrenaline thumping my veins, my nervous system is going for a toss, I close my eyes one last time and then open it to the flashes of the thousand lights.

"I present to you, the debut performance of ENVY the band." is the last thing I hear before Nick starts off with the guitar...

***

Five minutes later...

I didn't know the reaction. I didn't look back when I left the stage after the song had ended. Nick was still out there in the podium, he was playing the lead of *Summer of 69* and I could hear the yelps and the cheers.

I'm numb; my face is hot with the excitement I just felt. But somewhere, I knew, something wasn't right.

I couldn't think; it was like brain freeze.

Vicky is all chirpy, "How was our performance, Aakash, did you hear the cheers? I mean, I was so into involved my performance, I lost track of everything else."

Nick enters backstage, "I bet we made some mistakes. I could see people showing the thumbs down, damn it, we ruined it ... I forgot the lead." he slaps his head in frustration.

"We did great", I broke into fits of laughter, "We nailed it, guys."

"We did?", Vicky's face sparkled.

Nick was surprised, "Really?"

"Oh, yeah, we did, really." I danced, losing my grip, "You guys were like the real rockstars...hats off."

"Yaay," Vicky was jumping up and down in excitement. He sprinted up to me and hugged me, Nick joined in. And, brothers in arms, I lied again, "We did just too good. People are really going to envy us for years to come..."

"They will?" Vicky asked expectantly.

"You bet." I welled up with tears, "But hey, on a serious note, I know these guys, they might discourage you and all, but don't listen to them. Trust me, we were great down there, they might just be jealous." I kept on lying, deceiving them.

I didn't care about a show, about victories and defeats when it came down to my best friends.

I didn't care about the truth or lies.

I just had to make sure my friends were happy, 'cos they had the choice.

LIE 019

7th September, 2001
8:45 pm

The star rises on the stage. As the entire audience watches in rapt attention, he calls a random guy up to the stage. He has to show his last trick for the night, he gifts us his million dollar smile as his heavy voice fills the auditorium, "Boys and girls, get ready for some magic."

***

8:10 pm (15 minutes earlier)

"Let's get to the stage, some supernatural stuff." the host announces to a cheering crowd."I give you, the magician ..."

I cheer like crazy. He did accept my request. He came. Paritosh Sorkar climbs up the stage, his golden overcoat with multi-coloured dots, swishing behind him. In his charming manner, he comes up to the centre. Then, he waves his hand at us and the next instant, rose petals fly up all around from nowhere. I am breathless. It's gonna be a great show, I can tell.

But as Paritosh speaks, I know something is definitely wrong.

"Hello, everyone, I'm Paritosh and I'm here to spellbind you." He winks at the crowd, but somewhere I can feel that he is not his usual self, there is this wary serious shadow all around him, and I can tell he is hiding his feelings more than ever tonight.

But nobody can make out. People applaud with anticipation.

Paritosh started showing his tricks; he was a master in making things disappear — coins and birds. Then, his card tricks continued, there was the "needle through the thumb" trick, the scotch and soda thing, the aquarian illusion, the origami trick, but he really started going down after the first ten minutes, in the mental calculator magic. He made two mistakes and students booed. Paritosh started losing his concentration, he looked nervous and after one point he almost stopped most of his interactions with the crowd.

When he went backstage to get his instruments for the next trick, I made my decision....

✱ ✱ ✱

8:47 pm .... (present)

The random student is asked to sit on a chair, and concentrate on a dangling locket. To everyone's surprise, Paritosh was going for the kill, he was going to hypnotise the guy.

And, everybody had their doubts.

"Alright concentrate on this locket, your eyes are getting heavy now." everybody is stupefied as the guy's eyes start blinking; he looks like he's in some kind of a trance.

There's pin drop silence and the ambience is suddenly serene.

"You are getting dizzy now. You're going to sleep. Relax now." Paritosh looks menacing and the crowd is on the edge of their seats.

The boy has grown quiet now. He's petrified and looks stoned.

"Now, dear boy, please sing 'Mary had a little lamb to us'."

There's a reverberating applause down the crowd as the boy starts singing the nursery rhyme in his shrill voice, his eyes closed, still in a trance.

"Wow, that was melodious," Paritosh winks at the crowd, his enigma dazzling their eyes.

"Okay, now test subject." Paritosh continues, "Tell me something personal, name your best friends."

In a wink, the boy recites the names of his best friends. The crowd is hooting now, more applause.

"Let's see, how about your crush."

The boy is quiet.

Paritosh realises that he has made a mistake.

✷✷✷

8:40 pm (7 minutes back)

"What is wrong with you, Paritosh?" I enter backstage, out of breath.

"Who ... oh Aakash," Paritosh sighs, "I don't know, I don't think I can carry on the show anymore. I'm tense."

"Hey, you're the best magician I've ever seen, though I've seen very few." I squeak in a hurry, "But that's not the point, I just know you are good at this, what's there to fear?"

"It's my daughter." Paritosh sighs, "She got a proposal for marriage from our village in West Bengal".

"What's the problem, then?" I'm confused.

"I don't have enough money even for the tickets."

He bursts into tears. The valiant magician is troubled tonight and I don't have a solution.

"Paritosh, don't cry, you're going to set it right. Trust me, I know you." I pause to think, "For Christ's sake, you saved me twice buddy, you're like a guardian angel to me, you're that good. Just trust me, you will figure it out."

Paritosh looks at me, there's a small smile of hope on his face, though most of it shows signs of a broken heart.

"Thanks for the faith, kiddo." he starts walking off to the podium.

"Listen, what're you going to do now?"

"I have one last magic trick, you know the one in which I swallow blades and stuff. I guess I'll perform it right tonight."

"What if you fail?" I shuddered at the thought, "Listen, maybe it's not such a good idea."

"Well then, what should I do, huh?" Paritosh was getting more and more depressed, "I've disappointed you guys enough, this risk's worth it."

"No, trust me, it's not." I need to stop him.

"Well, do you have a better idea?" Paritosh snaps.

I pause for a while.

"As a matter of fact, I do."

***

8:48 pm

"I think you didn't hear the question, Aakash." Paritosh is tense now, "Name your crush." Then he adds, "Please, I can't change the question now," he whispers.

Oh darn it. Of all the questions in the world, this guy had to ask me this one question in particular! And that too for saving his ass getting kicked. I mean, first he asked me to sing a kindergarten song, then he asked me personal questions and now!

I felt agitated, but I had promised to help. There was no getting out now.

With my eyes closed, and my act still intact, I speak out the name of the first girl that comes to my mind,

"Anisha."

Whoa ... there is huge applause in the auditorium. I can feel the success of this trick.

"You son of a...," I hear Aditya swearing, and it's followed by hooting and laughter.

That does put me back into his hit list, I scowl.

"Alright now, on the count of three, Aakash, you'll come back to your senses. You'll wake up."

***

We celebrated that night, all of us.

Paritosh even introduced us to his daughter and we all enjoyed the story of how-I-nearly-got-drowned.

But as I started for home, Paritosh walked up to me, and then he patted my back and said,

"You're no less than an angel too, you know, kiddo." I could see tears in his eyes.

"Are angels allowed to lie?," I winked at him, then I got a bit serious, "hey, it's because of what you said the other day ... that there is always some good in our hearts, I just tried to stop you from being an escapist, after all, you're my personal hero ... so you can never back away."

Paritosh gave his handsome smile, then waved me goodnight.

"I'm proud of being your hero, won't let you down."

I never knew it was the last time I was gonna see my personal hero, my guardian angel.

LIE 020

"Hey, dude, why's your dad packing up all the things in your house?" Nick looked shocked.

"Oh, that! Yeah, it's nothing. He had to clean the apartment and all, so you see." I made it up.

The truth was, we were leaving, leaving this place forever. And, there would be no coming back. Only four days were left and I had still not gathered up the courage to reveal it to my friends.

"Hey, Vicky, you look distracted." I tried to change the topic.

Vicky seemed lost since today morning.

He stood up with a start.

"Look Aakash, there is something I need to tell you."

Hey that was my line! I had to tell them about my departure somehow!

"Yeah sure, go ahead." I said curiously.

"This doesn't feel right." Vicky was pensive and frustrated.

Oh no ... he knows.

"What ... err...," I tried to behave normally, "What doesn't feel right?"

"The truth," Vicky was all filmy now. I could imagine a scene from Sholay where Dharmendra asks for a justification from Amitabh Bachchan for his lie, so Vicky continues, "I'm sorry, Aakash, but I need to tell you this, apparently there's a love triangle here."

"Love triangle?" I was confused, "Vicky, can you be a bit more specific, for Christ's sake?"

"Oh ... you know what I mean Aakash, I'm in love with Anisha, too." Vicky is shaking now.

"What!" I chuckled, "Oh, man! So, this is what you were trying to say, gosh, you gave me a heart attack there."

Vicky looked bewildered, "What! Aren't you sad?"

I couldn't care less.

"Sad? Oh, of course not ... why'd I be sad?" I felt light-hearted, "I'm happy for you, Vicky. She's a nice girl. You guys make an amazing couple."

"Gee...really?" Vicky was welling up with happiness.

"Yeah, Vicky, I swear!"

"Well, all that's good, but there's a slight problem."

"Yeah, what's that?" I said packing my painting stuff.

"Anisha loves you."

***

I sit at the gate of Gandhi Park, waiting for Anisha. She's having her favourite dish, *pani puri*. She has been having it every Saturday at this very same stall for the last seven years, since I have her —known and every time, you get to see those same expressions on her face, expressions of joy, of immense unbound happiness.

After another five of those spicy mouth-watering delights, she pays the stall owner, then she starts walking towards the exit, her eyes bent on the road, her shy smile in place, her gentle demeanour, it's just as perfect as it was the last time I had seen her, walking home from this place, two years ago.

She stops ten feet from me, suddenly out of breath. I can see her eyes sparkle and a soft smile play her lips. I can see her elation at the knowledge of my presence. I can see the excitement, that tingling sensation of butterflies in your stomach; I can see it because I feel the same. It startles and amuses me at the same time.

Get a grip yoursely, Aakash!

"Oh, look who's here." she beams, "I thought you had forgotten Gandhi Park."

"Oh, no ... I hadn't." I replied, "I love this place, it's just that I changed the schedule a bit. Every Sundays."

"Oh, I see." she went quiet.

"Voila, I'm here on a Saturday now. Does that make you think of something?"

She looks up at my joyful face, and then smiles again, "Yeah, someone forgot to check the calender."

"Very funny!"

"So, what brings you here, my first official-boyfriend?"

"His first official-girlfriend," I look into her eyes. She knows I'm telling the truth. She gulps.

"Wow, that was some reaction. Don't worry, I'm not a serial killer back from the grave."

She chuckles.

"Hey, why don't we take a stroll inside?" I suggest.

Two minutes later, we're walking down the brick pavement towards the joy rides.

"Like good-old-times," she mumbles.

"Yeah, good old times," I whisper.

"Hey, I never got to say it, but I'm really sorry for what my brother did to you once. That punch must've hurt."

"Oh, you bet it did." I winced just at the recollection, "Hey, but it's okay, I guess he did the right thing. He cared about you unlike me who really made such a mess of our friendship."

"That's okay, Aakash, you boys are always a bit immature about such stuff," Anisha smirked.

"Oh, yes, we are. That lie was immature; I mean I've become so much more convincing now."

"Yeah, sure," Anisha retorted.

"I really missed you," Anisha whispered after a while.

I felt a lump in my chest, I felt broken.

We took a detour down the small lake on the periphery of the huge park.

"So, you wanted to say something?"

"Yeah Anisha, I guess." I didn't know how to put things in place, so I went with it, "I'm leaving, Anisha."

We stopped on our tracks.

She turned grim, "Wait, what do you mean?"

"I'm leaving Port Blair forever."

She stood there, her face expressionless. I couldn't make out her emotions, "Why tell me?"

"I err...," I didn't have an answer, but I still spoke, "I felt like telling you first. You were one of my oldest and best friends and I wanted to say goodbye."

"Aakash I...," Anisha's voice trembled, "I ...."

"You don't have to say anything, Anisha," I had to stop her, "This is just to let you know that I'm really sorry I couldn't be a great friend. I guess I'm just unlucky and a coward. Shouldn't have listened to your brother." I sighed but continued, "I want you to be really happy in life and you never know, maybe just two days later, while walking through the corridor, you end up crashing on some stranger, who with some magic and a bit of destiny, might turn up to be your best friend for life."

Anisha laughed sadly, "How do you come up with such stories, Aakash?"

"I have a gift you know." I wink at her, though the humour is long gone.

We stroll quietly for another five minutes.

"Chalo then, I got to go, pack my things and all." I felt like my part was over here.

"One last thing, Aakash," Anisha said, "Tell me something Aakash, that day while hypnotised, you said that I was your first crush ... do you still love me?"

I felt my heart skip a beat.

"I did adore you once, Anisha," I mumbled, "but it was a long time ago, before that punch, you know. Now, you're a good friend to me and I like you that way."

Anisha just kept on looking into my eyes. After some moments, she spoke. "That's all I wanted to know. It was nice meeting you Aakash. Have a great life. And, you are still a good liar."

"I don't know what you're talking about, Anisha, but I guess I'll leave it at that." I managed, "Take care Anisha, you're a special girl, always remember that."

I walked away.

See, every time I had lied till now, it felt good somewhere. I felt like winning, but that day was the first time I got caught red-handed and it was the first time I understood the ramifications of lies, how understated they are, and how tormenting it is to live with them.

This is an ode to Anisha.

The girl who was more than just a friend to me.

And, when I said "no" to her that evening, it occurred to me, it hit me like a train of thoughts, that I still liked her, that I liked her even before I had first lied about us being in a relationship, And, that it really felt bad when you broke somebody's heart.

✱✱✱

Two days later, walking across the porch to her class, Anisha bumped into someone. Her books fell off just like in those mushy sweet romantic movies and the guy helped her to pick them up. That was the day, Vicky and Anisha became friends, friends for life.

LIE 021

15th September, 2001

It's the day we left Port Blair.

I never broke the news to my friends. They got to know through the neighbours. It's that one day, that has made me hate the month of September for the rest of my life. I mean I was never good with emotions, you put me in a situation, I would never be able to figure out how I was supposed to react, whether to cry about it or get angry or just to delve into oblivion.

Our departure made me angry and not sad. I felt outraged, just at the thought of leaving behind and I couldn't even face my friends for a last goodbye.

I didn't want to meet anyone of them on the last day. I wanted to be left alone, wanted to practise estrangement once again, 'cos somehow the thought of Calcutta gave me a creepy feeling. I thought of it as an alien land, a place I wouldn't ever be able to jot down as my home.

They called me up on the final eve.

"Hey."

"Hey, Pritish."

"I just called to ask when your flight is."

"Oh … umm, at six," I replied morosely, "but why are you asking?"

"'cos we're coming to see you off."

"Hey you don't need … "

"Just shut up, Aakash…," Pritish yelled, "You don't get to tell us what to do, you stubborn ass."

"Okay fine, meet me tomorrow evening." I too shouted.

"It is then fine." he hung up.

"I'll miss you guys. Goodbye."

***

"That guy broke my sister's heart, got me thrown out for an entire term, ruined my image, and got me beaten up by my parents." Aditya grunted, "And he thinks I'll just let him walk away like that."

Aditya laughed smugly. He was going to take revenge.

"When's he leaving?" Aditya asked one of his fatso gang mates.

"Anisha was saying tomorrow evening at six something." the stupid bloke guffawed.

"Alright then, Aakash, brace yourself for our final strike!"

***

It was 5 when we left for the airport. It was an orange sky outside with faint stars. The breeze chilled me to the bone.

So, this was it.

I looked back one last time at my house up above the hill in Jungli Ghaat. The bungalow looked beautiful, like a brother (I have a strange imagery!). I felt like going back in, climbing up the stairs and into my room, jumping off to bed and sleeping under the quilt. I sighed, "So long, my friend."

My dad was busy waving at the neighbours, having some final words. Everybody waved us goodbye. They all stood there, in front of their houses, at their safe havens, at their own lands, wishing us all the best like we were soldiers on a war.

Suddenly it struck me, Paritosh Sorkar! His house was just a block away on the right. I had forgotten to tell him about our voyage!

I had to say bye to him, the magician.

As I sprinted towards the right lane towards Paritosh's house, I half-prayed for Paritosh to run out of his door, his fist clutching a magic wand, which he would move. I woke up from this horrifying nightmare.

***

"Hold on to your weapons," Aditya commanded to his friends, "Anytime now, I'm sure he'll come up this way to bid farewell to his old friend, that ignorant magician."

Aditya and his friends hid under the bushes, with hockey sticks and stones in their fists, all ready to hit.

"Anytime now," Aditya glanced at his watch, 5 pm. The sky turned orange and the stars started coming into view.

✷✷✷

I find the magician's door locked. It frustrates me some more, but then, on the doorknob, a small note is stuck.

I bent to read it.

It says,

"BLESSED ARE THOSE WHO'VE NOT SEEN AND YET BELIEVE...

AND BLESSED AM I FOR I UNDERTAKE THE JOURNEY BACK HOME."

"You were always weird, quoting strange stuff." I said to myself, "but I am really happy for you, magician ... bless you".

✷✷✷

"Aditya, it's 5:30, why hasn't he shown up yet?" the gang is getting impatient.

Aditya flexed his temple, "It's too late; we'll have to go to the airport. We missed that scoundrel again."

✷✷✷

They all stood at the gate. Pritish, Vicky, Anisha, Nikhil, all waiting.

Aditya made it in time.

"Alright, we're going to beat the shit out of him now." Aditya said scathingly.

"Here in front of the whole town, with cops and taxi drivers", Aditya's friends yawned, "We'll be chased, caught, beaten up and put into rehab."

"So, what're you trying to say?" Aditya was furious.

"We think we'll just pass, your plan sucks Adi ... seeyah." and they all left him, his most trusted so called friends, partners in crime.

"Okay, go away, you morons, I don't need ya." Aditya threw his hockey stick away, "I'm going to punch you again, Aakash. This is how it ends."

And then, Aditya sprinted towards the airport.

✷✷✷

"Dad, let's go inside. Nobody's coming." I retorted.

"But weren't your friends supposed to come? I heard them talking about your farewell gift or something yesterday?" Dad was suspicious and all worried.

"No dad. They're not coming. Look at the time. It's 5:40. we don't have time. Let's go."

As I entered the airport, I took one final look at the place, those silent roads, those dreamy mountains, that beautiful island.

✷✷✷

"We have to ask the guards." Pritish's voice was sober, "It's six now."

Nicks and Vicky were shocked and tense as they ran to the airport security guards, "Sir, could you please tell us when the flight to Calcutta leaves"

"Calcutta?" the guard was taken aback, "Well, I guess you'll have to wait till tomorrow. No more flights tonight. Only one flight leaves for Calcutta every day."

"And, when does it leave?" Anisha gulped, her voice freaky.

"Oh ... the flight leaves every morning ... 6 am sharp..."

✷✷✷

The flight took off.

I sit with my dad, my face on the window; looking down at the island I treasured the most.

"I'm sorry, guys, I lied. I know you won't understand me...," I swallow away the disappointment.

I never got to know how my friends felt that day, when I ditched them all. Didn't even give them a last chance to say goodbye, but only if I could understand that I wouldn't see some of those faces ever again, maybe I could've understood the worth of it, all my life.

The flight left my fairy tale behind, in a puff of smoke...

This first part of my story is to you guys,

Pritish, Nikhil, Vicky, Anisha and Aditya...

You people rock.

VOLUME 2

Calcutta Diaries

LIE 022

PROLOGUE:
28th May, 2006...
Darjeeling

It has started snowing and darkness descended over the hill station like death.

But all my mind could register was the accelerating heart beats, as I sprinted through HillCart Road.

The highway kept growing and there were no twists and turns. Only a steep fall of 10,000 feet ... I kept up with the sprint. The cars followed.

The sirens buzzed in my ears and they approached.

Right near Park Lane, I cut across the highway and paced through the deserted streets of the urban colony. It is then, I realised I had completely lost track of the path to the farmhouse.

It started snowing and the darkness descended over the hill station like death.

I couldn't stop; I had to run all the way. The pills were lulling me to sleep but I couldn't make this brain stop buzzing. I pulled out another tablet and swallowed. I had forgotten the count. I just knew half the bottle had emptied.

Why then! Why couldn't I remove that piece of information from myself, why wouldn't truth fade into a lie? Why couldn't I do it! Why didn't the lie materialise? My legs gave way and I fell, on my face, over some pebbles.

I start fading out. I can't run any more as I collapse on Hill Cart Road.

"Hey, kiddo, you okay?" I heard someone.

My eyes opened for a split second, I saw the solitary moon, I remembered Katie telling me how the best flats in Darjeeling were right here on this street, where I lay dying now. How she wanted her home here.

Everything flashed back and my head was fuzzy again.

I swallowed the last pill as I broke into a fit of laughter...

Lies. All lies. The friendship, the promises. Love square.

Two of the things that I loved the most were being snatched from me, and the world wanted me to follow on the rules.

"Well, fuck ya!"

My eyes flickered.

I was going straight to hell, I laughed.

LIE 023

15th September, 2001

Our flight landed at around 8:30 am at Netaji Subhas Chandra Bose Airport, Calcutta.

It was warm outside.

I looked up at the exit door of the airport and my eyes didn't register them at first. Then I recognised my grandparents from an old photograph we had in our hall. They stood there, their eyes moist, happiness overwhelming them. My uncle stood holding my grandma's hands, his eyes sparkling with fondness and nostalgia.

Just as we exited, granny and grandpa hurried towards me and embraced me in a tight hug. I didn't know how to react to it, it was so strange, so alien, so new to me.

I had not met my grandparents or any other relatives for the last eleven years and every memory of their existence had quite vanished from my mind. So, they were kind of out of my comfort sphere. But meeting them suddenly on a mournful day like this, I couldn't get a hold of my feelings anymore.

Uncle drove us to our ancestral house at Shakespeare Sarani, around twenty minute's drive from the airport.

However, the first thing I noticed while driving through the city, was not the huge roads, or the ancient structures, it was the traffic. It was like a massacre out here. Taxis, cabs, trucks, hand drawn rickshaws, automobiles, it felt vivid. The roads were jam-packed and even then, the cars would somehow manage to move. Every now and then, a bike or an auto would swish away with a dangerously negligible distance, and you could hear the crowd cursing each other. It felt scary, the city of lights.

By the time I reached home, I had a headache just from watching the angry mob. As soon as we entered the huge bungalow, I was surrounded with a stream of relatives and man! it was as titanic as the traffic!

"Hello, Aakash, remember me, I'm your aunt!" Every second minute somebody would hug me or pat me, or would slap my shoulders. It was spooky and I was exhausted with the fake smile I kept putting up.

"Aakash, go take a shower and freshen up, breakfast is ready." Some other aunt of mine told me.

My room was pointed out to me, to which I was accompanied by a lot of cousins who were either elated or super-excited and asking me infinite questions of a wide spectrum. Somehow, amidst the talk and chatter, I slipped into the bathroom. I look up at my face on the mirror. The noise has muted now. I turned on the shower and closed my eyes to the soothing cold water soaking my body. It came like a whirlwind.

The memories ... Pritish playing his video game, Nick trying out his guitar and Vicky giggling like a sweet girl ... I could see the pirate ship once more, I remembered the sea beach again, the silence of the sea shores, the graveyard behind K.V., Cellular Jail, Havelock, the lanes to JungliGhaat and my first ride on the bus to my school, it all came back to me.

"Hi, I'm Pritish." the fat kid smiled at me, as he extended his arm ...

"You're still a good liar, Aakash." Anisha smile, sadly.

I opened my eyes and gasped. My tears went unnoticed in the stream of cold water.

✳ ✳ ✳

"Aakash, you look sad beta, is something wrong?" granny broke my train of thoughts.

Everybody at the dining table was looking at me and that really unnerved me.

"Err...," I tried to speak.

"He's tired, that's all", dad said.

Everybody nods in understanding. I concentrated on the cereals.

"So, Anshuman, what's your plan now?" Uncle asked my dad.

I was quite passive to whatever boring discussion was on the air right now, but what grandpa said next, comes as a real shocker.

Grandpa announced in his thick voice, "Yeah, Anshuman, why don't you go back to being a journalist?"

I raised my eyes and dad was looking at me, too. He looked like a thief caught red handed. Everybody else sang in chorus, "Yeah, why don't you join the *Anand Bazar Patrika* again. You were such a good columnist."

"Err...umm ... I don't really think it's a good time to discuss." Dad was still staring at me and my look turned from amazement to cold.

How could my dad hide this from me? All these years of lies! That is when it dawned on me. Maybe, I was never interested in my dad's life. I had always been a lousy son to him, and the sudden realization depressed me some more.

"Oh, c'mon Anshuman, don't be a killjoy, tell us what're you going to do next? We're really looking forward to you writing articles for the next World Cup. Remember your brilliant piece in 1983, it was so splendid." Some relative of mine delved down memory lane.

"Aakash, have you read your dad's articles, they were so acclaimed, you know?" Uncle asked me.

Here it goes...

I kept silent for a while, then shook my head, "No, I haven't. He never told me."

Everyone went hush-hush.

Dad cleared his throat, "See, I'm not interested in that profession anymore. Writing stuff is boring and a lazy man's profession. Doesn't pay you heavy bucks, too. I'm happy working for the ministry of Finance now." He went back to his breakfast.

***

The next morning, we set out for our flat at Salt Lake City. Dad drove his Maruti-800 casually through the sleepy city. We reached the gate of an old building after a one hour drive. As I got out of the car, I realised it was a very tiny society!

We carried our luggage to the second floor. Dad was searching the key when I asked, "Why didn't you ever tell me any of this?"

Dad turned expressionless but his face gradually turned a bit pale. He kept on fidgeting with his bag trying to find the key.

"I mean, you never even had me talking to my grand-parents for my entire childhood. You never told me about you being a journalist. You kept it all under wraps. You had no connection to this life of yours. Who were you hiding from, dad?"

Dad finally got the key.

He sighed, then clicked the door open.

"This is what I've been hiding from."

LIE 024

It was an old small 1 bhk. There were cobwebs all around. Faded yellow curtains lingered around rusted window panes and the room was badly lit and had a filthy smell. I coughed as I made my way through the layers of dust that floated in the air. That's when I saw it.

The prizes, the medals, the photos, the articles. It just hit me on the face. I saw an old laminated copy of the "1983 World Cup article" hanging above the dining space. I read the name of the writer.

Soon enough, I recognised this room. It's where it all started. My life. This was my real home. I remembered it from the few pictures I once found on my dad's study.

This was where the 'then young' Anshuman Roy and 'the ever charming' Radhika had once taken refuge after fleeing from their parents. This is where their story started and eventually ended, too.

This place was more than just walls and old things.

There was a huge golden trophy kept over an old, antique almirah, on which the phrase "Best Journalist of the Year" was scribed. Right beside it was a medal and a trophy where you could read the inscription of "The Dadabhai Naoroji Award" for Journalism. Beside them all were more paper boards hanging on the wall with articles such as "The Communist's Tales" and "The Budding Controversy" displayed on them.

"Dad, it's your name written all over!" I was astonished.

"Did you...err...win all these?" I turned to face my dad.

He was lost somewhere else. His eyes were on the small showcase kept below an old black and white television. I gazed at the photo frame he was looking at.

It was a small cheap plastic frame, but laminated inside was the photo of a priceless love story.

I looked at the beautiful young face of my mom. She looked like an angel, fresh from wonderland, innocent and dazzling as she flaunted her million dollar smile and on her side, my dad winked at the camera, he had the Rajesh Khanna expression all over him. Their flamboyance was just surreal.

"What happened, dad?"(Let me remind you, I haven't yet had the chat with my uncle over the cup of coffee that churned out all the "mom-dad" stories you've already read. So, when I asked dad an explanation for such a beautiful relationship's falling apart, it was perhaps my first trespass into this entire matter and the outcome was the most significant missing piece to the puzzle).

"What killed your relationship?" I repeated.

Dad's face fell. He went over to a small closet beside the fridge and from it he extracted a small old article.

"This killed it, Aakash."

I looked at the old newspaper piece, the words were etched out in bold, "The once 'Most Honest' Journalist sued on charges of treachery."

I glanced back at dad, "I don't understand!"

"Your mom left me for a reason, Aakash. She left me because her dad told her the truth. The truth about my lie." a tear trickled down my dad's cheek.

"Maybe, this is not the right time, dad. I think we should go back to grandpa's place." My voice trembled as I panicked. In my entire life I hadn't seen my dad so withered. He looked broken, as if flooded by haunting memories.

"NO, I WON'T HAVE THE COURAGE AGAIN." Dad's voice was resolute and firm, "You have to bear it out, Aakash. You deserve the truth, no more lies."

LIE 025

On a cold midnight of December 22, 1949, some police guards were fast asleep under blankets and sweaters ... Their snoring reverberated through the barren lands of Ayodhya. They were oblivious of any trespassing, after all who would breach into a mosque at the middle of a winter night! The lights went out five minutes later.

It's then that they went inside the mosque. They were dressed up in orange cloaks and had garlands all around their necks ... they were committing a sacrilege after all. With wary and chivalric strategies they placed the idols they had brought along at the corridor where the Muslims offered their prayers and off they went.

The Babri Masjid issue started the next day.

Prime Minister Jawaharlal Nehru had the power to issue strict orders and clear out the idols of the Hindu deities that were placed in the mosque, but he knew protecting the Hindus and his party was the greater good for him.

✳ ✳ ✳

1983

Anshuman Roy was the most legendary journalist to have joined the biggest regional newspaper of the country, the *Anand Bazar Patrika*, that had a readership of 64 lakh. He was the most controversial Columnist of all times. A die hard communist, when he joined in 1977, CPI (M) was at its peak in West Bengal. And, his revolutionary ideas shot him to fame overnight.

He was super-intelligent, a genius with numbers and predictions, he called it all observation, but he could predict every result of the elections months before they were declared.

He was the whiz kid of *Anand Bazar Patrika* and his article on the 1983 World Cup and why India would definitely win it was his greatest piece ever. They said when India won that season, people lined up in front of a bungalow at Shakespeare Sarani and hailed Anshuman Roy; he was the role model of West Bengal, a person who proved the strength of the pen and words. They compared him not to Rajesh Khanna or some other Bollywood hero, he was then just "Anshuman Roy", the name that was written with gold in every Communist's heart. He fought for the common man and ensured that Calcutta would continue to be the city of rebellion. They knew that he was going to create history some day.

And, that he did ...

✱✱✱

1985

The Vishwa Hindu Parishad and the BJP had it in mind. Rajiv Gandhi did the honours. He ordered the locks of the Hindu Janmabhoomi, the Babri Masjid's gates to be opened to Hindus. He saw it as their right to have their temple back for the age-old belief that the land belonged to a temple that was brought down by Babur once.

What was to follow in a few years' time was no more science or guess work, but we were not man enough to write down the controversy. Nobody wanted to go against the Hindus, the majority.

In Calcutta, CPI(M) was going to lose this year. The opposing party had its leader Mr Abhirup Roy, a man of immense wealth playing the cards of religious issues gaining sympathy from the Hindus at large. And, he was unstoppable. The country was with him. He had blindfolded Calcutta.

That was when he stood in the way.

The whiz kid committed his biggest act of courage. Anshuman wrote his next prediction. He wrote how the Babri Masjid would lead to the biggest Hindu–Muslim riot in Indian history. It was his best article till date, his masterpiece. Anshuman expected his readers to behave logically; that's where his predictions hit dead ground.

He was stoned, beaten; he was convicted of acting treacherously against the political party for his own vested interests.

The *Ananda Bazar Patrika* had to declare a lockout. Protestors and extremists charged at the press office and half the building was burnt down. One year down the lane, things came back to normal.

But something had changed. Anshuman Roy was a traitor now. A person, who betrayed his own religion, he was as good as dead. He was fired from the newspaper, his career was sealed. The last people heard about him, he was spotted in a small government office, working as an accountant. Anshuman Roy and people moved on.

But the world missed a chunk of the story.

LIE 026

1985 was a year of miracles. A person who fought for the country was admitted to the ICU after being attacked by his old fans, the citizens of Calcutta.

But some people see light, even on the coldest of nights.

The mob saw reason. The burnt effigies of an honest human being had done the magic again. Though critically scorned, but the article, the master piece was noticed.

The truth was sung out loud. It just needed some time to sink in.

Anshuman Roy was a genius. He had predicted it again; he was just waiting for the change, lying awake, fingers crossed, in his hospital bed.

And then the miracle happened. CPI (M) won under the most unexpected circumstances.

Calcutta was shocked by its own reaction. The intentions were clear no more.

The pen had worked again, a blessing in disguise that even the people couldn't register.

* * *

That day, the man stood outside the gates of the leader of the losing party.

Anshuman Roy, beaten, injured, weak, stood there, firm, his eyes glinting with pride. His career might've been finished but he had achieved what even a lifetime worth of success couldn't have given him. He had created a Communist in every citizen and when he stood facing Abhirup Roy, the latter was stumped.

"We did it again, Abhirup Roy," Anshuman smiled, exposing his broken lip.

"You think you won, Anshuman?" Abhirup Roy, a middle-aged power hungry man growled, "It is my blessings that your life was spared. If I wanted, I could kill you at this very moment in front of the entire city and people would still hail my name. All in the name of religion, you see."

"The people are innocent, Mr Abhirup Roy. They never realize what is in their hearts. And so, every now and then, someone has to step forward and bear the torch." Anshuman's voice was full of pride.

"Change." Abhirup Roy hissed, "You are nothing but a naive philanthropist brought up in some idealistic utopia and you think you stand a chance to alter religious sentiments? CPM won by a twist of fate or even better, maybe because it was all evil play too ... why don't you make some more predictions about the reality, Einstein ..."

Anshuman Roy retorted, "CPI won, not because of foul play, they won because of those little things they've been doing. Look at the roads, the parks, and the electricity. Abhirup Roy, the whole country wants is a little shelter, some clothes and food and then you and your politics can go to hell. Gods are remembered at times of need, not at times of murder."

"Poor people like you, who require scholarships for even mediocre degrees cannot think beyond this. This is what your levels of understanding will always be." Abhirup Roy laughed mockingly, "You middle class philosophers, were never at par with the upper rich classes like ours. So, screw you very much for explaining the national sentiments, but let me tell you, these boundaries still remain. The rich vs the poor. Money will win again, Anshuman and I'll see to it that we win, if not by tactics, then by money. We know the rules of the game and we know how to alter them. Now, if you please." And with that Abhirup shouted for security. Next moment, Anshuman was dragged out of the rich man's castle.

"You will never win. You know why, it's because of that mindset of yours. This is my last prediction, or better still, my promise. I'll ruin you,

Abhirup Roy. And, I'll ruin every corrupt leader," Anshuman warned before he was punched senseless.

The story died, but the rivalry didn't.

It just grew when Abhirup's daughter Radhika ran away with a middle-class government employee a year later.

***

"Abhirup Roy believed that I stole his daughter to avenge my injuries," dad mumbles softly.

I'm still amazed by what I have heard in the last one hour. I had no freaking idea, of my dad being a rebel once and all of it seemed so unreal.

"Then, why didn't you tell mom about your true intentions? That you were not a revenge seeker."

"Because, Aakash..." dad went pale, his head hung low, "...that would have been a lie."

"What?" I shouted with such intensity, I heard brakes outside our flat.

"I was young then, Aakash. Every day as I worked inside those old buildings of National Savings Institute, I felt only stagnation; I felt the fire fading. It was like caging my heart. And, all because of those shrewd politicians. They ruined my life, Aakash. I was called a traitor. I wanted revenge, just didn't know how."

Dad sighed, "That's when she walked in. The girl who was always on page 3 of *Anand Bazar Patrika*, Miss Radhika Roy, a fresh, young girl out of Harvard. She was so unlike her dad, Abhirup Roy. She was an innocent, sweet and free girl, who had nothing to do with politics, who just loved life and wanted to work in a small office like ours, just because she thought it would be fun."

Dad went quiet.

"So, what happened next?" I was getting impatient now.

"I didn't understand her. The first day I saw her, I was so shocked, I spilled ink all over myself. "Dad chuckled softly, then continued, "I wanted revenge. Wanted to prove Abhirup Roy wrong. Prove that money could've bought him silence from my side, but it was justice that would win."

"So?"

"So I played the oldest trick in the book. Impressed his own daughter, made her fall in love with a middle-class bloke like me and then destroyed the old crook's life by snatching her from him. I destroyed the rich monetary boundaries the guy was so proud of. See, the day Radhika Roy ran away with me, it was not our love that won. It was only me."

Dad looked at my eyes now and sure enough he saw the anger, "I did something wrong, son. But then I did end up loving your mother more than my life, more than my vendetta. She was all I ever wanted, I realised so late. I never told her any of the truth. She was not in the country when the old things had happened, so she was oblivious of my past record and the rivalry between her dad and me. Her dad too feared that telling her the truth might actually make her go against him. But one day the truth had to come out. It happened when that monster Abhirup Roy fell ill and Radhika was summoned to help her ailing father. The heart-less tyrant told her the story, garnished with hundreds of lies and brainwashed my lovely little gift. He took away my most priceless possession. He won, son." Dad started crying in earnest, "Never gave me a chance for explanation. I waited, Aakash. I waited for her all my life."

We stood there, quietly for a while.

"I hope you forgive this old man of yours," dad said between muffled sobs.

"Don't worry, dad, I'm proud of you. You will always be my hero, no matter what."

✳ ✳ ✳

1985 might've been a time of change, but you know the thing with change is that it's not always for the better. While Calcutta was saved, a revolutionist's life, his mindset was all drained away. Nobody cared.

LIE 027

I watch Pritish walking away from me in the examination hall, I try to say sorry, but can't, I turn around, I see Nick, Vicky and Pritish sitting under the banyan tree and then someone cracks a joke about ghosts, I try to laugh, but it hurts and then Aditya punches me to the ground and I'm back at my house, under the quilts and the bus honks like mad.

"Yeah, yeah." I say irritated, and then I hear my own voice, before I squat shocked on my bed, my nightmare vanishing, forming a new one.

The bus honks louder this time, I see it from the small window of our hall.

"Wait", I try to yell at the school bus which has started.

Damn it ... first day of my new school life, and voila, I have already missed the bus.

***

"Dad."

Dad is sleeping again with his head on the table, newspapers and articles all around his face.

"Um ... dad," I said, two notes higher. Dad woke up with a start.

"Oh ... wha ...", he looked at me, then at the wall clock, "oh, sharks! your school!"

"The bus just left." I yawned, "Drop me to the school, will you?"

"Er ... yeah, I'll do that." dad scratched his head.

"And, I know you've not made any breakfast, so I'll take just a minute." I said as I went to freshen up.

Some little things never changed, though life did ... it was like a half circle, like a chord !

✶✶✶

The strange thing about Calcutta was that shops and malls had the same appearance, with their names written in clear Bengali letters, most of them dedicated to the gods and goddesses like Durga Boutique! and Shiva Electricals!

I even found a shop named Shubhodeep Jewellery! Strange choice of words!

It took me the next ten minutes to figure out that the shops didn't actually have the same names, in fact they were the same ones and that dad had been circulating across the same square. It took my dad another five minutes to realise he was lost in his own city! Amazing!

So, we took dozens of detours, somehow saved ourselves from running down a crazy dog that kept following our car to pee or something! And yeah, there were some additional heated arguments with the other sinister drivers on the road, who had the feeling they were driving planes.

I reached my school, SMI, around an hour late.

"Oh, I have a sense of De-ja-vu." I said as I waved dad bye. Late again.

I was a good athlete, I sprinted very well, you know it reminded myself of how Shah Rukh Khan would always run through the bridge to the summer camp in *Kuch Kuch Hota Hai*, you know I quite aped the style well, apart from the fact that I always crashlanded!

I fell on the huge bushes near the assembly ground of this private institution.

The school looked grand and stylish. It was a four-storeyed building and something suddenly made me self-conscious as soon as I entered the campus, as if I was close to something, real close. Although I was limping after my great fall, I hurried towards the gate,

"Do you know in which floor class 9 is?" I asked the guard, a thin, frail, vulture-faced Bengali.

He looked at me thoroughly, his expressions changing from disgust to puzzled to sympathetic...

"What happened to you?" He pointed to my torn trousers and stared at his watch, chewing *paan* (betel leaves).

"I'd love to chat, but please tell me where class 9 is, I'm in a bit of hurry." I made him see the obvious.

"Oh, that...," he thought hard, which was a time consuming process, too, "Yeah, it's on the third floor."

"What the...," I slapped my forehead.

"Dammit, Aakash, you're in for a treat." I limped up the stairs.

✱ ✱ ✱

"May I come in, ma'am?" I was gasping for breath and my words came out in an incomprehensible squeak.

A fat woman, with intense and excessive makeup glanced sideways at me with contempt, and then without any comments, she went on teaching.

I was indecisive. I looked at the fifty students inside, who stared at me, all of them checking me out with expressions of amusement and mockery.

I felt that I was stinking. I was sweaty, my trousers were torn, my light yellow shirt had some classic stripes of green slime from the bushes and I looked exhausted and seemed the most uninteresting thing in the world.

Oh! I suddenly remembered I had even forgotten to wear my tie. All the others had ironed dresses and they had well-combed hair, round Bengali faces and looked like sincere, wise pandits!

I shrugged as I requested for permission to enter the class one more time and was again unnoticed.

A front bencher, with his face gentle like a sheep gestured me to come in. As I looked around, three more boys nodded to the bloke's suggestion.

So was that it? Are the Bengali teachers like this only ... they don't even reply to your pleadings to enter the class?

I thought for another minute and still all I could hear was more jostling and muffled laughing and the fatty madam's boring lecture.

So, I made my first mistake of the day, I entered the class.

The next minute, the old lady went all haywire.

"What the hell do you think you are doing?" she screamed in a deafening voice.

"I...err...," I was petrified.

The students had started laughing now. They were all having a great day. The smug first bencher just winked at me, his mischievous grin broadening.

"Ma'am," I tried hard, "he said I could come in." I pointed at the first bencher.

I don't know what the joke was, but that made the class convulse with more honest laughter.

"Oh, him!" The old lady had a sudden change of voice, "The most sincere, honest and best student of the class asked you to come in. Wow, is that true, Deb?"

She eyed him with a strange look, and I was shocked when I realised, she kind of revered that particular superhero of the class.

"No ma'am, I swear I didn't." The guy put up an innocent face, his gentle voice felt so honest that for once, even I had to recollect the incident.

"Well, we've heard the justification, now time for your punishment, new boy, what's your name?" the lady became serious, her eyes filled with serpentine glee.

"Aakash Roy." I shrugged.

"Very well, Aakash, let me see, you're late, you are wearing a dirty uniform and you even forgot your tie and ...", how many 'ands' were there, I wondered, "and, you also ruined my mood, so you know, I want you suspended."

I looked at her, bewildered.

"But then, considering the fact that you are a naive new comer from some rural island something Blair I've heard, I will save you the torture. Just kneel down for the entire day."

"Ma'am, I'm sorry but please, I'm hurt, I've a limp because I fell downstairs. Please, spare me this one time." I pleaded.

"Shut up and do what I said, you liar." she almost howled.

I bent down on my knees, adding insult to injury.

"He's telling the truth, ma'am, I saw Deb asking him to come in." it was an unusual female voice. It was quite shrill, but still felt supportive.

In the crowd of the fifty students, I didn't even see her face. I was already on my knees, I could only see her legs.

"Are you 100% sure?", The old lady had turned grim now. Deb, the smart son of a gun, looked flabbergasted.

"Yes, ma'am, I definitely saw him." the shrill voice with beautiful legs was back.

"Alright then." she said with a serious disappointment, "I know what to do, Deb, you too, kneel down with the new fellow."

"But ma'am ..." Deb went white.

"Do what I said, now."

The entire class went quiet as Deb rose, came and knelt down with me.

He looked at me, expressionless.

I winked. The leg suddenly stopped hurting. Shockingly, he winked back.

Ma'am now looked at the girl with the shrill voice who sat on the last bench. Then, she uttered the most shocking name ever.

"Thanks for telling the truth, Katie."

LIE 028

The girl with the cowboy boots, the pink jacket and those curly turls of soft hair.
"Hey, how do you know my name ... wait a min ... Katie?"
"No, Bond ... James Bond ..."

✳ ✳ ✳

The memory surfaced like a whirlwind and kept me occupied.

So, was it destiny back on track? I tried my best to peek at the girl but still saw nothing but her legs!!

That's when the bruise registered. It hurt like hell and I looked at my swollen knee. It enraged me a bit and my eyes instinctively moved to the other guy kneeling down beside me, Deb.

His eyes were on me too, and I was amazed to find that he was enjoying the punishment. His face had this calm written all over it and I felt that I could really use it as a punching bag. I grinded my teeth at which Deb smirked some more.

"What's so funny?" I whispered.

He kept on staring at me, his face straining to resist the urge of bursting into a crackle of laughter.

"You know," he whispered, "I have been using the same old trick for the last four years with every new boy, it's our own way of ragging, but guess what, you're the first one to have dragged me along."

"Yeah, I've a nasty habit of dragging people to hell with me." I grunted.

I sighed at the increasing labour I had to put up with.

The period ended with the electric buzz deafening my ears.

"You remain as you are." The teacher pointed at me sternly, then she turned all soft as she faced Deb, "And you, go back to your seat. Don't repeat it next time son, we've a lot of expectations riding on you."

Expectations, my stinking sock!

"Yes ma'am, I apologise. Never again, I promise." Deb had his innocent face back on display and I was again amazed by the levels of this chauvinist as he took a fake oath.

Deb rose in a perfectly swift manner, his athletic body flexed back to form a striking pose which was applauded by his classmates, who seemed to be his blind followers and then waved a flying kiss to them and what the hell, the cheers were magnanimous!

Where am I! A coven of some frenzied fanatics!

Enough of the truth...Now was the time for some lies, I had really done a lot of injustice to my poor left knee. I apologised to it. The knee looked up at me like a sad puppy.

The next teacher entered the class and his eyes drifted to me at that very instant. He was quite fat too (what was up with these teachers and their sizes?), and he wore a kurta pajama to class, it reminded me of our traditional day at K.V. He observed me for a moment or two, I noticed he had crazy eyes and his face was filled with such a huge moustache that there was hardly any space left for the eyes, nose and mouth to stick in.

"What happened?" He looked perplexed.

"I had an accident." I couldn't believe my ears even as I said it.

"How?"

"I was coming in an auto and it collided with a parked car at the gate of the school."

"What?? Then, why are you getting punished?"

"I don't know. I guess it was the previous teacher's car or something. They towed it." Was this even a story, I mean which kind of a far-fetched lie was this!

"Oh good heavens!" The professor burst out laughing, "Get up, boy and go to your seat, you've had enough of the punishment."

I rose silently. I couldn't even believe my ears. Had I really done it! Pulled off another lie.

I looked at the entire class now, my eyes scanning every student, it first rested on Deb, who did a thumbs up and winked, man! Something was wrong with his right eye; he kept winking like a maniac! My eyes pursued the search for the girl now, for Katie, I looked straight at the bench where she sat. Alas! Some other girl sat there now, her oiled hair tied up in a braid, her eyes bent low on some notes she kept jotting.

"What're you thinking, new boy, you can go back to your seat and I'm proud of you, what's your name again?"

"Aakash, Sir." I mumbled as I limped to the seat where this strange unknown girl sat.

"May I sit here?" I asked her. The entire class had their eyes on us.

She kept scribbling in her notebook, oblivious to my question, avoiding me on purpose. I felt like I had become a non-living object.

"Ooooh ... new friends, huh?" Some fellow classmates sang in mockery.

The girl who was silent till now, grimaced at those boys and next thing you know, she snarled, "Mind your own business, morons."

"Whoa." I took a step back; even my left knee helped!

The boys went mum immediately, their eyes back on their books. The professor looked at the girl.

"There there, Katie, don't lose your nerve again. Didn't I ask you to meditate?", He chuckled.

Katie dismissed Sir's joke and resumed writing.

Katie!!!

Yeah, that many exclamation marks formed in my head.

I sat down beside her. My eyes were on her face. This was not the Katie I had met in Delhi. This was somebody else just with the same stupid name! Dammit! I kept staring at her. Finally, she looked back at me with limitless acrimony.

"Er ... are you Katie?" my mind was still on the same rail track.

She stopped writing, her nostrils flared and instantaneously I realised what a blunder I had made, the volcano was alive again.

"Sorry sorry, you know what, don't answer that question." I put up my hands in surrender.

She continued with her work.

I suddenly felt heartbroken. What was wrong with Calcutta! Right from the first minute I landed in this city, it had been knives and daggers at me! Damn it, the rate at which I was getting devastated, I would soon be axed by some chipmunk!

The professor started teaching. After some ten minutes of futile efforts I realised we were reading the first chapter of organic chemistry.

I glanced back at Katie from the corner of my eye.

"Is the subject that boring?" she said and I was suddenly taken aback.

"Um ... err ... " I was at a loss of words. Embarrassed, I looked back at the empty blackboard.

I heard her chuckle softly.

"I ... err ... actually, wanted to thank you, Katie, if that's really your name, Katie." I stressed again on the name, my heart wanting her to refuse the fact, give me some optimism.

"Don't thank me; it was a mistake on my side."

"?"

"I shouldn't have saved you."

"Wow." Where was this headed, "Why?"

"Because I hate liars ..."

For one second, I had the feeling that I should grab my books and find another place to sit, I mean, somebody just got turned off by my greatest virtue.

"But how do you know I lied?" I kept up the small talk, though my interest was dropping like sensex.

"Kavitha ma'am doesn't have a car." She said in a matter-of-fact voice.

The fat madam didn't have a car!

"Oh." I looked back at the fat hairy professor, "then why did he let me sit?"

"He's a kind person, that's why." Katie mumbled, "He doesn't punish anybody. That's why he was proud of you." She stuck her tongue out at me and suddenly it reminded me of Anisha. I went quiet at the sudden thought.

"Good for me." I opened my notebook.

"You should apologise." she said after a while.

"What? why?". I was bewildered.

"To Sir, you lied after all." she was serious, "You know, a little sorry would do good to me, too."

"I'm not sorry." I said and we went quiet.

"So, why do you hate liars?" I said after a while.

"Because they stink." She reminded me of how sweaty I was at the moment.

✳ ✳ ✳

SMI was filled with rich millionaires and most of them were all spoilt brats. On the first day of school, I met some three guys, one was Sobhanjan, he had a very effeminate way of presenting himself, his hands always danced whenever he did his nuances and *nakhras* and I kind of avoided him when he insisted on showing me his Barbie collection! I met Subhojeet Ghosh, the guy was a classical singer, tall, spectacled and looked crazy, too. I mean, the first thing he talked was about how tablas worked and asked me whether I knew Carnatic music!! He was really disappointed in me.

And then I met Deb.

"We never introduced ourselves to kiddo." Deb stretched out his hand, "So, you're from an island I suppose?"

"Not interested." I stared out of the window, distracting myself on purpose.

"Easy there, boy." he laughed, "I know you're pissed, but hey, we can be friends. You know I'm really interested in knowing about the pathshala or Vidyalaya they say you have been raised in."

"It was K.V. and I'd rather respect you as the enemy." I gloated, looking straight into his eyes.

The guy remained as callous and stylish as if I had apologised to him or something.

"Well then, I guess we'll surely have fun." He completed his dialogue and his friends applauded again. He gave me the feeling he was some Rajnikant. I half-expected him to take out a cigarette and toss it to his mouth.

I cursed and grimaced when he left and then my eyes met Katie's. She was also cursing Deb.

That did make me laugh. The girl hated a lot of things, and we both had one thing in common.

✱✱✱

I returned, all tired and exhausted, to our 1 bhk at Salt Lake City.

"How was school?" Dad asked me. He was typing a letter or something.

"I don't want to talk about it." I opened the refrigerator and grabbed a bottle of water.

Dad looked at me, "There must be one highlight? One silver lining?"

"Nope, not one." I shook my head.

That was the first night I dreamt of a paradise sorta place and the new Katie.

LIE 029

Ties are idiosyncratic objects. I wondered what they really stood for. They hang from your necks, like pendulums without any meaning or purpose whatsoever. No matter how much I tried, I could not fathom the art of wearing the strange thing.

"Dammit dad, how do you wear it?" I declared defeat.

"Well, that Aakash, has been the biggest debacle in our family heritage. I mean, your great grandfather, Mr Avinash Roy, nearly choked himself to death while trying to wear that jinxed thing and later we found out it was a bow tie, I mean, how could he even ... so anyways your grandfather, used to wear sweaters to his meetings so that he didn't have to wear the tie."

"Dad, quit stalling and get to the point, will ya?" I got impatient.

"Yeah, well, the point is, my son, I never learnt how to wear the tie. It was your mom who would always adjust the knot." Dad's voice went down a key.

"Hey dad, am sorry." I meant it, "But how do you tie it to your office now?"

Dad looked at me and smiled, "Never let go off the knot. I have had the same knot for the last twelve years ... "

"Dad, why don't you sort things out with mom?"

"Let's keep that for some other time, kiddo." Dad said as he went downstairs for some tea.

But how does he wash his tie? I dismissed the doubts. Whatever ...

I looked back at the mirror. A thin, pimpled and silly, a bit handsome (a very less insignificant bit) boy looked back restlessly, his hands curled around a piece of cloth!

Focus Aakash, it's just a tie.

***

"Ma'am, this thing beats me; I can't get the knot right." I said to a fuming Kavita ma'am. She frothed with relentless anger.

"You really are that dumb, aren't you?" Ma'am spoke coldly in front of the derisive class.

I looked away at the doors and the windows. I had the feeling one of these days, Kavita ma'am would suspend me for sure and bless me, and she was also the class teacher!

"Okay, here's what you can do. Katie, help him with the simplest thing of the world and teach him how to get it right."

Well, even on the second day, I had planted myself beside the short-tempered girl. I somehow thought it would be best for both of us. Because somehow she hated talking and I shared the feeling.

She looked at me with such intense aggressiveness, it freaked me out.

"It's just a tie." I whispered trying to put out the fire.

Damn It ... how the hell did her name end up as Katie ...

She scowled taking away the tie from me, then twisting and turning it in proper oriented directions. A minute later, there it was, as polished and smooth as in the movies, the perfect tie.

"Thanks," I smiled, "and sorry, too."

She looked up at me.

"You know, for the other day, I shouldn't have lied." I lied calmly.

"It's okay," she went back to concentrating on Kavita ma'am's boring doctrine.

I sat and looked around. So many new faces! It was my favourite game. Reading faces. Like I could tell from the drooping eyes of Sobhanjan that he really had a lot of gossip yesterday over the phone with some girl as they discussed how to put Barbie to sleep. I looked at Subhojeet, he looked lost, maybe, in some sitar concert where he was playing the tabla at the centre stage with people yawning and trying to die. Beside him, sat a guy, brown hair, eyes concentrated on a triangle he had drawn in his exercise book. I observed the figure properly, it was a triangle and he was deriving a formula out of it. Trigonometry. I quietly calculated, the chapter was still to be taught in class. My eyes went to Deb, and he as usual, sat there with his innocent face back in place, the fake poster boy, I hated him.

My eyes went back to Katie and I found her smiling.

"What's your problem? Don't you have anything else to do?" she asked immediately.

"I wasn't looking at you, I mean, how do you do it? How do you know I was looking at you?"

And then, it dawned on me, "Hey, were you looking at me, too?" I was suddenly shocked by the realisation.

"You say it as if it's some crime." she stammered, "and it doesn't mean I was even giving you a side glance stupid."

"Oh, you liar!" I could read her eyes trying to look away, her posture suddenly tense. She was lying.

Then, something strange happened.

She rose from her seat in the middle of the class.

Oh, no! You're so dead now, Aakash!

She gathered her books and went to another bench and sat there stiffly.

The entire class now looked back at me.

Hey! Here's another of my sucking introductions!! I am that bad with girls!'

3

Days, weeks....and two months down the line, I was still an unknown foreign entity. I mean I spoke Hindi with Bengali kids out of habit, I was not familiar with a single Bengali slang and knew no dating places in the area, my dad had a Maruti 800 and I kept on showing up with unkempt dresses!

I faltered even in studies. The school had CBSE affiliated to ICSE Board and the syllabus was strikingly new to me, It was very different and

I couldn't cope up without help from my classmates, which unfortunately did not materialise. Even my attempts at joining the guitar class or the music academy in the school had succumbed. The student head of the music academy was Deb Roy. He was everywhere, captain of the sports team, student of the year, junior editor of the school magazine. They said he was just too good.

There was just one exception. See somehow, he was not the best. Every year he came second in the class. It had been happening since the last eight years, since he joined the school.

Enter Robbie Andrews – the south Indian Christian. He was, rightly put, a genius. They said he had appeared for an IQ test as a kid and got some stupendous result, something that was kept under wraps, something that showed a 200plus, which really appeared far-fetched to me.

But yes Robbie Andrews was different.

I met him to join the science group of the school. Robbie Andrews was its head, the only exception to the reign of Deb.

He was busy drawing some figures and stuff. The same kid I saw some days ago trying out trigonometry.

"Hey", I said, but was interrupted by a woman who had been wiping and cleaning the science club dorm.

She suddenly came up to Robbie and started in Bengali.

She said, "Beta, could you please help me like you did earlier? I really need your favour, beta."

Robby looked up at her, then at me.

"Err...I don't understand Bengali...can you please translate?" He asked me with a humble smile.

"Yes," I said and listened to what the lady said.

"Beta, I need some money for my kids. I have to pay their school fee."

"She's lying." I spoke in English to Robbie. I could read the lady's mind. She was lying. Her eyes bent low and her voice trembled at times.

Robbie said, "What does she want?"

"Money."

The lady continued with her tale of a drunkard husband who used to beat her up and about how all the money she had saved got wasted on him. She cried as well.

"Ask her how much she wants." Robbie said, as he took his purse out.

"You don't have to give her money, Robbie, she's lying. Don't let her get into your head. These people don't work hard enough. They're losers. Don't listen to her. She's lying." I tried to impress Robbie, the genius with my clear understanding of lies; I was a detective at that.

Robbie glared at me and I went quiet with the shock.

"What's your name, mate?" he asked.

"Aakash!" I said, still confused by his reaction.

"Aakash, why do you think she's lying?" Robbie asked in a soft voice.

The old lady became quiet and I looked at her. She looked frail and thin and fatigued.

"I don't know; she's surely a loser. That's why."

"That's not reason enough on why she lie, Aakash? Think and answer."

"Because she wants money," I concluded.

"No." Robbie took out a hundred rupee note and I gaped at him. "She just doesn't want it, dude." He paused and looked at me," She needs it. It's the money she's lying for and that's all I needed to know."

He handed her the cash. The lady welled up with tears and blessed him.

I stormed out.

Robbie was crazy or just super-rich but he was not a genius anymore to me.

Two days later, as I walk across the rusted rail track to find the right path to home, I realised what Robbie meant. The rains wash my face with the lies of the heavenly graces.

LIE 030

December 11th, 2001

I felt lost. I boarded the train to escape, I watched the Howrah Bridge fade away in the distance, it was a windy day and there were signs of a storm approaching. Small ships canalled through the old docks near the Howrah Bridge, sailing on for refuge but I was lost, out of plans.

"Where to?" the bloke at the ticket counter asked.

"Belur." I racked my brains to reach the conclusion.

He gave me the ticket, a small rectangular token, I pocketed it and walked across platforms for the local. I saw people pushing past me. I saw the fruit seller's discontent, I could read the signs of the bookseller, his broken hopes. I saw the beggars sitting over dirt, handicapped, looking at us like we were gods, their eyes praying for a coin.

I finally found the rusty old train, wearied out and jam packed. People hung on from its doors like cliff-hangers and even then, more people gathered for some more cliffhanging. The train whistled.

I tried to find an empty compartment, running through the length of the gigantic thing, but no space for a needle in the haystack. Disappointment clouded my mind as the engine rumbled and the train started moving. Suddenly, a hand held me and without any prior notice, pulled me through a filled compartment door. There was one hit, a collision, as the cliff hangers move hither thither and next second, out of breath, I was inside the compartment, into a mess of a thousand heads. I looked up at the owner of the guiding hand. A thin, athletic Bengali 30 something old looked at me and smiled, "See brother, it's simple. You just have to fight through." I looked at his faded jeans and the stained shirt. He was now looking out for a place to sit, an impossible task. I followed the person in suit and I don't know how even in the rush, the memories came back.

✳✳✳

December 10th, 2001

I had been waiting all day. Deb was an expert guitarist. And he pulled it off with extravagance like those rockstars in movies. Girls would applaud and cheer, while boys would support and then, our superstar would send flying kisses all around. They would keep on recording the songs, most of which were in Bengali. So, it was quite hard for me to understand all the words, I had been out of touch with the language for some eight years after all. And anyways, if you were eaves dropping on practices from an old cellar room door near the music studio of SMI, it was really hard to keep track.

They were having auditions for the new members today and this was my last chance to make it to the group, but things were like a bitter-sweet symphony between the selectors and me, with Deb being the head.

So, all I did was wait for the right time, *any moment now.*

✳✳✳

December11th, 2001

He stood alongside, took out a cigarette and lit it up with flamboyance.

I concentrated on the outskirts of the city flipping by. The paddy fields, the small brooks, the bamboo forests and the villages – I was witnessing the real West Bengal for the first time.

"I'm Rakesh." He introduced himself, bowing his head, in a dramatic manner.

"Aakash." I shook his sweaty palm.

"You an outsider." Rakesh spoke in broken Hindi.

"Yeah, sort of." I replied in Bengali.

He smiled.

"I was in Port Blair for the past twelve years, you see." I tried to make my point.

"Port Blair? Oh my God!" The guy had his hands over his mouth, like he was looking at a tarantula.

"Andaman Nicobar islands, you're from that corner of the earth, so how come you are here?"

"Just going to meet an old friend." I said, "Guardian angel." I mumbled to myself.

"Something wrong? I see your mind is elsewhere." Rakesh was now getting on my nerves.

"How did you know?" Then I continued anyways, "No, I'm fine actually."

The guy broke into laughter at my contradictory statements.

"Cheer up, brother, it's your first experience of the most twisted thing in Bengal and you have your mind on something else, enjoy yourself, brother", he called a vendor who stood at the opposite gate.

The vendor had a tray filled with food items.

"Here." Rakesh grabbed a packet of chips and popped the packet open.

It had Lais written over it, with a picture of Shah Rukh Khan, a very bad duplicate of Lays.

"No, thank you." I refused but he kept on insisting.

"Sir, the money", the vendor interrupted Rakesh's futile attempts.

"Oh, yes." He took out his purse."How much?"

"Eight rupees."

"What the hell, brother? These were five rupees last Sunday. Have you guys like lost it?" Rakesh yelled at him.

"You are talking about some imaginary Sunday, Sir." The salesman also shouted.

And next thing, the war of words was on. The audience enjoyed the sight with rapt attention.

✳✳✳

December 10th, 2001

"I'll grab some water and be right back." Deb said as he walked out of the studio.

"My turn," I smiled and tiptoed inside.

Everyone looked at me bewildered.

"Why're you here?" A girl named Madhura popped in the question. She looked like the captain of the gang.

"I want to audition." I said in a confident tone, this was my last chance.

They broke into fits of stupid laughter.

"Hey, I can do this, okay." The mockery was making me irritable.

"Okay, okay", Subhojeet now came forward in his whimsical way, his face twisted with malice, "Why don't you sing us something and we'll see." He looked back at the crowd, his body bent like a sitar.

Some of them nodded with unenthusiastic sighs.

"Okay, great." I grabbed the small microphone and started the song that ANV had composed, *'Jo thi dil ki khushi'*.

"jo thi dil ki khushi,
bujh gayi woh hasi,
sapnein they kayin, jab gum tha nahin..
dil toota magar, dard bhi na hua,
dost chutta magar, maine fir bhi sahaa,
maine jaanu naa, kyun yeh huya"

"Hey, hey, stop, stop." Subhojeet was furious. "Where's the classical rhythm man?" He looked furious.

"What." I was astonished. "Hey, this is not a classical song. It's blues." I tried to clarify.

"Blues, my foot, idiot." Subhojeet started wailing with inaudible doctrines of how disastrous and hurtful my song was.

"Get the hell out of here, you stupid villager." Subhojeet shooed me out, "and never ever dare to sing, you suck at it loner."

Everyone laughed.

Alright! That was it.

It happened like a flash.

I sprinted like a racer. The next thing, Subhojeet went flying over the trash bin in the corner of the room.

The students shouted all around in unison, screaming names at me, like "Satan" and "vile" and "monster".

Frankly, I found it poetically delightful.

✳ ✳ ✳

"Hey hey, it's okay, Rakesh." I took out a 10rupee note and gave it to the seller, "I bought it. Don't you worry."

The seller took it and next moment, he was gone, without even giving me the change.

"What, why'd you do that, Aakash, you should never ever listen to these people's whims." he went haywire, "Hey, come back you asshole."

"Relax, Rakesh, it's not a problem." I counted the 3 hundred rupee notes in my purse and placed it back in my pocket.

Rakesh grabbed another chip and crumbled it with anger.

"You know when I was young, Aakash." Rakesh mumbled, "I'd always take this local to get to school, and every day I saw people trying to dupe each other, with their lies, I promised that I was gonna rise above it. That someday, I would be off this vicious cycle. I would walk 5 miles, 5 miles, brother, to get to my school and every step exhausted me, but I'd encourage myself with that indelible idea, with that one single shred of hope, of being rich."

I looked at his sad face.

"But then, see, I've become part of this cycle at last. Couldn't escape my fate, could I?" He smiled as he took another drag from his cigarette, "I still take this train everyday to work at a small factory that makes crackers and I still walk five miles to work, I still fight with the system, but the only change has been the realisation that I've already conceded defeat somewhere."

I kept quiet. I was bad at consoling.

"And today, when I see kids like you, I feel happy." Rakesh continued, "But yeah, a bit jealous, too. I mean, I'm that shallow now brother, envying a fifteen year old", He mocked himself with despair.

We kept quiet, listening to the sound of the whistling train.

"See, I made a mistake, Aakash." Rakesh started again and this time he was really pensive, "I shouldn't have dreamt of going above the system. I should've dreamt of changing it by being a part of it. Be the change you wanna see in the world, Gandhi said I suppose." he winked at me.

I was surprised by the poor man's wisdom.

"How can we change the system, Rakesh?" I didn't have a clue what a system was for starters but I asked anyways.

Rakesh smiled, "See, I'll give you an example." He threw out his beedi and focussed on me, "Suppose you have a BMW, that's what the name is I think, of that costly car."

"Yes." I encouraged.

"Yeah, so the day, Aakash, the day you're powerful enough not to keep it for showing off, but you have the strength of gifting it to an underpaid clerk, that day you'll change the system."

"What", I laughed out loud, "That's absurd Rakesh, why'd I do that?"

"Exactly, it's so absurd, that it's the only thing that would ever make sense, brother", he patted my back.

Rakesh was insane.

Why would I ever gift a car to an underpaid good for nothing? I mean I earned it. It's my property, dude.

***

10th December, 2001

"You really think you can come here and create this mess and walk away?", Deb pushed me so hard, I slipped and fell.

I stood back to face his burning aura.

"Never again, should I see you here, do you get that?" His yell deafened me and I was shaken by his power.

I nodded like a stupid twp-year-old and then out of shame, or embarrassment, or anger, I don't know what, I stormed out of the studio.

Deb had won again.

SMI was a mistake.

* * *

"Hey, run, the ticket checker is coming." A mate of Rakesh announced.

"Oh, shit." Rakesh swung up, then he looked at me, "I gotta go, pal, your stop's just two stations ahead. All the best, brother!"

"Hey, what happened?" I didn't quite understand the entire scenario of people running away to the next compartments all around me. They seemed panicky.

"No ticket, mate." Rakesh grinned, "Welcome to India, brother."

"Hey, but here's something I wanted to give you." He put something into my shirt pocket and hugged me.

"What's this?"

"*It's the last shred of faith I could give you. Just believe that we are not that bad.*" He smiled and then in the cloud of the storming passengers, he vanished.

I took out the small ten rupee note from my pocket.

I smiled.

Two stations later I got out of the train. A beggar stood in front of the bogie. I checked for my purse to give him a coin.

I could not find it.

The shock came unannounced.

I ransacked my pockets, shuddered with the dejection. Oh, man! Pickpockets.

I closed my eyes to trace the events and my mind played back the cards.

I remembered Rakesh hugging me. I remembered taking out the purse in front of him and counting the 3 hundred rupee notes.

"Oh, you thief, you liar." I grunted with the sudden anger boiling through my body.

Rakesh was the true master of this game, lying and deception. For not even one instant, did he let any doubts arise in my mind and look at me now, I was left shaken, my faith vanished ...

LIE 031

Broken promises

Belur was a small village in West Bengal, famous for the Belur Math, the headquarters of the Ramkrishna Math and Mission, founded by Swami Vivekananda. Located on the west bank of the Hoogly River, this place has always been proclaimed "A symphony in architecture". I had come here looking for someone, someone who used to dazzle us all the time, whose hands wave spells, who was my guardian angel.

"Do you know a magician, Paritosh Sorkar? He must be showing magic tricks here at the station in the evening?" I asked a fruit-seller resting at the far corner of the station.

The guy looked at me with hostile despicable eyes, scanning me. Then, he opened his mouth with a very exhausted air, "Now, the news channel has journalists your age? Surprising."

I was left confused. "Sorry, I'm just a friend of Paritosh, a very close friend." I always cherished our friendship. Paritosh Sorkar was one of my favourite persons in the world.

"And still, you come so late?" The old fruit-seller now smirked smugly.

I was frustrated. What did he mean? I mean, how could fruit-sellers be so abstract, popping out sarcastic and undecipherable statements one after the other.

I started to move to the other stores at the far end of the station.

"His house is at the northern end of the station. You'll find a chawl beside the rail tracks. Ask anybody. Your friend is famous now, he is." The fruit-seller yawned.

I turned and smiled at him with gratitude which was repayed by an unapologetic grimace, then I nearly jogged to the small chawls, houses or rather boxes made of cardboards, irregularly shaped bricks and polyester roofs, with sheets and joints sticking out at all the odd places.

I could see small kids playing in front of them, collecting waste stuff from the nearby dustbins, poverty emancipating from their frail bodies. When I approached them, they looked up, stunned.

"Umm ... do you know Paritosh Sorkar?"

They nodded in unison.

The guy always had a rapport with the kids.

"Can you point out his house?" I asked hopefully, knowing the answer would be affirmative.

Soon, I was walking to the depths of the small town of the chawls, facing the strange truth of poverty on the face of it. I could see Hoogly River flowing by, far in the distance, its edges covered with dirt and garbage, the beautiful river, a stinking mess.

I remembered the handsome and gentle face of the magician. It had been around Five months, since I had set eyes on the guy who had saved me once from the pirate ship and before that, on the night of Diwali. I remembered how he popped out a lotus from thin air, how he made the dove vanish and his million dollar smile. I was really low in spirits and seriously needed to meet a character from the past, just cherish old days and talk.

See, silence is overrated. You might keep mum with all your feelings, bury them deep, lock them up in some dark part of your heart and ensure yourself you'll never reveal them, but one hour with your best friends and the locks all broken, your secrets disclosed. I really needed some advice, and more than that, some chat today. I mean, I had been rejected by every group in my school, I was humiliated by the most popular guy of our school, got punished on the first day by the class teacher, seriously face a fear of suspension any day now, and I even ended up finding a girl whose name was Katie and who was the worst kill joy of all time.

"Oh my God, look who this is." My heart accelerated as I heard the familiar voice. It was Paritosh's daughter, Kiran. I had met her on our Foundation Day, after the magic show, back in Port Blair.

She came up and hugged me, her eyes welled up with tears, and that left me dazed!

"Hey, I'm happy to meet you too, Kiran di." Her happiness surpassed any bounds.

"So, Aakash, how've you been? Dad always talked about you, so much, he did. How did you find us?"

I suddenly felt her voice go down a scale but still I didn't understand.

"I'm good. How are you people? Where is he? You guys finally made it to Calcutta." I said, breathless, "He had told me about your house at Belur and that he would be showing magic tricks at the station when he got back. You know when I got down here at the station, the first thing I expected was Paritosh Sorkar, showing off his tricks to the mob! He promised me that I would always find him at Belur."

Kiran trembled and that suddenly stopped me.

The story started then. The story of a broken promise. Of a lie.

LIE 032

The magician's tale
22 September, 2001

Ravi knew he wasn't drunk, but he swayed anyways. Maybe, it was the fatigue, or the restlessness. He was tired with the daily news of how the sensex was dropping like a meteor. How two giant planes out of nowhere suddenly came down at the twin towers, and destroyed his career. His was a business, a life of a stake holder and he had been doing his best, finding out every loophole, looking out to grasp every blessing in disguise to keep his business afloat, or more still, at least his job and somehow, Ravi knew now that his career as a businessman was probably down in the stale waters of the overflowing gutter.

As he got out of his office at midnight, he knew he might end up missing the local, and to top it all, the rains spoiled the night. It was a storm out here.

"Goddamn rain." Ravi somehow walked the mile to the station. It took him 10 minutes more than usual in which he constantly cursed the roads, the potholes, his boss and Osama bin Laden. His were international curses!

He missed the train by a minute. He shouted with unfathomable anger, and then went up to the bench at the far corner where he normally found the fruit-seller everyday and then he sat there.

He pulled out a packet of Wills cigarettes and lit one up. He took two long drags, and then rested his head on the wall behind, closed his eyes ready to wait for the next half-hour for the train, at the empty station.

Ravi was twenty-three, a passout of Jadavpur University, who had aced in his class, was real famous back then. Today, he was a loner, on the verge of losing his job, his shares were all gone, he didn't have a girlfriend and he was still a virgin, out there cursing Al Qaeda, blaming the sucker for his failures.

Ravi opened his eyes, and sighed. If only he could let his wrath loose, he would have burnt this entire world down.

That is when he saw the guy in those multicoloured robes.

A clown maybe, he sat there, packing his stuff below the display board that showed the time. It was 12:35 am.

Ravi observed the man. The eccentric person looked tired, no wait, it was disappointment with a tinge of sadness, Ravi could read it.

He took a last puff of the toxin in his hand and then caromed it away. Then he cleared his throat. The clown was still uninterested, he was busy packing strange things in his sack.

So, Ravi stood up, unzipped his rain coat, then wiping off the water, he went to the stranger.

"Hello, I'm Ravi."

The guy looked up; you could see his red eyes and his expressions of exhaustion. The bloke was having a rough day, too.

"Sorry, but can I help you with something?" The bloke asked.

"Oh, no." Ravi said, "But I was just curious, you know. Never saw you here before. I always take the 12:30 train."

"Aah, I see." The bloke replied with his heavy majestic voice, "No, actually I leave at nine every night. I just waited a couple of extra hours tonight. Wanted to make some more money, you see." The bloke sighed.

"So", Ravi asked, "Had any luck?"

The guy shrugged, "Nah, not much". His voice shook with sadness.

"I'm sorry." Ravi looked away, "What do you do to earn your bread?"

"Why, I'm a magician." The bloke smiled.

"Oh ... that does explain your strange robes." Ravi chuckled, he just wanted to take his mind away from the problems of his life, so he went on, "So, Mr Magician, why don't you show me some tricks and I will see how much I might help you."

The magician lowered his head, "Sorry Sir, but I have already packed my stuff. The show's over for tonight. Got a daughter at home. Need to return."

"Now, now," Ravi said with utter disappointment and a bit more derision, "That really doesn't sound like you have any intention of earning some extra cash. Look at me, my job gets over at nine, but every night I stay up till midnight and even then I'm getting fired. Learn something from my life, do that."

The magician kept quiet for a while, then hesitantly, he started unwrapping the sack.

"I'm doing it because I have a daughter I've got her to get married and I really need a lot of money for her dowry. But I'm gonna charge 40 rupees for my ten minutes show."

"Done." Ravi was anyhow going down, so he didn't care whether he was being duped anymore. He was no more a businessman. He was the spendthrift.

"Alright then, sir." The magician smiled. Then, he took out the pack of cards, cages of birds, flowers and cups and matchboxes and rings. Soon, the magician started pulling impeccable tricks. He was an orator as well, Ravi observed, and he was really good in his profession. Ravi was soon giggling and applauding. The sullen silence of the empty station had suddenly been energised. And then, the ten minutes were over.

"Hey, I wanna see more of those tricks!" Ravi scowled as the magician started packing.

"Sorry Sir, but I need to go. It's late. My daughter must be waiting."

"Hey, but I'm paying you, am I not? what's the problem?"

"Sir, I need two thousand rupees by tomorrow. Your extra hundreds ain't gonna help. My daughter won't get married by that. I really need some time on my own, to figure out some way." The magician had gone all pensive.

"Oh, chuck that and hear this out ... No ... no ... better still, wait." Ravi reached for his purse, and then he took out something.

The magician's eyes were blinded by what he saw.

A thousand rupee note!

"See this," Ravi smiled, "Show me something indelible, something out of this world, and I promise you'll have 1 grand as a gift."

The magician looked dumbfounded. He stood transfixed his eyes watery, as he stared at the note.

"Which magic can bestow me with such an amount?" He tried to think hard. He had no such amazing trick.

"Something irresistible, something unreal," Ravi chided.

"I don't know, Sir." The magician scratched his head, "I mean, I can make birds vanish and I can guess any number you are thinking of. I can calculate any equation, no matter how big the numbers are, what do you wanna see?"

"Bull shit." Ravi was dissatisfied, "Show me some magic that would be surreal. Your best till date."

The magician thought hard, then he mumbled, "I apologise Sir, but these are the best ones I have. I don't have any masterpiece. I'm sorry." Tears came to his eyes.

"Oh, c'mon you idiot." Ravi was irritable again, "See, I've had a bad day and I need something good to relax. So if you want your daughter to get married, want to pay the dowry, be a good father, then you better get your ass straight and show me a real trick." Ravi fanned the note in his hand.

That's when Paritosh Sorkar heard the whistle of the Shatabdi Express. He had to make the decision, make it now. He looked up at the sky and thanked God for this blessing in disguise.

He wanted the money, more than his life.

"Alright Sir." Paritosh Sorkar, stood. "Tonight, I'm going to show you the greatest magic trick ever."

"Now that sounds good," Ravi grinned like a five-year-old boy.

"You hear the approaching train, Sir?" Paritosh queried.

The faint siren of Shatabdi filled the silent night.

Ravi nodded.

"Sir, what I'm going to do, is dissolve away."

"Err... what does that mean?" Ravi rubbed his chin.

"I'm going to vanish and you see the masterpiece would be that I'll vanish in front of an accelerating train."

"Oh, good Lord!" Ravi was stunned, " Can you really do that?"

"Yes Sir, as long as you promise to pay those thousand bucks."

"Oh, I cross my heart." Ravi looked at his watch.

12:50 am.

"Alright Sir, see here's what you have to do." Paritosh was shaking now.

"Right, as soon as I vanish, you place that note in this box, lock it and keep it here in my sack and go away." Paritosh displayed a silver box, and then repeated the instructions.

"But why can't I just give it to you when you reappear?" Ravi was confused.

"No Sir," Paritosh Sorkar smiled sadly, "See, there's a problem. This is very complex wizardry and once I disappear I might end up somewhere else," Paritosh exaggerated.

"Oh, okay." Ravi agreed, "You really are a true magician, aren't you?"

"Oh, yes, I am," Paritosh beamed. He really could fake those expressions, "But swear to God that you'll pay the cash."

"Obviously man, trust me." Ravi patted Paritosh's shoulders.

"Alright then, Sir."

The siren neared.

The two men could make out the lights of the approaching Shatabdi Express.

Slowly and steadily, Paritosh sauntered to the third rail track, farthest from the station. He stood erect, soaked in the incessant downpour, his eyes looking down at the rail track, all shimmering with the wet waters washing the dirt away.

The train was real close now. He could feel the track shaking.

He looked one final time at Ravi. The guy looked back at him and popped up his thumb with anticipation, his mouth opened, his eyes glinting for the magician's last trick.

Paritosh sighed and then concentrated back on the track.

Then, he saw his daughter, smiling down at him, he saw her in the marriage veil he had bought for her. He smiled and remembered what a small kid had once said to him in the corridors of Cellular Jail.

"Magic is lies in perfecting lies."

You were right, Aakash. Lies then, it shall be.

The train swooshed away at 250 miles per hour, Ravi saw the flash of light, he saw the magician standing there on the track, his body at peace, rigid, waiting for the moment, and then the train zoomed by. The magician vanished in the sudden blur.

Ravi clapped his hands to his mouth in awe.

From the right side, on the first track, the local emerged.

"Oh, shit," Ravi whispered; he had to board this train. He didn't see where the magician had disappeared from the track far away. It was not visible anymore in the rain, but he knew the guy did vanish.

He looked at the silver box, and then he looked at his thousand rupee note.

Ravi was in a Catch 22. He looked one final time at the third railway track, then without hesitation, he ran towards his local. Shatabdi fainted away in the distance. It was 1'o clock.

"Sorry, magician, the trick might've been awesome but you'll have a lot of publicity in the coming years anyway. So, now that you are not here to check on me, I better keep the thousand rupees to myself. See, businessman we are." Ravi smirked and boarded the local.

As Ravi decided the magician's fate, he never knew those thousand rupees were worth **a life**.

✷ ✷ ✷

11th December, 2001

I look at Kiran. She's going to get married on Sunday and I see henna on her palms.

But I can't ignore those tears in her eyes.

I walk away.

It has started to rain and I'm walking down the same track where Paritosh stood four months ago on a windy night.

The ten rupee note in my pocket is getting wet by the downpour and I realise all those hundred million lies of the world.

I realise the tears and the lies of the woman at SMI to whom Robbie had given the cash.

I realise the deception of the pick pocket, Rakesh.

Money it is, then.

I see the beggar in the ground, handicapped, his arm stretched, looking up at me like I were some god who could eliminate his sorrows. I give away the last ten bucks to him. Can't see him die, I can't.

Paritosh was a magician, a guardian angel, he was the guy who made me realise that one decision that changed my life.

That day I decided, all I ever wanted was to be rich, super rich...

For me, Paritosh never died. Magicians don't. They just vanish. I would rather believe in another lie than accept a truth I couldn't live with.

LIE 033

Lie, steal, plead.

My first year at SMI was the loneliest year of my school life. I had no friends, none at all.

Deb Roy was still the proclaimed superman of the class. The other Bengalis had this issue with my non-Bengali ethos, for example, I was an eggetarian! And, a semi veg Bengali did not exist for them!

Robbie had not spoken to me since the last encounter where I had misbehaved with a poor old lady (Robbie didn't talk to the entire class anyways! Half the time he had all these notes open or he'd be reading Stephen Hawking).

Katie didn't even look at me anymore. She had developed this habit of looking straight through me, as if I were a block of ice or a puff of smoke (it felt scary!).

So, basically when the tentative dates for the annual science group project were displayed, I knew I was gonna flunk, for the first time. I had no group, no innovative ideas and I really didn't know how to make dummy models out of card boards for science exhibitions.

So, I had to strike up some new idea.

"Hey Katie, hi." I stopped Katie in the canteen. She looked uncomfortable at my creepy presence, but I went ahead anyways.

Lie RULE 32–(WHEN IN NEED, Lie ... steal ... plead)

Pleading part...
"Whoa, look who this is? The Andaman boy!"
What was wrong with that place anyways!

"Yeah, cool," I scratched my head, "Um ... err ... actually Katie, how're you? Long time, no see." I was on the crafty lines. She looked unimpressed.

"So?"

"Err ... nothing. I just felt we should catch up like friends do." I tapped her shoulder. Now that did piss her off. You could literally see her nostrils flaring like a baby dragon, ready to incinerate me.

"What do you want, Aakash?" Katie grunted through clenched teeth.

"Oh, nothing yaa. I just felt like talking to this friend of mine with whom I sat on the first day of class 9.", I winked sheepishly.

She rolled her eyes and started trotting away.

Plan-a backfired...
Plan-b

"I was wondering ... err ... if we could ... umm ... team up for the ... you know ... science project!"

Oh! boy, it felt like asking her out for prom night!

Her face suddenly turned into a smirk, a strongly smug one.

"So, the doofus is looking out for help", Katie's voice was like that of a vulture.

"Err...," I sighed, "Yeah, I could really use some help." I lowered my head, begging.

Her face suddenly turned all soft; into an expression that was quite a complex one.

"Umm ... Aakash, I already have a team, so ..." she said slowly.

"Oh!" I felt a lump in my throat, "Yeah fine, not a problem at all." I started to leave.

I heard a small voice mumble from behind, "Sorry."

✳✳✳

Stealing and lying part...

Robbie sat on the deserted science lab beside the garage, all busy. He had a pile of things all around and from what I could see, he had cut out wood, forming tracks, all pasted over a wooden board, which were further connected to a speaker (strange!) and then through a small balloon, to a pendulum and other weird stuff.

"Ahem." I cleared my throat.

Robbie looked up at me, "Aakash Roy, the Bengali translator!" he said in a tone of delight, beaming. That shocked me a bit.

"Hey man! Wassup?" I entered the classroom with wary steps.

"Oh, I'm fine. Please, take a seat."

I perched on the desk and looked at the dummy. There were copper balls and white plates and electronic stuff, a lot of them.

"Robbie, first of all, I want to apologise for the other day. I know what you think of me."

"I don't think of you," Robbie's comment suddenly unnerved me as I tried to grasp the sense of it.

"Okay, anyways, I'm sorry man! I know my mistake. I shouldn't have behaved that way with the poor lady, should've respected your decision."

"Oh, that," Robbie recollected, "Don't be sorry, it's a vague word, if there's anything one should say, it's thanks."

"????"

"Obviously, because I made you see some sense." Robbie winked.

"Yeah, that's true." I still wasn't sure whether it was Robbie or my trip to Belur that made me see the truth, "Thanks."

We went quiet as Robbie observed the sun and recorded time and stuff while I inspected the huge apparatus on the table.

"By the way, Robbie, what are you making here?"

"Oh, that," Robbie looked at the tracks and silver balls, "It's a contraption. It's like a complete chain of energy transformations, starting with potential to kinetic energy, movement of a ball down the track, which then leads to initiation of vibrational energy by switching on an amplifier that leads instead to kinetic energy and then magnetic energy and oscillation energy of a pendulum, which goes on further to generate ... "

"Wait a minute." I was all confused. "I don't get it."

"Well, good. Now, try to." Robbie restarted.

He was going to design a model for initiating a chain of events, through the push of a small ball, which would finally move a small car down a race track, with many intermediate steps that would explain the 'energy remains constant' model with a demonstration of energy conversions. Seven energy conversions in total.

The idea enthralled me. I could tell this was one hell of a project. So, all I wanted was to get my hands all over it. The project was still in its initial phase, so I struck up a deal. I was gonna help Robbie with the project in the days to come. Help him complete it. I still hadn't specified my conditions because I knew a genius like Robbie would never agree on my terms. So, I simply lied. I was gonna play on my own terms.

Every day after school, Robbie and I would tiptoe to our secret deserted classroom and make the magic happen, our project had a lot of flaws at first, but with an IQ of 200 + and some 100 something combined, we were sure to succeed.

Robbie Andrews was a great guy, a very honest, cheerful innocent lad. He would laugh at the simplest of jokes, knew nothing about adult stuff, would never care for his clumsy style of clothing or be proud of the amount of cash you'd always find in his purse. He even told me he'd introduce me to his dad, who was a famous teacher to get all my doubts in mathematics cleared. Robbie Andrews could have been a great friend, if my intentions at our small pact would've been at all good. Robbie would never ask for a team mate, his projects were always solo, so that made me an unwelcome guest. However, I had a plan of my own.

We completed our project two days before the due date and then the testing phase began.

At times, we would get exhausted and while I ate chips or listened to music, Robbie would sit near the glass windows recording some details in his pocket diary with his small disc that he always carried with him. The guy was mysterious.

I stole the project one night before the presentation. I knew the entire concept now, I knew all the formulas, all the steps of construction, and every scratch of the model was a boy's book to me. So, that night while Robbie had left for the washroom, I grabbed the entire structure, hailed a cab, and then I was off.

✳ ✳ ✳

Mine was the first presentation the next day. Robbie had not even arrived in the class by then.

I explained to Kavita ma'am the entire concept, showed the entire demo and the car did make it to the finish line. The class was filled with applause.

See, the thing with professional liars is, they're always good with expressions.

I beamed and smiled and bowed my head, though the guilty conscience was burning my soul deep down...

Deb Roy had made a model on volcanic eruption with a lot of chemical reactions involved. The thing would've been appreciable if it hadn't blasted at first go.

However, even in the puff of smoke and the flames, all Deb would receive was astounding cheers and hoots. Students loved fireworks.

Robbie arrived last. Every eye was on him as he went to the centre stage, with empty hands.

Here it comes, the complaints. I braced myself for the trial!

It was then that Robbie unzipped his bag and took out the circular disc.

"What's that, Robbie?" Kavita ma'am looked at the cardboard clock.

"Why, it's a sundial, ma'am."

Question mark faces.

"Alright, since the beginning," Robbie explained in his generous voice, "animals and human beings have been dependent on the sun for telling the time. This sundial here does the same; it tells the time through the shadows of the small dial I've fixed at the centre. I've tested it every day for the last month and I've etched the hour and minutes properly. See this here." He proudly displayed the disc, "It is as good as any of your battery-run watches."

There was applause. I was amazed and it made me smile.

Robbie looked at me and then he grinned with utmost happiness, the same expressions a best friend would convey to the other.

I was ashamed.

✳ ✳ ✳

"I'm really sorry, Robbie." I told him after class.

"Don't say that, Aakash, sorry is a vague word, makes no sense, never helped anyone." Robbie said casually as he read 'a brief introduction to space and time'.

"But aren't you angry that I stole your 'contraption'? Your idea."

At that, Robbie looked up at me, his face sparkling up with queries, "Stole? Why'd you steal your own project?"

"What?" I was abash all over again.

"That was your project, Aakash. You worked on it for so many nights. I just helped, that's all I can say."

"But, but…," I could feel an adrenaline rush, "It was your idea. I just put some efforts."

"Doesn't matter. Ideas are nothing unless utilised. Frankly, I couldn't even dare make such contraption at this age, it's so complex and tiring. It was your enthusiasm that made it happen."

My face altered into a surprised smile. I couldn't regress my emotions anymore, "Thanks, bro."

We shook hands, though I felt like hugging the guy.

✱✱✱

"You know something, Aakash, you have a quality." Robbie once told me.

"What's that?" I said oblivious, eating an apple.

"You make believe." Robbie said seriously.

"Oh, that." I smiled, "Yeah I do … I lie".

LIE 034

I had read about Mr Dennis Andrews somewhere, in some book. He was this famous professor at the Indian Statistical Institute. Well, somehow he happened to be Robbie's dad.

"Listen, I don't think it would be a great idea to go out there to your dad with my silly mathematics doubts."

"Oh, don't worry. You would be fine." Robbie said as we arrived at 24 Parganas, where Robbie lived. They had a small cute yellow house with pink hedges. It shone in the sun and looked exceptionally sweet. Robbie was playing with a prism in his hand that kept glimmering as he walked with me to his house.

An old jeep was parked on the corner in the car shed. We trotted through the small lawn while Robbie chatted.

"Listen, here's the deal. My dad takes classes and stuff for students our age. So, you can get yourself enrolled or better still, you can say you're a friend and have the classes for free."

"Okay." I nodded, "Okay, so I'll say I'm a friend of yours, I think that'll work."

"NO." Robbie panicked, "DO NOT SAY THAT. Don't say you're my friend. My dad doesn't like my friends. He thinks I befriend all nerds. In fact, don't even mention my name."

"Well!" I wondered about my personal opinions.

"I'll tell you what to do. Say you're a friend of Katie's and never ever take my name in there. I am the topic you never wanna raise in my house, not with my family."

"What? Why? And Katie?" I was confused.

"Yeah, do that." Robbie went on, "Do not tell anybody you're my friend or something. Never ever mention my name, got that?"

"What's this about? Some personal dispute?"

"It's a secret Aakash, and promise me you'll keep it, or we won't be friends anymore."

"Yeah, yeah, chill." I shrugged.

"Alright then." Robbie pressed the door bell, then he trotted towards the backyard, the prism still shining in his palm.

"Where are you going?" I was getting bewildered now.

"Oh, my room is at the back. Show you some other day." Robbie waved bye to me, "And remember, do not even utter my name."

"Yeah, I got that." I put my finger over my lips and didn't even notice the guy who stood facing me on the door.

"Talking to somebody, lad?" The middle-aged gentleman looked outside in the garden, where Robbie had just disappeared into.

"Oh, Rob ... no ... err nobody." I managed quickly, holding on to the strange promise.

The guy looked at me suspiciously, waiting for more. He wore a suit, had a pipe in his hand and wore wire-rimmed glasses. He looked vintage.

"Um, I'm here to study." I said, expressionless.

"???"

"Err ... Na wait, see I'm a friend of Katie's."

Does that ring a bell! I looked at the guy for some response.

He beamed in reply, "Oh, come on in then, lad."

Man!! Katie was famous. I still didn't understand the connection, not until I entered the huge hall which was all designed in the 1980's style. There was an old rifle on the opposite wall and huge portraits of some old Englsihmen hung on the walls. A grandfather clock stood facing us, its magnanimous structure towering over me. On the side wardrobe, over the showcase, was a photo frame, and although it took me sometime to register the stunning beauty captured in there, I realised, I really did know this girl. She was not in her bad mood here, not scare mongering anymore, her straight hair, not oily anymore and her dimple visible, her eyes alive with a magical innocence that glued my eyes to the photo even more.

"Well, looks like we have got a fan of my daughter here." The guy said in a soft voice, his chuckles quite subtle.

I flushed, then I looked up at him, "Katie? She's your daughter, Sir?"

"Yes son, I'm Dennis. Your friend's dad." He stretched out his hand.

"Hello Sir, I'm Aakash Roy." I said after the handshake.

"Alright then fella, take a seat."

"Sir, actually I have been having some problems with maths, and Katie said that you might help me with ..."

"Oh, that, don't you worry about that. We've plenty of time to discuss that. First, lemme get your friend for you. I bet she'll be happy to have you here." Dennis beamed again, and for a second he reminded me of Dennis the Menace as he shouted over the top of his voice, "Katie, look who's here."

That was it. Now this freaked me out. Katie didn't know about my sudden intervention here and I had already lied on her behalf.

And, I had a pretty definite feeling that she'd hate to find me here. Damn, I'm going to be thrown out of this place in a minute.

I heard footsteps on the wooden staircase above and then, with trepidation and butterflies, I saw her again, for maybe the hundredth time, but yes, it did look like this one could actually make the first dazzling impression on me. Katie, the always frustrated, short tempered girl came and stood right before me, her eyes rested on mine, and I was amazed by the beauty she suddenly imposed on me. She was not sporting her uniform, instead, she wore a silvery orange gown, her hair flew behind her, it reached her waist, her face had an innocent expression that did kind of stop my breath and I had to pinch my wrist to realise I hadn't walked into a dream.

Katie and I beheld each other, She shocked, I scared.

"Look who's here." Her dad said with bubbly happiness, cradling the fire. She continued with her shocked stare, "Aakash." she mumbled.

"I should go." I whispered as I rose from my seat.

"How come? Why're you here?" Her voice was low and soothing to the ears, but Katie was erupting with questions, and her former self kind of returned but even then, amidst all her prying, I still found her cuter than ever.

"What do you mean?" Dennis was a bit confused, "He said he was your friend. Came for mathematics doubts. Isn't it so, Aakash? Why Katie, he's your friend, right?"

She kept quiet for a moment as she tried to figure out my latest trespassing. I just kept looking at her, speechless, both from my wrecked situation and her beauty (see a guy's mind works in strange ways).

Finally she spoke, and this time I gaped.

"Yeah, oh, hi Aakash." She smiled, her face that of the cute innocent girl, "What took you so long? I was kinda expecting you all day long."

Now, that did stop my heart beat all over again. I couldn't react.

"Imolost." I said gibberish that sounded more like molestation or something, though I meant to say, I'm all lost! She raised her eyebrows and then, I saw her grin heartily for the first time.

"Alright then, kids, I suppose, this is it then, I've made my decision." Dennis broke our conversation.

We turned our attention to him (In my case it was partial, see I couldn't take my eyes off his daughter!).

"Alright, Aakash, although I take batches and tuitions and my classes start at 6:30 pm, but do a thing, you be here at 4:15 sharp and you'll study with my daughter, the two of you, friends together. What say?"

I was transfixed again. What was up with the stars? I felt a rush of adrenaline that also brought in a stream of happiness as millions of endorphins were generated.

I nodded in appreciation of his idea, and what gave me almost a cardiac arrest was that even Katie nodded with a super cute smile at her dad.

Get a grip, buddy!

"Alright then, dismissed." Dennis said in his high army-happy voice, "You guys have fun today. We'll start with classes tomorrow. Katie, why don't you show him your room and then, maybe later, you guys can go play outside?"

Katie and I exchanged glances of nervousness. "Okay dad," she said in a gawky voice.

She pointed me to follow her and then we ascended up the stairs. I could hear soft notes on the piano in the background. Somebody was playing soft romantic music outside somewhere as I followed the silhouette of the girl I hated even twenty minutes ago, and now I was stunned by her beauty! Strange life!

We tiptoed to her room and then she opened the door and I gaped all over again.

The room kind of shone, nay, rather glittered with exquisite cleanliness. The white-tiled room was crystal clear. I could see teddy bears in lines, I could see books and table lamps, a soft bed with multi-coloured quilts, posters of Miley Cyrus, Hillary Duff, Peter Parker and John Abraham everywhere. I went inside warily.

"Do you live here or have you just put it up for display?" I spoke to her for the first time, and that "imolost" part really didn't count.

"What do you mean?" She said, with a question mark on her face.

"I mean, your room has no signs of a present human being, it's so." I tried to explain.

"Clean?" She ended the line for me, "Yeah, I do my room, like thrice every day. It's my favourite pastime."

"What!" I broke into a soft smile.

"What's funny?" She swelled with her usual anger, "I like it that way. And, you're the first guy I've ever shown my room to, so respect it."

"No, it's nice, good work." I faked an imaginary applause. She bowed her head with a sweet smile.

"Hey, I'm sorry. I took your name in there. Actually I needed help so I ..."

"It's fine, I figured that out." She said, stopping me mid-sentence, "And anyways, your plans amaze me. How you used my name for free classes." She stuck her tongue out.

"Umm," It was not my idea, I wanted to bring in Robbie's name but the promise played back in my mind.

I shrugged, then ended up with a cover smile.

"Hope, you're okay with your dad's plan, or you know I could take up his classes, that evening batch." I said half-heartedly.

"No, it's okay." She said, looking away, but I could feel her smile.

"Anyways, so if you're done with my room, let's go outside, I wanted to have an ice-cream." She said swiftly.

"Sure." We walked out of the house, bade farewell to Mr Dennis for the day, then strolled up the lawn, as Katie kept on talking about how her dad generally was praising him as a teacher.

She would always speak Hindi and English with me. She didn't know Bengali. She was a Malayali Christian.

"My dad is very strict too, you know." she said putting on a sad face.

"Really," I said stopping at the ice cream parlour," he looked kind of sweet to me. I mean, he was really happy to meet me."

"There's a reason for that," she mumbled as we looked up the flavours.

"One black current double sundae."

"One black current do...," she looked at me with surprise. We had made the same weird choice, "Same pinch." she winked and pinched me. "Make that two," she said to the shopkeeper.

We savoured the ice cream.

"You know I'm a quiet girl in class," she said.

"Oh, I know that. That's why I sat with you on the first day." I smiled, "I like quiet people."

"Ohho, Mr Aakash, then I'm sorry, you're for a real bad treat. I'm not silent by nature, okay, I talk too much, I mean half my carbs are burnt in the process. I just don't like it in school. So, I keep quiet."

"I know why." I smiled.

"You don't." She mumbled, taking another bite.

"Oh of course I do. The Bengali clan, the big language difference."

"Wow Mr Aakash." She looked at me with fondness, "I'm impressed, coming from a Bengali, that's new!"

"Oh tell me about it." I smiled, "I too am on the border line here. I'm a semi-veg Hindi speaking Bengali. I guess that makes me some sort of an alien." I faked two antennas out of my head.

"Oh, my gosh ... you're veg!" She broke into fits of laughters, "That really calls for punishments."

"I bet that does." I shrugged.

We were quiet for two minutes as we concentrated on the ice-cream.

"Hey don't be sad. See we could team up." She winked.

I smiled, however, she had grown pensive, "But only if you want to, I mean you know, I'm the talking type." She explained.

"Hmmm ... that's true." I said with sarcasm, "But then, anything for free tuitions."

She punched my back.

"Ouch, looks like this friendship's going to be injurious to health."

"Oh, you bet." She laughed.

We sat on the huge paddy field outside, the Hoogly River in the distance, looking at the beautiful sunset.

"It's Katherine." she spoke softly.

"What?" I looked at her face that had turned orange, reflecting the sky.

"My name." she smiled at me, "It's Katherine Andrews."

"Katherine ... Katie, oh." I smiled with amazement.

"Friends." She stretched her hand out, I took it.

✷✷✷

Four years down the line, I hug Katie and she slowly brushes my hair with her hands, "Hey, it's okay, Aakash."

"I'm a bad friend, Katie, You would never realise."

"No Aakash, you're not, trust me." she wipes tears off my face.

"I should go now." I suddenly detached myself from her arms, "sorry, Katie."

"Hey, Aakash", her soft voice stopped me. I swayed, my head all dazing with a hundred million thoughts.

"You remember, how my father had smiled and laughed the first day you came to our house four years ago on a winter eve of December?" she asked expectantly.

I tried to remember, but my mind was all messed up. I shook my head.

"Military Uncle smiled at me once?" I smirked sarcastically.

"Oh yes, he did, you know why?" Katie said, her voice wavering, "Because you were the first friend I ever made in Calcutta. You were the first guy to have walked into my life and you did come unannounced as always." She smiled, all nostalgic.

I turned around to face her, knowing I would forget it all when I woke up.

I looked at Katherine, her eyes are all wet, too.
How did it feel so real!
 "You were always special, Aakash, you just never understood."

LIE 035

So we all have had those bad times when things weren't pretty well, we were all let down and started hating a place, and thought these were 'the worst days of my life' but then something, maybe, a small flicker of happiness, a moment of rejoice, it might be that small smile, that outstretched hand for friendship that suddenly lightens up life and it all turns hopeful, all over again. You might even be unlucky enough to miss out on those little things, give up those small threads that would tie you to the magical universe, those unforeseen events, but I didn't.

This is the story of that silver lining.

* * *

"Hi, Robbie, what's this now?" I sat on my usual desk at the old deserted science lab of SMI as I looked down at resistors and transistors and other such over the top stuff, that Robbie toyed with. He looked kind of absorbed, but then he always had time for me. He put the tester down, switched his table lamp off and then looked at me and yawned.

"I feel like sleeping, but this thing is really cool, so I guess I have to get it done." Robbie showed me all these diagrams and flow charts.

"Err ... quick question. How come you never told me you were Katherine's brother?"

"Unimportant stuff!"

"Er ... what exactly are you making?" I gave him my usual puzzled look.

"Well, I'm making a, let's see, I call this the 'turn off'."

"What?" I suddenly had a different thought in my mind, however, aware of Robbie's little insight in that field, I quickly responded, "What does that mean, Robbie?"

"Oh ... it's actually a jammer, a TV-jammer, a computer jammer, you know." Robbie moved his hands in the air, "It's like you could actually put out any frequency by using this jammer. It kind of catches, or fine tunes into any certain frequency and then it can be used to 'turn off' the frequency completely, you know, put out that frequency."

"?????????", I actually had more question marks than I just currently used.

"Okay, see two decades ago, this guy Steve Wozniac made a TVs jammer through which he could switch off or blank out any television when he could fine tune to its perfect frequency. I'm trying to make an advanced version of it. It's like those devices that could render any display useless."

"Man, that is awesome." I now realised the plan, "It's evil, too." I smirked.

"How is that evil?" Robbie was confused.

"Oh, c'mon, think of all the fun we could have with it, you know like turn the television on and off, disturb the other students when they are like at the climax of a movie scene! Oh, man! It would be evil." I grinned with malice.

However, Robbie had gone quiet. He went grave as if I had played the wrong string of Beethoven's symphony.

After two more minutes of silence, I finally got impatient and looked down at my watch, it was 4:00 pm.

"Oh, sharks, I'm late, I've to go."

"Huh? Where? School just got over." Robbie focussed back at me.

"Your dad's classes, listen I'll catch up with you later, buddy. Make that crazy thing for me, okay." I finished my sentence in a hurry as I stormed out of school.

"Best of luck buddy, you need it." I heard the distant statement of Robbie.

***

Damn it, this is unfair. Why does she need to look that cute all the time?

Katie sat cross-legged on the sofa, wearing a blue top and her hair all tied up in a knot, as she sipped coffee out of this huge mug.

"Oh, you done with your room?" I smiled at her as I entered.

She looked up at me, and her face flushed with a glow so sparkling, it could actually light up the entire street, "Oh, Aakash, you and your pathetic sense of humour."

"Funny." I sat on the opposite chair facing her, as I unzipped my bag and brought out my books, "It made you smile, alright."

Prof Dennis entered the very next moment, hereby restricting our warm up talk.

"Hello, Sir." I smiled at him.

"Evening, boy." Dennis took his seat at the centre, like our focal lengths, equidistant calculations. His voice was all stern and his greeting suddenly turned the evening ominous.

"Alright, so let's start." He set a timer on the alarm clock at the table, timed it precisely at 60 minutes and started a countdown. I kind of smirked at the funny time stamp he kept, however little did I expect that the timer was going to countdown the most ferocious time of my study life.

Alright, so Dennis was a menace with teaching! *Yup, dude, he could really compel you into euthanasia.* He was scary, he was strict, he was fast and erudite and he never repeated anything he taught. Right on the very first day, he scolded me five times, predicted my failure in the coming term, took a test of mine for self-assurance, and failed me on purpose, giving out zeroes because I skipped a step while calculating!

Katie, on the other side, was the fighter. She would argue with her dad, ask him doubts even on silly stuff, turn a deaf ear to his scolding and stick her tongue out at places, too.

Yeah, she was an expert at it. She was strong and rough with her dad and now I knew how, she had turned aggressive in class. She had just inherited her dad's genes and was this split personality, laughing and jumping and crazy at one moment, and then the next moment, she would explode into Goddess Durga or something and terrify you.

The father and daughter duo should really give meditation and yoga a shot, I thought!

Man, the 60 minutes were terrible, in fact they were frightening.

I could really sense a brain freeze approaching by the end of the class. All I could concentrate on was the timer, as it ticked in slow motion, counted down to zero after some decades or centuries of atrocity.

✱✱✱

"Oh, man!" I had my hand over my head trying to ease out the headache, as I used the other one to taste the chocolate ice-cream.

"Yeah, I know." Katherine sighed, "I guess I should've alerted you. But you know, I kind of didn't want to, I don't know why."

We sat in the ice cream parlour near Katherine's house, trying out new flavours.

"Oh, trust me on this. You should've like really warned me, lady." I sulked.

"What can I do, my dad's like this only. He was in the army earlier." Katie squeaked, her face swelling up with anger again.

"Yeah, I saw that army jeep outside your house, I wish I had read the signs." I sighed.

"So cool, don't come from tomorrow! It's not compulsory, and anyways, your trigonometry doubts were clarified today." Katherine said with some more of cynicism.

"Yeah, they were." I shrugged, "Just that now I'm left with bigger doubts about my career, your dad's a real motivator, military uncle!" I said sarcastically.

"Oh, please, don't blame my dad, you were all depressed anyways."

"Not that I needed an upgrade on it, but anyways." I vented some more of my bad mood.

It happened spontaneously. Katie's ice-cream came flying at my face. The cone aimed for my head, and the next moment I could taste mango syrup all over my face. *B.E.A.U.tiful.*

"May I have a tissue?" I asked the shop keeper, who watched the scene with rapt attention.

"Here you go, kiddo", he handed me two dozens of those paper napkins, "You need it, mate."

By the time I wiped my spectacles, Katherine had already gone off the site.

"Brilliant, simply epic." I speculated, as I paid the shop keeper the extra bucks for Katie's ice-cream.

So, this was it. I grabbed my bag and started walking through the meadow, taking in some fresh air, waving a final goodbye to 24 Parganas! What kind of a locality name was it anyways! 24 Parganas!

That's when I heard her scream.

Suddenly, my confused and stupid questions didn't matter anymore. The Rajesh Khanna from the 1970's was back on track, and I ran to her. Katherine's scream had me going haywire. I ran fast as if I could really beat Usain Bolt on this one. I cut through the bushes, the shrubs and then there I was at the source of the commotion.

I looked out for a hurt, injured, or maybe, trapped Katherine, but hey, what did I get to see?

Katherine bent low near the surface of the weedy pond, her eyes over the other edge, her face twisted into that innocent smile of hers!

"What the hell, Katie?" I shouted in frustration.

"Shhh, you'll scare it, dufus!" she put her finger over her lips and grimaced at me and then looked back at her prior focus.

"What? Scare?" I looked at the spot she had been staring with constant concentration and then I saw it, a small puppy!

The puppy looked all muddy and ugly; and honestly, I hated puppies. They were filthy, they licked your toes and stayed awake all night eating your head.

"So cute na," she whispered.

"Yuck."

"Oh, shut up, Aakash. Listen, we need to save him." Katherine now said in her I'm-real-serious voice.

"Save him ... from what? trees and bushes?" I was confused.

"No duffer, the puppy might drown in the pond, it's all alone. Look at it, the poor thing; we need to get it over here."

"Accepting all your hypothesis and on-the-fly plan, how do you propose the escape route? I mean, it's on the other side of this jinxed pond. How do we get to it?" I was already bored but I kept talking as

I didn't want unkempt water all spilled over my face again. Enough of facials for today.

"Oh, it's simple, Aakash, we don't get to the puppy" she simpered, "You do. You swim to the other side and get the puppy."

"What? No, I can't do that." My hydrophobia just geared back in with full acceleration. Remember the ocean-drowning episode!

"Why? You were on an island for seven years for God's sake." She was irritated.

"Nope, it's not gonna happen, Katie. See, I've this problem with water. I've this ... er ... fear." I back stepped with growing fear that she might actually kick me into the pond!

"Please, for me." She made the cutest face possible on earth.

"Still no, I'm sorry." I said reluctantly, my eyes absorbing the last shreds of her divine expressions.

"You're such a ... ", she trotted to the pond, "jack ass!".

And then, she jumped into the water.

"Oh ... Katherine!" I watched her in awe and shock all cocktailed together as she swam across the dirty pond, her hands cutting through the weeds, as she moved towards her target. It took her a couple of minutes to swim to the other side, all soaked and filled with sea weed, she reminded me of Catwoman!

I watched her slowly walk to the puppy, then squat near it, as the puppy was frightened to death, its leg was trapped in a small shrub and it couldn't set itself free. It really was trapped by the bushes, I pondered over the irony!

Katie slowly approached it, her face all calm and soft and her hands slowly untangling the poor thing. Once free, the puppy made a sudden knee jerk reaction, it ran off like a wild leopard.

We were amazed, and Katie turned sad. Her face was all sober and weepy.

"I guess I'll swim back then." She rose and looked at me.

"Yeah, do that, and it was nice in there, what you did" I faked an applause. She smiled and bowed her head, like she always did.

"By the way, how're you going to swim with one hand?" I queried.

"One hand? Why?", Katherine was confused.

"Look behind you, saviour." I beamed.

Katie's expression suddenly changed as she processed my explanation, and then she turned in a full swing, to behold her gift; the puppy wagged its tail as it looked at Katherine.

"One more fan," I whispered.

***

"We need to make it a house!" Katherine was all perked up and super excited. Her joy knew no bounds.

"You can keep it in your place." I suggested.

"Oh, no. That's not gonna happen. My dad only likes German Shepherds or Labradors. And, it's a small Pomeranian. He'll kill me with this dog. He hates cute and fluffy stuff.", Katherine explained, her eyebrows all etched up, as she somehow completed the statement, "What about your house?" she fired back.

"Oh, I live in a 1 bhk with my dad and trust me, we can't even handle ourselves, forget the dog." I shrugged thinking of my dishevelled room.

"Okay, so we need to find it an alternate home."

"Well, why don't we make it a house out here in the meadow? It will be safe. This place is deserted all the time and we will supply it with surplus food", I said keeping a safe distance from the puppy, which was presently licking Katherine's ears as she kissed it on a periodic basis.

"Okay, fine, but I don't know how to make all those construction kinda thing."

"Um fine, don't worry, I can handle this matter, remember the contraption." I winked.

Soon, we were out there, gathering wooden planks, getting hammer and nails, sitting cross-legged in the sunset, fixing up the "Dog-house".

Alright, the house was pathetic. I mean, even the puppy scowled when it first looked up at the mess, but with some supply of biscuits and milk, it went inside the wooden contraption alright and sat enjoying supper.

"Hey, it's 7, I should go." I looked up at Katie after a while, as she still cuddled the puppy.

"Um ... yeah, even me, too," she stood and put the puppy back in its refuge.

"So, I guess I'll see you tomorrow in ...", and then she suddenly paused as she realised the unfortunate truth.

We looked at each other, and sadness engulfed us. The truth was, I wasn't coming to this locality again, not for those stupid classes, my venture to this part of West Bengal was over. Katherine looked at the puppy and back at me, like a helpless single parent, but then I blinked, and she had again turned back to her former self, strict and strong like her dad.

"Good night, Aakash." she said, as she walked away.

"Night, Katherine." I shrugged.

"By the way, thanks Aakash." She turned one last time, and although her face was no more visible in the growing darkness, I could make out her expressions, "Thanks for the help. "

"My pleasure," I mumbled.

"So, this is the final goodbye then." She vanished into the darkness and I stood there, all alone again, the Aakash, I had always been.

✳✳✳

"Nice dress." I entered Katie's house the next day, accurately at 4:15 pm.

"You?" She looked up at me, all surprised and her face again welled up with that floodlight glow, "You came".

"Yup, I did. I kind of missed the puppy." I lied.

She smiled, "Me, too." She lied back.

LIE 036

February 24th, 2002

School was kind of fun now a days. I'd always sit with Katherine and we would chat all along, talk about movies, about pending homework, I'd tell her about Port Blair, and she would bring alive to me, the shores of Kerala. By the end of the month that we had been sitting together, I could actually tell you her native address, her favourite restaurant in Kerala, her crushes, and some of the Malayalam words such as "*engngane irikkunnu?*" and "*namaskaaram*", "*illa* " and all that stuff.

"Well, you know tomorrow is the school annual fete." Katie said all stirred up.

"So?" I never really understood why the brother and sister were always over excited.

I mean, half the time, Robbie would be jumping up and down with his weird inventions, of the likes of "turn off" etc., and Katie on the other hand, would be spiced up by normal events like a stupid puppy or some school fete ... I mean who gave a damn!

"I do." Katherine boiled up, "I give a damn about it!".

Oops, did I say the last part of my thoughts out loud?

"*Kshamikkanam*" I apologised in Malayalam, "I'm sorry."

"Oh, you better be ROY, dufus." She became jovial again. Her moods were like Cherapunji, ready to rain down or hail at any point.

We sat quietly for ten minutes as I completed (copied) the homework from Katherine's note book.

"Okay, so you better be prepared for tomorrow." She said sharply.

"For the fete? What'd I do in there?" I looked at her, bewildered.

"That's for you to figure out; I've already submitted our name in the entries for stalls and guess what?"

"Oh, shit! We got selected did we?" I was terrified.

"Bingo." she beamed.

"What in the hell are we going to sell?." I was dumbfounded.

"That's for you to decide ... I'm not into the business thing, you see." she hummed happily.

God save us ...

***

February 25th, 3:45 pm

"So, how's the 'turn off' thing going?" I tried to stay as calm as possible. Robbie didn't know yet. He had been in this lab the entire day.

Robbie shrugged, "I quit on that thing ..."

"Why?" I was aghast.

"Aakash, I don't think it's a good idea to make that TV jammer, after all. I mean, you only said it was evil, didn't you. That got me thinking."

Oh, my big stupid mouth!

***

February 25th, 9:30 am

We put up our stall in the extreme right corner of our school premises, Katherine and I together pasted the posters that we had prepared all evening at Katie's place.

We had decided on playing a game called '7up'. It involved tossing two dices, and if the sum of the digits that'd turn up exceeded 7, then the guy who's playing the bet, gets rewarded with double the money he had invested on the game. You could bet any amount, and if your dices summed up to anything more than 7, you would get the double of your money, and similarly if you lost, you would have to pay us double the money you paid earlier. It sounded like a profitable game to me and I never took any chances.

The night before, i.e. on 24th, I sat for an hour sharpening the bases of two dices on the sides with big digits, i.e. the numbers 4, 5 and six had their bases extra smoothened, so that they always ended up inverted! That would be the trick with the help of which we were always going to be on the winning side,

But apparently, I made a mistake ... *I couldn't stop my big mouth!*

I told my cheat code to Katherine, and while I bragged about my winning tactics, the volcano erupted again. Oh, she was flabbergasted! See, girls have this thing, they're always good with scolding, I mean, they have a sharp taste with words and once they're knives and daggers at you, you're one way or the other, *seriously in trouble ... dude ...*

"How in the world have you turned out so bad, Aakash?" she continued screaming as the other students from different stalls looked at the despicable me, "I can't believe you end up lying at everything you do, can't you ever be honest?" she was in no mood to stop.

After two more minutes of sheer torture, I put my hands up in declaration, "Okay, alright, I apologise, it's a bad idea, it's in fact pathetic! Happy now? Kshamikkanam." I was on the verge of dissolving from the face of earth.

"Don't you kshamikkanam me, dufus." she indexed me with extreme intensity.

✳✳✳

February 25th, 3:49pm

"Hey, that was a mistake. I mean I misunderstood the "turn off" thing." I requested, "Listen, I think it's a great idea and you should really work on this thing, man! I mean look at all this research you have done." I flipped the flow charts and the diagrams that Robbie had crumpled off.

Robbie shook his head, "No Aakash, it's not gonna happen. The jammer thing might be great, but it's unethical."

"Hey, so what? At least it's an exciting thing. I mean, why do you brother and sister always have to be truthful sons of Jesus!" I punched on the desk with aggression.

Robbie looked at me and I could sense fear in him. He was not used to angry people, except his dad, I guessed.

"Alright, for the thousandth time Robbie, I apologise, but please say yes to this. It's important."

My eyes scorched into his and I could see him in the Catch 22, maybe for an IQ of 200+, this was the first time.

✶✶✶

February 25th, 10:30am

We played a fair game and to be frank, it really felt good. I mean, the first guy who turned up bet for Rs. 30, lost, as the sum of the digits turned up to be 5. So, he had to pay us an extra 60 bucks. Ninety off the first player; we high-fived.

The second one bet 20 bucks, and he lost too, scoring only 3! So now we had another 60.

a hundred and fifty on the first ten minutes. This game was turning out legendary.

"Make it for 100." Deb Roy stood in our stall, sporting a white John Players, a Tag Heuer watch, his face whiter than milk, his smile in place, the picture perfect boy!

"You're not playing with us, sorry." I waved him bye.

He looked at me, aghast.

I stared back.

"Ahem, Aakash, we can't say no to our customers." Katherine intervened softly.

"Hey, we can change rules." I replied. No way, I was going to let Deb Roy play.

"Don't be a spoil sport, Aakash. I know you have this very big problem with me." Deb Roy chuckled, as calm and callous as a turtle, "But come on, how's the struggle gonna survive, if you don't give me a chance."

Katherine handed him the dice.

I grunted. Back stabber!

And, sure enough, the jerk did win! He made a perfect twelve! I just couldn't believe his luck. There was applause all around as the crowd cheered the youth icon.

Katherine took out the 150 of our savings from her purse and added an extra 50. So, here we were, all our morning's savings gone in a jiffy.

I sighed! *Deb Roy was my bad luck!*

"Hey no, you guys keep it." Deb Roy smiled, "You guys deserve a great start. And anyways I was a wildcard entry, so I don't think I should keep it."

"Oh, shut the fu ..." I was irritated.

"Aakash, school, remember!" Katherine!

"Hey, Aakash, c'mon relax, dude." Deb was playing cool again, "Listen, I need to talk to you anyways, clear some air."

"Well." I played back the day I auditioned back in mind three times before I went on, "You know what, the only thing we need to talk is how bad the fight is gonna be."

Deb's calm face shifted to form a new image, "Is that so?" I saw his fists clench.

"Hey, guys, what are you doing?" Katie shouted now and we both backstepped with the shock. "Shut up, both of you jerks. Listen Deb, just take your money and get going."

She handed him the money, "We really don't need donations. Bye."

Deb looked at her, his face grim, then his eyes shifted to me, and stayed there for another twenty seconds.

"Pack up guys." Katie yelled again.

**

Two hours later, we were broke. Katie's pocket money of a thousand something was already gone and I had to part with two hundred bucks. That left us with very little scope for business.

"This was a bad idea." Katherine shrugged, "I think I'll have lunch and then I'll be back in fifteen minutes. You handle the stall till then, and after that we might get going. This ain't working well."

I nodded silently. Two hundred bucks! I was really pissed now.

My idea was not bad at all. It just didn't get implemented.

"Hey Katie. don't worry, go have lunch, get some rest, enjoy the fete and take your time. I'll handle it here."

Katie smiled at me, her killing smile, "Awww, you're a sweetheart." She strolled away.

I smiled, "I'm no sweetheart girl." I mumbled and swapped the dices as she walked away.

The game begins now.

***

February 25th, 4:00 pm

"I'm sorry, Aakash."

I stared at Robbie as the last hope faded.

"Please." I mumbled. Robbie didn't listen. I couldn't explain the gravity of the situation to him. The truth could not surface today.

***

February 25th, 1:30 pm

Katie returned half an hour later and her mouth fell open.

"Shut the f…," she controlled herself, "front door! how in the world?"

She eyed the two thousand bucks I held out for her.

"Just my luck," I winked at her.

She jumped and hugged me.

Alright guys, okay for the record, this was the first time, I, Aakash, got hugged by a girl! And that too in front of a crowd of 300 students!

She realised what she had done a second later and let go, embarrassed. She was all red in the face, as we shied away and rifled with useless objects, trying to hide the spontaneous thing that just happened.

I swiftly swapped away the dice back and Katherine remained as innocent as always.

One hour down the line, we had made excellent business. I was amazed at how we ended up making 5 grand! We were on a rampage and our team was the most successful.

"Alright, partner, I'll go grab a bite. When I return, we'll pack up and leave, okay? It's enough for this year. We were great." I told Katie.

"We were great." She beamed, her floodlight glow back on display.

I strolled around the stalls, casually whistling. Today was my lucky day.

So, there I was, having biryani and French fries and coke, completely oblivious to the twist in the tale.

I returned to find a worried and jumpy Katie.

"What happened?" I asked.

Katie looked at me, her eyes bent low, and she shrugged, "I'm sorry, Aakash, I've made a mistake. Please, forgive me."

I looked at her open purse. All the money gone.

"Blimey, you lost it all, did ya?" I couldn't stop laughing. The overconfident Katherine sucked at business. Frankly, I didn't care about the loss, I was so happy with the reasons I could tease Katherine with now.

"No Aakash, that's not what happened", Katie's voice shook. And, a tear rolled down her eye.

This is where I got worried.

"Sobhanjan and Subhojeet and some other guys from class had come half an hour back."

"So?" I went tense as I recollected how I had thrown Subhojeet into a dust bin the day he had criticised me in the auditions.

"They told me, Kavita ma'am wanted to find out how much business we made. She would keep 20 percent of our total sale with her for the stall and the rest would be ours. That's how this fete works." she went quiet.

"Tell me, what happened then, Katie?" I shouted at her now. I knew something bad was coming.

She started weeping, "I gave them the money to show to Kavita ma'am. I trusted them and now they just denied the entire thing in front of Kavita ma'am. They said that we had been losing all day. They personally verified and told her that we have made zero profit and you know ma'am, no matter how much I told her, she didn't trust me. Those scums took away our money. They insulted me so much." Katherine wept.

This was it!

I didn't know when it happened, what were the thoughts that led me to do it, but there I was, storming through the corridors, my fists clenched, my heart pumping, anger boiling through my brain. I found the gang eating samosas at the last stall. Deb Roy sat between the crowd, joking, laughing and cheering.

He was the root of it all, I could backtrace to him offering us the Rs 200 rs back, because somewhere he knew it was all gonna come back to him. The rascal.

I grabbed a wooden club from the ground and the next moment, before anybody even saw me approaching, I remember knocking Deb Roy out with the wooden club.

It was one swift stroke, as Deb was lifted from the chair with the hit, blood spurted out of his nose, and he fell with a deadly thud to the ground.

***

February 25th, 3:40 pm

My dad sat inside principal's office requesting him for some mercy. The panel had started with ideas of rusticating me, but now they had come down to suspension for a month.

Turned out, Deb somehow got a minor injury on his head and was getting treated now. The positive thing that worked on my favour was me getting beaten up, too, by the gang. Blood soaked my face and although the pain was incessant, it did help. See, the teachers couldn't punish me severely now. It was fault at both ends.

However, these were not the things that buzzed in my head. All I could think now, was what a month's expulsion meant. It meant I was gonna miss out on our first practical. I was about to flunk. The practical was 29 days away from this unlucky day of mine and I thought hard for one good idea.

That's when it struck me.

***

4:00 pm

"Okay, fine Robbie, don't make that thing of yours. I just need one favour." I said.

Robbie turned. He was as yet unaware of the events of today, and so I knew I could get away with the lie, before he got to know the entire backdrop.

"What do you need, Aakash? Tell me." Robbie asked kindly.

"I need all your research work. I want to read about the jammer. Everything about it."

"You're not planning on making it yourself, are you?", Robbie became suspicious.

"No, no, I'm not. I won't be working that hard, Robbie, and I don't even have the brains for designing such a device." I maintained, "I just need it to kill some time."

"So, you promise." Robbie asked as he took his file out.

"I cross my heart." I lied.

LIE 037

There's a silence so condemning, it feels almost grave. I stood there, thinking of how in the world a day as great as this, when I got hugged, made 5,000 bucks, and was having some irresistible biryani, ended up like this. I almost could smile at the joke, just that I didn't feel like it anymore. See, when the joke is on you, you just don't feel like laughing, no matter how crazy or classic it is. As my dad and our principal looked at me with abhorrent eyes, I kept up with my interest on the floor and the small ant that tried to climb the table.

"Look at him, he doesn't even look ashamed." The principal said through clenched teeth.

The next moment, a tight slap almost pinned me to the table. My eyes went blurred with some aqueous fluid, but I didn't let them out yet. Do not display what they want to watch, the apathy really pisses them off, it does.

"Sir, on behalf of him, I apologise. Forgive us. Give him one more chance."

My dad glanced at me with one last shred of huge disappointment and I resumed with the ant struggling with its tiny world.

29 days left for the *coup de grace*.

* * *

I sat there, reading the charts and diagrams. I was going to try the myth today, try to realise it, and that too without the help of a genius. I felt sorry for lying to Robbie. But guess, the "TURN OFF" was meant to be turned on. So, there I was reading the docs and making the jammer.

Twenty-five days to go.

***

"Hey, I heard you got suspended." Katie's dad Dennis looked at me with an amused expression.

I nodded silently, wishing Katie would join us soon so that we could start with the proper classes. Katie had been ill, some headache, and I didn't even know whether she was angry with me or just too hesitant to even call me a friend. Was my retaliation a cause of her headache or was it just an outcome of the shame of befriending a lunatic of my kind.

So, I left the thoughts in mid-air, and concentrated on the quadratic equation and got it wrong, the fourth one in a row.

"Why don't you take a break today?" Dennis turned a bit soft and I instantly nodded. This was the first time the guy had shown some leniency and I was overwhelmed.

He switched off the timer and left his seat.

"By the way, Aakash, I heard what had happened." Dennis said as I started packing my stuff.

We paused. I was quite expectant of some more words of advice.

"I'm proud of what you did in there." Dennis said as he lit his pipe and walked off to his study.

I sat there, confused, shocked, amazed (oh ... how could I explain my feelings! It was such a shocker). I realised all army men loved some action.

"And, for the record." Dennis stopped near his study as he chuckled inaudibly, "Katherine hates you for that."

***

I wrapped a coil out of some thick wire I had, turned it into a mesh, and then I soldered on a little tap halfway down one of the turns and put a capacitor there.

The whole thing was just as small as my index finger, it was petite. I built on top of the case a 9v battery. There was a small clip on top of a 9volt battery, I stripped it out, soldered it to the connectors on my little TURN OFF circuit and then I could plug another 9 volt battery in as my power source. So, I was able to carry the 9 volt battery case with the jammer on it totally concealed. Only there was this six inch wire that acted as the antenna, which I had to stick out to transmit.

And, there it was, the 'turn off', all set.

I ran to the hall and switched on the television. I held my breath as I powered the jammer on. There was a small static on the screen, it was there for like a wink of the eye and then the television happily displayed the channel.

I had failed with the jammer.

Twenty days to go.

★★★

Katie looked sick. Her eyes were red and her face was swollen. She looked weak and thin, her face had lost its glow.

We sat on the grassy paddy field, looking at the sunset as was our customary habit.

The small Pomeranian played on her lap as she cuddled it. The sun's dying light shone on her face and I saw tears.

"It was all my fault, Aakash, I shouldn't have gotten you involved." she sighed.

I kept quiet looking out at the birds sailing home, the west wind brushed through the birds diverting them from their paths as they struggled against it to fight their way back.

"We have our computer practical on 25th March; you would be on suspension then." She put her hands over her head as she sobbed.

"I'll figure out a way, Katie. It's not your fault." I looked at her now, "Don't worry."

She grimaced.

"Hey, why haven't we named this puppy yet?" I tried to change the topic.

"Oh, yes, I was thinking of Pluto or Dallas?" Katie looked up now, wiping off her tears.

"How about Sabith?" I looked at the small fluffy puppy. It looked nothing like a fighter, but somewhere I felt it should have a warrior sorta name.

Katie raised her eyebrows, "Sabith?"

"Yeah, like Sabith the warrior?" I now wanted the name in earnest.

"Umm...," Katie looked at the puppy which now was lying down on its back, its paws flying incoherently in the air.

"We need to think this over."

I shrugged.

Katie and I exchanged glances of decision-making and indecision for the next five minutes, after which she slowly mumbled, "Sabith".

The dog jolted from its stupid position and stared right at her as if hooked by some spell. It looked at her, confused, its tongue sticking out.

"Sabith it is." I smiled.

✶✶✶

It was 3 o'clock in the night as I attempted for the 50th time to turn off the television frequency and all that I ended up doing was just creating a small flicker.

I slammed my fist on the wall and immediately regretted the decision.

"Aakash." The voice suddenly unnerved me as I turned to face my dad. He looked serious and sleepy at the same time. He hadn't talked to me for the last 18 days, since my suspension.

We had been silent, grave like some robots with no emotions except for the eating, bathing and the sleeping part.

He gave me the disappointed Rajesh Khanna look. I half-expected him to break into the, "I hate tears re" dialogue, however dad cleared his voice and pointed me to sit.

So, it was ultimately the time. *We were going to have the "TALK".*

I shrugged and imagined myself climbing from K2.

Ten minutes later, Dad had not even come to the point. He explained how hard he had worked as a child, how he would walk 20 miles to school and how he would ace every exam. Both of these were lies, grandpa had later told me.

(*Dad's school was two blocks away from his house and Dad never topped, he was somewhere near the 50th rank.*)

Then, dad talked about how he had dreamt of me becoming a scientist, getting the Nobel Prize!

I yawned and my eyes blurred with sleep.

"Aakash, I know I won't be able to make this fact dawn on you, son, but know one thing, you can't beat up a guy and become superior to him. You can't buy a Mercedes and win over some poor fellow, what you need is the right platform to compete and that, Aakash is education. You people might've been born with different situations, financially and emotionally but there was this education that was the same for all of you. So, why don't you beat them where you can fight as equal?." He looked at me trying to figure out whether I had understood his kind-of-war scheme.

I nodded slowly, looking back at the jammer that right away sucked!

Dad sighed, then he stood up and patted my back, "Promise me son, never again. No more of such deceitful activities ever again."

"Dad!" I said irritated.

"Promise me, Aakash." my dad almost pleaded now and that really disheartened me.

"I promise." I said, my fingers crossed as I lied.

Eleven days to go.

✳ ✳ ✳

It was my birthday today and I lay quietly on my bed, trying my best to sleep. No friends, no school, and a plan that just didn't work.

My dad had forgotten my b'day again, but it was quite usual for him, *he did that even with himself!*

I closed my eyes and requested my brain modestly to shut down as I turned on the 'turn off' once again out of sheer habit. It was midnight when the phone rang.

I suddenly felt my heart beat accelerate.

I tiptoed to the hall and picked up the receiver before dad awake.

"Hello ... err ... is it Aakash?" The voice was hazy but it froze my heart alright.

"Pritish." I couldn't believe it was him.

There was static, a lot of it, but even then the indistinct voice was a very familiar one, like the sound of my heart beat.

"Happy b'day, buddy." Pritish's voice was loud with excitement and happiness.

"Thanks dude, you remembered." I chuckled.

"Nah ... actually beamed on Orkut! It did." Pritish laughed from the other side.

"Oh yes, computer freak." I pictured my best friend Pritish again, eating a burger and playing 'Need for Speed'.

Then, we laughed and forgot our worries for the ten minutes we talked.

"Dude! it's a whole lot of static. Is something wrong with your line?" Pritish complained.

"Something wrong with my life, buddy!" I shrugged as I explained to him with a lot of recantations, the past few events of my screwed up life.

"Hey, c'mon Aakash, ups and downs happen, I mean, you left us even without a last good bye. Imagine how hurtful it was. We disowned you for a while and I dialled your number so many times, but then hung up as my alter ego took over. So, something bad was supposed to happen to you too, you see, Karma."

"Ooohhhh ... Pritish getting philosophical, huh!" I teased him smugly.

"Nah, I'm just saying look at the bright sides, too, now. It seems like a little crush you have in there, Katie."

"She's just a friend, sicko." I blushed as I retorted.

"Yeah yeah, cool." Pritish's voice was filled with sarcasm, "but anyways, you fought for her. You are like hero of some bad Tollywood movie."

"Chuck that, she hates me for it." I sighed.

"Aah, that's just her sense of righteousness speaking. She so adores you for this, buddy." Pritish got playful every minute now.

"Yeah, sure," I yawned.

"Alright buddy, now it's really hard to hear anything ... listen, many happy returns of the day and wish you a great life ahead ... all the best, dude. Make us proud there." Pritish said before the line went dead.

I still held the receiver listening to the dial tone and the static that engulfed the phone.

"Thanks, bro." I felt my eyes go moist, "And, I'm sorry".

I knew I was gonna lose as I walked towards my bedroom.

Two days to go now.

I cursed BSNL as I moved into my quilt.

That's when it dawned on me. The static!

I suddenly realised that I had the "Turn off" switched on.

✷ ✷ ✷

Final act ...

The computer practical exam started at 9 am sharp.

I stood by the door where no one could see me.

Careful now!

I could see Ramesh Sir giving students the tokens that had the programs which they were supposed to perform.

The exam was of 100 marks and missing this meant you were gonna flunk, for sure.

I hyper-ventilated. *Last chance.*

With one last prayer, I clutched the "Turn off" in my pocket. Its 6-inch antenna stuck out of my jeans like some tail I had grown.

My dad's promise flashed before my eyes like some effigy of Gandhi.

Sorry, dad!

Here you go. I clicked the button.

There was a small flicker on the screen and for a moment I was sure the thing had failed again. I was too used to its failure, you see.

But then, the magic happened.

Right before my eyes, 40 screens went blank.

Students and teachers stared at the screens, bewildered.

I felt my pulse reach 500.

"What happened?" I heard Katie ask Ramesh Sir as he looked helpless, pressing the keys without any idea whatsoever.

Soon enough, three more teachers ignored me as they entered the lab and tried their best to fix the computers, but the screen just wouldn't come back to life.

The frequency from the remote server was lost, turned off. The wifi was all messed up.

I warily hid the "turn off" still switched on behind the doors of the lab, where it would continue jamming the server.

I looked at my watch. 9:45 am.

I smiled as I wiped the sweat from my face. Then, I turned.

"What is that?" Deb Roy stared at the place where I had hidden the jammer.

I stood numb as I faced him, caught red handed.

"Oh, my god, is that the jammer you were talking about in class with Katie once? "

We looked at each other and then Deb understood.

I heard a voice in my head sigh.

You're so gone, dude..

LIE 038

Deb here …

Deb's Diary Entry 403

*S*o, *yes, how was today? Well it was good, actually wait, it was more than just good … it was a blockbuster, man!*

I got punished for the first time in my entire life, I mean, I, Deb Roy, the epitome of perfection, really had a hard time today.

All credits to a new guy from Andaman.

Thin, handsome and malicious Aakash, he's one bad ass :D. Right on the first day he took me down with him and that too on my own game. Yes, it was my same old trick I have been pulling off for the last … I don't even remember how many years! I instructed that innocent fresher to enter the class without taking Kavita ma'am's permission and as usual the rat fell for the trap!

As with every victim, he got yelled at, punished and scolded, but then the epiphany happened!

I got caught red handed for the first time.

As I knelt with this full-on-attitude, dude, I really had this revelation. I mean, not since ages have I seen a guy with such powerful eyes, such aggression, such focus. I googled Port Blair and the place looks awesome.

I think Aakash is gonna make a damn good friend of mine, he just has this spark, you know …

Chalo, signing off tonite.

Luv all (flying kisses to all the ladies)

***

Deb's Diary Entry 427

Just another normal day, BTW I proposed to Madhura today in the "truth-or-dare" game.

As expected, the poor girl took it seriously and accepted!

Now, I'll have to take her out on a date something. I think I'll take her to Hyatt. Dad said they make really awesome Thai food!

And yes, other highlights, I had a chat with Mr.Aakash Roy today. The guy is still not ready to be friends with me. I think he just doesn't like my attitude or something. And, anyways I cracked a joke about Port Blair, too. Wish he could realize all I had in mind was frank humour. There's a clash of ego somewhere. If only he could understand, I respect the guy. He's all so silent and not the show-off types (so unlike me ;-)), and still he has some real spark in him, and he's from Port Blair, too, man!! I overheard him talking about a jammer something with the boring Katie, his new best friend!

I mean, the guy was talking about making a TV-jammer with which he could jam off any signal, i.e. turn off TVs and computers! The concept is just wow, man!

Though I have my doubts as to whether it's even possible.

Chalo I'll update you ppl more abt this protege that Aakash is!

✳ ✳ ✳

Deb's Diary Entry 433

Bad day ... oh, it was one let down of a day!

We had our auditions today and there we were singing and having real fun ... recording amazing stuff and then I went for some fresh air and when I was back, guess what I saw!

The studio was totally messed up, the microphones were all thrown hither thither, everyone scattered with fright, Subhojeet lying flat over a dustbin, fainted. I mean, the poor guy had to be taken to the hospital for he was so panic-stricken, yaar!

And, guess who made this entire mess! The prodigal newbie! Aakash Roy!

I was literally shocked and disappointed in him. I still don't know what actually happened. I just remember throwing him off the studio, I was so pissed, you know.

I guess we're going to complain to Kavita ma'am tomorrow about him. He is in for a suspension!

Dammit! I really hoped we could be friends ...

✳✳✳

Deb's Diary Entry 434

We didn't complain. And, I was so glad you know, I could've hugged Madhura for tha ;)

Remember, how we record all our auditions in the studio!

So, Madhura gave me the record of yesterday's studio auditions and I replayed the part that I had missed, and man oh, man!

What I heard next was the best song in years.

Some "jo thi dil ki khushi." It was stupendous, I swear to god!

What a talent Aakash is and what a loser Subhojeet can be sometimes, I tell you.

The guy actually insulted Aakash after such a masterpiece. I mean, I felt irritated listening to the cry baby that Subhojeet is and although hitting Subhojeet didn't sound like an intelligent decision, but then, not all people are idiots like me.)

Aakash, hat's off to you, yaar! I already regret hitting you yesterday!

I'll apologise and make it up to him, I think, what say?

Chalo, it's 3 am.

Love u all,

Deb

✳✳✳

Deb's Diary Entry 438

Haven't yet apologised to Aakash? I actually keep on listening to his track – jo thi dil ki khushi. I am working on a rock version of the song. I guess that's how I'll apologise to him:

BTW, Aakash stunned the entire class today with his project contraption. It was a stroke of a genius, I tell you, and even then ma'am had to find a flaw.

She refused to grade his project saying contraption was not in our syllabus!! The old fatty :-X.

However, Aakash keeps on surprising me. He had something else in wraps for us.

He turned up with an alternate project, a sun-dial, it was breathtaking as usual.

Kavita ma'am was so dumbfounded today! You should've seen her face ... lol.

I made a volcanic eruption and it really erupted, man! It was the rockstar stuff, you know, show off, just my cal. J)

✳ ✳ ✳

Deb's Diary Entry 450

Just came from the hospital. Had three stitches in my head!

Man, it hurts and yet I'm still confused what caused the entire feud for all I can remember is praising Aakash and their game that they made in the fete ... 7up was a nice idea ...

And still, he convicted me! Me of stealing some 5,000 bucks! WTF!

The guy didn't even have the guts for a fair fight. The bastard hit me from behind. He needs a rehab!

Anyways I'm so tired tonight, I might just passout in the couch! no energy left, yaa!

Last I heard, Aakash got suspended for a month. That means, he is gonna miss the first practical and hence fail. I think he deserves it. Aakash would never make a friend, he won't even make a fair enemy, I really overestimated the boy.

Man, I have a bad taste in my mouth ... those pain killers ... how do you make crying smileys!

✳ ✳ ✳

Deb's Diary Entry 466

Feel cheated. Had a fight with my closest friends. How could they steal Aakash's money. I don't know whom to trust anymore.

Sobhanjan, Subhojeet, Pratik!
Liars they all are ...
Aakash shouldn't have come to Calcutta, yaa!
Think what he'll say about us when he goes back!
Betrayers and thieves we all are!
I'm ashamed of myself.

✳ ✳ ✳

Deb's Diary Entry 477

Oh, today was one hell of a day, man!

You just wouldn't believe what happened!!

Remember Aakash's suspension and how he was going to flunk?

Well, today was the final day of his suspension and the day of our first practical examination!

I was feeling so guilty as my mind kept wondering what would happen to poor Aakash. I felt so sad, man!

But then as always, I underestimated Aakash Roy.

That son of a gun actually cast a spell on me today.

He came up with the jammer. I mean, can you for Christ's sake even believe it!

He jammed all the PCs in our lab ... made sure we could not give the exam without him.

Exam's postponed till tomorrow...

And, I'm super excited; nay that's an understatement....

I'm thrilled.

I caught him while he was jamming the entire network.

I witnessed a genius at work today! How does he do it? I mean, we're in class 9 for heaven's sake!

He was so frightened when he got caught red handed at the crime scene.

He thought I was going to report him to Ramesh Sir.

That fool, doesn't even understand, what a big fan I'm of him.

I didn't say anything to him, just smiled and left.

Aakash buddy, I don't know if I'll ever tell you this, or if you'll ever read my diary, but I respect you, man!

Can't wait to have you in our band!

P.S. Didn't I tell you Aakash had a spark? See, I knew it right on the first day.

✳ ✳ ✳

Present day ...

I placed Deb's diary on the stone steps as I sat near the Grand Canyon. Just a one day trip from Los Angeles. Grand Canyon is an amazing and a lonely place all the same.

The zephyr roared through my ears and I felt broken again.

See our mind is one big liar! It just framed views of others and stored them in our long-term memory and oblivious of the truth, we went on loathing those people, not even knowing how important they actually were.

I wish I had understood Deb for the friend he was to me.

And, all I had of him today was this small diary.

The ink looked faded, but I still remembered the callous look. I could still hear him laughing or throwing flying kisses at the crazy audience.

I plugged my I-pod in my ears and played my favourite track.

jo thi dil ki khushi — rock version.

LIE 039

*Y*ou *just knew some things, you just trusted them without reasons ... It was like a superstition, a blind faith.*

As the taxi raced down Diamond Harbour Road towards the old palace, where the princess once lived, I could sense her presence, could feel the connection getting stronger again.

I didn't remember how she smelled, how her hug might've been, how her lullabys were my favourites as a child. I just knew I was gonna meet her today.

***

A week ago

I stood facing Deb Roy. My hands trembled as Deb eyed the jammer, his pupils dilated as it sank in.

"Is that the jammer you and Katie were talking about?", Deb Roy's voice was really loud and it freaked me out. I could bet even the teachers inside the lab might've heard him saying it.

My index finger moved right to my lips as I begged Deb with my eyes to lower his voice.

"Oh", Deb's voice lowered a key as he chuckled with some more curiosity pulsing through him, "I'm sorry, I forgot."

"Okay, yes, it's the jammer." I whispered after a moment or two, acknowledging the fact that any time now I was getting rusticated for sure. My dad was gonna throw me out this time, "But listen, Katie has nothing to do with this. Please, don't get her into this. Don't report her."

"Who said anything about complaints?" Deb now turned back into his callous and careless self.

"So?" I was shocked to hear his comment. If it were on Facebook, I'd have liked it!

"So yes, this is super, awesome, man!" Deb looked at me with appraising eyes, "Man, this is like the best prank device ever made. I mean, think of all the fun we could have with it."

"Err...we?" I was really getting confused now.

"Hmm, about that," Deb's eyes now turned playful, "how about let's just say it would be only me having the fun then, though you're always welcome to join in, too."

"???????"

"See, I'm not gonna report you ... as long as... ", And, here came the conditions, I was sure there were a lot of em! at scoundrel.

"As long as," Deb continued, "you gift me that jammer of yours as a penance for hitting me a month ago, it still hurts jackass."

"Oh ... okay." I was not at all sad to think of a future sans the "Turn-off", as long as I had a future with a degree!

"And ... " Deb continued.

There are always 'ands'.

✳ ✳ ✳

"Why don't you swim, Aakash?" Katherine was completely off the track with my thoughts.

I'm not a fish!

We sat together, our backs supported on each other's, as we squatted beside the old mangrove near the pond eating Cornettos.

"I have hydrophobia." I took another bite, "I nearly got drowned once. It was horrible." I suddenly had goose bumps, as the old pirate ship and the black waters flashed.

"But hey, you have to get over it someday, right?" Katherine was always mentoring me, annoying!

"So, I guess I'm not flunking, after all." I thought out loud, changing the topic.

"Of course, you are not." Katherine elbowed me, "In fact, I think you might end up topping. You really had my dad impressed with your edge in algebra. All your papers were better than mine."

"Yeah, I so like proving military uncle wrong." I smirked. "Remember, how he predicted I was gonna go down in maths."

"Yeah, show off, I remember." Katie teased.

"But I won't be topping, nope, with you and Deb and Robbie in competition, I don't stand a chance." I savoured some more ice-cream.

"Robbie?" Katherine took her brother's name more like a question, as if she had heard it for the first time or something.

I suddenly remembered the promise I had once made to Robbie that I won't raise his topic ever in front of his family. That made me go quiet.

"Oh ... um ... nothing, I was talking about you and Deb, you people are better than me, trust me."

"Yeah, whatever doofus." Katie had gone oblivious as she concentrated on the sunset now.

"Hey, listen." I said after a while.

"Hmm", Katie's voice sounded distant, although I kept talking.

"It's about Deb."

"What about him?"

"That day when I jammed the servers, he spotted me pulling the entire thing off and he wanted a favour from me to keep his mouth shut."

Katherine was now all ears, I could tell.

"He wants me to join him and his irritably moronic friends for a picnic they've planned as an after exam revitalisation something."

"Why'd he want you to accompany him? I thought he hated you."

"Oh, that he does." I looked out at the silent waters of the pond trying to chalk out Deb's plan.

"You must not go Aakash ... it's a trap." Katherine's voice had a hint of dread, but more of it was the care that made me happier.

✳ ✳ ✳

"There you are." Deb had his long hair tied up in a band, his look resembling Kurt Cobain, Nirvana. I sighed just at his look.

There was his entire group, Subhojeet, Sobhanjan, a fat kid Kapil and Madhura, all of them had this smile of malice and treachery somewhere.

Now, I didn't know how I felt right then. For one thing, I knew today was going to be a bumpy ride.

However, what happened next actually made the ride suddenly horrific.

"Hey, Aakash, we've a surprise for you." Madhura said, "See who's here".

And then, I saw her, Katherine, hair tied, lips pursed, eyes on me, a small tense smile, "I thought I'll accompany you all, too."

"What?" I was really frightened now, "Why Katherine?"

"Hey, hey, let the lady decide, okay? If she wants to come join us all, it's an honour." Deb as if sealed the deal.

"I need to talk to you, in private." I called Deb.

The next second Deb was walking with me, his face glinting with mischief.

"Yes, Aakash? Go on", Deb said, as he took out some gum and offered me.

"Listen, I want you to ask Katie to go home. I don't want her to be in some kind of danger. She and I don't know you people much. She's here just because she wants to safeguard me and I can't put her in some sort of a risk, I mean, it's me you hold a grudge against."

"Huh?" Deb looked at me with an expression of confusion, that turned into pity, and then it turned into a fit of laughter.

"Oh, my gosh." He guffawed, "For heaven's sake, Aakash, who do you reckon we're? Gangsters?" He held his stomach as he tried to calm himself but he was choking with laughter.

"Yeah, whatever." I rolled my eyes. I felt embarrassed now.

"Okay, see." Deb now quietened himself with herculean efforts, "I know we've had our differences, but I'll cut it short for you, all I invited you here for was spending some quality time and making friends. I think it's high time, you got to know us all."

"But ... I."

"No if's and buts, dude, let's go now, otherwise we'll miss the book fair."

***

The Calcutta Book Fair was the first thing that made me fall in love with the place. It was held at a huge ground, Maidan, they called it, was totally crowded up with book stalls forming a compendium of exotic and extinct books altogether. The Fair was majestic. We had to catch the metro to go to the place. The underground tube, the metro, the feel of it all, and Katie by my side, it was extraordinary. Subhojeet and Sobhanjan avoided me as they indulged in useless talk and display of their wisdom about international authors.

Well, now I was this guy, who never had interest in books. I mean, I lacked the patience. I could never make it to more than twenty pages. I was kind of restless with pages and intricate descriptions and complex English words. I always wanted to grow up and write a book that would be a thriller and a page turner, although I really think we should not delve into that now!

"Hey, that's the Harry Potter book everyone's talking about." Katie nudged me.

I followed the direction of her index finger and there was the wizard with his round spectacles and magic wand.

"I wanna buy that book." she cried.

"That one ... with that fancy cover and all, you sure about that ... I really don't think it's a famous book or something." I gave my opinion that had no effect. Katie was already at the desk picking up the copy of Harry Potter and the Philosopher's Stone ... quite a lengthy title.

"It's a best-seller, Aakash." She stuck her tongue out at me.

"Hmmm ... and here I am, wrong as usual.", I accompanied her to the counter.

"Let's have some lunch, shall we?" Deb announced as we all sat in a circle, I and Katie at the loose ends, our eyes on the exit gate, anytime now.

"Alright, what have you got, mate?" Kapil asked Madhura as he took out his lunch box. He opened the can and brought out pooris and dum aloo and an amazing aroma that made my stomach growl!

"Nothing I would share with you, fatso." Madhura said with narrowed eyes and opened her lunch box. Biryani. " My mom's just the best at this. Yaay." she smiled.

"Wow, that's just too good." Deb said as he too took out some rolls and then his eyes moved in my direction. "How about you, Aakash, what did you get for us?" he smiled.

I shifted in my seat.

"Yeah, what did your mom make for us?" Sobhanjan asked innocently, the guy really looked optimistic.

"Well I … err." I hadn't got anything but some money to buy junk food. It was simple to say that out aloud but my mind was somewhere else right now.

"Oh, c'mon man! You didn't get us anything, you bloody avenger you." Deb laughed as he appeared to be complaining.

"Yeah, err … " I tried to speak but there was this lump somewhere. No sound came.

"I … err … asked mom not to … you know, I just…" I stammered as I lied and was shocked by my own lack of convincing power. They looked at me like I was stoned.

"It's okay man! Hehe … we're not gonna abandon you for that. Just buy us something, okay." Deb was a bit afraid of my sudden petrified look. He winked nervously.

I felt a hand clasp mine. Katie was looking at me now, her eyes filled with an understanding that was fascinating. How could she read my mind?

"Yeah, I guess … err … I'll do that." I said as I concentrated on the grass near my feet.

Everybody went back to their conversation after that.

Luckily for me, things turned out quite comfortable after that sudden frenzied reaction of mine. There were no more such awkward reactions the rest of the day. By evening I had made friends with everyone and it was turning out to be a great day. Deb was not bad either. In fact, he appeared to be like the real jolly fellow, cracking the best jokes, coming up with new fun plans, the guy was good, I couldn't help observe.

We were really tired when we returned.

"I guess this is where we all depart." Deb said as we stood at the crossroad.

"Well, we're really glad you joined us." Deb continued.

"Pleasure." Katie smiled back.

I nodded with a small smile.

"Hey, one more thing by the way." Deb looked at me now in particular. "This, Aakash, was our way to apologise to you."

"Sorry, what?" I never thought this day would come!

"Yeah, we ... err ... about your song." Madhura spoke now, "We listened to "*jo thi dil ki khushi*" again and again after the fiasco you made that day."

"We record, that stuff in the auditorium, you see." Deb chuckled, "And, we wanted to witness the punching and stuff again, so we accidentally stumbled upon your song."

"And, though I think it sucks, personally." Subhojeet added, at which both Deb and Madhura eyed him with anger, he continued, "but looks like the majority has an altogether different opinion."

"Yeah, we loved it, dude." Kapil ended the statement.

"Wow." I was surprised, "Did you guys rehearse this before?" I smiled, "I mean, everyone took turns and made it pretty convincing."

Deb smiled. "Yeah, well, we are also into the drama and acting group of the school, you know." he winked. "But no, really Aakash, we'd love to work with you. What do you say?"

"Say yes, Aakash." Katie whispered, her hands gripped mine super, strongly and I feared she might fracture my arm in her excitement.

"Well, I ... err ... ", I scratched my head, "I guess".

"'I guess' is good." Deb smiled, "'I guess' is pretty nice. We'd be expecting you in the auditorium next Saturday. We're starting afresh with a new album idea. Do come."

I nodded hesitantly.

"Bye guys, and thanks, it was fun!" We waved the rest goodbyes as I and Katie got into the bus back.

"Well, that was a fresh breath!" I stroked my chin.

"Yeah, that was." Katie exhaled, "I'm all excited about this."

"So, you think this is a good idea?"

"Trust me, I can almost see it. It's a great idea Aakash, you're gonna be a good singer!"

Katie hugged me. I sighed with relief for things did look a lot brighter than I had expected. But my mind was still somewhere else.

"What're you thinking?" Katie said as she could sense my thoughts.

"Oh ... nothing important, I was just wondering whether we should buy the tickets or just avoid the conductor," I lied to her.

But she didn't smile. Katie could always make out when I was lying. She had caught two of my lies that day, and I knew she knew what it was that kept me thinking.

LIE 040

I was sinking down the black water, I choked ... The pirate ship adventure was a bad idea!

I saw Aditya standing in front of me with an electric guitar, his malicious smile widening, as I gasped for air... I saw Paritosh Sarkar twisting his hand and producing a blue lotus out of nowhere...

And then ... It all faded out but she remained.

Standing on the other side of the glass door, she looked at me, as she mumbled a silent prayer.

A tear trickled down her face and I woke up.

***

"Sabith is really a handful I tell ya." Katie said as she patted the Pomeranian that was our pet now.

I was looking at the small huts that lay miles from the paddy field where we sat every evening.

My mind was elsewhere, so much so that I couldn't even register the puppy licking my fingers and then ...

"Ouch!! What the!!", I pull my hand away as the dog bit it all of a sudden.

"This thing's a monster!" I felt like strangling the puppy as it started dancing.

"Don't be a spoilsport, Aakash" Katie yelled, "You were not giving it attention! It was bound to happen!"

"Why on earth would I give it attention? It's not Pink Floyd!" I said irritated, looking at my middle finger that was swelling up.

"Okay, let's clear this out, Aakash! What's been up with you since these few days? Where are you lost all the time?" Katie had her eyes on mine now and her intensity was blinding me...

"No ... It's nothing." I tried to avoid her, concentrating on my finger that I so wanted to raise at the dog.

"Oh, c'mon Aakash, you added the question number with your answer today in Maths. Don't you think it's clear that something's wrong with you?"

"It was a mistake." I retorted, "And, it's nothing Katie, just some nightmares and stuff."

"Why do you always get to be so dark and mysterious?" Katie said loathingly trying to provoke me.

"It's nothing you should know ... you ...," I tried to say but Katie's shout made it impossible.

"Spit it out, will ya!" Katie went haywire. Sabith moaned with fear as it ducked its head in a small paddy bush!

Some warrior dog!

"Okay, see here's the thing." I sighed as I tried to explain, "Lately, I've been having all these thoughts and nightmares, you know."

Katie was all ears.

"I mean, you remember that drowning incident I experienced once in Port Blair ... that day something weird had happened at the hospital."

I tried to recount the events and the image flashed right before my eyes.

"At the hospital chamber, as I was gasping for breath and kept drifting in and out of consciousness, I swear to god, I had seen my mom. I remembered it perfectly. I saw her there, standing outside the ICU, her head at the round glass window." I broke off; my eyes again back to her face.

"You sure it was not a dream, Aakash?", Katie said after a while breaking my train of thoughts.

"I ...," I breathed in the sadness, "I don't know Katie. I just don't know."

"Then, why don't you find out, Aakash?" Katie was all excited now as she sat on her knees, her hands pressing mine.

" Umm...wait a minute...what?" I was bewildered.

"I'm saying, why don't you get her address and go meet her or something? Just see her for once and talk to her, maybe?" Katie was all hopeful now, but her idea was eccentric to me!

"Have you lost it, Katie?" I had gone all cold with just the idea of facing my mom, "That's impossible! I can't meet her. It can't happen, that's just ridiculous!"

"Why Aakash?" Katie pleaded, "Just think of it, Aakash! It makes perfect sense, she is in the city, you too are ... It's so possible ... Just do it Aakash."

I stood up suddenly, Katie stumbled.

"You're making no sense, Katherine, I'll meet you later. I shouldn't have told you this entire thing in the first place." I started walking away, my hands trembling as my heart beat incoherently.

"Please, Aaakash," Katie tried, "I know you can do it, please stop," her voice a little...

"Please, Aakash, for me."

✳ ✳ ✳

"Have you been sleeping all afternoon?" dad woke me up, "You missed your class, Aakash."

"Ohh ... I was just ... err ... kind of tired." I shifted under the covers, as I looked at the alarm clock!

"Ohh, sharks! Katie will kill me!" I started!

It was 6:30 pm.

Katie must've been waiting for me in the field for an hour now.

I dressed up like crazy and the next thing, I was running off for the bus!

It started raining by the time I made it to our meeting place!

I saw her silhouette from far away and that made me sprint to her.

She was crying and it unnerved me. Just as Katie registered my presence, she dropped Sabith from her lap and started running away.

"Katie, I'm sorry." I begged as she stormed away towards the horizon.

I started running behind her, trying my best to stop her.

She was inconsolable and I was shocked by her tears and the sudden outburst of sentiments.

"Katie … stop please, let me explain." I tried to outrun her, and then it happened all of a sudden.

Katie's leg slipped and she fell head first into the lake, filled with seaweeds at the right corner of the field.

"Ohh, shit." I stopped in my tracks.

The pond had filled up with rainwater and in the twilight, it was so hard to even make out its edge.

There was displacement of water as Katie slid down the surface and the water rippled under the pond's dark cover.

I stood there frozen to the ground, my hydrophobia gearing up, waiting for her to emerge from the water, swim back to the edge and then punch me in the face.

But it didn't happen.

Katie was not coming up.

Adrenaline and fear gripped me as I shouted her name, deafening the night.

"Katie!", I started shivering as drops of rain poured on me.

And then, I saw her, trying to unscramble herself from a weed that had clung to her leg.

She tried to rise up to the surface, but the weed won't budge!

"NO... no Katie." I shouted with terror! As I moved towards the water body, the sudden hydrophobia kicked back. I stepped back!

Katie struggled with fear, she tried to make it out of the mess, but the weed wouldn't cut loose, she was sinking now. Her eyes moved to mine, and then stayed there as she pleaded.

Couldn't let it happen. My weakness and my fears couldn't turn me into such a coward!

It was all a blur, as I jumped into the lake, my body hit the water, streamlined through its cold levels and all I could think of, all my heart could register, was Katherine.

I dived in deeper, my eyes scanning the waters, my hand outstretched as I tried to hold her.

Her fingers touched mine, and I pulled her up with all my strength.

It happened like magic. The weed snapped and she glided behind me as I swam up to the surface.

Panting and heaving, we made it to the boundary and then, coughing we lay down, the raindrops pouring over our face.

"I thought for a minute I had lost you there", I said, breathing in oxygen.

"Me, too." Katie whispered, her voice all sand papery.

"Hey, Katherine, don't ever do that to me again." I now held her as I wiped the water away from her face, "Don't ever be mad at me like that. I'm sorry I hurt you yesterday and I'm sorry that I didn't make it here early but trust me, I didn't mean to offend you like that."

I grew quiet as our eyes meet.

It was a spontaneous thing as her eyes closed, her face moved, closer, and our lips touched, stayed there for a while.

Her breath warmed me up and I just couldn't let her go.

It felt like a dream, washing away all the nightmares.

She shifted and we parted, both surprised and taken aback by what just happened.

"Um…," we both started to speak, grew quiet, opened our mouths, then grew quiet again.

Then, she said softly, "I knew you would save me … I knew you could do it."

Four years later…

"You can never lie, Katie … You don't have the guts," I teased Katie as she grinded her teeth.

"Ohh really, Mr Smarty Pants … you think I have never done it, huh!"

"I bet … never in front of me, at least! You can't fool me, lady Katherine.", I smirked.

"Misconceptions and that ego of yours would never make you see the light I assume, Aakash. So, let me just recall an event!!"

"Fire away." I chuckled.

"Remember the night we kissed." she whispered.

"Ohh, that … yeah your first kiss, haha." I grinned.

"Yours too, doofus." she retorted back.

"Whatever, so what 'bout it?" I yawned as I looked at the watch. Pune was boring at nights!

"Yeah, so do you really think that I got stuck at that pond that night?" Katie's eyes glinted maliciously.

"What do you mean ... of course, you were stuck, your legs had got tangled in the weeds."

"Or, it could just be one small attempt, Aakash, to make you realise that you were more than your fears ... that the stupid hydrophobia thing was all in your mind!"

"You're not making sense, weirdo!" I said half-seriously now.

"C'mon, Aakash, think of it this way. You were not gonna meet your mom, you were not ready to face your worst nightmares. Someone had to do something for poor you!", she smiled.

I was all silent. Man, the hookah must've gotten to my nerves something!

"And, holding my breath for someone like me, ain't that difficult after all" she winked as the last bus arrived at the stand.

"Catchya later, Aakash." she climbed up into the bus.

I was confused, unable to speak.

"Have a haircut by the way Smarty, you look all messed up." She stuck her tongue out as the bus started to move away,

"For me, Aakash ... "

LIE 041

O kay, so here's some impromptu for all those people who by some eccentric, bizarre and twisted accident have forgotten their first kiss (those who still haven't had it, my condolences) — Right away after your first kiss, you're blurred for the next 24 hours with just this thought, just this visual replay of that magical moment, that sweet chocolate-moistened kiss of yours, and mind you, the thing plays on and on in a loop.

For me, that night was all about that kiss. I couldn't eat, couldn't sleep, couldn't think straight, I even spoke gibberish when questioned and the world was spinning on its axis at 24 dizzy rotations per second!

But it was the next morning, that with the break of daylight, I saw reason!

Katie was my best friend!

I didn't have anything as remote as love for her ever! I mean, yeah, I loved her hair and her eyes and her dressing sense and everything, but hey, that's what guys do! We look out for girls, God just made us that way! And, this confused me. I wasn't as mature and evil yet then that I would consider cheating on her or something of that, sorts; but somewhere I could feel I had crossed a line that I shouldn't have. One kiss and I was afraid of my next step here! I mean, how do I excuse myself, what if Katie felt something more about me? The questions petrified me and I had no answer, I definitely needed someone with superior brainpower!

* * *

I met Robbie at the deserted lab.

"Hey, there, Port Blair boy, long time, no see...", Robbie came and hugged me before walking back to his table and opening up another file.

"I'm really sorry bro, but you caught me on a wrong day! Making some serious notes, you see", Robbie said before drifting to his books, "And anyways, you never visit this old geek anymore, what's the matter with you?"

"Hey, the holidays are still on! What important research are you carrying on at this point of time?" I looked at him, the eccentric scientist in his making!

"Oh, some computer shit, you wouldn't care...," Robbie kept on looking at the journal, "Now, get to the point, loser, and tell me what brings you here?"

I sighed. I knew Robbie wasn't the guy to chat with, so I went on with the truth, "I kissed your sister."

Robbie turned the page, then scratched his scalp, gave a small laugh, then turned to me, "You kissed my ... what!?"

"I err... kissed your sis..."

I didn't ever imagine in my worst nightmares that Robbie had such infinite strength apart from his academic head! It happened in a wink. He leapt at me, for three split seconds he was airborne and then he crashed on me!

"What!" I flew off the floor and hit my head along with Robbie!

Both of us fell flat on the ground with our backs and heads aching like hell.

"What the hell was that for? Ouch!" I tried to gain my balance, shocked and spread-eagled!!

"You moron! Of all the people in the world, Katie kissed you! I mean, look at you! What's wrong with her? I'm gonna scold that...," Robbie squealed angrily!

"Don't tell her that you know ... Robbie! Please don't." I stopped Robbie midsentence, "And, if it's any consolation to you, I really didn't mean to kiss her and we're not even serious."

"What?" Now, I could seriously bet Robbie was on the verge of a heart attack! "You, son of a..."

"Hey, watch your tongue, man! What is wrong with you, Robbie!",

I gasped, "Man! I really need your advice right now, that's why I came to you and you do this to me."

"Oh, don't you use those cheesy lines on me, you ... err ... umm ... scum!"

I knew Robbie couldn't swear!

"Alright listen, I apologise for this um, mistake of mine. Now, please will you help me for God's sake! I mean I came to you, dude."

Robbie groaned as he sat up, balancing himself. The guy looked pathetic, fatigued, and now, disgusted.

"Okay, relax now!" I assisted the guy, trying to console him, "Count to five, man! Breathe in, man!"

"Yeah, water." Robbie grabbed his bottle and took multiple sips!

Then, he gasped some more, flexed his neck, massaged his ankle which he had injured from his comical leap! Then, he looked at me.

"Now tell me your stupid story!"

✳✳✳

I met Katie later that evening at our favourite spot.

She had this amazing thing going on with her features. She literally glowed, Katie. She looked extremely beautiful that day.

As I went there, something played back somewhere in my mind all over again.

I went back a year.

I had stood in front of Gandhi Park as Anisha walked up to me.

"Come here, sit with me." Katie waved at me as she smiled like a princess.

It was like a dream with just one flaw.

"I thought you had forgotten Gandhi Park!" Anisha said as she beamed.
"No, I hadn't."

"I thought you wouldn't show up today! I have been waiting for such a long time." Katie whispered slowly as I kept zooming back and forth in time.

"So, you wanted to say something." Anisha said.

"I'm sorry, Katie" I gulped as I went with the truth, "But what I did yesterday was a mistake. I shouldn't have."

Anisha looked at me as her eyes sparkled up.

Katie was quiet. Her eyes were on the sunset.

"Katie." I said after a while, worried now.

"What doofus?" Katie chided "Lemme think of a plan how we're gonna arrange a meeting between you and your mom!"

"What!" I suddenly felt a lump melt away in my throat.

"So ... err ...," I continued, "You forgive me?"

"Of course", she dismissed me with a wave of her hand, "After all, you saved my life there and…" She became quiet.

I waited for her reply.

"And, anyways, I never had any such feelings for you either, so it's good we're even!" She faced me now and winked.

I couldn't say whether it was the dimming light as twilight approached that caused her glow to fade.

"Any how!" she clears her throat, "Looks like you're still lost with yesterday, let's devise our plan tomorrow." She stands up and dusts grass off her jeans, "Bye."

"Hmm." I beam with joy, "No probs, best friend." I wink at her.

"Yeah, I can see how we've grown similar. This friendship is something, I tell you." Her words made no sense to me then.

Nine years after that ominous Sunday, I realised it.

I had somehow made Katie like me that day.

I had made her into … a liar.

LIE 042

It's the story of two calls that had made all the difference...

Call 1:

"Wasup, bro?" Deb's voice over the line caught me off guard.

"Hello ... err ... Deb ?" I was shocked, "How did you get my number?"

"Hmm...," I heard him chuckle, "I made some calls ... Not important anyways ... Now listen."

What Deb told next was something out of the box.

***

Call 2:

"Hello, ma'am, how're you today?"

"I'm fine now, now you tell me about the future", The lady said, hiding her emotions. Her hands shook as she grabbed on to the dial.

"Ma'am, err ... why don't you come to my office right away? It's important.."

"No, I don't feel like. Let's deal with this over the phone. It's just yes or no." the lady spoke with confidence, "So, spill it out, doc."

She had a feeling today was going to have some shocks planned out for her. She just hadn't predicted how big!

***

Earlier that day …

"Okay, here's the plan." Katie said as she opened a huge folded sheet of paper and laid it on the plain ground.

"What the hell is this?" I looked at the huge map with all the landmarks and hundreds of locations marked on it.

"I tried to find your mother over the telephone directory, but she's not listed there, and her father's phone number is long dead."

"Hmm", I sighed, "so what now?"

"It leaves us with two options." Katie explained with seriousness, "Option 1: you ask your dad."

"Nope … let's keep my dad out of this." I said spontaneously.

"I could see that answer coming. That brings us to the next choice. Remember, during the year 1985, when your dad's article on the Babri Masjid issue came out about which you told me once?"

"Um … yeah, what about it?" I still hadn't figured out the plan, although I could remember telling Katie about the entire episode of my dad's rebellion against my grandfather Abhirup Roy in 1985…

"Yeah well, remember how your dad protested in front of Mr Abhirup Roy's house when CPI(M) won the election that year? How he was thrown from Abhirup Roy's house …"

"Yes, I do." Now, I was listening to her intently.

"So I guess, with the political unrest at that point and your dad's super controversy, that news must not have gone unnoticed…", Katie said, her voice trembling with excitement, "And, it must've been covered by *Ananda Bazar Patrika* at that time and …"

Now, I could see where she was going.

"And …," she continued, "Somewhere in that article, they must've provided the address or the location where the entire story took place! That is your mother's home!"

I nodded, speechless.

"So now." Katie flattened the edges of the map, "We have to find that paper excerpt from somewhere, and since it's such an old article, there's only one place we could search for it." Her fingers moved along the straight lines in the map, to a landmark.

I looked at the small heading with concentration, THE NATIONAL LIBRARY.

***

Call 1:

"You remember our deal about you joining our band, right?" Deb said in his callous voice.

"Yup, you know but I don't think it's the right time to discuss it, I have something else." I was stopped mid-sentence.

"Dude, It's now or never, I have news for you." I sensed thoughtfulness in Deb's voice.

"Okay, go on." I had to say.

"We've got an awesome opportunity to perform."

***

Call 2:

"Ma'am, see, I really think it's hard to explain over the phone. I mean, it's not a straight answer anymore. You understand that there have been a lot of exceptions and there is still hope."

"So, it's that bad, huh." The lady coughed over the phone.

"No no ... I've said this to you a hundred times now ..."

"Not with such an intense tone doc, not until now." The lady managed to chuckle.

We went to the National Library the following day, Katie and I.

It was on Belvedere Road, Alipore, a two-hour journey from our place.

It was huge, filled with infinite rows of books, journals, old vintage theses and dust all the way over the polished wooden benches and tables.

Luckily, Katie had a library card, and I could enter as a guest for the day.

"Hmmm ... ", Katie walked to the far end to the corner where a dozen 15-inch long rows of newspapers were piled up, "Let's start here."

Two hours down the line, and we were still nowhere close to the article. The newspapers were not in order and the heat of the day had started to give me a headache.

"We'll never make it!" I moaned.

Katherine paused for a while, looked at me with her stereotype can-you-shut-up look and went back to it.

I sighed, flexed my muscle, and moved away to take a stroll. The library was empty except the corners where boys and girls hid at the corners talking or making out. I was shocked by the entire epiphany! It reminded me strangely of my own personal experience and I looked back at the corner which I couldn't see anymore now, where Katie stood searching for the newspapers. The girl whom I kissed first! I was unnerved at the sudden thought, so I turned away and concentrated on the section I was now in. It was the modern literature section. I scrambled through some local Indian authors looking out for books and then a particular book grabbed my attention. It was the illustration on the cover that took my breath away. My painting, that I had once drawn years back and won a silver at the lion's club (The painting I had titled "The wait") in Delhi, flashed as the cover of the book.

I grabbed the book off the shelf and read the title, "Catching Up with Time".

I read the author's name now.

Mrs Radhika Roy.

I was petrified, numb as I held on to the book and read the name over and over again.

"Aakash." It must've been two minutes later that Katherine came along, "What have you been doing here ... what is that?"

I handed her the paperback. There was a whoop of delight a minute later which had us thrown out of the library.

✱✱✱

Call 1:
"It's a show called "rockstars" that MTV has decided to launch this year. They're holding their auditions at Darjeeling, too. That's the nearest to Calcutta we got and I guess there would be less competition in Darjeeling

than in Calcutta, so we've decided to give the auditions there." Deb squeaked.

"Hold ... just hold on a minute, that's a lot of information." I scratched my chin, "There's an audition huh?"

"Yes."

"At Darjeeling?"

"Righto!"

"And, you're asking me to join you guys there?"

"That's correct." Dev sounded glad that I had figured out the entire thing.

"When is it?"

"This Thursday."

"That's three days from now!"

✳ ✳ ✳

Call 2:

"How much time do I have, doc?" The woman coughed again.

Silence on the other side.

"Oh, c'mon doc, give me some figures now! Months, weeks, hours! ... hehe ... secs?"

"Err...," the doctor paused for another moment before saying it, "Some weeks now ..."

The woman put down the receiver and looked out of the glass window. A taxi zoomed past and all she could make out was a boy looking at her for an instant before she drew the curtains.

And, it was all dark after that.

✳ ✳ ✳

As the taxi raced down the corners of the Diamond Harbour Road towards the Princess's Castle, I could feel the connection getting stronger again. I was going to meet my mother for the first time today after all these years. I felt goose bumps. For a moment, I wished Katie were by my side, But then, I knew I had to do it alone.

We had found Radhika Roy, my mom's address from her book, "Catching Up with Time".

She lived at her paternal house, here in Diamond Harbour.

The car now took a turn and I could see some bungalows from the rear end. For an instant, I saw a woman come up to a window and look down straight at me. It happened like a dream, I felt a strong thud in my heart and stared at her, but the moment was gone. She had drawn the curtains and I couldn't understand why I was suddenly restless. I didn't know her, I couldn't say.

The taxi now drove through the road and we stopped in front of a huge iron gate.

Beyond the gate stood a mammoth white building.

I read the name, "Mr. Abhirup Roy" on the golden plate that was plastered beside the gate on a huge boundary fence.

I paid the cab, then with slow steps went on to the gate, where a guard stood, his eyes on me.

The middle, aged guard asked me as I approached, "Who are you looking for?"

"Er ... I want to meet Mrs Radhika Roy." I said in a dry voice. My heartbeats were trumpeting now.

"And who, may I know, are you?"

"I ... err ... I'm her son."

"Wait there for a moment."

The guard picked up the dial of a black telephone he had with him at the small table where he sat. He dialled an extension and then spoke, "Ma'am, here's a boy who says he's your son." Then, he looked at me, "what's your name again?"

"Aakash." it took me a staggering effort to squeak my name out.

He listened on the phone for another minute, then nodded and said, "Yes, ma'am."

Then, he hung up the phone.

"She's not here right now."

"What!" I was taken aback by the reply.

"She's gone abroad for a few days."

"But you just called her." I was appalled and confused by this reaction, "Why doesn't she want to meet me?"

"Sir, she's not here at the moment, I called her office number."

"You're lying. Let me talk to her." I don't know why, but I had started crying up there like a fool.

"Sir ... sir, please understand, she is not here right now. If you want, then give me your number. She'll call you back when she returns."

This never happened. The tears! I cried for another minute before calling a cab.

"Sir, you could give me your number, in case...," the middle-aged guard looked apologetic.

"That won't be necessary."

★★★

Call 1:

"Thursday, that's three days from now." I looked up at the watch. It was 6 in the evening, two hours now that I had returned from Diamond Harbour.

"Yup, dude ... we have to leave for Darjeeling by the day after tomorrow anyhow!" Deb sounded crazy.

"That's a very short notice." I spoke slowly.

"Dude, c'mon, this is our only chance, just forget all that and come with us." Deb was at his pleading best.

"We don't even have enough songs." I thought out aloud.

"We will manage that!"

"I don't think I can make it at such short notice. Dad won't agree."

"C'mon dude!! I'll talk to him, or even better make my dad talk to your dad! Ask for the permission!" Deb was overflowing with excitement!

"I just...," I looked at the book, "Catching Up with Time", at my top shelf then. And, it suddenly paused me.

"Hello, Aakash...hello...you there?"

I kept looking at the book and a fresh outburst of tears dimmed my eyes.

With a broken heart, I made my decision.

"I will come."

VOLUME 3

Darjeeling Diaries

LIE 043

Darjeeling Diaries...
May 2001
Prologue

"We're running out of time." Vicky punched the white wall of the dressing room.

Madhura was walking round and round across the room, her mind accelerating, her heart freaking out. Subhojeet sat beside them, his face sweaty, his hand clasping the steel of the chair, and the sense of defeat finally settling in. He constantly mumbled curses, the guy who always had his reservations.

The crowd went ecstatic out in the front. There was a gush of applause and frenzy drowned into the night.

The lead of 'paranoid android' killed through the ears and the audience shouted more than ever.

St Joseph Church had never been more crowded.

The moon was clear and distant and shining, the white orb, more clear than ever, as if trying to ignite the freezing night, but only for that ounce of cloud, right there, drowning it in from the left, the atrocious vapour clouding the glory with spite so resplendent, it hurt.

His eyes were focused, never stirring, never lost, as if captivated, as if in a trance, Deb sat quiet, transfixed in his chair, his muscles loose, his heartbeat calm, his mind silent, the timid numbness dissolved, as he urged for reason in his own way.

The music stopped in the distance, some more cheers, and then finally the inevitable moment.

"Now, let's call up on stage … guys and gals, I present … E.N.V.Y.", the host shouted in his high pitched voice.

Vicky, Madhura and Subhojeet now turned in his direction.

Deb sat there, quiet and miles away, his train of thoughts intermingled and tranluscent at the same time.

"He didn't show up", Madhura whispered as if to herself.

"He didn't come." Deb spoke for the first time in the last half an hour. "Why?" He looked up at the three of them one by one, his face plain without emotions but curious, all the same, "Why didn't he come?"

The unhinged, super-charged lady Patrische entered the room, running and out of breath.

"What're you still doing here? They called out your name."

"Ma'am, please, give us some more time, he hasn't showed up yet, Aakash." Vicky begged.

"There are 10,000 people out there who have paid for every single second of this show. It's your only chance. Now or never, boy."

"Ma'am, but," Madhura started.

"Stop Maddy." Deb spoke firmly.

Madhura looked back at him, confused.

"We will perform." Deb picked up the guitar.

"But … but", Vicky stammered.

"Don't you see it?" Deb smiled sadly, his face grieved for the first time, "He lied."

LIE 044

It's all a gamble. Life is an enormous pack of cards, with permutations and combinations etched, hundreds of those 52 versions repeated over and over again, marking a new one for each day of our lives, just a matter of chance, which card you're gonna have today, ace you win, joker you die ...

Dad drove me to the railway station, making no attempts at small talk on the way. He was disappointed and quite annoyed by my sudden vacation venture and the phone call request made by Deb's dad. He didn't have his say on the entire plan of my auditioning at this music show at Darjeeling and frankly, I could contemplate his answer. Ever since Dad gave up journalism, he was not the guy who believed in the other side of the road, the idle lifestyle, he'd say.

I kept looking out of the window all along the journey, the Howrah Bridge, the Victoria and the traffic. Calcutta was familiar now, the hostility gone. Although the city didn't cherish my hopes, it did bring some surprising people in my life. Katie's rain-washed face flashed out of nowhere and the train of my thoughts was broken by the honks of the car. We were stuck in a traffic jam.

"Damn the mob!" Dad hissed angrily.

Then, he took out a cigarette and lit it up. He was frustrated, I could see, and it was not the mob I could tell.

Dad didn't look at me when he said reflectively. "The problem with dreams is, they don't work in real life."

I was shocked at the sudden exclamation.

Dad went on. "We live in a country with the second largest population in the world, with no land, no emotions, where death is like common cold, do you really think the country gives a rat's ass about your dream?"

His question was more of a statement. I kept quiet. Long lecture coming!

"Nobody cares and it has always been like that. You find your own share of life or see others snatch it away. People dream for a life too, Aakash. I know you've lost me by now."

Dad sensed my growing interest in the Mercedes Clk stuck two cars away from us.

"Look at the car, Aakash. Don't you want to drive something like that around someday, live a happy life? You know as a kid we all want to be noticed, be special, but as we grow up, we realise what was important was to have a normal life, a beautiful and normal life, which really guaranteed nothing but happiness. "

I looked at dad now and for a split second I could actually realise the pleading in his voice, the confrontation of a middle-aged guy with his son, an understanding that might determine the fate of that child's life.

"You see, Aakash, the world runs by a system, where there's a defined procedure for success and failure. You study hard, the only place where you get to fight with others as equal, based on your own knowledge that you acquire, then you get a job based on your own quality, it's your strength, it's what makes you proud, you earn your own bread and you live. And then," Dad sighed, "There are your dreams. Rockstars and all that sort. You should never be confused between your profession and your hobbies. Never make your favourite hobby, your way of earning bread. It just turns your favourite thing into a business."

"I love music dad, but I would never do it for the money."

"Aren't you participating in a competition which helps kids like you sign up deals for recording music and being rockstars and stuff."

I nearly laughed, "It ain't that simple, dad. Thousands of kids and just one winner."

"My point exactly," The traffic had started to move and Dad now concentrated on driving once again, "Why compete with something you love. You might just lose it in the process."

"Dad, don't worry, I promise I'd never use music for money. Never bring in competition and narrow mindedness in something I love."

Dad didn't say anything after that.

We reached the station in plenty of time. I found Deb, Subhojeet and Madhura waiting for us at the station. They looked excited, nay, hyper. Deb, however, maintained his callous look somehow. He winked at me as I got out of the car.

"Alright then." Dad sighed.

"Yeah", I nodded. "Catch you in ten days." I smiled at him.

"Remember the promise, Aakash," Dad said pressing on the gas, "and yeah, remember how the world runs. The system."

"Yeah, yeah," I yawned, "education ... job...normal life. I get it"...

Dad drove away but he left me with a memory.

Dec 2001,

I remembered Rakesh, the guy I had met on the train on my way to Belur, the pick pocket.

And, I remembered what he had said. The Mercedes stopped coincidentally right beside us. A young guy in his thirties, out of it, he looked like a star.

"How do I change the system, Rakesh?"

"I'll give you an example, suppose you have a very costly car, BMW sorts. Instead of showing it off, you gift it to an under-paid clerk at your office, that's when you change the system. You play with its rules."

I started walking off with my friends, shared some chips, sat on the platform bench and waited for the train as we cracked jokes and people kept clashing and walking by.

But somewhere I realised that I had not listened to my dad that day. That the promise was nothing but a lie to me. Because somewhere, I had started to create my own version of the world. Somewhere my system didn't have those cycles ... Education ... job ... normal life. Nope. I was gonna frame my own system.

Life was a pack of cards but what if you didn't play the game according to its rules.

What if the joker was not the loser in your game. What if the aces didn't count. What if reasons were not reasons enough ...

LIE 045

"Okay guys, so here's the thing," Deb spoke now. "The auditions for MTV Rockstars start tomorrow. We will go through three selection rounds to get qualified for the television show held in Delhi. First, where we as a band present a performance in front of the judges, if we clear it, we're in for the second round, where we compete with other bands from West Bengal, which will happen in three days time. If we succeed, we will perform in front of a 10,000+ crowd at some school here, and if we make through that one as well, then guys! We'll be officially in the competition in Delhi!"

Deb sipped his cup of coffee with not even the slightest bit of trepidation. While the rest of us gaped at him.

"What?" he noticed us after a while.

"How, may I ask?" Subhojeet asked cynically, "Do you plan to perform all of this without a proper band, with no songs rehearsed, with nowhere to stay? How?"

"Bro! Do me a favour, will you? Breathe, relax", Deb savoured the coffee.

"No, he's right Deb, how're we gonna do all this?" Madhura sounded anxious too.

"Oh, not you too, Maddy," Deb now looked appalled. "I've got it all figured out. Just trust me." Deb winked at her.

I didn't counteract. I was in no mood actually. A lot was running through my mind.

Mom ... Katherine ... dad's promise and my life ... It felt all messed up. I felt I was lost at this crossway, with nowhere to go ...

The train was 4 hours late …

Though the journey was poetic. It was beautiful, as the train slithered through the clouds, with sights of ice-capped mountains far away across the horizon, with tiny hints of snow in the atmosphere, with tea bushes, lush green and moist rocks all around.

I didn't remember falling asleep but I remembered the vivid dream. The snowy castle, the tower and the girl … I remembered how she waited. She turns …

✳ ✳ ✳

"Let's go," Deb patted my back, breaking the story.

We reached Darjeeling at five in the evening. It was already dark in the small hill station. I got down the train along with my friends, then we all went and sat on the nearest bench.

"Okay, wait here." Deb said looking at the main gate, "While I go and get the status on my driver! Dammit, he should've been here by now!"

Half an hour down the line, we still didn't have any updates on Deb's imaginary driver! Deb looked lost, trying to make calls and searching for network.

We sighed while Madhura shivered in the cold.

"Wait, I'll get us some tea", I said as I stood up, stretching myself. Then, I walked to the small shop on the far end of the station. There was a small crowd of tourists there, all in jackets and sweaters and overcoats and mufflers.

"*Bhaiya, teen adrak ki chai!*" I waited for my order as my eyes shifted to the other platform right opposite ours.

That's when it happened, without a prior notice, with the highest amount of odds, it all fell in place and there I was, back at peace with the universe.

I was dragged three years back.

And, I swear it was so real, so authentic, so naturally surprising, I could feel it in my veins.

Catcher in the Rye … The girl with curly hair, pink shiny jacket and black shoes.

I went numb. She stood just twenty meters from me, her back at me, as she talks to a guy, her voice warming me up, I feel goose bumps as her curls fly away with every stroke of the air.

"Katie", I muse inaudibly. White smoke escapes my lips and she fades away in the dark.

"Sir jee, chai", I'm suddenly jerked from behind.

"Wha!" I turn back to face the tea vendor.

"Fifteen rupees Sir."

"Yeah," I pay the guy, place the three cups in my hand, drop one in oblivion, and then turn back to look at the platform on the other side.

But she's gone. Like a walking dream, she has disappeared. I'm back at the crossways.

"Aakash, right here." Madhura waves from the far end.

I nodded and approached them.

"Hey, Aakash, let's go," Deb shouted from the main gate.

I turned and then I dropped the remaining two cups.

Deb walks over to me, "What happened, bro?"

But my eyes are on the people who accompany him. A handsome, young guy, apparently some years older than us and a girl gracefully standing beside the guy.

"Oh, I forgot to introduce them. This is Daniel bhaiya, he is gonna drive us to the resort." Deb points at the handsome bloke.

Then, his eyes fell on the girl beside him. My eyes were already locked in hers. My mouth opened in a comical manner, tea stains all over my jeans, my eyes unflickering as if I was in a trance, I stared at the girl beside the bhaiya named Daniel.

"Do I know you?" The girl looked at me, confused.

Subhojeet and Madhura had joined us with the bags and Madhura cursed me for spilling the tea but I still am staring at the girl.

"Um ... Aakash," Deb was a bit perplexed now, "She asked if you knew her."

"What! Er ... ," I came back to my senses, then I became silent again as something weird struck my mind.

I was back at the Intercontinental Hotel, Delhi for a split second as she walked up to me for her blue cell phone ...

"Um.. No I don't." I lied. There was an awkward silence as the girl eyed me with apprehension, others with bewilderment. "Ahh okay then." Deb cleared his throat finally killing the awkward situation, "Aakash, meet Daniel's sister….. Katie". "Katie." I smiled …

LIE 046

Daniel and Katie Thomas were the children of a business tycoon Mr. Heath Thomas. And, Deb's dad turned out to be a family friend, or more precisely, a potential business partner. Mr Heath Thomas owned hundreds of tea gardens in a small hill station and soon enough in the jerking drive we realised that Mr Heath Thomas actually had his hands on half the lands of Darjeeling.

Daniel drove an open Jeep, six halogen lights attached in the front and top, a spare wheel clamped at the rear, it was a macho machine as it roared through the cold night. We were freezing on the windy roads that slithered and bent sharply, snaking up the mountains. It was pitch dark at 6:30 pm in the evening and all we could see were lights from towns far below as the jeep honked its way through the mountains above.

"We've booked two rooms for you guys, at Hotel Mayfair, it's a nice place and the room I booked has this lovely sight from its left balcony." Katie spoke loudly over the jeep's grunting noise for us to hear.

"That's great, thanks yaar!" Deb said, his polite smile up for display.

"It was a pretty darned task to book those rooms you see, all the hotels here are already booked, lots of crazy teens piling up in the name of music, big time suckers!" Katie rolled her eyes. I couldn't avoid but notice the golden highlights in her curly brown hair, as it waved in the wind, creating havoc in my heart.

"Ouch, Kates." Deb made a face, "I always thought you had a thing for musicians."

"Musicians, not maniacs." Katie retorted, "It's more of a mockery now, petty bands trying to ape beatles and the eagles."

Deb yawned, "Well, taking up the entire world into picture is considering a wide scope, you see!"

"My point exactly," Katie said. Taking her I-pod out and plugging it into her ears she added, "Why take chances when you can have the best?"

Deb playfully poked Katie and the next thing Katie was poking him back.

I caught Madhura rolling her eyes, clearly annoyed by the display of such intimacy. Somewhere I too, felt a lump and wondered whether I too, shared her feelings.

We reached Hotel Mayfair at 7:30 pm. We were tired, cold, freezing and pale.

Mayfair was quite on the northern elevated mountains of the city. That meant, a small trot on the right towards the boundaries before the cliffs, and you could actually view the entire town of Darjeeling lying down below, blanketed in a cloud of mist, peaceful and sleepy.

We got down from the jeep and collected our bags. Katie and Deb were catching up on some old tales. By now, I had realised that Katie and Deb were childhood friends, the best friend sorts.

Another thing that I realised soon was that Katie was quite different from the mental picture I had painted of her.

The first shocker was when she took out a cigarette and lit it up, its smoke depressing me.

"Katie!" Daniel shouted, as he got out of the car, "How many times have I asked you not to do that."

Katie took a long drag as she kept on looking at the horizon in oblivion.

"You promised you'll quit, young lady!" Daniel was furious now.

"I did." Katie yawned over another puff, "I did give up. This present part, however," she looked at her brother with sarcasm, "is called resuming."

It took Deb another second to snap that cigarette and next thing, it was gone.

Katie slapped Deb's shoulder in disgust. "So caring, huh! Where were you then for the last three years?". And, with that she stormed off to the jeep.

Deb looked at us, then at Daniel, then shrugged, "Guess, she is still pissed!"

"You were her best friend, Deb," Daniel mumbled audibly, "shouldn't have left her and gone away like that moron."

"I know, Danny bhaiya!" Deb said sadly, "But that sister of yours, has turned into a real spoilt brat, I tell you. "

"I know," Daniel looked really worried. I wondered what this entire fiasco was turning into. I felt hopelessly out of the loop, so did Subhojeet and Maddy, who looked totally exhausted and bored.

"She's fifteen, for heaven's sake." Daniel said anxiously, "Deb, only you can handle that girl. Talk some sense into her, bro."

Daniel gave a small sad smile while Deb nodded, then looked at the rest, and waved goodbye.

"You'll get your keys at the reception. Enjoy the stay guys, and all the best."

"Thanks." we chorused.

***

We were fatigued and out of energy but we still needed to practice. The auditions were at 9 am the next day and we still had not decided on a song.

The MTV Rockstars had this unique rule that every song sung has to be one of the band's original compositions, that is, no classics, no old movie song covers, just innovation and creation.

And see, there lay the problem, we had not composed a single song together. We didn't have the lyrics, the music, the rapport and most importantly, the inspiration, well, that just went away from my heart with a puff of smoke!

The dinner was comforting, with some delightful courses, and an amazing service, which pleased everyone except for Madhura, who sported a killjoy attitude throughout the evening. I, however, on the contrary, kind of started liking this free tour over the first plate of the hot soup. Deb's dad had arranged this entire trip for us and the stay at the hotel was free of charge for all of us.

Post dinner, we sat with pens and notebooks, but no lyrics. We sat with guitars and keyboards, but no music.

We had some ice-cream from a glass bowl that came complimentary. It sat right at the centre table, and every second minute, out of frustration and the irony of ice-creams in the cold made us dig more of it.

"We could attempt at '*Jo thi dil ki khushi*'?" I put up after another spoon of the ice-cream and our failed attempt at a song for the last two hours and too many complaints from the hotel authority about the dissonance.

"Yeah, it's a great song." Deb admitted, "But there's a slight problem. The chords are real hard to memorize in such short time and I haven't even figured out the proper lead."

"How about 'you make me'?" Subhojeet asked, blood rushing into his round pimpled face.

"Yeah I guess we'll have to go with it", Deb nodded his head, "But we never went up with the entire lyrics, I mean, what was it again?" He moved his fingers over the strings of his electric guitar, and it formed a tune.

Subhojeet started to sync the keyboard to the tempo, and Madhura started humming the lines, all bored.

"Love your eyes, makes me see my dream,
I love your touch, takes me to the extreme
I love your charm, filling these blanks above
I want you girl, you make me fall in love… "

Madhura kept singing the mushy romantic pop song, as Deb magnificently displayed his guitar skills, while Subhojeet kept going out of sync, and scowling!

"So," Deb looked up at me, after they finished the entire thing, "What do you think?"

"Umm … err." I really didn't know what made me stammer and express my true emotions, but Madhura looked suddenly offended.

"Just tell us whether you'll be able to sing it properly. I am not looking for an approval from you." Madhura nearly yelled.

I looked at her, wide eyed.

What had gotten into the girl!

"Maddy, where are your manners?" Deb's voice was slightly loud, but filled with strictness.

Madhura rolled her eyes, while Subhojeet scoffed and gave me a YOU-DESERVED-THE-SCOLDING look.

The guy had a problem with me since I had dropped him into that trash bin, half an year ago. He annoyed me and I kind of guessed the feeling was mutual.

"Hey, Deb, it's okay." I didn't want an argument right on the first day of our stay; I could, of course, see a lot more coming in the future.

"And," I continued, "Madhura, I think I can sing the song, and um … it's lovely." I covered up.

"Whatever", Madhura looked at the ceiling now, totally uninterested, while Subhojeet started playing the keyboard in the highest volume, possible.

"Well, then, let's take it from the beginning and Maddy, be a bit more enthusiastic, will you." Deb had a tinge of anger in his voice, and being the carefree guy he always was, the tinge kind of felt very distinct.

And, that is when Madhura snapped. Next thing, the glass bowl of ice-cream was air-borne. It crashed right at the door in a big thud shattering glasses and ice-cream on every corner.

The next minute, the door bell buzzed us awake from the shocking episode!

"Ohhh, what the hell Maddy!" Deb threw his spoon away, as it too went flying out of the balcony.

I looked at mine and wondered what was coming next.

"Someone open the goddamn door!" Deb said as he unplugged his guitar.

Well, it was when the door opened, that the first tragedy of our Darjeeling trip began!

It was the hotel authority. Some suited, aged, spectacled guy and other waiters behind them.

"Sir, I'm the manager of Mayfair and we have been having complaints about noises of musical instruments from your room for the past two … and … oh dear God!" The manager was bewildered as he scanned the room. Broken bowl, shattered glass, ice-cream on the drape, and a crying

Madhura and furious Deb. Subhojeet and I looked weird anyways, didn't need mood-swings for that.

"What in the name of Jesus is going on here? I demand an explanation." The guy was furious now.

"Sir, see, I can explain, we just..." Deb tried to persuade but the manager went on, "Why is that girl crying? Ma'am, is there a problem? Please, feel free to tell me."

Madhura sobbed hysterically and her crying didn't help at all.

"No Sir, you're getting it all wrong." Deb made up his super, innocent face as he tried to convince the man some more, "Sir, we're guests of Mr Heath Thomas."

"I couldn't care less. You people are vacating the hotel in 15 minutes, or I'm gonna report you misfits." The man shouted at the top of his voice and my ears went deaf for a minute.

And, in that minute, Madhura cried some more, Subhojeet swallowed some more nails, Deb requested, nay, he nearly begged and some more ice cream fell from the ceiling on to my head.

✳ ✳ ✳

It was 12:15 am, when we stood outside Hotel Mayfair, shivering, in the cold, with nowhere to stay, with network problems on Deb's cell, making it impossible to contact the Thomas family, with a sad Madhura and an irritated Deb.

"What happened in there, lady? Huh?" Deb could actually slap Madhura any moment now.

Madhura had her head hung low as she sobbed more. I personally felt bad for the girl. She needed some immediate help was my opinion.

"Why in heavens, did you make a mockery out of us at that hotel? We're standing here, with no clue of any place to sleep, because of your foul mood." Deb continued, while Subhojeet tried to stop him, "No ... shut up Subhojeet, I want an answer from this idiot. So maddy." now Deb grabbed her elbow, pushed her close to him, and spoke, grinding his teeth, "Look me in the eye and answer, Miss Madhura Ganguly, what went wrong?"

Madhura cried some more, as Subhojeet and I tried to calm Deb down.

"Answer me now." Deb yelled.

Then, finally she spoke.

"Katie and you."

For a minute, I could bet I must've heard it wrong.

"What?" Deb went haywire as he let go off Madhura, "Katie and me, what do you mean?"

"She is the girl you always talked about Deb, your crush, isn't she? And, you still love that bitch!" Maddy now started moaning and crying like a lunatic.

"Oh, God", Deb had his hands over his head. "So, your little ego is hurt, is it Maddy?"

But by now, my eyes were on Deb, too. I was completely astonished by the sudden turn of events.

"I love you Deb, you know that!" Maddy said between tears.

"But I don't, Maddy. Grow up. We're just friends. You and me. Katie and me, all of us!"

"You're lying." Maddy said, unsure, herself.

✻ ✻ ✻

"I don't lie, Madhura. Katie is not my crush. There's nothing between us." Deb whispered in Madhura's ears as they both sat together with Maddy's head on Deb's shoulder, her hands wrapped around him as we waited on a bench outside a small church near the auditorium where the auditions were to take place this morning.

I was an insomniac, and amidst Subhojeet's snore, I realised that although Deb had a friend in Madhura, Madhura loved Deb, and tonight, she was heartbroken.

As I stand at that graveyard, on November 2010, I watched my first love for the last time. Everyone remembers their first love.

LIE 047

I couldn't recall falling asleep. But I knew I was dreaming because I saw them together. The two Katies, hand in hand, whistling and dancing around. Katherine looked at me, and my heart was filled with a tinge of sadness. There was a question in her eyes, as she said softly, "I waited for you, Aakash. Why didn't you come?", I saw a flash of our favourite place, the pond, the dog, Sabith, the huts in the horizon, the rainbows and 24 Parganas…

Then, Katie lit a cigarette, her hair flaming red, as she looked at me and said, "Did you know the guy who killed John Lennon had a copy of *Catcher in the Rye* when he shot Lennon dead?"

* * *

Katherine closed her eyes and rain drops lit up her lips as I kissed her.

"Is that you, Aakash?" I opened my eyes and the cold registered. In fact, it's freezing, as I shiver to death.

A young bloke was looking at me, his face lit up with excitement, as he sipped a hot cup of tea, put on an eerily comic expression of enormous and boundless joy.

"I can't believe this, Aakash!" The stranger was drunk with elation.

"What, me lying down on a bench on a street with my friends, homeless in a hostile hill station! Yeah, it's a shocker." I sit up, sarcasm in my face, as I looked at the clock, it was 8 am and still there was mist all over the roads, so thick, you couldn't see anything 20 feet away from your location.

"No … no … not that." the guy jumped up and down, enthralled, " Yeah, a bit of that too, but, but … ", then he paused, "Don't you recognise me?".

I cleared my eyes as I made the effort to recognise him.

And, surprise surprise, I was dumbfounded.

"Vicky." I stood up so suddenly that Deb and Maddy whose backs were supported by mine, are pinned to the wood of the bench.

"Ouch, what the...?" Deb opened his eyes while Maddy squinted, rubbing her head.

"What are the odds man?". I looked at him, aghast. Vicky hugged me.

"So...?" Vicky said after another ten seconds.

"So". I cleared my throat, "Umm, how come you're here all of a sudden, so far from Port Blair?"

"Oh, that", Vicky boomed, "We have some of our farmhouses out here, so I come here during the summer vacations every year. I also have my relatives here."

"Yes, right." I suddenly recall Vicky telling me and Nicky about his farmhouses and property one night before our performance in the school farewell, the day I had gotten pissed off cos they kept playing, "*tum toh thehre pardeshi*" in a loop.

"And, what brings you here?" Vicky kept up with the small talk. "Wait, lemme guess", his eyes moved to the guitar and the keyboard and then my three fellow mates who completely ignored him.

"The rock show, MTV rockstars, eh?" He answered his own question.

"Guilty as charged." I nodded.

"Aakash." Deb piped in, "auditions start in an hour, we should get going."

"Err... okay then, Aakash, I'll go now. But wait, here." Vicky took a pen and jotted down his number on my palm, "Call me once you get done with all this. We'll meet and catch up. It's been two years, isn't it?" I hugged him once more as he jogged away in his sweatshirt and shorts. Yup, two years and a completely different world, it has been.

***

It was an unruly crowd in front of the town hall, where the auditions were taking place.

There were something like 500 kids out there, with musical equipments, fighting their way inside. How many people were actually auditioning for this show! It must be a jungle out there if we took the entire country into the picture.

We freshened up at a small café nearby, and deposited our bags and stuff to the cashier because we had nowhere to keep them. We had been thrown out of Hotel Mayfair, after all.

We had coffee and sandwiches at the café nearby, while Deb filled our audition forms.

"Okay, we have four members in the band, out of which Aakash is the vocalist, Madhura will play the chords while I would be the lead guitarist and Subhojeet, you're playing the keyboard. "

We nodded in unison.

"Damn this!" Deb mumbled looking at the form, "They've asked us to provide a name for the band."

"I don't understand." I exclaimed, "You people had a band at school, didn't you?"

"That we did, but ..." Madhura sighed, "Our band at school had a Bengali name "Appekhha ", the wait. "

"Yes." Deb added, "We can't use that name here, you see, loses appeal!"

"I differ." Subhojeet protested, "I mean, it still stands, it's authentic, it's real." I knew this was going to come out of Subhojeet, his traditional values were his talismans, after all, and Subhojeet sans the values and the Bengali classical heritage, was a concept undefined and inexplicable. I could bet even the name appekkha must have been Subhojeet's brainchild.

"Yes, Subhojeet, I understand all your creepy sentiments" Deb concurred, "However, it just won't do, man! Look at the competition; we won't stand a chance with that name. We need something global, something like ... er ... like "The denizens " or ... um, maybe, ", He kept on thinking while Subhojeet gave up his sandwich in raw defiance.

"The zephyr." Madhura suggested, "I love that word, what do you say?"

"Um..what does it mean?" All three of us asked together.

She frowned as if she expected cheers and toasts at her strange suggestion.

"Guys, it means a soft soothing breeze, or the God of West Wind, something like that."

"No, no, it's too hard and alien!" Deb shook his head, "wouldn't work."

"How about e.n.v.y.?" I said after two minutes of indecisive names.

"Envy?" Subhojeet looked at me in sheer disgust, "That's so negative."

"No, wait a minute." Deb stopped Subhojeet mid-sentence, then wondered for a moment, "Envy, huh?"

"Yes." I said, quite defensive now.

"It's not bad." Madhura spoke softly, "I mean, it's quite trendy a name Alright".

"And, it has this mischief and witty vibe somewhere inside, you know?" Deb remarked.

"Precisely." I smiled A short name, stylish enough to withstand publicity if we ever get any".

"Yeah well," Madhura commented, "We've not rehearsed our song, I am still not confident about the chords and you, Aakash, don't even know the lyrics."

"Because they are incomplete, too." Subhojeet complained bitterly.

I felt wretched. We were homeless and needed a bath, I mused.

"Well, in a nutshell, we're in deep shit." Deb smiled fearlessly, "And, you know what, that is a USP for us, we're on a completely different level from the entire crowd."

"Yes, they're all prepared and confident and are sporting their best clothes, while we look like perfect vagabonds." Subhojeet fumed.

"Oh, c'mon Subho, give it a rest, will you?" Deb tried to cheer us up, "See, why to accept defeat even before the war begins. We're here to have fun, remember. So, let's just charge up and go out there and create history." His voice had a warmth that I observed for the first time.

"You would make a good manager, dude." I smirked, "You never accept the truth."

He smiled smugly as we left the café.

We should've packed some more sandwiches with us, only if we knew what was gonna happen to the entire day ahead.

Six hours down the lane, we were still waiting in the line, with another 20 fellow auditioners expressing expletives at the entire system.

We hadn't rehearsed anything yet, c'os the queue was too long up to do anything in. It was humanely impossible for us to play the guitars and the keyboard with the amount of noise around.

TV news channels would show up every hour, click pictures, ask questions, glamourise the entire ordeal and go away.

I felt hungry, tired and my legs ached ceaselessly. Beside me, Maddy rested her head over Deb who somehow still managed to look handsome and fresh. The guy was a different league. Subhojeet's face was glum as ever and I noticed he was super-close to a full blown panic attack.

And after, what seemed like an eternity, our name was called.

✳ ✳ ✳

"E.N.V.Y.", a voluptuous blonde woman shouted our name and approached us as we stepped ahead.

"Alright kids." Her hands swayed incoherently instructing us, "Here's the drill, you go straight through that passage, there's a small dressing room on the right, where you can freshen up before the audition starts, you have five minutes before the staff guides you to the judges. Now, scoot!"

We thanked her and sprinted to the dressing room.

It was a small blue air-conditioned dressing room with neon lights and steel chairs and mirrored walls.

We sat there quietly, the sound of our rising heart beats audible as we looked at each other and then at the mirror.

We showed every signs of being lame losers, fatigued and unworthy of attention or cameras, for that matter.

"Alright guys, buckle up." Deb's heavy commanding voice resounded, "Those judges in there don't know how tired we are, they have no idea, how bad our preparation is, for them we are still mysterious people who haven't even made a first impression."

He continued with his monologue, "So, what we gonna do is…", he paused for a while letting the pressure build up, "We gonna give them the best audition we can, we gonna pretend we're all fine and fearless and that we know what we're doing, and you know how we achieve that." He smiled with his lordly air, "We achieve it by this simple lie to ourselves that we are the best. So, Aakash, just go out there today and sing with all your heart, forget the world. Subhojeet, be the guy you're back at all your classical performances where you play with no discrepancies, be the weightless child who sways with all the pure ragas and whose life is music, and Maddy, just know you're the sweetest girl I've ever met and you still look beautiful after all this turmoil and exhaustion." He winked. And, we broke into wild laughter.

It was always easy to be a victim of lies.

Lies … the most natural form of hope … where you're not bound, not restricted, just free, the unburdened child, without baggage , running around the world, lost in your ecstasy, prepared to conquer.

We were guided to the stage a minute later.

The cameras flashed from all corners and we had the attention of the judges.

And, it started …

LIE 048

We walked to the podium. I faced the three judges, an acclaimed musician Mr Rajiv Malik, a Sufi singer Murshid Ali, and the lead vocalist of a famous Indian band "The Sufi Saints", Ravi Kapoor.

They all looked optimistically at us, wisdom and experience staring out of their faces.

The perfunctory introductions were done.

"So, what are you guys going to perform today?" Ravi Kapoor asked in his heavy voice.

"Um..we have this song, "You make me.""

"Hope it's not another die-hard romantic thing ruined and drained in rock beats, c'os we've been hearing a load of that shit since morning." Murshid scrounged up his face skeptically. Rajiv and Ravi nodded in agreement.

We exchanged nervous glances for two reasons.

First: It was a super-romantic pop song.

Second: The lyrics was clichéd and again agonisingly romantic.

I thought about how demoralising it would be to board a train to Calcutta the next day, back to our apartments, with nothing but dissatisfaction and all our rock dreams shredded into unrecognisable scraps. I thought about facing Katherine and telling her how my mother refused to meet me, how I was denied that birthright to know her. I thought about the promise that I had made to my dad of never resuming music as a profession once this trip ended.

I didn't want any of that. Not now.

I rushed to Deb and Maddy who were busy checking the power

supply to the electric guitar, while the judges looked at us in a state of bemusement.

"Just play the lead and chords and let me worry about the song. Just embrace yourselves for some surprises and play on for the second para, I'll figure something out. Just follow what I go with." I whispered to the bewildered band members, who tried to figure out what I had just said.

"But …" Subhojeet objected.

I hushed him. No more arguments. For the first time I was gonna trust this gut feeling of mine.

"So, shall we start then?" Murshid Ali asked impatiently.

"Yes, Sir." We nodded.

Deb played the lead a couple of seconds later.

I blinked, as my mind accelerated through the lyrics and when I sang, the verses were different.

"I hate your eyes, they can see my soul inside, I hate your smile, as you mock all those times I lied, I hate your world, it shadows the heavens above …I hate you girl, you make me fall in love …"

After the first stanza, I knew I had changed the entire song, almost completely, but it felt right somehow, more ironic, more poetic.

Madhura surprisingly handled the transition pretty well and her chords went flawless, while Subhojeet played the keyboard with utmost delight.

Deb's electric guitar cut in the end of the first para, and took the song up a key.

" And I know, and it pains inside, That you hated me, every time you cried … So, I hate those fights, and that you were right, And, I hate myself, and this solitary night… C'os in the rains, when I search that moon above … I hate you, girl, you made me fall in love"

The song continued for about 2 minutes.

I didn't notice how elated I felt as I sang the last few words. We exhaled, as the music stopped and we stood there, stupefied after the best performance of our lives.

There was a moment of silence, as the judges exchanged a few words. Then, they looked at us gravely.

"E.N.V.Y." Murshid Ali spoke with a tone of mystery.

We crossed our fingers, I could feel the goose bumps, and for a second, I felt a panic attack threatening me.

"Bravo guys!" Murshid Ali boomed, "You were fantastic."

"Utter flamboyance, you guys carried it with intricate finesse." Ravi Kapoor was overwhelmed, "And, the lyrics and music, hats off, guys."

"It is one sad ballad, beautifully penned for the modern era." Rajiv Malik expressed.

For me the lyric was a random bunch of lines, that I had just tried to rhyme, and had almost forgotten most of the poem by now, the song seemed just a moment's thought that was impasse now.

"So, Sir? Are we selected?" , Subhojeet stammered, expectant.

"Oh, you bet your asses you're selected." Murshid Ali smiled.

There was a momentary pause, followed by a loud cheer from all of us in unison and then there was hugging and laughing and celebrating the moment.

"Excuse me, sorry, I hate to interrupt", Ravi Kapoor interjected, and this time his face was indeed, filled with quite a gloomy expression, "There's a slight problem with your band that I hate to point out is not in accordance with the rules of this show."

We looked at him terrified.

Dammit, every single time! God!

"You are missing a drummer in your band."

"Yes, Sir, but we don't need a drummer", Madhura retorted, "Our songs are mostly with the guitar and keyboard."

"I'm sorry, ma'am, but that's not allowed. The rule book here says you have to have a drummer in your band."

We were appalled. Was this how it was going to end?

"Sir, but...," Deb tried to protest.

"I'm really afraid but I'll have to tell you that we can't do anything in this matter. You're a good bunch of musicians with potential, but...," Rajiv Malik sighed, "tough luck, kids."

One minute ago, we were celebrating our selection, and then these morons had to point out this flaw, to kill all the fun, all these moments of laughter.

I felt cheated, as if I were denied my share of happiness.

It intimidated me, all these rejections. My mother, my friends, this superficial show!

I had to follow Newton's third law now. I had to lie back.

"But Sir, we have a drummer indeed …" my voice was firm as I made my choice.

"Sorry?" Murshid Ali looked at me along with the other two judges and the cameraman, who pointed the huge apparatus at me, recording my first lie for the world.

"Yes, Sir, he was sick so we couldn't register him earlier, but I can assure you he will be present for our next performance."

"Wait a minute, so you're telling me you guys haven't listed this drummer guy of your band here in the form and you assure his presence in your next performance, provided we select you?", Rajiv Malik spoke more like a lawyer.

"Yes, Sir.", I replied on behalf of the rest of my band members who were stunned with the turn of events.

"But, but you understand that's against the rule. How could we probably arrange it?"

"Sir …" Deb added to my lie now, as if in silent understanding, "One leap of faith."

"Please, Sir…", Madhura chided.

"Okay, let me look into this … " Murshid Ali scratched his brow. "What's your drummer's name again?"

"Vikas Malhotra."

Vicky.

✳ ✳ ✳

October, 2010

I replay the video in Youtube. "The auditions of Rockstars — Darjeeling auditions."

I see a young me lying again and again, with no hint of a doubt. He was confident of what he was doing.

He had no idea, not a shred of suspicion how this was going to affect his life forever.

I just wished we got rejected right then and I left Darjeeling.

"Alright guys." I saw the judges finally declaring their result to ENVY, "You people are hereby selected. All the best, guys."

There was a roar of laughter and the video stopped. It paused as a young me jumped up in the air with a smiling victory on my face.

LIE 049

"That was great. What you did there, Aakash..." Subhojeet whispered in my ear while we headed for a restaurant for some snacks. The gracious remark from the person I least expected kind of made the lie worthwhile in a strange fashion!

"Calls for a celebration, guys …," Deb chuckled as he ordered four cappuccinos and muffins and burgers and french fries.

"It indeed does … " we agreed.

We wanted to laugh out loud and play some more music or call up our friends and tell them the selection thing but we were literally exhausted by the toll the day had taken on us and felt too drained to do anything.

Eventually, as the order arrived, all we could do was sink in and eat. The energy came back gradually.

"So … " Deb said over a sip of cappuccino, "What was this entire thing about that Vikas Malhotra guy? Who is he?"

"Well, Vikas Malhotra is an old friend of mine. Remember, the guy we met today morning?"

"Oh, that guy in those hockey pants." Madhura looked up, " Vicky something?"

I nodded as I bit into the burger.

"So, can he really play the drum?" Deb asked curiously, "I mean, I thought you were making this whole thing up out there like you know, you made the song up."

I smiled.

"No, his declaration at the audition might've been a well, scripted lie, but the rest holds true. And, as a matter of fact, I need to borrow your phone to make a phone call." I looked at my palm as I held the blue Nokia in my hand.

✳ ✳ ✳

We took a cab to the farmhouse where Vicky had asked us to meet him in an hour after the phone call.

As my eyes drooped with fatigue and the beautiful zephyr lulled me into a small nap, I sleepwalked through the dreamy lanes of Darjeeling. I saw the habitants of the place, mostly Nepalis, dressed in colourful woollen dresses, witnessed hundreds of tea garden, returning from the day's work, counting their wages, making small talk to each other, wearing red and blue sweaters and with small baskets in their hands. Small shops lit with small bulbs that sold kerosene and wood for cooking purposes and Chinese toys in abundance hung amidst small tuna bulbs. There were foreigners and Bengali tourists and mountaineers who would take photos of every scene they saw. White sheep ran everywhere free and haywire. We all had gone to sleep by the time the cab had reached the farmhouse on the other side of the town. The cab driver woke us up.

It was pitch dark outside and all we could make out was the fading orange horizon far away as night approached.

I looked at the watch. It was 6:30 pm.

We paid the cab, collected our belongings and started trotting towards the silhouette of an ancient manor around half a mile deep amidst a bushy tea garden. Halfway, we were sure we had taken a wrong path to the castle which emitted a haunted vibe.

The thickness of the bushes summed up with the darkness of the night would give you an illusion quicksand anywhere now or any moment, we might end up slipping down some unprecedented cliff, falling miles down the hills.

Mosquitoes buzzed around us and the sound of crickets jammed our ears as we kept walking through the field.

It turned out we had definitely taken the wrong path, because as we reached the farm, house, we saw the mud road that actually existed just some metres on the right of the path that we had carved through the tea garden.

"Aargh!! I already have a creepy feeling about this place." Madhura complained while shooing the mosquitoes away.

We ascended the eerie cracking wooden steps to the old wooden mansion; its colour faded, a filthy moist greeny layer over its wooden structure now, at the verge of collapsing any moment.

I rang the bell.

A loud ding-dong hammered through our hearts.

Madhura grasped Deb's hand in apprehension while Subhojeet was close to breaking into cold sweat.

A minute later, Vicky opened the door.

He looked surprisingly handsome, his pimples had faded on his pale face, and he sported a hint of moustache. His hair was well gelled and he looked as if he had just taken a bath. That's when I realised how badly I needed a shower, too.

"What're you waiting for, hop in." He guided us into the hall which was gigantic.

I was meeting Vicky after almost three years and I felt close and distanced from the chap at the same time.

"On the phone you mentioned your problems at Hotel Mayfair, so I arranged this place for you. It's our oldest farm-house here. Sorry, but that's all my grandpa permitted me to have my hands on." Vicky said, as if embarrassed.

"Ohh ... this place is ..." I moved my eyes to catch up with the messed up fireplace, the creaky ceiling, the gravelled porch and the broken stairs, "majestic!"

"You think so?" He asked me earnestly, clearly unaware of my growing sarcasm.

"Yeah, absolutely."

"Well, thanks man! I personally used to consider this a shit hole, but whoa, grandpa always said this place was an architectural paradise." Vicky exhaled, "Guess, he was right!"

I nodded, "Hey, by the way, meet my friends, Deb, Maddy and Subhojeet."

The perfunctory introductions had now become a customary routine!

"Wow!! So, well, you people can stay here for as long as you need."

"Yeah, well, thanks a ton Vicky. I'm really trying to contact my friends here." Deb said, "But something wrong with the signal! Just can't get through. The last I could get was messaging them the address of your farmhouse. Hope that helps."

"Ohh no, it won't. Cell phones are scrap metal here." Vicky said matter-of-factly.

"Okay, well, let me show you your rooms and then I can leave for the night. Dinner has been cooked. The maid has already made it and left for the night."

"Um … Vicky", Madhura asked in a sombre voice, "Are there any guards here? Any watchmen you know. "

"Oh no, Maddy. There is no need of watchmen here for there is no fear of thieves at this estate and there are no inhabitants here for an entire circumference of five km. It's all tea gardens guarded by German Shepherds, my favourite dogs!"

Madhura literally shivered with the thought of barren misty mountain open lands with grumpy dogs howling!

I saw her almost dig her nails through Deb's hand while he scowled a bit!

"Don't worry though, guys. It's the safest mansion here, a bit old and weird, but practically awesome. Wait till the morning to realise the fact."

"Hey, Vicky, I had to talk about something with you before you left, man!" I finally said after he had shown us into our rooms and prepared to leave.

"Yeah, let's take a walk, Aakash and you can tell me on the way." Vicky said as he wrapped his windcheater.

We walked down the muddy road under the light of the full moon. I couldn't resist but feel demented with the eerie howl of the blowing wind that felt like a bloody tornado fast approaching.

"This place sure as hell gets a bit haunting at night." Vicky smiled maliciously sensing my trepidation.

"Yeah, I can tell." I said through clenched teeth as the freezing wind touched my face fiercefully, "And, the creepy silence is over the top man!"

We burst out laughing.

"So, long time, eh?" Vicky spoke after we calmed down.

"Yup, man, How's everyone at Port Blair?"

"Great. Pritish is really getting fat by the hour." Vicky said, "And, Nikhil has become super-serious, pensive half the time. And, he plays the guitar genuinely brilliant now I tell you."

"Great yaar. And, how're the brother and sister, Anisha and Aditya?"

"Well, Aditya is one pain in the ass though last time I checked, he got beaten up by some fellow students of Carmel School."

I smirked just thinking about that guy.

"And Anisha." Vicky kind of stopped mid-sentence.

"What about her?"

"She's a great girl." Vicky smiled, "And, a close friend now."

"Whoa, hold on a minute!", I stopped with a widening smile at my face, "Don't tell me!! You did it? Impressed her?"

"Well, no ... yeah, kind of, I mean, we're just good friends, mate." Vicky blushed and I chuckled.

"Amazing, man! Proud of you! I knew you'd be great together."

"Yeah well, I'm still trying, she's hard to get!!" Vicky flushed with a shy smile.

"Awesome buddy! I'm sure you'll woo her.", We had come to the end of the mud road where it met the main road. Vicky's scooter was parked there. That brought me back to the real matter I had to discuss.

"Vicky, I hate to ask for another favour, but I really need this one!"

"Anything yaar, just tell me." Vicky had changed, I noticed. Maybe, it was Anisha and his growing friendship that had made the crazy rich spoilt kid into a generous guy.

"Okay, I'll be honest with you. We really need a drummer in the band for Rockstars and the best guy I can think of is you."

"What?" Vicky gaped. "No." He shook his head vehemently, which showed signs of tearing off any moment now.

"Why?"

"No, dude, never. Trust me, I have had bad experiences with that idiotic thing. I gave up drums just a month ago after public humiliation and there's not a chance in the world that I resume it."

"Dude, just because you screwed up one time somewhere doesn't mean you'll just quit your favourite obsession like that. Chicken out like that!"

"My obsession! Says who? And, more than once, bro." Vicky was resilient.

"I, dude", I fired back, "I believe in you and I think you're just too good a drummer."

"Yeah, right." Vicky stuck his tongue out which weirdly reminded me of Anisha. "Dude, try as you may to hide it, but we all know our performance at the School Foundation Day was gross! It sucked right away."

"It doesn't matter what others think, Vicky. Someday you'll have to prove them wrong. And, you remember how happy we were the day we first performed."

I suddenly realised the truth behind the statement. Singing did make me happy, in fact, those were the best moments of my life, the two times I had performed.

"You're really hitting solid wall here, dude." Vicky strapped his helmet, "You can't persuade me."

I went quiet.

So, truth won't do it again.

"Fine then. Hide away, Vicky. Leave the ground and take a stroll in your solitary confinement. I mean, after so many years when I met you, I really kind of hoped I'd meet the old Vicky and you know what, I'm really disappointed in you man!!" I could tell Vicky was getting sentimental now, "I mean, what happened to the old Vicky who would dare to spend an entire Diwali night out in the open amongst graveyards and below haunted banyan trees!? What happened to the guy who had the guts to ask any girl out and was self-obsessed!? The guy who sang *"tum toh thehre pardesi"* with pride?"

"Dude, first things first, I'm still the same." Vicky tried to protest, "And, in my defence. On Diwali night I was forced to have the night out, and *"tum toh thehre"* is a personal favourite."

"Oh, kill me!! Really?"

"Dude, you know my answer, so let's leave it at that." Vicky now started the ignition as the headlight flared.

"Do it for Anisha's sake then."

"What?" The scooter stopped and so did I.

What did I just say!!

Bull's eye.

"Anisha, dude." My voice was dramatic now, like Shahrukh Khan from *Kal ho na ho* as he read the empty diary in front of Preity Zinta and lie subtly, "The girl who fell in love with you right at the moment she first saw you up there at the dais, playing your heart out. "

"She loves me? Really? How can you be so sure?" Vicky was blinded by the sudden twist in the tale that I had created. "Wait a minute, did she tell you that?"

I stayed quiet, making it almost unbearable for the Romeo out there.

"Tell me, please." Vicky was earnestly desperate now.

"If that is what you want to know, then maybe, I'll have to break this promise that I made to Anisha three years ago. What I'm telling you dude, is purely confidential, you get that right. You can never reveal this to Anisha!"

"Oh, I promise I won't!" Vicky's eyes glistened as he looked haggard to know the truth!

"Very well, then." I said decisively, "I must admit then that yes, she indeed, confessed on our trip to Carbain's Cove, that she has had a big crush on you since the day she saw you performing "*jo thi dil ki khushi*" at school."

"So, do you think if I propose to her, she would accept?"

That's not the point!! Jack ass!

"I'm not sure, but I know one thing." I went silent arousing his curiosity again.

"What are you sure about?" Vicky looked thirsty for love.

"I can assure you, Vicky, that if you resumed drumming and if by any chance we made it till the end, then Anisha will be yours for eternity!"

"Oh, dear heavens!" Vicky's face glowed with hope!

"Yes, mate." I could see the potion working.

"Very well, then." Vicky tried to make an attempt at thinking. "Gimme one night, I'll tell you my decision by tomorrow!"

As he left for the night, somehow I just knew he was gonna be there with his drums here, first thing tomorrow morning. See, the best thing about love is that it is a make-believe concept, and for liars, it's a forte.

LIE 050

The wind roared through the mansion, shaking it like a house of cards. As I lay there on the creaky wooden bed trying my best to sleep, turning a deaf ear to the constant demented howl of the tempest, the incessant bark of those cursed German Shepherds constantly made the entire effort an attempt in vain. The rustle of the huge tea garden, the squealing wind, and the eerie ambience of the place felt ominous.

So, I sat upright and started writing, to keep my mind off the stupid happenings around. I didn't know how the idea popped up in my head, but I just started jotting things down in an empty diary that I had brought along for the music notes and lyrics.

I started writing strange stuff, right from where it all began. Port Blair Diaries.

And at one point, I lost track of time.

I wrote down all about my first friend, Pritish, about Anisha, the pirate ship and Kendriya Vidyalaya. One story led to another and I was back down the memory lane.

That's when I saw it. A shadow through the north window. It floated by, zooming like a spirit and the impact unnerved me to the core. My dilated pupils were stuck at the sight, scanning the darkness outside the window. No movement. I sat there, stiff in my position, fixed, like a ragged doll, a cold sweat forming near my temples.

Another gust of wind and the window pane came crashing. It was a brutal noise and my heart hammered. That's when I heard it. A small cracking noise as a door opened somewhere in the hall.

"Not good." I mused, trying to figure out what this mansion was up to!

Slowly and steadily, one eye on the half-closed window and the other on the door to my bedroom, I crept down the stupid bed.

Crackkk!!

The old bed made such a creaking noise, it almost echoed in the silence.

"Dammit." I whispered in despair. I stood now, petrified, letting the sudden noise fade out. I knew I had made my quiet movement public now.

Footsteps down the corridor.

I tiptoed to the edge of my door, trembling all over.

I had once had a close encounter with ghosts before, at Port Blair, on a Diwali night. And, this time, things did look like a playback from the old pages.

The entire place had gone quiet again, but I felt restless, I could feel a presence somewhere and I felt like being watched. I couldn't decide whether to scream, to alert others or latch my door, or my eyes shut instead.

There was a huge distortion as the pendulum in the front room clock came to life the next minute. It struck three, and the sudden noise catapulted my panic. I felt like acting out one of those hundred stupid scenes from some Ram Gopal Varma flick, however, the sweat and the tension did kind of kept the fear real.

A moment of Catch 22, in a moment of fear and anxiety, I pushed my bedroom door open as I peeped outside staring at the hall right in front of my room. I knew, Deb was just on the other side of the dark hall in the master bedroom where he shared bed with Subhojeet, while Madhura must be fast asleep upstairs. So, if I made a run for it, I could still end up knocking on Deb's door.

But the thought of invading the hall felt like mission impossible. It felt like some death trap, a black hole.

I gulped, my eyes searching for the source of all the commotion and then I found it.

My worst nightmare.

The image was distinct, clear and horrifying.

My eyes fixed on the lady in white who stood 20 metres away from me, on the east side of the huge hall. Her eyes drifted towards me, the alien aura stupefying me, my legs trembled and the next thing, my hand moved towards the bedside lamp. I don't know what had gotten into me, but I raised the lamp, which jostled as the wires came popping out of the switch board. In a twist of fate and stimulus, I aimed it right at the ghost which swayed, its eyes ripping my soul out.

There was a shriek. Breaking glass and then, the moment of truth.

I stood there, clueless and petrified, as the lights turned on, my eyes staring at the broken remains of a mirror, whose few remaining fractured chunks now reflected the distorted image of Madhura, panicky and freaked out, standing on the stairs opposite the mirror, taking in the entire mess that had taken place.

Deb stood across the hallway, scratching his chin, trying hard to calculate how expensive the mirror, I had just shattered was.

"What ... err...," Subhojeet said, his face and voice, both visibly shaken, "Was that all about?"

I looked at them, dumbfounded.

"I heard something run past the house." Madhura spoke after five seconds of awkward silence, "And, that kind of scared me a bit." She continued, "So, I got out of bed and was walking down the stairs to your room." She pointed at Deb, "When I saw Aakash opening his door slowly. Next thing you know, he took this lamp and aimed it at that mirror and I kind of squealed with terror."

"Why would you do that?" Deb looked at me with bewilderment.

"Err...," now I realised. Damn those horror movies!!

I had accidentally seen Madhura's reflection in the mirror and thought it to be a spirit or something! It was the sound of her door opening, that had gotten me worried in the first place and now I kind of felt ashamed and embarrassed, and out of explanations, too.

"Err...," I tried to think.

"Say something." Subhojeet was annoyed at losing his sleep, "Will you?"

"I saw something there. That thing, moving through the bushes outside, guys." I tried to make up for my stupidity, "There was something I tell you."

Silence.

Now, I could feel everyone getting tense all over again. The lie worked as long as it kept people out!!

"Dude!!" Deb finally spoke, "Get some sleep. You must've been dreaming or something. There's nothing here. "

The bang on the door couldn't have been more perfect.

All four of us literally jumped at the sudden clang. The door banged again, and it continued.

"What the hell!" Subhojeet stammered.

Did that just happen, did I just enrage some lone pissed off spirit by my lie who had come hunting for me now.

"Deb, don't open the door please!" Madhura cried, tears streaming down her eyes, her hands held tight against the locket of some god she wore.

"Nothing will happen, okay" Deb's eyes widened as he stepped towards the door.

I looked back at my room, trying to find another weapon to throw at any moment now. I pictured a headless man standing outside, ready to chop us into tiny beheaded dead kids with his axe!

It was 3 am in the night ... we were in some haunted mansion in the middle of nowhere, with hungry dogs and no human presence for miles. And, someone was knocking at the door. This was, not good!

Six pairs of eyes watched, as Deb grabbed a club from the fireplace, then slowly and steadily unlocked the door which had gone haywire from constant banging.

Another silence, as the door opened, a stream of wind hit our face, and for a second I had to blink just to keep the dust off, that it brought along.

"Shock shock!!"

It was the voice I least expected.

Katie stood there, puffing another cigarette, as her eyes strolled on to our scary faces, her face glinting with a smug smile and a pure dose of sarcasm.

"Howdy, scared people ... And Maddy, you can let go off that locket now. I'm not gonna bite you." She winked.

"How did you find us here?" Deb was surprised, his voice, doped with elation.

"Ahh…one of your SMS's got through. The one where you had texted the address of this place and so I came looking!" She gave a hollow laugh, as she trotted in. I could see that she blinked, and almost knew instantly, she lied.

I didn't know whether it was her reflex action, but she immediately looked at me, as if sensing my doubts.

"At 3 am?" I thought out loud, and realised my slip of the tongue.

"Why? Is that illegal? Am I gonna end in prison?"

"You are a good liar by the way." This was the first time she had addressed me and I was shocked at the accuracy of her statement.

"What do you mean?"

"I know you had seen the reflection of Madhura in the mirror and thought it was some ghost."

"What…," she had caught me off guard, "How did you … know?"

"Relax, dude." she said moving away, "I was the one whose footsteps you must've heard across the window. I was in the porch, while you carried out that entire fiasco of shattering and shrieking. I laughed my lungs out the whole time. It was a good show." She chuckled mocking me.

Deb and Subhojeet guffawed. I was finally caught red-handed.

"Whatever." Madhura was evidently pissed off to see her nemesis Katie, as she climbed back to her room …

"Sorry for eavesdropping." Katie yawned, "Sue me."

✳ ✳ ✳

Katie had finally stepped into my life, the girl of my dreams, my love, at, first, sight story.

But now that she was here, and she was startling me with her intuitions, I was lost … I didn't know what was to happen next.

LIE 051

Sleep had long fled and the tea gardens covered with mist and fog that turned golden yellow with every ounce of the sun rays at the break of dawn was an outstanding sight, too good to be missed.

I sat at the porch, a blanket wrapped around my shivering body, as I let smoke escape my mouth, my breath all vaporised, white mist adding up with the clouds. The place felt peaceful, in fact, now that the howl of the wind had stopped, I noticed how sullen the silence was; it could make your ears ring like crickets. I saw a few German Shepherds, too, beastly creatures springing by, chasing invisible victims, lost in paradise, and the more I looked, the more I delved into oblivion, into a strange peace, my eyes started to droop, and the lights kept on fading.

"Are you always up this early?"

I woke up with a start.

"Wait a minute. Were you sleeping here?"

My eyes looked up at her dazzling smile, and I feared she might hear the increased heart beat. Katie stood there, a cup of steaming hot coffee in her hand, her eyes red, her face a bit tired, but beautiful as ever.

"I just sort of...," I tried to make sense.

She looked at me with amused eyes as her interest rose. So, I finally gave in after a bit of confused indecisions.

"I kinda fell asleep while waiting for the sunrise."

"Ohhh ... so you didn't sleep at all earlier?"

"Nope, I didn't."

She jumped to the part where I sat and couched beside me.

"Me neither. Just couldn't sleep. Fled from my place just for some respite in the middle of the night, but bad luck." She frowned, then smiled.

"Why did you flee?"

"You want some?" She pointed to the cup, avoiding my question.

"Nope. I'm fine." and soon realised I badly needed the coffee...

We sat there silently for the next five minutes as we watched the sky turn from dark yellow, to flaming orange and then blue streaks painted the sky gradually.

"You want sunrises? You should come with me sometime. There's an awesome place here, they call it the Tiger Hill. Best sunrise spot ever." Katie said softly but with confidence.

"I'd love to." I said, surprising myself. Through the corner of the eye, I saw her smile.

"So, you play something in the band?"

"Um ... I'm the singer and the lyricist for now, and a bit of the chords here and there."

"Ohhh, so you write, huh? Poet!" She spoke in a voice tinged with sarcasm. The golden streaks in her hair furled, a strand of hair touched my face, and I realised how close I was to my first crush right now. That didn't help though.

"Sounds weird when you say it like that. I just mince words, follow some pattern and rhyme stuff with music, that's what I do. I'm no poet."

"Apparently, this Shakespeare is humble." She mocked some more.

"At least, he admits to the crime."

"Hmm, so you think you know about me." Katie sensed where I was headed.

Yes, I knew she was a painter who had beaten me three years ago in a stupid painting competition that she had no recollection of, with a spell binding painting captioned "Atonement" and I also knew that she loved *Catcher in the Rye*. Two plus two, she loved literature!

"I'm just assuming. You've yet to clear my doubts."

"You have a lot of questions, I have some, too, but mine are not for you, so why don't we both be in a doubtful sense of life for the moment."

"You can't always get what you want." I thought out loud.

"Rolling stones. Good song." she smiled.

"Are you always this good at catching a person?" We laughed. "No really, I mean you caught me two hours ago with that mirror thing, you're going to get me into trouble, Katie."

"I'm just good, you know." she winked at me, "bond."

Both of us went silent at the sudden revelation.

"I should go, wake Deb up. A lot of catching up to do."

She stood up abruptly. A few drops of the coffee spilled.

"Why did you refuse to recognise me, Katie? Why did you lie?"

Her eyes now fixed into mine as I felt a lump up my throat.

"Why didn't you call me, Aakash? I thought we both liked 'Catcher in the Rye', food for talk. I thought you rifled through the entire hotel that day in Delhi, searching for me. Why did you lie?"

I tried hard to answer, tried hard to figure out the reasons, the explanations, tried to tell her that I loved the envelope of dreams and that reality strangled me, that I never called her because even as a kid I knew how perfect that entire story was and that if she didn't pick my calls up then, maybe, a child's wonderland would've been devoured, the dream would've been lost … but she was long gone, Katie had subsided into the room, her perfume still lingered and the sun rays now hurt my eyes.

✳ ✳ ✳

I always had her number. Katie's. Was I her first crush, too?

Was I responsible for her declination to recognise me? Because I never called her. Because she came to the railway station that day in some other world, and I didn't even try to get back to her?

Was I ever going to get another chance? Does life work like that!

LIE 052

It was getting hard to focus with the rise of the day and as the jamming sessions started, I literally shuddered with an abominable headache.

We had qualified for the second round of Rockstars. Now, we had to go through the elimination round where we had to perform along with other bands that have been selected in the competition. The performance was three days later, and we had opted for blues.

At around ten in the morning, Vicky showed up. Alongside dangled, sparkling new drum sets.

"You know why I am doing this." Vicky whispered to me.

"I do dude. And, I respect that." I faked a salute.

"Why is she still here?" Madhura mumbled to me as she eyed Katie, who sat alone by the corner smoking another cigarette.

"Katie, how many times, huh?" Deb scowled at Katie angrily.

"Sorry, daddy", she rolled her eyes, threw the thing away and drooped, almost as sleepy as I was right then.

"Katie, did you tell Daniel bhaiya that you're here?", Deb asked.

"Slipped off my mind."

Deb stroked his temple, frustrated as he again started texting in his cell.

"So", Subhojeet enquired, "what are we going to play for the competition?"

"Well, about that," Deb pressed the send button, then placed his cell over the table as he took his guitar, "we could play the song we did in our school festival last year."

"Thy magic?" Madhura asked.

"Yup, that's the one", Deb smiled as he tried to play the lead.

I had no idea of the song and somehow I didn't have a lot of enthusiasm too, about the song, maybe it was sleep, or general disinterest. "Ohh, that one sucks. You had mailed it to me, I remember." I looked up at the stark reply from Katie who had her head bent on the table as she spoke.

"What do you mean? It was highly appreciated", Madhura protested with chagrin.

"I'm surprised you even call it a song," Katie sat up right now, as her eyes focused on Madhura who was knives and daggers at her by now.

"What's there to hate about it?" Subhojeet scratched his head.

"Well you fused classical with rock and then sang a ballad ... what're you people? Losers?"

I suddenly had a strong urge to burst out laughing. I needed a sleep or I could really get slapped!!!

"Hey you mind your words gal...," Madhura cletched her fists.

"Hey hey girls ... relax please," Deb had to stop Madhura from literally throwing something at Katie.

Katie looked at me and winked instead.

For a minute, my heart stopped and my sleep deprived eyes widened.

"Hey, Katie, as much as I thank you for your kind words, but we're going to stick to the song." Deb tried to settle things.

"Ohh, trust me," Katie smirked, "You've already changed your mind, Deb."

We practised "Thy Magic" all afternoon and soon realised there was nothing magical about it.

The only thing that kept me going though was the sleeping beauty beside me. Katie slept through the practice sessions, her face calm, peaceful, a small smile somewhere and a hint of a dimple in her cheek, as she gently breathed, lost in dreams. Her strong lavender perfume wafted through my heart and I couldn't help but steal glances at her periodically.

For the fiftieth time, Deb repeated his mistake on the seventh note and then he stopped.

"Enough of this! I'm done with this song," Deb declared keeping his guitar down.

"What do you mean?" Subhojeet picked his hairs in annoyance.

"That this song is out of the list. We're not playing this. It's stupid. Don't you see."

"Why? C'os your girlfriend thinks so?" Madhura's voice was filled with sarcasm.

"She is not MY GIRL FRIEND!!" Deb said through pursed lips and a flare of anger.

Katie shifted in her chair, her eyes still closed, fast asleep.

"If I may", Vicky squeaked breaking the awkward silence, "You guys are not helping. What are we going to do now should be the matter of the debate and for the song", he raised his drum sticks in defeat, "That girl there was right. It sucks!!"

"Why don't we make a new song?" I suggested.

"In two days?" Subhojeet asked skeptically.

"Well", Deb went pensive, "What do we make it about? We would need inspiration."

I don't know how, but I knew the source of my inspiration even before I really thought about the matter.

My eyes went for the nth number of time to the girl I was infatuated with. Katie's eyes fluttered and poetry was made.

***

"Thy magic is a good song, you know", Katie whispered to me as we sat at a Dhaba on the outskirts of Darjeeling, eating alu parathas. Twilight had settled and I was exhausted.

"What? But then, I don't understand, why did you lie in there today morning?" I was amazed by this girl and her mysterious acts.

"That Aakash is not a lie ... it's make believe," Katie took another bite, "And, I did it to get back at Deb and you."

"Umm... I'm lost here?"

"Well, for the time being, let's just say I want to know how good are you at poetry and lyrics," her eyes shone with malice, "Or, is it just pure old wives' tales that you're feeding us."

"You know, we both are good at lying."I ate another piece of the heavily buttered oily and delicious alu paratha.

"Ohh, trust me. You suck", she rolled her eyes.

"So ...," I paused weighing my next step, "Can we just forget the past and be friends?"

"I'm sorry but forgetting the past is an impossible concept," Katie responded strictly, breaking my castles of sands, "but then", she continued, "You never did harm me, anyways. I was already emotionally damaged. Self-loathing poor little bastard I'm", she spoke obliviously.

"Err...," I looked at her with my last shreds of hope.

"What? ... Oh yes, Aakash. We're friends alright."

That was the day I penned the second song of my life.

LIE 053

It was around six in the evening when Daniel Thomas, brother of Katie Thomas, stormed into our mansion. He was furious, and beyond any consolation.

"How dare you, obnoxious girl," He boomed visibly shaking everyone in the room, "Have you got any idea how much you've worried me with this hackneyed behaviour of yours? You should be ashamed. You deserve so less."

A tear trickled down Katie's eye.

"Daniel bhaiya, please calm down." Deb tried his best to stop the feud, but things had evidently run out of hands. Daniel Thomas looked baffled, fatigued and aggravated.

"Oh, why not Deb. Absolutely. My brazen little sister is out all night and one entire day with no hint of her whereabouts. The servants are out there in every nook and cranny of the town looking for this rich spoilt brat and you ask me to calm down. How sweet of you!" He grinds his teeth as if he's gonna hit Deb.

Deb is out of counter-arguments as Daniel strides to Katie, and then slaps her.

"Where were you all night, Katie? I know you came here at 3 in the morning. Deb messaged me, so you better not lie and tell me right now or I swear to god, you're off to Pune at Dad's place. No more of Darjeeling for you. "

"I was here." Katie wept as she spoke in a sandpapery voice.

"Oh, don't lie, don't do that to me."

"She was here, Sir." I hear myself speak. Everyone turn their eyes at me with pure astonishment.

"What did you say, what's your name?" Daniel now approached me, his eye balls bulging, his face contorted with rage and confusion.

"I'm Aakash ... er", I squeaked as my brain toiled hard thinking of a lie to tell.

"Aakash, so you're telling me that Katie was here right from 9 pm yesterday with you? And not 3?"

I nodded slowly.

"Explain then, why Deb has a different theory for the night?"

I stared at Daniel's face, searching for an answer, any crafty lie, anything that had some resemblance to a true story. I could tell, the room was waiting for an explanation. Through the corner of my eye, I saw Deb, bewildered, Katie looking earnestly at me for an escape, Madhura shell shocked and Subhojeet all sweaty again. Vicky had no clue what was going on around his grandfather's farmhouse.

"We're waiting here, Aakash." Daniel scoffed.

Think something stupid!! Think now!!

"Er ... Sir, she met me in the porch while I sat there and worked up a song with her."

"What?" Daniel was flummoxed. So was everyone else.

"Yes Sir, that is why Deb never got to know Katie was here. She was helping me with the lyrics for our song. "

"You really think I'd believe that?"

I felt stoned. Daniel didn't buy my story and I didn't have a back up. See, the problems with lies are once they've been leashed, there was no coming back.

"He's speaking the truth, Sir," Madhura's voice surprised me as Daniel turned at her now.

"And, what makes you say that?"

"I saw them working up the song yesterday night. Katie really helped a lot."

Daniel stayed in the same position for one whole minute, before walking to the nearest sofa and sitting, his head, under his hands.

I sighed with relief as I realised I had sweated my shirt.

Deb rushed to him, and patted him on the back.

"It's okay, Daniel bhaiya. She is safe as long as we're here. Don't worry."

My eyes went to Katie, who sobbed quietly in the corner.

She went with her brother after a while. We never got a moment even to say good bye to each other. And somewhere, I wasn't even sure whether I would see her again. Katie had walked out without a prior notice like she had done three years before, leaving me alone again.

"Hey, thanks, Madhura." I smiled at Maddy, "You really saved my ass there."

"She's way out of your league, Aakash." Madhura rejected my words, with a wave of her hand, "I can see what is brewing here."

✱✱✱

It was late in the night when I wrote the first few lines of the song we wanted to compose for the show.

"Tumhe na jaanu main ... Naa pehchanu main, Naa yeh bataun main, ki reh na payun main, Tumhi se din mere, Tumhi se raatein hain Tumhi se yaadein meri, Tumhi se baatein hain."

It all was for Katie, the stranger who had suddenly brightened up my life. Was she just an excuse I was using to cut off from all the issues of my life, was she an escapist's delight, or was she the whole concept of soul mate and destiny ... I didn't know ... it was like a jigsaw puzzle with its pieces lost, beyond repair.

"May I come in?" Deb knocked at the door of my room, breaking my train of thoughts.

"Hey buddy, wasup?" I closed my diary and smiled at Deb politely. He appeared worried.

"I just wanted to thank you, bro." He said as he opened a pack of Good Day cookies and offered one to me, then took another himself and sat on the couch.

"For what?" I kind of knew the answer.

"For everything you did in there to save Katie. You really are a friend, man! I'm proud of you dude."

"Oh ... that was nothing, Deb."

"Naah, man, you seriously helped us in there. And, I know you really think that Katie is all wasted and an arrogant girl, but it's not true, you know. She was never like that."

"Hey, man ... I really don't think such things about her." I tried to clarify and wished that I could tell Deb how thankful I was to him instead, for making me meet up with Katie. It was because of him that I was here today getting a chance to see Katie and talk to her.

"No, Aakash. I think it's time I owe you an explanation about what really happened to Katie. You know" Aakash, I used to come to Darjeeling every summer holidays for two months and stay at the Thomas Manor. Mr Heath Thomas, Katie's dad, has been a family friend for so many decades now. "

Deb paused and ate another piece of the cookie before he continued.

"So, it started when I was a kid, right in first standard. Every summer vacation, I would come up here to Darjeeling and meet Katie, who soon became my best friend. We would play all day long and listen to fairy tales every night straight for two months. We would roam around the hills of Darjeeling and the place soon became a boy's book to us. And then, I would be gone for another year of studies to Calcutta, missing her all the while. I remember calling her every night before sleeping and asking her what story her parents told her that day. This continued for about six years, before things changed. My dad went through some rough patches in business and it was because of some wrong deals with Mr Heath Thomas. This led to small arguments and then gradually, it resulted in dropping the idea of visiting Darjeeling altogether. And so, our friendship eventually hit rock bottom. "

Deb sighed and his expressions were that of grief and regret.

"And, what was to happen next was complacency. I got stuck with the cobwebs of Calcutta blues and my new friends while Katie was estranged, left out. I stopped calling her and we got distanced from each other. It was last year when I visited Darjeeling again and to my utmost shock, Katie had changed. She had gone rough, had developed an ego and was no more my best friend. So you see, Aakash ... ", Deb looked at me and smiled sadly, "You can put the blame on me. Maybe, I'm responsible for how Katie is now and trust me, every moment that I face her, it aches inside to see her like that, self-destructing herself."

As Deb stopped, it dawned on me. I remembered the painting that Katie had made three years ago at the Lion Club painting competition. It was of a girl, standing at her balcony, anxiously looking at the moon. She had called it "atonement". Amends. She had been waiting for her best friend all along. Deb.

I had not slept for more than 24 hours, but even then, it was hard to melt into unconsciousness.

Somehow, the truth had startled me. It was easy to imagine Katie as a totally alien character, as something larger than life, but now that I knew her roots, it had suddenly started hurting.

I remembered what Deb had told about how it ached inside to realize katie's pains. I suddenly knew what he had meant ...

LIE 054

"**M**orning sunshine." I almost smiled at the sparkling voice in my sleep. I shifted in the cozy bed, deep in slumber. Then came along the sudden knocking on my head.

"Wha!!", I opened my eyes as I tried to understand reality and it came like a surprise.

"Hi." It was Katie.

"You!!" my sleep had vanished, "Here!!".

I looked at my watch. 4:30 am.

"What're you doing this early?" I was confused as I sat up.

"Dude … no time for explanations. Now freshen up. And hurry. We'll miss it otherwise."

* * *

Katie was a rash driver. I realized it within the first two minutes. The cold froze me to death while Katie was determined of finding other ways to do the same, i.e. crashing, cliff diving in the car, dashing against trees or just burning the engine out with a bang!

She drove at a break neck speed, zooming through the tea gardens, cutting across through uneven roads, dissolving amidst the mist, and escaping from the clouds unscathed. The jeep roared through the dark night, killing the silence of the winds, as it fluttered past new undiscovered ways.

I still had no idea where Katie was taking me, and gradually it was getting creepier.

It had all happened in a wink. Moments ago, I had been wrapped in blankets, exploring my dreamland, when suddenly she had jerked me out of bed. Everyone in the mansion were fast asleep while we had tiptoed to the window, through which she had trespassed into the farm-house, and moments later, we were out in the open, just the two of us, sprinting through the huge dewy, all wet tea gardens, towards her jeep.

She didn't speak when she started the ignition; neither did she blink when the jeep zigzagged through the hilly slopes while she pressed onto more gas, giving me little heart attacks, every time we neared a narrow pass. Nor, did she answer my query as to whether she was even of the age to get a license to drive this monster. She was just fifteen after all. Every now and then, through the darkness, I would see the steep edges of the mountains through which the jeep moved, The small tiny huts kilometres below our elevated roads. One wrong slide, and the car could be air borne, aiming for a free fall under gravity.

Fifteen minutes of drive later, Katie finally killed the engine and got down. We had driven up to a huge cliff and had reached an edge of the mountain.

There was a thick mushroom of cloud ahead and I couldn't even see what laid ten metres away.

"Finally, we're here", Katie looked up at me, her face the brightest thing in the peripheral vision of mine. The sky was now turning a bit bluish black as I got down the jeep, shivering in the glacial wind.

"I ne ... er ...h .d ... a de ... ish", my teeth were chattering due to the extreme frigid temperature and I couldn't phrase my words.

Katie burst out laughing, "what did you say?" she chuckled as she came closer to me, "Here, tell in my ear."

Her face came closer to mine, as I felt the heat of her skin and my heart did a drum roll.

"I didn't have a death wish...where are we?", I finally said.

"Ohh ... you will know", she beamed with excitement and mischief, "Now, come with me".

"Where?" I looked at the cloud she had started walking towards.

She is going to get us killed! That suicidal self-loathing angel!

I stayed petrified in my position, too scared and frozen even to run for the jeep.

Katie looked back at me, then laughed some more, "Ohh, don't be a baby now, Aakash. Here, take my hand."

We held hands as she took me across the clouds. It felt like a dream, except that it had goose bumps and excessive teeth chattering involved. My face and my entire body got soaked as soon as we got inside the white sphere of mist. I could no longer see anything. Everything was pure white, all my sensory feelings cut off, just a slight hint of suffocation and a bit of panic, but Katie's firm grip as if reassured me that I was in safe hands. We moved along the cloud, my eyes closed, just trudging behind her. In another world, I could've been sleeping the same incident, with just a pleasant ticklish feeling in my head.

"Aakash ..."

"Hmm ..."

"Open your eyes ..."

Infinite sky, Orange streaks across the horizon silver lining the black sky which viscously turned yellow, and out there, right across a far peak, a small orb of pure orange, The sun ...

It was breathtaking, the serenity and the spellbinding beauty of nature that I witnessed.

The perfect sunrise.

"This ... is Tiger Hill", Katie whispered in my ear, "See, I kept my promise."

I nodded as a smile spread across my face. It felt magnificent, like I was looking up at the heavens, surreal and highly refreshing.

We stayed there for a while, all along watching the dawn breaking, beholding the sun rise, a blue morning.

I was still quiet with the spellbinding sight as we hit the road back to the old mansion.

"Thanks for yesterday, Aakash." Katie said as she drove through the snaky path.

"Thanks for today, Katie," I said.

She smiled.

"And, in case you're wondering where I really was on Sunday night from 9 to 3, I'm going to reply, 'It's none of your business'," she tweeted.

"I was not going to ask." I focused on the road.

"I know you think I'm all messed up and a bad kid." She said as we crossed another narrow turn while I held my breath, "And, I know you already regret being friends with me."

"Are you that bad at reading faces?" I retorted and looked at her now, "I am no one to judge somebody, Katie, and if I were to mouth my thoughts, I'd say you're really a nice and a beautiful girl and...", I abruptly stopped as we both blushed.

"And...?" she smirked.

"Um ... err... ", I didn't know what to say.

She kept on smiling through the rest of the drive.

We reached the mansion at around 6.30.

"I got to head back home right away." Katie didn't stop the engine as I got down, "See, my brother doesn't know I have a duplicate of the car keys and that I'm not in my bed room right now, snoring."

Both of us burst out laughing.

"No seriously, I'm grounded, according to him. Only Deb can come visit me in the afternoons."

"Man!! If Daniel gets to know this, he would be really pissed."

"As if I care." she rolled her eyes, "And anyways, I had to meet you, after all." She winked, "Show the poet some Darjeeling."

I grinned.

"So ...," she said.

"So...err," I suddenly realised she had to leave, "Aren't we going to meet again? I mean, I'm sure Darjeeling has a lot other places that a poet might admire!".

She guffawed, "Why don't you just say you want to see me again?"

"Err....."

And, why am I always at a loss of words!

"I will catch you tomorrow ... same time ... but you got to promise me that you won't tell anyone."

"I cross my heart." I was elated.

"Alright then, *adios amigo*." With that she was gone.

I don't know how long I stood there in the porch, staring at the piecemeal disappearance of the tail lights. Her lavender perfume still lingered in the air ... Katie ...

"Aakash!!" Deb shook from behind, "What're you doing here, at this time of the day?"

"Ohh, Deb." I look back at him as I lied, "Nothing, man ... Just got back from a morning walk."

"Wow! Great, bro ... So, how is this place?"

"She's amazing…"

"She?"

"Err…," I smiled, "It's amazing."

LIE 055

We started with our new song, "*Na jaanu main*", a Hindi blues in the afternoon of our fourth day at Darjeeling.

I had penned down the first four lines, and we were trying to compose the tune. Subhojeet suggested a lot of cold play influenced piano strokes, while Deb tried A-minor.

"Alright guys, let's just patch this thing through," I said after a while, "I'll start with the song on a low key, let's see where this goes. Maddy, play some exuberant chords." I smiled at her.

And, after a lot of refusals and corrections, arguments and acceptances, coffees and sandwiches, if's and buts, finally we had the music.

It was beautiful. Deb's guitar strokes were sloppy and just added flamboyance to the song.

We still needed to have a proper end and add another stanza to the lyrics that continues with the same music, but we were quite confident it was going to turn out great eventually.

***

"Hello. Who is this?" Mr Dennis Andrew's strong baritone came from d chthe other side.

"Err… This is … Aakash." I spoke after a while.

"Who Aakash?" Mr. Dennis pondered for a while then before I could re-introduce myself, he boomed on the receiver, "Oh, Aakash huh! The lazy chap! Yes, yes … where, have you fled to? Missing tuitions like that? I was going to call up your dad any day now. Even Katie here has no idea of your whereabouts."

"Is that Aakash?" I heard the faint voice of Katherine from the other side interrupting her dad.

"Yeah, it's him, Aakash, talk to Katie." Mr Dennis handed Katie the phone.

I was mum, out of explanations.

"Hello, Aakash?" Katherine's expectant brisk voice came along.

"Kates, how are you?"

"Not well, but don't worry, I know it doesn't matter to you." Katie's voice shook a bit.

"Please, don't say that. I'm really sorry for not telling you before I left for Darjeeling."

Silence on the other side.

"I'll be there in another six days, Katie."

Katie coughed on the line. Then, she spoke softly, "Please, come back sooner, Aakash. I have to tell you something."

"I will, that is if our band got rejected, you know, out of the competition." I chuckled trying to cheer Katie up "So, got my fingers crossed here Kates..."

"Yeah, I heard you people did great at the auditions." Katie squeaked in her sand-papery voice.

"We managed somehow."

"So, keep managing, Aakash. I know you can do that. "

"Hey, about that thing you had to tell me, Can't you tell it to me over the phone, if it's urgent."

Katherine paused for an indecisive moment, then she snorted, "Naah ... It's not that important you know. It can wait."

Katherine lied.

✷✷✷

I kept awake till 3 o'clock in the morning trying my best to end the song, I wanted one perfect line but it seemed difficult. Nothing could fit in. The song was too beautiful to be messed up with and try as I did, I couldn't recreate the charm.

What had happened all of a sudden?

Was it the lack of perspective, or a confusion settling in? Had I lost my inspiration, or was I just not sure enough. I didn't know.

That night I dreamt of Katherine. I saw her playing along with me and I felt annoyed when military uncle, Mr Dennis appeared out of nowhere in my perfect world and from his pocket, popped his timer.

"Your one hour is up." He shouted at me and the buzzer jolted me awake.

4 am ...

✳ ✳ ✳

I followed the jeep's flaring headlights in the haze.

"Hey, sunshine." Katie winked at me, "You're fifteen minutes early." She checked her watch. It was 4:15 am.

"So are you ..."

She smirked, and then nodded.

"So...?" I said.

"Well, hop in." she announced, "Let's leave for some adventure."

We took the highways today, and the speed flickered around a good 80 miles an hour.

"This is the Hill Cart Road." Katie informed me, "I love these roads. They take me straight to the Park lane, the most beautiful houses out here."

"Hmmm...sounds like some future plans here."

She smiles, "Nope. Not my check list. I'm not the trad princess who follows the book, you see."

I looked back at the roads.

"You look a bit worried or is it just the early morning?" Katie said after a while.

"I don't know ... I'm just a bit in a soup with this lyrics of mine ... somehow I can't find the proper end."

"What is it about?" Katie asks, "Your song?"

"It's about a stranger...," I try to figure out the song myself, "You know ... It's like this song where the guy tells us about this girl, he has just met, whom he doesn't even know enough, but somehow, it as if intrigues him."

Katie listend quietly, so I continued.

"It's like he described how life brightened with her in the room, how every single moment spent with her was so special, but." I stopped.

"But, what?" Katie slows the car down a bit, as we passed a small fountain, white droplets of water from the shower oozing out, moistening our faces as the jeep passed.

"Somewhere it's all more like a dream, a sweet fantasy, and somehow there's a home where the guy had to go back one day, those special moments were fleeting, and it was just surreal. "

"Unreal...isn't it?"

"I always wished life was like movies, you know, Katie." I said, "Where true love happened and serendipity and soul mates were common terms, but we all know that's just pure clichés."

"Hmm," She nodded as I thought out loud.

"But what is important is we still love the concept ... and somewhere we want it all to happen. If not in a real story, maybe just in a song."

"So, you think the song should've a happy ending but you're afraid that's what happens in every second song?", Katie put it starkly.

"Pretty much."

"Well, here's an idea. Why don't we just get real in your song for a change? I mean, Jim Morrison would do it, Elton John or even 'the killers.'"

"Do what?"

"They'd let it live with just the confusion ... The soup that life really is. The song would state your state of mind and it won't conclude. You know which are the best stories?"

"Which ones?" I looked back at Katie as she stopped her car and faced me.

"The one's which doesn't have an ending ... which gives you the chance to pick your own version. Like life."

When I got back home, I wrote the last two lines of the song ... the English translation of which was

"And even so ... I'd never say That without you, I'm lost, in search of a way And even so ... we might never meet This heart would live, but just won't beat ..."

LIE 056

The competition just got tougher.

We sat there re-playing the song in our head, Deb's fingers played an invisible guitar as he calculated the strings in his mind, Subhojeet was busy wiping sweat, while Vicky was super-nervous and Madhura couldn't decide whether her make up was fine or not.

Breathe in ... Breathe out ...

I was tense as I noticed how the other bands performed, the singers so confident, long haired, tattooed dudes, as they rapped and shouted and smiled.

I couldn't do just that stuff.

It became harder to remember the lines as the goosebumps returned and so I closed my eyes and went back to my dream ...

* * *

11 hours back ... 5 am

"Big day today, huh?" Katie looked up at the sunrise through the pine trees.

I had no idea where we were just that Katie took some careless turns on the way, hit on a sandy road, then trespassed through prohibited forest land and here we were ... on no man's land.

"I really think there can be snakes out here, you know, those really poisonous ones." I inspected the site, thick with shrubs and wild bushes, surrounded by pines.

"Yup, I know." Katie shrugged callously, "And Deb would come up here often, we saw this rattle snake here once, right where you're sitting now."

I stood up instantaneously and Katie broke into a fit of giggles.

"You're not helping", I sighed.

"Don't worry, dude, snakes are more afraid of us and I know this place through and through." she assured, "been here a thousand times."

"What's so special about this place?"

"Um ... just some stupid myth."

"Tell me about it ..."

Katie looked into my curious eyes and uttered the name.

"Love square..."

***

"And now, we have the band from Calcutta, E.N.V.Y." The ever so hyper, short lady Petrische pushed us to the stage as the host asked for a round of applause.

We ascended the stage.

"Alright guys." Deb looks up at the crowd of aspiring singers and musicians, "Hello there folks, I'm Deb, this here is Aakash, we've Madhura on the base guitar, Vicky on the drums and Subhojeet on the keyboard and we're gonna have *"Tumhe na jaanu main"* on your lips for the rest of your lives." He winked at the crowd.

There was a huge round of applause as I suddenly realised we just had the best introduction amongst all our competitors. My eyes moved on to the judge's seat as I saw the trio, Rajiv, Murshid and Ravi hopefully looking at Deb who was confident as John Lennon had been in each of his performances.

Deb looked at us, then he smiled, "Let's rock and roll, guys," as he blasted off with the lead of our song.

The keyboard played a minute later and I held the microphone close to me as she popped back up in my head.

***

11 hours ago…5:10 am

"Love square, what's that?" I was sure I had heard that name for the first time.

"It's just a stupid myth around Darjeeling. People here often speculate about having been to that place. They say it's the most beautiful square in the world. Covered in snow, the paradise for true lovers and shit. They say only true soulmates can find it. It's like this sacred place, like the fountain of love."

"And, you've never been there?"

"I hate to break it to you, but it just doesn't exist."

"Maybe, you just never found it."

"Oh, trust me, I've been through these forests in nights and days, trodding alone, at late nights and all I could find were more and more spaces of darkness ... the myth says love square is surrounded by pines and thorns and this is the only place in the entire hill station with pine trees, and so far ... nothing ... Utopia just doesn't exist." Katie shouted to the wind.

"Is this where you were the night you dropped at our place at 3 am?", I was suddenly struck by the revelation.

Katie was stunned though she attempted to ignore my remark.

"All stories of finding neverland and it's just pure humbug," she speculated.

"Is that what you really think?" I challenged Katie as she stopped at her place, "You've been here a thousand times trying to find this Love square of yours and have failed over and over and even then, we're still here. What do you call that?"

Katie closed her eyes as she inhaled the fresh breath of air and exhaled with a smile, "I thought you loved hope."

✶✶✶

I sang my heart out. We were lost in the performance as Deb blew everyone's mind with his guitar and smiles.

And then, I saw her there.

Just for that split second, just right on that last line … Katie Thomas standing right in the first row, smiling down at me.

The camera flashed and she faded away. My walking dream.

My hope.

As the music stopped, I was struck with two realisations.

1>

"That was awesome. Simply brilliant piece of music there. Is it yours, Deb?" Ravi Kumar asked excitedly.

"Yes, Sir, he made the entire thing, that guy." I heard myself lie as Deb looked at me, completely shocked.

He looked at me, with utter confusion and then Murshid Ali answered his question, "I think I can see a star there." he smiled, "I have a feeling that you're going to be a rockstar, Deb. You've it in you."

We cheered as we hugged Deb.

Yes. It was Deb, the rockstar material, the looks, the style and the charm. He was the face of our band, I could see it. He was our U.S.P. … and for that he had to have a song to himself.

I could always copyright another of my song.

As we headed back to the dressing room, Deb suddenly patted me from behind and then hugged me tight, "Thanks bro…We owe this success to you…thanks for making E.N.V.Y. win dude."

Madhura and Subhojeet hugged me, too. A lot of hugs today!

***

11 hours ago, 5:30 am

"You know, maybe, I could help you find your Love square."

Katie burst out laughing, "Ohh, you cute optimistic guy!! "

She walked up to me and hugged me.

And, a warm feeling spreads all over.

It's so strong it feels part of my soul. As her arms wrap around my shoulder, it gets clearer.

***

Through the cheers, the second realisation dawns...

2>

I was irrevocably in love with Katie Thomas.

LIE 057

"Thy soul shall consummate kosher love Egalitarian, Pine woods, the solitary blench star above."

I read the excruciating couplet over and over again, but it was erudite and beyond comprehension for me. So, I gave up and handed the book back to Katie as we trotted in the pine forest, all confused.

"You were right, Love square is a myth," I sighed.

We had collected a dozen books that covered almost every tourist spot in every hinterland of Darjeeling, and all we found about love square were just these two lines.

"See, this is the only detail that I ever got about Love square." Katie exclaimed, "I mean, there are references to the place here and there, but if you backtrack, all you can find out about its location are these two lines that cannot be comprehended."

"Looks like it's going to snow any moment now," I shivered as I looked up at the sky.

It was five in the morning and the entire hill station was lulled into morning dreams as the white moon was the only star in the sky.

I could never figure out how appropriate the moment was, all penned down hundreds of years ago into two small lines…

***

The night before…

We could not be stopped. We were ecstatic, brimming with joy as we cheered.

284

We were one step closer to Rockstars now. Our group had been selected as one of the finalists from eastern India.

Now, we had our final performance at Saint Joseph's College, Darjeeling.

If we qualified it, we would move on to the national level competition, to be aired live on television on MTV.

This was our big claim to fame, and we had completed half the journey.

Rumour had it, that the live performance at Saint Joseph Church would have an audience of around 10,000.

That brought butterflies in the stomach every time my thoughts catapulted in that direction, but the happiness of victory was sweet enough to make the fear desolate.

"Okay, guys." Deb now stood up, "First of all, I need to announce something." he said clicking his cup of hot cappuccino. I knew the entire crowd in the café had their eyes at us, but I chose to be in oblivious of the fact, these moments were too precious.

"I am raising this toast." Deb chuckled, "To my dearest friend, Aakash."

At this, Vicky, Madhura and Subhojeet banged the table in appreciation as they hooted with joy.

"The guy who composed one of the sweetest songs of our band. Here's to the man who made me the hero of the day." Deb smiled and winked at me and the rest applauded. It felt incredible. This was the first time, that I had been noticed for something appreciable, something honest, and it felt warm, for the first time, I was proud of myself, in a funny way as I sipped the hot coffee.

I looked at Deb, who was beaming with innocent happiness and pride and I felt glad that I had a selfless and modest friend like him.

I felt sorry for all the times I had misjudged him.

***

"So, you're telling me that you sneak out of your place every morning, you've been doing it for some years now and your brother doesn't even have a clue about the whole affair?"

Katie smirked smugly and nodded.

"See, my parents are at Pune, so it's only me and Daniel here, and frankly, that castle of mine my rich parents created, is too spacious and lofty for just the two of us. So, it's too difficult for my brother even to make out that my bed is empty."

"But even then, it has been years now and never even once?", The thought of Katie slipping out every dawn startled me, as we walked through the edge of a small creek, in the pine wood forest, trekking deeper into the woods.

"Alright", Katie finally exhaled a huge ring smoke, as her voice turned mischievous, "Let me show you something." We both halted as she dug her hands into her pocket and out came a small bottle, with some small white pills inside.

"What's that?" I asked curiously.

"Sleeping pills." Katie winked, "Add one to your dinner stealthily and you won't wake up until at least eight in the morning."

"Ohhh, dear Lord." I couldn't believe what she had been doing. "All these years, you've been mixing pills at that poor bloke's dinner so that you could explore snowy mornings?"

"Argh, for god's sake." Katie rolled her eyes, "It's not that big a deal. These pills relax you, soothe your nerves. And, one doesn't kill."

I was mildly aggravated by Katie's lie and was going to protest some more when it happened. Out of the blue, small dots of white show touched our faces.

I paused with the sudden intervention and looked up to see my dream materialise.

Two minutes later, the entire town was dazed with the snow fall.

"This is pure beauty." I whispered as Katie and I held hands watching the cool breeze bringing in a compendium of snow along side that blinded the entire place.

Katie shivered a bit by my side as the wind roared.

"Here, have this," I gave her my overcoat. I wore a sweater under it and another sleeveless sweater over my t-shirt while Katie wore a sleeveless t-shirt, her body being super adapted to the cold. No wonder, the goosebumps!

She wrapped the overcoat and I tried to walk over the edge of the creek to her right. That's when I slipped over the snow, and skidded.

*** *** ***

The night before…

"Hello, dad!" There was high static on the other side and I could not make out dad's voice. He tried to say something but it was inaudible.

"Dad, can't hear your voice. Just wanted to tell you that we got selected for the State finals. It's on Sunday. I will call you again soon. Bye. Take care."

I hung up and walked back home. It was more of a one-sided conversation.

Only if I had heard what he said. Some shocks just await the perfect timing.

*** *** ***

I slipped through the forest, and rolled down the sloppy hill. As I skidded down below, everything blurred, and I cut through the bushes, delving deeper into the thick forest. I could hear Katie scream from behind as she sprinted to save me.

The sharp gravels and the stems cut through my shirt and my body, and it ached all over as I finally dragged to a stop.

My head spinned as my eyes kept fazing in and out of focus.

"Thy soul shall consummate kosher love egalitarian, Pine woods, the solitary blench star above…"

Pine woods, the forest…blench meaning white and snowy, star above…my eyes focused to the lonely moon high up as I tried to sit up. The blench star above!

"Hey, you okay?" Katie ran from behind and then she clasped my hand trying to hold me up.

That's when it dawned.

"Where are we?" I was transfixed as I saw the small valley that I had slipped into in a complete coincidence and the four snowy dusty sand roads colliding at the point where I had skidded down to.

"It's a square…," Katie slowly uttered, as her eyes went to the small dried up fountain built at the centre of the four untravelled abandoned roads, "It's Love square … "

LIE 058

L ove square lay there right before our eyes, as real and as beautiful as those references and those couplets expressed. In flesh and blood, Katie and I, witnessed the dream of Katie materialise that dawn. The snow fell over our hair, as if in sheer appraisal from the heavenly graces, as we walked over to the old dried up fountain, built in white marble right at the centre of the square, with a small statue of Cupid over the structure, his arrow pointed at the heavens, as his closed eyes and subtle smile reassured the fact that I was definitely with my beloved out there, as if history and the paradise had written this page in our lives, as if this love was immortal, as if Katie and I were destined to meet, soulmates ... Katie took my hand, her eyes met mine, and slowly she whispered, "Thanks"... I couldn't stop beaming, as I held her hand tightly, reading the caption in the white marbled structure,

"Lines in palms and in stones white ... shall not be erased, try as much the tempests might... And, if the crossways are where thou shall meet Love square shall lighten your path to embark each feat"

Below those etched lines on the fountain, hundreds of names of boys and girls had been carved over the stone, couples who had discovered love square earlier.

I desperately longed to etch our names, too, "Aakash & Katie". However, Katie checked her watch and gasped.

"I have to leave now. It's late." Katie shrugged, "Let me drop you home Aakash. You're a bit injured, too. You need to get some first aid."

She drove me back to the farmhouse. We were both silent throughout the walk back home. Then, as we reached the old mansion, she said,

"Aakash, I might not make it in the mornings for the rest of your stay here. But we sure had fun, mate." I felt a lump in my throat at the thought of facing solitary mornings sans Katie.

"And, don't be sad. I will stay out with you people the entire day on Sunday. Your final day of performance at Darjeeling. We will have fun then."

She winked as she drove away in the haze of snow.

So, it had to be Sunday, right before our final performance, that I could confess my love for Katie.

As I traced back my path to the old creaky bed and lay there for the rest of the morning, I couldn't sleep. I kept going back and forth amongst all those precious moments that I had passed with Katie, her round green eyes, the highlights and that lavender perfume, her smirk and that mischief that she flaunted, it drove me crazy. Three years ago, I had fallen for this cute little princess at first sight, Somehow the feelings had strengthened over the years.

***

We kept practising "Jo thi dil ki khushi" at a stretch for the next three days. It was exhausting but somewhere it had this pump of adrenaline attached to it. The crowd, the live performance and the best shot at music and Rockstars were reasons enough to keep us on our toes, putting in the best efforts.

Every night as we went to bed, I could hear Deb strumming his guitar. He was preparing for a surprise end, the best lead and an alternative version, that he had tailor made for the live performance. It was all under wraps, and all we knew was that it had a lot of electric and distortion in it… That was more than enough for us. Deb was our trumpcard for the performance and we counted on him.

***

And then, all of a sudden, Sunday came knocking at our doors.

We were pumped up, all anxious, and determined to win. However, for me, meeting Katie after three days was the biggest highlight of the day. She was my inspiration, remember. And, with her by my side, I was kind of assured to blow some minds away at the show. Katie met us at 9 in the morning. She looked drop-dead gorgeous. She wore a black jacket over a red tee and her hair was tied, smelling of lavender, she stole my breath away, while she just winked and smiled at me.

We re-rehearsed "*Jo thi dil ki khushi*" for the thousandth time and Katie was impressed, I could tell.

We had lunch at the café nearby and then we took a stroll to the museum at Darjeeling. Then, we visited some churches, prayed for luck and by 2 in the afternoon, we were all perked up.

"Hey, guys." Deb asked us, "Why don't you people go to the farmhouse, take some rest and then meet me at Saint Joseph Church by 5:30 in the evening. We can practise one last time then, check the mikes and sound arrangements before the final performance at 7 in the evening while I go drop Katie and chat with Daniel bhaiya?"

We nodded and waved goodbyes to Katie and Deb.

Before leaving, Katie came to me, and whispered to me in the ear, "I will be there at the show cheering you all. Just in case I don't meet you before the performance, know this that you're my favourite singer and poet of all times." She winked at me, "And, I know that you're going to do well, infact, do great."

"Ohh, you little sarcastic liar." I smiled back at her, as she climbed on to the cab with Deb.

"Bye, Aakash..."

✷ ✷ ✷

I sprinted through the pine woods. It was 4:30 in the evening. I had to hurry back to Saint Josephs, but before that I needed to do one last thing.

I remembered the line inscribed over the stone hedge at the fountain of Love square.. "Lines in palms and in stones white ... shall not be erased, try as much the tempests might." I was going to write Katie's and my name there, make this love immortal.

I slipped, skidded, fell, but I kept running for the square.

I was elated, overjoyed, it was like this happiness spreading through me and then I stopped abruptly.

I saw Katie and Deb there, right before Love square.

A mix of confusion and sadness engulfed me.

They kissed.

For a few moments, I could not place it all as my head jumbled with the hard hitting reality.

There were no words to explain, it cut through me, I went numb, my heart as if turned into lead. I was baffled, petrified, as my best friend and the love of my life, kissed passionately right before my eyes, unaware of my presence.

"I love you, Katie." Deb said as his lips parted for a fraction of seconds from hers, there were tears in Katie's eyes as she wrapped her hands over his shoulders, and smiled heartily, "I love you, too Deb. I've always loved you, even before I knew the meaning of it."

They hugged and they laughed, they cried and they smiled and they wrote their names on the white stones, while I stood stunned there, hidden beneath the thick pine woods.

It cut me like a sharp knife, cut through my veins, and still the betrayal that love and life had played on me mocked some more. My tears were frozen, and I couldn't express the shock and despair anymore.

All I could do was, wait there, as I watched my dream become someone else's for ever.

*** *** ***

I lost track of time and couldn't tell as night crept in. Katie and Deb had long left, the love square was deserted and the snow fall showed no signs of abating.

I sat back, and sighed. I was oblivious, lost and thoughtless. My hands reached for my pockets that I wore and then I found something.

It was the bottle of sleeping pills that Katie had forgotten in my jacket three days ago when I had lent it to her.

I opened the small cabinet and as if to stop the bizarre storm, took a pill, in subconsciousness.

I stood up after a while, took a look at the watch. It showed 6:30 pm.

The show would start in half an hour. I knew somewhere in another world, Vicky, Subhojeet, Madhura and Deb were waiting in apprehension, but I couldn't care less.

It didn't make sense anymore.

I started walking through the cold dark road, lost in nothingness, as if high, as if doped.

I hit the highway, as I took another sleeping pill and swallowed it.

Half an hour later, I found a STD booth.

I picked up the receiver, I needed to talk to Katherine. My only friend. Tell her what happened.

My head was heavy, and it was a strain even to stand there. I dialed a wrong number. Hung up. Dialled again.

"Hello, Katherine...," I asked for her.

"Aakash?" the unknown voice enquired.

"Yes, can I talk to Katherine, please?" I begged.

"Aakash...," the voice paused, and then resumed, "I'm your mother."

LIE 059

"We're running out of time." Vicky punched the white wall of the dressing room.

Madhura was trotting round and round across the room, her mind accelerating, her heart freaking out. Subhojeet sat beside them, his face sweaty, his hand clasping the steel of the chair, and the sense of defeat finally settling in. He constantly mumbled curses, the guy who always had his reservations.

His eyes were focused, never stirring, never lost, as if captivated, as if in a trance, Deb sat quiet, transfixed in his chair, his muscles loose, his heartbeat calm, his mind silent, the timid numbness dissolved, as he urged for reason in his own way.

***

I had dialled my dad's number instead of Katherine's by mistake. But the voice on the other side froze my hand as I grasped onto the receiver with the sudden shock.

"Mom." I stammered as I said the word for the first time in my life.

There was silence on the other side of the phone. Then, finally she spoke.

Radhika Roy.

The princess of this book. My mother. The one whom I had always thought of, who my dreams were made of.

"Aakash, my son." Her voice shook and there was so much pain in it, that it terrified me.

I had a feeling almost immediately that things were coming down. That my world was crashing, I just didn't know how badly yet.

✲✲✲

It has started snowing and the darkness descend over the hill station like death...

But all my mind could register was the accelerating heartbeats, as I sprinted through HillCart Road.

The highway kept growing and there were no twists and turns or any detours. Only a steep fall of 10,000 feet... I kept up with the sprint.

I couldn't stop; I had to run all the way. The pills were lulling me into sleep but I couldn't let this brain stop buzzing. I pulled out another tablet and swallowed. I had forgotten the count. I just knew half the bottle had emptied.

Why then? Why couldn't I remove that piece of information from me, why wouldn't truth fade into a lie? Why can I not do it? Why didn't the lie work?

✲✲✲

The music stopped in the distance, some more cheers, and then finally the inevitable moment.

"Now, let's call up on stage ... guys and gals, I present ... E.N.V.Y." the host shouted to the world, in his high pitched voice.

Vicky, Madhura and Subhojeet now turned together in his direction.

Deb sat there, quiet and miles away, his train of thoughts intermingled and transluscent at the same time.

"He didn't show up." Madhura whispered as if to herself.

"He didn't come." Deb spoke for the first time in the last half an hour. "Why?" He looked up at the three of them one by one, his face plain without emotions but curious, all the same, "Why didn't he come?"

✲✲✲

"I'm sorry, son." My mother wept in earnest now and my heart thumped as the curiosity charged up.

"What is it, mom? Tell me. Tell me why didn't you call me all those years? Why didn't you let me inside your house that day at Diamond Harbor?"

I swallowed another of the tablets as my train of thoughts accelerated.

"Aakash. Come here, beta. Please come back soon. I don't have a lot of time, my love." She sobbed.

My heart sank.

"Mom?"

I never thought that I'd ever have this chance of talking to my mother in this lifetime of mine and today when I had this blessing, why had it suddenly turned into a curse? I almost knew something was wrong. Something forebode grief.

I shivered. Please, God.

I begged to the skies as I pleaded for mercy.

"What is it? Tell me, mom."

Amidst sobs and tears and static, she whispered.

"I'm dying, Aakash."

✳ ✳ ✳

My legs gave away and I fell, on my face, over some pebbles, and my eyes squinted.

I started fading out. I couldn't run anymore as I collapsed on Hill Cart Road.

"Hey, kiddo, you okay?" I heard someone running towards me.

My eyes opened for a split second, I saw the solitary moon, I remembered Katie telling me how the best flats at Darjeeling were right here on this street, where I lay dying now. How she wanted her home here. With Deb by her side.

I remembered how my mom had denied access to her house when I had cried and urged for acceptance at her gate.

How she had come for me to the hospital years ago as I had nearly escaped drowning in Port Blair.

Everything flashed back and my head was fuzzy again.

I swallowed the last pill as I broke into a fit of laughter ...

Lies ... All liess ...

Two of the things that I loved the most were getting snatched from me, and the world wanted me to obey His rules.

"Well, fuck ya!!!"

My eyes Flickered.

I was going straight to hell. I laughed.

✷ ✷ ✷

The unhinged, super-charged lady patrische entered the room, running and out of breath.

"What're you still doing here? They called out your name."

"Ma'am, please give us some more time, he hasn't showed up yet, Aakash." Vicky begged.

"There are 10,000 people out there who have payed for every single second of this show. It's your only chance. Now or never, boy."

"Ma'am, but." Madhura started.

"Stop, Maddy", Deb spoke firmly.

Madhura looked back at him, confused.

"We will perform." Deb picked up the guitar.

"But ... But." Vicky stammered.

"Don't you see it?" Deb smiled sadly, his face grieved for the first time, "He lied."

He started walking towards the stage when his cell phone rang.

Deb picked up his cell. Listened for a minute and then dropped his guitar.

"What happened?" Madhura asked, anxious and frightened.

"It's about Aakash." Deb's face had turned grim and he stuttered and his fists started shaking.

"What about him?" Vicky asked.

"He's gone into a coma."

LIE 060

"Hey, you really scared us there." It was Katie.

She sat there, her fingers entwined with mine as I lay in a cloud of white. Her face was as beautiful and as poignant as a fairy. She smiled down at me and it felt like a blessing, the best gift that god could endow me. Tufts of her hair flew and created havoc in my mind as I kept staring at her face like a boy fascinated by the white orb on a full moon night. Flawless, divine, my dream ...

"I missed you, Aakash." Katie's voice was soft and touched every vein of mine making me realise how strong a feeling true love was. A tear formed somewhere in my eye, as the image got blurred.

I blinked.

"Aakash, my son, I'm dying."

"I've always loved you, Deb, even before I knew the meaning of it."

The thoughts fluttered back and the spell broke ...

"I love you, Katie." I didn't know why I said it, or maybe it was the valium. She was surprised as she tried to process my words.

"I love you too, Aakash." she smiled, "You're my sweetest friend."

I closed my eyes.

"I love you just a bit more than that."

✳ ✳ ✳

I had never been to Shanti Niketan earlier. They say, as a kid Rabindranath Tagore didn't like classrooms. He didn't like closed spaces, restrictions, his favourite seat was just beside the window, as he would spend innumerable hours just watching the grassy fields, the clouds, the azure sky, the horizon and the infinity that lay beyond.

So, when he grew up and super rich, as he already was, he made his sorta school, those kinds, which didn't have restrictions, where classes were held in open space, under the sun and the peepal trees and where they taught you literature and cultural events where you were free, like Tagore always was. He made his window again, Vishwabharati.

I walked through the red brick porch as I heard women chant Rabindra Sangeet (the songs composed by Tagore).

I heard them sing, "Anandaloke", my favourite Rabindra Sangeet and I couldn't smile.

I grabbed my back pack, as I check the room numbers in the dormitory.

99 ... 100 ...

I sighed and prepared myself for the last goodbyes.

There was just a slight problem ... You see, rather irony ...

This was my first visit to Radhika Roy, too.

101   ...

I knocked at the door.

There was silence.

Then she answered, "Come in, Aakash."

I had cold feet. My heart thumped as a strange vibe engulfed me. I suddenly felt part of that voice and it was startling, how even after so many years of estrangement, the magnetic pull was magical.

I stepped in, and my eyes fixed on the fragile lady in bed. And, I was spell-bound by the beauty I saw.

She was still the same. Like in those old photographs and in those mom–dad stories. She wore a white chiffon saree with red border as she lay under the sheets, and a diamond pendant adorned her neck. Her forehead had creased a bit and I noticed that she had become thin, but nevertheless, the spark was there. Just like old times, I suddenly remembered, as some unseen, unfelt memories from some forgotten childhood, came rushing.

"Mom." I uttered the strange word.

Her eyes had filled up, but she wiped them almost immediately.

"Ohh, I've awaited this moment for so long now." Radhika Roy's voice was sand-papery, "It feels like my destiny."

I sat there right before her and we just looked at each other for the next few minutes. Time flew by.

Then, she smiled, "You know, you're my dream right. "

And, you've been mine for the last 15 years of my life.

"I wish I could go back in time and buy all those moments back. Relive it all you know. Life's too short. But you know that ad of master card right. Money can't buy everything." She winks trying to cheer me up.

I smiled.

"I read your book." I said after a while, "Catching Up with Time."

"So, did you like it?"

"No. It had a sad end. I hate sad ends."

She beamed, "You know, I hate them, too. Takes away all the fun. Leaves you feeling gloomy for days. I mean, why write if all you can gift the world is sadness."

"Then, why did you end the book on a sad note? Why does the protagonist, Radha, never come back in the end?"

"See, the problem with my book and with every grown up killjoy person is that by the time we hit our thirties, we're all dangled by a mess of maturity and practicality and then, all we're left with is truth."

I listened intently to her as if trying to capture and lock away all her words somewhere close to my heart.

"And ultimately, even in fiction," she smiled sadly, making a face, "life happens."

"I hate truth." I said spontaneously.

She went quiet as she watched me for some time, filled with wonder and amazement for some unknown reason and then she took my hand.

"When you write a book, Aakash, do give a happy ending." she smiled.

"Why didn't you come to me all these years?"

She gulped her tears, then she spoke softly, "Because by the time, I was over my sentimental issues and that angst with your father over his lies, I had long lost you both. My father died two years after you all left and by that time, I had decided to move on. I kept waiting for your father's call, kept waiting for him to apologise, but he never did. And, somewhere that little ego of ours ruined what otherwise could've been a beautiful tale. I did my Ph.D. from the United States, came back to Calcutta and became a professor at Shanti Niketan. I was preoccupied in this bubble life of mine, I was complacent with settling in a world without my sweet heart." she kissed my face.

She sighed with grief, "I was so wrong, Aakash. Today, when I lie here dying, I realise that I could've spent my entire life just beholding you ..."

She coughed and the stark fear hit me. She choked for a second as she gasped for breath.

I panicked, but she held my hand tightly and smiled even in her pain.

"Nothing to fear, Aakash. You've the entire world to win. I can see it, son."

I looked at her face, and knew that she could actually believe what she said. As if she knew things that nobody did.

"Hmmm ... We're getting all mushy here." She tried to sit up, but failed. There was a fraction of disappointment, but she was really good at hiding her emotions, I noticed.

"You know how Anshuman proposed to me?"

I shook my head and shrugged. How little I knew about my parents.

"He planted this entire garden of roses in front of our house at early dawn." She broke into giggles like a ten-year-old kid, as she blushed, "He was so dumb." She closed her eyes and giggled some more, "He was really so cute, you know."

I nodded, my eyes glistening with tales that I had never heard.

"What about you, huh?", Her face suddenly brightened up, "You got a crush?? A girl friend?", She winked.

"Nopes." I shrugged and she broke into laughter again.

"Shy, are you? Like your dad." Her face was glowing with this happiness, it dazzled me.

I kept quiet.

"Hey, you know, I've something for your … Um … Letme see." she pondered for a moment while unhooking her diamond pendant, "How do I explain this to a fifteen-year-old kid?!"

We looked at each other in utter confusion, then finally she placed the pendant in my hand.

"This is for your wife." She looked at me hopefully, "You like it?"

"Mom, but, I … I don't have a wife!!"

She broke into another fit of laughter.

"Someday, you'll have one." She brushed my hair.

I blushed, for minute the world and the fears had taken a back seat.

"Come here, son." She hugged me and held me close as we went to sleep.

✷✷✷

"It's time." The nurse said.

My dad kissed mom one last time and before she even tried to speak, he stormed out.

A tear drop shone on her cheek as she looked at me.

"Come here." She whispered.

She grasped my fingers and said, "Ohh, Aakash, remember you're my dream boy. When in trouble, come back home, son."

She was finding it difficult to breathe and it made her cry.

She looked at me and I looked back and she urged me to lie.

"It's going to be fine, mom."

✷✷✷

Dad cried hugging me. He shouted and yelped.

"I am so sorry, Aakash!" Dad sobbed and wept as he shivered with me in his arms.

"I want her back," he pleaded, "please."

I couldn't cry. I didn't know why. I had gone numb.

I walked alone, the necklace dangled in my hand, and the world was all dark.

I wished I could end mom-dad story happily too … make them live a little more … give them one more shot at life … But there were no happy endings … Life was always like that.

VOLUME 4

Pune Diaries

LIE 061

Prologue to the 4ᵗʰ Volume.

"This changes everything." Robbie can't stop smiling.

I nodded, trying my best to fake a smile.

"Aakash," Robbie actually broke into a nerd-dance, "we're gonna be famous, bro."

I raised my glass to him.

Then, I took another sip of the poison.

I needed a lot of alcohol to do this.

"You know," Robbie too took a swig, "I never thought we could achieve this. And, you always did, man!! I respect you, friend. You are the best thing."

And then, he came and hugged me.

It caught me off guard, and I tried to free myself but he was too drunk to notice.

He wept on my shoulder.

"You made me realise my dream, Aakash. God bless you, yaar." he said with such honesty that it stung me.

"Naah", I made another glass of the strong vodka for him, and then slipped the small capsule inside as I handed it over to him.

"No blessings here, Robbie." I laughed at my own self, "I'm too rotten for anything as optimistic as a blithe."

"No man!!" Robbie was not convinced as he sipped the drink, "You know what!! I agree to disagree."

We both broke into fits of laughter.

"We'll be famous, man! We'll change the world." Robbie whispered as he fell flat on the floor, unconscious, The adulterated vodka spilled over the ground.

"Yeah, bro, that we will." I lied to him one last time.

I looked at my watch. I didn't have much time.

I tiptoed to his desk; his laptop screen was on, unlocked. He was just using it, minutes back.

I wrote the commands.

The last file got deleted 10 seconds later.

Then, I opened the bottom shelf of his drawer.

The last CD titled, "MINDMAP", lay there in the cabinet, with all those thousand mathematical equations and logic diagrams.

I picked them up and out came the cigarette lighter.

I set it all ablaze, as Robbie's dreams fade into dust.

I looked at Robbie for the last time as he lay snoring on the floor, beside the ashes of his hard work.

"So long, my friend."

It felt cold but the monster in me was furious. The monster killed the last remains of Aakash that night. As I left the country that night, I left the old me too...forever.

LIE 062

"Is...," I couldn't breathe, it was suffocating me from inside. "Is Katherine home?"

"Aakash." Mr Dennis Andrews was evidently frightened by my hyper ventilation, "is everything okay?"

I didn't respond. I felt nauseated and my hands were red where I had the pendant clutched stiff. I was swaying on his door, like a drunkard lunatic.

Katherine came running down the stairs even before Mr Dennis could understand of the present dilemma.

"Aakash, finally," she started even before she noticed me, "I thought I won't see you before ..."

Katherine stopped in front of me; I can see it in her eyes, immediate fear and worry.

She grabad my hand and walked me to the field where we would sit everyday.

"What is it, Aakash?" Her voice strained with trepidation, as I shivered.

I can't say it. I just can't.

She's no more.

It's so hard, to live without that little fragment of hope that someday, a guardian angel would come knocking at your door and hug all your tears away.

Katherine shook me, as I swayed.

"Aakash!" she screamed trying to hold me as I cowered on the grass.

"I can't do it, Kates", I looked at her, as if begging of her to save me from this curse. "I can't cry."

I shuddered as if in a frenzy.

"Here," Katherine's palms closed on my face, "Aakash, Aakash, focus. Look here."

I heard her as if from very far as my brain got fuzzy.

"I'm right here, Aakash. Nothing to fear, Aakash. Calm down.", she said all panicky.

"I can't cry, Katherine," I plead, "Please, make me cry. Just one tear."

And then, she held me. She hugged me so tight I felt her there.

Mom ...

"Don't Aakash. It's okay Aakash. breathe."

And then I cried.

I shouted and wept and couldn't stop.

We stayed there, in one another's arms, for eternity, as she let me free.

***

We sat at the café nearby the entire afternoon. I didn't say a word. I was lost.

And she never asked.

She just sat by my side, her hand holding mine.

People came and went and the questions remained unanswered.

Katherine just kept looking at me, sad and tearful.

My thoughts were confused, my mom, all her stories, her last few minutes with me. It played in a loop.

I tried to escape from my thonghts but could not. So I looked at Katherine, as she sat there, gloomy and honest as only a true friend could be.

I felt her hand in mine for the first time in the afternoon, and I know I couldn't thank her enough.

"I want you to have this." I said after so long that it jolted Katherine.

"Huh?" she looked at me, confused, then her eyes followed where I pointed and it set over the small diamond pendant.

"Aakash?" Katherine didn't understand, "Whose is this?"

"It used to be my mother's. It's her last souvenir that I got." I shrugged.

Katie moans as she suddenly realizes the truth, and covers her mouth as her eyes well up.

I looked at her. The mascara in her eyes scatters around as the tears came. I pressed her hand, and shake my head.

"Don't Katherine." I hushed her, "Don't".

"I'm sorry Aakash." she said between quiet sobs.

"Just keep it with you", I hand her the pendant, as she refuses.

"I'm sorry. I can't. ", she refused, "It's hers. It means a lot Aakash. I can't have it. She gave it to you."

"But see there lies the problem," I said, "she is killing me Katherine. I can't hold on to her every moment. This..", I looked at the pendant with anger, "this makes it so damn difficult for me to lie to myself."

"I don't understand Aakash. It's her last gift you've got. You can't just give it away.", Katherine protested.

"It's a constant reminder Katherine," I exclaimed with pain, "And I don't want the reality to sink in anymore. Lies...are all I need now."

My voice was firm and I could sense her worries but I was sure...my journey had begun.

Hell was calling....

"Lies Katherine," I couldn't even recognise my voice as hatred and self pity made me vicious, "Lies are my objective reality."

And I gave it away to Katherine.

My mom's last memories too.

We walked back to her home.

At her porch, she looked back at me, came closer and kissed me on the cheek.

"Take care of yourself Aakash."

She sighed as her eyes tried to hold on to me. Her glow was long gone and I could sense a sadness building somewhere. She opened her mouth to say something, and then stoped.

"I am sorry Aakash. Hope you forgive me."

I didn't understand her.

Then she pulled the pendant out of her pocket, "And I know you'd want it back someday Aakash. I'd be there to give it back to you. I'd come for you Aakash. It's a promise."

"I have to go now Katherine." It was twilight and I felt weak and shattered.

"Just promise you'll forgive me."

I nodded, still lost. I didn't know what she was talking about, but I didn't ask. I had no more strength in me.

I left her standing at her porch.

I had no idea then that unconsciously, I had lied again.

P.S. *I would never forgive Katherine for what she did next.*

LIE 063

I woke up to the dark night.

It was 4 am.

I had got accustomed to waking up everyday at that time.

Memories of Katie flooded back and the sudden events of the last few days clotted my head.

I moved to the wash basin and washed my face. Then, I looked at myself.

And, for the first time in my life, it felt like staring back at a stranger.

Dad had fallen asleep on his sofa. I saw a photo frame he had in his folded arms as he snored.

I tiptoed to my room.

I had nothing to do.

No Katie, no mom, no Rockstars, no dreams.

I settled with the silence of the sullen morning.

***

The entire class was staring at me.

I felt like I was back in standard one. I felt like the weird kid again. There were hushed gossips, revolving around me.

I was the topic of every lunch discussion; strangers walked up to me and offered me condolences. They knew my sad story, although most of them had no clues of my existence a day back.

Katherine was absent that day in school. So was Robbie.

What came as a shocker was that every teacher in the class already knew the fact; they didn't even call out the two roll numbers.

Pre-meditated skip.

The absence of Katherine beside me led the awkwardness and loneliness.

"Hey, Aakash." It was Deb.

I refused even to glance back at him, forget replies.

I kept staring at the floor, trying to be oblivious of his presence around me. Anyways, he just grabbed the next bench.

"Hey, bro," he called again, his voice at its soft-best, this time there was a small tap on my shoulder.

"Yup." I gave up my attempts at nirvana and faced him. Deb looked at me with a serious and sincere expression, "Really sorry about what happened."

I shrugged. "Me, too. I mean, about the whole Rockstars thing. I'm really sorry I wasn't there."

"Dude," Deb was appalled, "You were not there because you were in a coma for heaven's sake. I mean, please don't apologise."

I nodded.

"And, I felt so bad we were not there when you needed us the most." Deb continued, "You had to live with the news alone while we were out somewhere else on a stupid show."

"Yes, but still …" I had to say this somewhere, "I feel bad it had to end like this."

"We all do, Aakash." Deb said softly, "But not for the show, for you. I mean, you never showed up because you had just got that call and god knows how shattered you must've been." He paused, "Let's not go into that. I'm here to tell you that we're all here for you, man … every single minute from now on."

I didn't know how to respond to Deb's generosity. Somewhere I knew that even earlier when I had got that call from my mom that night, I had already decided not to be on the final performance.

Somewhere, only I knew that my reasons for not being there at the finals of Rockstars were already determined when I had lost my love. When I had lost Katie. It had nothing to do with the news of my mom that I had received later in the evening when I had already taken all the sleeping pills.

But now the realisation dawned that my group E.N.V.Y. had no idea of that fact. How they had all come to believe the lie that the events of the night had forged for the world.

Deb patted me on my head as the bell rang declaring the end of the recess. He got up to leave, then he turned back and said, "Hey, mind if I sit with you from now on?"

"Er, dude" I was reluctant, "I was kinda saving it for Katherine, you know," I explained, "Katie."

Deb was awestruck, "You don't know?", He stuttered, "She didn't tell you?"

"What?" my heart hammered.

"Katherine Andrews", Deb swallowed, "She has left the school."

"Sorry?" My high pitched voice suddenly silenced the entire cacophony of the students as they stared at me in confusion.

"Yeah, man!" Deb squeaked, "They left the city, Aakash. They're gone."

✳ ✳ ✳

I sprinted through the lanes of 24 Parganas, to spot Katie's pink and blue house.

I couldn't breathe as I reached for the door.

I stopped. The lock shone mocking at me, as my jaws dropped.

"No," I screamed, "No, no, no, no, no."

This couldn't have happened.

Katie's voice reverberated in my head, "Just promise me you'll forgive me, Aakash."

I hit the door with all my strength.

My knuckles bruised and the sprain tore me up.

And then, it hit me. Katherine had disowned me forever. She was gone too, just like everybody else whom I loved in my life.

Her door was closed too, like the innumerable doors that I couldn't peep through anymore.

It felt suffocating, the sudden realisation.

I walked back injured and alone, to my favorite place for the last time. The grass field, the small pond, the sunset and Sabbith, the dog.

I didn't remember how long I sat there alone, estranged from the universe, but it was long enough to dry up the Aakash who had broken into tears just a day back.

LIE 064

Meteorites …

The result of the board exam turned out pretty good. I finished with a decent 90 percent, while Deb topped, 6% ahead in the race. And then came the summer vacation, then the rains. The winter hit somewhere down the line and the first few months of higher secondary went unnoticed. I had lost track of time and life.

Deb, Madhura and Subhojeet would make futile efforts pleading me to get back into the band every once in a while. Deb would make endeavours at even being my best bud. I ended up getting calls from even Vicky and Pritish … But the enthusiasm had packed its bag and left. The inspiration was someone else's now and I had dissolved into nothingness.

There were days I woke up in a pile of books that I had planned to study but with not one page turned. I was going down. I had chosen computer science as my additional subject, and that turned out to be the only subject that captured my attention. I liked C, in a nerdy way! I liked making infinite loops and ending up in messes and then pressing the exit button. I loved recursions and the goto function, It was non linear, unbound and limitless.

I neither had a lot of hopes back then, nor friends. I had become reserved, more covert than ever. I would muse all the time and the world mattered no more. Teachers who once considered me brilliant started giving up the faith and moved on. I became neglected, another failed story, another needle in the haystack.

I fared real badly in Class 11th. I almost flunked in two subjects, and my overall aggregate was a meagre 60. It was computer science that saved my ass. I had scored 95 in that subject, the highest, and that surprised and shocked a few. I was the one who had got the shocker!

I couldn't recollect the nights that I had spent learning C and C++. All I remembered was "Iwoz", a book about Steve Wozniac and Steve Jobs and how their company, Apple Inc. started in a garage. At some mornings, it felt haunting to look at the notes and the programs that I had etched unmindfully. It was an unfamiliar feeling, as if I had started losing my edge.

Class 12th came on like a tempest with all these forms of JEE's and AIEEE exams. Dad had been really disappointed with my 11th mark sheet and he could still see a lot of potential in his young kid, which the kid had no clue of. So, he enrolled me into this institution called YUKTI that would guide me through the entire examination debacle. What followed next was intense shopping of heavy books that I was assured would end up sold at some grocery store, neat and unread.

Although his section had changed because he had pursued Biology in Class 11th, Deb would often meet me in the corridors or the playgrounds. He would invite me to all this cultural activities and sometimes even compel me to attend the functions. He would earnestly try to be my "best friend", but Katherine had done an impeccable job at that and somehow that quota was filled for infinity in my life.

At times, Deb would discuss Katie Thomas with me. It felt absurd to measure the intensity with how much I still loved that girl who was in some other world now, talking to her boy friend every night, love struck.

I failed in three subjects in the mid-terms that year. However, I had again topped in computer science with a perfect cent.

Dad took me to counselling sessions and even tried to have round table discussions with me at dinner. But all he got as an acknowledgement was silence.

Anshuman Roy silenced after that. He too, joined my league and turned into a pessimist.

*** * ***

"Hey, Aakash," Deb spotted me at the cafeteria and came running, "How've you been, pal?"

"Aweful", I sipped the black coffee.

Deb would do this every few weeks. Catch up on me like we were some great friends who had a lot in common. He was right, considering the person we both loved.

"Hey, Katie likes it, too", Deb stared at the drink with an amused expression.

"Maybe, that's where I started," I gulped some more of the strong caffeine, trying not to think of Katie's beautiful face.

"Okay, dude, so here's the thing. I have managed to get registered in the next season of Rockstar and MTV seems to have forgotten how we had ditched them in the final performance last time. So, I guess we still have a chance to make the magic happen again. Back to Darjeeling!"

I kept quiet and concentrated on the table fan that produced a blatant jangle.

"So ...?" Deb was excited, as he looked at me hopefully "What say Andaman boy? Maddy and Subhojeet are all in. They all want you to be our lead singer and make us win. How about another shot at this?"

I shrugged and took the last sip.

"Nope."

"What?"

"NOO," I nearly screamed, "Have I made myself clear?"

Deb was aghast as the whole cafeteria went quiet.

"Aakash bro," Deb's hand was at my shoulder, "What is the matter, dude? Relax. It's okay. Let's think this through buddy what say?"

"Fuck off, Deb," I jerked away his hand.

Deb's face lost its colour.

"May I know the reason of such retaliation at an old friend?" Deb's voice was heavy.

"How many do you want? You back stabber", I lost it finally, "Why don't we just start with Katie, the girl whom I loved and whom you snatched away from me."

"Wait a minute," Deb's face contorted with shock, "What?"

"Yes, you asshole," I continued, "I loved her, dammit, and it all remained because you had lied to Madhura that first night of the stay when you said you and Katie had nothing like love. You lied Deb and that one lie ruined my life. Just because you had the looks you got the girl, you became the face of E.N.V.Y. and you get hero worshipped everyday."

Deb went white as he tried to process my statement.

"And you know what, Deb", I laughed hysterically now and for a minute it gave me a feeling of the melodramatic actors, "remember the final night when I didn't show up. It was not because of my mom's news."

I paused for him to think and after 10 seconds he realised.

"You avenged your love," he whispered in shock.

"It was always personal, Deb."

Deb stood there petrified as the crowd looked on, anxiously anticipating a fight.

"Why didn't you tell me?", Deb's face unfortunately still had no sign of hatred, only a strong disappointment.

"Because I don't share stories with my enemies." I grunted.

Deb was no enemy, it was just plain jealousy, but the blinded me had exploded. That moment, I could've dragged a knife down Deb and not regretted, such was the fury of the monster.

Deb looked at me appalled one last time.

"I never thought our friendship would end this way." Then he sighed, "But I'm really sorry Aakash ... I love Katie and it stays." Deb walked out after that.

"I love Katie more", I threw the empty paper cup away.

LIE 065

"I have got the forms of WBJEE for you. You could take a shot at that. It's easier and you get to stay at Calcutta with me." Dad smiled stressing on the last few words, as he passed the mixed vegetable.

I nodded as I ate, my eyes on the plate.

Three minutes of silence.

"Things at work haven't been going good", dad's voice had a tinge of sadness, "and by the looks of it, I guess that's your story, too."

I shrugged.

Dad opened his mouth twice, and then shut back. Then, finally he spoke.

"I just want you to know, Aakash", Anshuman Roy said, "Together we could be a great team and soon, we'll get out of this rough patch, son", he brushed my hair as my eyes moistened a bit, but they dried before I even blinked.

***

School had become a constant source of torment. I was loathed, avoided and cursed everywhere. It felt as if I had somehow offended a Bengali cult god or something! Students used my name as a definition of backstabber. And, what could be more enraging! News had it that Deb Roy had left the school band. Somehow people were smart enough to do the math and get me into the equation.

The last one month of class 12, I bunked school and studied at home.

More or less doing nothing that is.

I remained in my room idling, reading junk software gadgets magazines that had no relations to my present course or watching movies.

The board exams sucked to the core.

I kept on guessing answers and writing gibberish in most of the papers.

I even feared that I might flunk in mathematics.

Then was the turn of the IIT's.

On the morning of the exam, dad drove me to this Hanuman temple before leaving me to the Centre of the examination.

He put this turmeric paste's 'teeka' on my forehead, made me eat coconut bits as the prashad, and wished me luck.

As I stood there, my palms folded, my eyes closed, facing the son of the winds, my head was still jammed with my mom, Katherine and Katie and everything that I didn't want to think about ...

And, I prayed for a different life.

✹ ✹ ✹

Around one hour into the exam, and I had already declared defeat. Forget answers, I could not figure out the questions.

I left the Centre and i walked through the Calcutta streets.

So much had changed since the day I first came into this city, my birthplace. I was walking beside Maidan, the place which my mom–dad had turned into a rendezvous when they had fled 18 years ago.

I could see the tower of Victoria Palace far in the horizon.

Calcutta had everything for me, everything except love.

AIEEE started off pretty well, I got stuck at one numerical and wasted ten minutes. Finally, I gave the sum up and hurried through the next. That left me puzzled over that, too. I was frustrated now and my focus kept on getting weaker. Soon, I was in a soup.

The exam left dad and me stranded for a week. He was tensed with my career now, I could tell. He was preparing for the worse.

The next week I gave WBJEE.

✹ ✹ ✹

I got disqualified in the iit - JEE exams.

AIEEE, I managed to get 125 marks, out of 320. Pretty bad. WBJEE, I scored well, getting 165 out of 200. It assured me a good college in the city.

Dad was happy with my WBJEE results and got me all the forms of the best colleges in the city. He also started looking for a bigger flat near Techno India College, a very famous private institution in West Bengal. He wouldn't care even if it meant that he will have to switch two locals to his office every morning. The man was excited with the fact that his son was finally growing up.

I filled my forms and finally got a college.

✳✳✳

Dad was really happy that day for his boss had assured him a raise in the coming months. He came home clutching packets of roshogollas and samosas.

He made tea and sat at the table, inviting me to join him.

He kept humming some Kishore Kumar song and savouring the snacks. I told him my decision and showed him my acceptance letter to the college.

"But you said...," Dad kept repeating, re reading the papers, his voice pleading, "I have already settled for the rent and that flat is really nice, it's a 2 bhk."

Dad left fifteen minutes later. He returned at around midnight and was drunk, I could tell.

Two weeks later, I left for Pune.

I had chosen MIT (Maharashtra Institute of Technology), Pune.

I wanted a different life, even if it meant breaking my dad's heart.

LIE 066

Pune Diaries....

Never been to the western parts of the country before, so when the plane started bumping and shifting, throttling through the clouds and the air pockets caused due to the extremely low air pressure, I realised that the western ghats were finally here and that in about 5 minutes we were going to land.

Pune looked less crowded than Calcutta, which turned out wrong eventually after it got ranked with the highest number of automobiles in the country.

It was cold outside, much cooler than Calcutta as I walked to the auto stand. Out of habit, I spoke in Bengali. However, the rickshaw driver realised the destination (names sound the same in any language) and asked for 350 rupees to get me to Kothrud. He asked a sum of 200 more than the real price but well, the stranger in the city was new in town and it was the autowaala's day today!

My father did not accompany me to Pune. He did not even come to drop me off to the airport. Maybe, he was bad with goodbyes, or maybe, it was just his disappointment and my lies that had enraged him. I didn't care.

I wanted the solitude and was satisfied with the silence I had to share now. Pune ... MIT, was my choice. I took it. Now, I was going to face it. Deal with it my way.

And, there were faces I knew I would never see again. I closed my eyes and they flashed again like a slide show. I opened and realised how wrong I was.

We crossed FC Road, I caught a glimpse of a Garware square. Then, it took a right on the next square, and then straight it marched towards Kothrud.

"Where in Kothrud shall I drop you?"

"Um ... MIT Collge of Engineering ... the one with."

"Say no more ...", the rickshaw driver smiled, "Another student, eh? Which year?"

"First. Came for the admission procedure."

"*bahutich padhai karenge yahanpe*", he said, in a strong Mumbai accent, which made me giggle, but I controlled myself.

"Yeah ... studies are all I have in mind!" I said sarcastically as I took in the fresh air.

My eyes focused on a girl and it was an instantaneous glimpse, but it startled me. I felt as if I had seen a ghost. Someone I had known earlier. She passed me like a gust of wind in some vehicle and I could not place her.

I focused back on the road.

MIT Pune looked like another big private institution, tens of buildings collaged together, leaving small places for lawns and trees, vibrancies of streams popping everywhere. Diploma, engineering, business, foreign studies and random others. It felt like a fete out here.

I carried my huge bags with me, dragging them to the college office built on the ground floor of the college library.

There were a few students over there. I was two days late, so I guessed that most of the students had already been enrolled.

A tall short-haired guy stood at the front desk talking to the receptionist in a pleading voice that had a slight hint of fury into it.

"Sir, please look at my certificates. I have been a topper for the last 6 years. Here is my AIEEE marksheet. I deserve the seat in MIT hostel based on my merit. They had assured me over the phone."

The lanky chipmunk looking receptionist was disinterested, as he kept looking at the computer screen at a video in Youtube on mute chewing tobacco. It appeared like he had noticed the small hint of fury, too.

"Sir?" the student asked desperately.

"NO. CAN'T DO", the receptionist shuffled the pages on his desk and smiled at another lady down the corridor, oblivious of the student who held his marksheets with frustration.

"Um", I intervened with my admission forms.

The disinterested receptionist stared at me with such disgust, I double checked if I was stinking.

Then, he glanced at the watch. 1:30.

"Lunch." he yawned, "Come later."

"Oh, okay", I started to turn, when the topper spoke, "But that's half an hour from now ... at 2." he protested.

"Dammit!", I said under my breath, as the receptionist flared flames.

"Are you teaching me rules?" he shouted, deafening us, "You know what! Come tomorrow. Office closed!"

"But that's", the tall duffer silenced abruptly as I stared at him with anger.

"Sir, please don't do that. I need admission today because I have nowhere to stay and I need the college hostel. I apologise on his behalf."

The bloke looked baffled.

"Well, let me burst your bubble then, snowflake." the receptionist said annoyed, "The hostel is already full. No more seats. Look somewhere else."

It took me another half an hour of persuasion that ended in rejection and a bout of anger as I stomped out of the office.

The topper was still there, as he followed me outside.

"They are liars. Someone must've paid more money to get those rooms, I tell you." He said from behind.

"And, who asked you again?" I retaliated gifting him my cold gaze, as he silenced.

"I was just trying to help." he defended himself.

"I saw how that worked miracles for me." I shouted at him.

"Back off, man!" He was pissed now, "Just tried to help you sir ... I've had the same problem. Now, I have taken up an old room on my own without roommates and will have to pay the entire rent of ten thousand out of my pocket money because of this idiot receptionist. I'm not in some seventh heaven right now, so buzz off."

"You buzz off." I spat.

"I'm outta here." he was gone instantly.

"Great start", I told myself.

*** ✳ ✳ ✳

I ate a double egg roll at Faaso's in the afternoon. Then, my enquiry for hotels at the neighbourhood began. The prices chilled me to the bone.

By the evening I was tired, exhausted and nauseated. I needed help and I needed it immediately.

And then, I saw the only student I knew around the entire place. It imploded like a cracker. The only genuine idea!!

"Hey, topper!!" I shouted at the top of my voice.

The tall bloke stopped at the distance. He was having a glass of cold coffee in a crowded dull looking café.

Durga Café. I ran to him.

"Hey, there bro." I stretched out my hand.

"Bro?" He looked at my face with amusement.

"Hey, about earlier. No offence intended. Can we just forget that and be friends?", I said, shrewdly.

"Um." He scratched his brow and sipped the coffee.

I made a puppy-eyed face. That always worked.

"Alright. What do you want?" The guy sighed.

"Well, I wanna be your roommate!" I beamed with the offer.

"Ohh", his face glowed as he considered the idea.

"But then again." He calculated, "What's your name, again?"

"Aakash Roy" I shook his hand again.

"Bengali?!! Non-veg!!" the guy backed off, "Sorry, no non-veg allowed."

"Ohh, but I'm not a non-veg, Pure veg man!!", The omlette-wrapped roll formed a savoury image in my mind as I lied.

"What? Bengali veg? that's new ...", He chuckled suspiciously.

"No, honestly. Never tasted a non-veg dish in my life."

"How come?"

"Um ... allergy." I made up another stupid one.

"Drinking? Smoking?"

"None Sir!! I'm clean." I reassured him.

He pondered some more.

"Um ... 5 thousand ... okay?" He finally said, taking another sip.

"Done." I said, "I'm thirsty. Can I have a sip?"

"Get your glass." He hid his glass comically, "And, I'm Sunny Lodha."

LIE 067

The initiation of boredom ...

I opened my new empty diary, the new add gel pen stuck to my lips, my eyes were on the board. Applied Science.

Ten minutes later, I zoomed back to focus at the board, the diary still empty, the pen still stuck motionless, my eyelids heavy.

The last bench was a safe place and I was attracted to it right on the first day of my college. My eyes scanned the alienated congregation, the unusual faces, the new flock. I saw Sunny Lodha right on the first bench, jotting down notes, concentrating on the blackboard, his lips whispering the answers as the teacher wrote them down on the board. My eyes wandered to the girl's row, the species surprisingly with a higher degree of fashion sense than those back in school, most of them over styled for college, in fact, even for parties. A girl had brought a Gucci bag to college. I kept looking for BMW car-keys in her desk.

My eyes moved to the last bench on the left side of the class. A short thin bloke had his head flat over the desk, in deep slumber. He had this smile over his face as he slept which could only equate for an angel-filled dream. It provided a certain absurd sense of confidence in me. I was not the only one bored after all. The next lecture was equally sleep inducing. It could put me into a coma. I kept on sipping water just to sit upright and focus on the mathematical sums of quadratic equations.

"Nitish Agarwal." the woman professor stopped abruptly at the twentieth minute of her morose choir. It suddenly brought me back from my somnolent state.

My eyes followed the professor's gaze, I had guessed rightly. The sleeping boy on the last bench was the accused. He has been spotted. The shepherd had picked the black sheep of the day.

But it hardly mattered to the kid who was fast asleep. If listened, you could hear him snore rhythmically. The class was dumb struck, silently observing Nitish. "Nitish Aggarwal." the woman shouted at the top of her voice. Nitish shifted in his seat, then slowly his red eyes opened. The first person he saw was me, who was directly on the opposite last bench to him. He sat upright, then stood up slowly, scratching his head.

"Er … is there a problem, professor?"

"Why don't you tell us that, Nitish? Looks like mathematics is either a useless subject for you or you must've misinterpreted my lecture as a lullaby."

"But, of course not." defended the wavering boy, "Mathematics is poetic and your lecture is music to the ears."

Students gaped at the randomness of the reply and it was a shocker no less for me, too.

"I would've counted on your words, Nitish." The teacher replied, "but the problem is that your recent actions don't quite set the foundations for your statement."

"Oh, that has nothing to do with the present situation. In fact." Nitish's eyes does a quick scan of the blackboard, "quadratic is an old favourite of mine."

"Why don't you prove your point this once and I'll consider your prior explanation." The professor kept the chalk over her table, as she pointed at the problem on the board. "What are the values of x and y? Tell me now, or explain your situation to the principal later."

I reread the question on the blackboard. If the lady had noticed my disinterest in class, the next victim could be me. For assurance, I was definite that Mr sleepy head was looking at a week's suspension at the least.

I was in the "given conditions" phase of my answer when Nitish's voice cut through the silent classroom. "x = 5, y = 8".

I looked up and for the first time Sunny Lodha turned his head at the back bencher. I saw in his face a similar expression as to that of the professor's wrinkled face. And, I knew Nitish was correct.

Nitish beamed, while the professor picked up the chalk.

"Wash your face and get back." was all she could say.

Nitish nodded as he left the herd amazed.

***

"That guy is a bloody genius." I said through my half-filled mouth.

Sunny and I were having lunch at the college canteen, Chandralok Garden. The food was spiced up and oily, and the chewing gum paneer was a revelation.

"Yeah, sleeping on the second lecture like that. He, sure, has some brains", Sunny Lodha squirmed mixing the gravy with the jeera rice.

"He was asleep even in the first lecture." I pointed out. Sunny shrugged.

"The teachers are good though." Sunny said, "How was your first day, Aakash?"

"Lots of lights and fans in the class." was all I could manage.

"You missed the first two weeks. Bound to happen." Sunny gulped down the gulab jamun, "But don't worry, You'll pick up soon. Not that hard."

"Hey," I scratched my brow, "I was really thinking of taking the day off. I've this headache."

"Right on your first day, Aakash?" Sunny looked at me with disappointment.

"Yeah ... I couldn't sleep that well last night ... so".

"Yeah ... happens", Sunny commented, "You must be missing your parents or something."

"Yeah," I added, "That must be it! So, will you do me a favour?"

"Yeah ... what's that?"

"Um ... Sunny ... today in class I noticed that all the profs would do is pass on this sheet of attendance record and all we had to do is sign on it. So, my roll number is 85073 ... if you could..."

"What?" Sunny looked at me in disgust, "Proxy ... on the first day? They cross-check, Aakash."

"Not always." I retorted.

"But dude ... That's wrong."

"Oh, what's the harm, man?"

"You're gonna lag behind, Aakash. That's the harm. You don't want that do you? I mean, I can get notes for you. We can sit in classes together, man. But bunking and proxys, that's not good dude." Sunny was trying hard to talk some sense into me.

I sighed.

"So?" He asked me pleadingly.

"Useless you are." I stood up and left.

✳ ✳ ✳

"Hey, bong."

I turned to face the thin short genius.

"I have a friend in class. He will mark your attendance. Tell me your roll number again."

"Ohh ... er ... 85073."

"Cool then." Nitish messaged his roll number and mine to some other guy, then beamed and started to leave.

"Hey ...You bunking?" I asked him from behind.

"Too." he winked back at me, "I've a headache in earnest. The vodka was strong."

"You were drunk today morning in class?" I said in utter disbelief.

"Nah ... that I was until 3 am ... it's been the hangover ever since. " Nitish chuckled and strolled off. I could see him sway a bit.

He had had one too many.

LIE 068

New Territory

I woke up on the floor. My head ached as if it had been hammered. My eyes dwindled and my throat was sore, as if even the air has been choked out of it. I squinted at the sunshine through the curtains. I looked at the table clock in my room. It was 1:30 pm. Dammit! I had missed class again. I tried to stand up but staggered and fell.

What in the name of the devil!

A sudden urge to puke jolted my empty stomach and I stirred.

Sunny.

I looked around the empty room, then managed to sit up. There was a bottle of water a foot away.

I sipped the liquid. It's O.R.S. The cold liquid ran through my intestines and I regained my senses. I picked up the phone.

31 missed calls.

Dad - 21

Sunny - 9

Nitish - 1

I looked at the date … bloody hell … It was not Wednesday … it was Thursday already. Had I been sleeping for two days! What the hell had happened? I closed my eyes and strained to think back.

***

Tuesday   ...

I attended the first two classes. Fell asleep in the third, bunked the last 4 lecs.

Bunking was fun.

Even strolling around the campus felt good when you were out of the class, skipping lectures. It was some sort of a declaration of freedom and triumph of malice over honesty.

MIT's library lacked novels ... They had the best collection of Pearson publications, Wiley and Harper & Collins but lacked Penguin and Rupa or Bloomsbury.

I left the library when I realised I was actually utilising my bunk-time.

I was a tourist and the whole city was penning down a welcome note for me. I took a bus, and landed at JM Road. Walked straight towards a big shopping complex, and stopped at Pune Central. Another hour of window shopping and then I headed towards E-Sqr. It was a multiplex with around five screens that was currently showing all the recent releases. Another hour of a vagabond's life, and I was back to square one.

It was around five in the evening that I stopped at Café Coffee Day for a cappuccino and some more self-introspection.

"Hey, Bong." the familiar lazy voice poked me from behind.

"Hey, Nitish, bunking class again?"

"Well what can I say ... You inspire me." He chuckled.

He sat alone on a chair by the corner, a small diary open, an ink pen kept at its tip.

He sipped some more coffee. "This bloody headache is a curse, I tell you."

"You've been drinking?" I didn't mean to trespass on his personal addictions, but the reply was spontaneous.

He chuckled, "Yeah ... some things don't change now ... do they?"

He rose from his seat and took the couch next to mine.

"What is that?" I pointed to his diary. He snapped the diary close in an instant.

"Jokes." he smiled.

I nodded analysing the lie.

"So, how come you're this far from your city? No good colleges back at Calcutta?", The change in topic was fluent for Nitish.

"I'm fleeing." I replied pouring some more sugar in the never-getting-sweet coffee.

"Oh ... join the league." Nitish shrugged.

"What are you running away from?"

He looked straight at me and then his eyes turned cold as if a steel knife had just been sharpened behind them, "Nothingness."

I nodded, already perplexed.

"Chuck it ... this ain't gonna work." He picked up his coffee cup. From his pocket a small bottle came out. He poured the liquor into the coffee as I gaped at him.

He sips, squints then sighs with relief, "ahh ... heaven".

"What's your story?" I was really curious now but he was a closed book.

"Not really a nice way of introduction, I believe." he looked at me skeptically.

"What's your take?" I retorted.

"Alright." His face lit up. "Let me introduce you to my kinda party. Everything else will be self explanatory."

✱✱✱

"Aakash." Sunny was deafening me with his screams, "You lied to me!!"

Somebody gag him!

He shook me as I opened my eyes to a blurred imagery. Can't control the urge.

I puked all over the tall guy as he backed up and I hit the thick ground.

"Arghhh." Sunny screamed.

"Ouch." I massaged my scalp as I faded away.

✱✱✱

I had never had hookah before. Was not fascinated with the idea, too. Frankly, I was never into the gang of experimenting–addictive – philosophical–chutzpah brats. There was a control freak in me somewhere.

But what happened when a superfast wave collided with a pebble with some motivated inertia?

Nitish was not just a fast processor when it came to mathematics, he knew the equations of manipulation way too well.

And, a little push was enough for the defender in me to declare defeat.

We sat at Co2 Club, a filled hookah beside us, loud music growling through the ears, the bass resonating through the heartbeats.

"Tell me what you read, Aakash?" Nitish shouted over the psychedelic music.

"C ... C++ ... Dennish Ritchi." I said over a swig of smoke.

The hookah was mint flavoured and felt refreshing.

"Read Osho, my friend." Nitish dismissed my reading interests with a wave.

"Osho? What's that? A book or something."

"No ... a monk ... a true philosopher."

"Boring."

Nitish avoided me, "You know, Osho said that we are all made up of organic elements. All chemistry in us. We're results of some weird complex chemical reactions."

"Huh?" I felt light headed with the smoke blinding me.

"Sex!", Nitish pointed out the obvious.

I nodded in vague understanding.

"So, that is one reason why we should believe in the intake of every pure organic chemical substance that the earth bestows upon us."

"I've lost you." I concentrated on the bubbles inside the hookah's base.

"This dear boy." and from Nitish's pocket two joints popped out.

"What the hell is that?" I suddenly realised where this was heading.

"Here are all the answers." he lit up one and took a swift drag, "Your turn".

"I'm so not having that." My heart pumped faster.

"Ohh cmon ... just one puff ... No biggie." Nitish insisted.

"What's in it?" I was completely ignorant of this territory.

"Just some divine herbs. They're good for your health. Liberates your inner soul." Nitish prompted me.

✶✶✶

"What the hell did you take jackass?" Sunny slapped me hard.

"Heyyy", I squealed.

"Hush hush." Sunny shut my mouth, *"You're gonna get us out of this place."*

I was being dragged. I heard a click, a door unlocked, a push on a floor of foam, and then it was a blur.

✳ ✳ ✳

The phone rang a good ten times before Nitish picked up.

"Hey, Bong!", His lazy voice crackled merrily over the phone.

"What the fuck did you give me that night? What the hell was that?"

"Why didn't you like it? You had both of them. You kinda loved it back then." Nitish sniggered.

"I said "no"! I remember." I nearly squealed.

"Everybody comes around. A little lie does the trick."

"What!!" I shouted over the cell, "And, you couldn't stop me!"

"Dude … I'm the initiator. And, you handled it pretty well I got to say. Sleeping for two days now. I'm impressed."

"I don't remember any of it. How I even got here!"

"Oh, I called up your friend to tackle the shitty part. He didn't take it well I can tell." Nitish answered unapologetically.

"Dammit man! I'm gone! You liar." I hit the dry wall.

"I can be your role model, Aakash." Nitish hung up.

✳ ✳ ✳

Sunny Lodha entered the room at five in the evening.

"Hey, man." I started to speak when he stopped me.

"No bullshitting, please," he changed into a pair of t-shirt and jeans, "I'm going to grab some snacks and finish some notes. When I return at night, I expect the room empty. Your rent is stashed on the bottom drawer. Get lost."

He stormed out, the door opened behind him.

LIE 069

Nothingness defined ...

"Welcome, Bong!" Nitish gestured with genuine elation.

"I just need a place to crash for the night." I shrugged, facing the heartless lazy wanna-be-philosopher.

"Happy to help." Nitish guided me through his huge apartment. It was at Koregaon, one of the posh areas of the city and it was a huge apartment, well decorated with luxurious furnishing.

"How many students do you share the flat with?" I asked settling my luggage on a small bed-room in the extreme left corner of the vast 5-bhk or something.

"It's just me." Nitish couldn't have been more subtle about the astonishing fact.

"What?"

"Oh, yes, and sometimes I bring guests over." He winked, "I follow Osho's lessons, if you know what I mean".

I shuddered. Drug addict, with a sex life, and a genius! Who had I run into!

"No, I meant, this entire flat. How do you manage the rent?", My voice could not hide the excruciating honesty and curiousness in my words.

"I don't." He chuckled, "Dad owns this place." Then, he gestured for zipped lips, "And, half the city, real estate."

All rich people in the country and the real estates! Deb Roy flashed in my mind and so did Katie Thomas.

"So, you live quite a life." I couldn't help but notice.

Nitish tittered, "I sleepwalk through most of it."

✳ ✳ ✳

It was 9:30 and Nitish was already two bottles down.

"Don't you eat?"

"Oh, you bet I do!" Nitish laughed, "Let me take you to this amazing place where they make some awesome parathas!"

"Um ... you're gonna drive us there?" I asked tensed.

"Duh!! Now you want a chauffeur!"

Chaitanya at F.C. Road was a miracle at parathas. The paneer cheese paratha and the chicken delights were amazing. And, the lump of butter to top it off. Amazing.

Nitish ate like a pig. One paratha and a chicken biriyani, then a double sundae and he returned with two large packs of wafers.

"I have to say, for a thin guy like you, that is mind blowing!"

"Oh, it's the alcohol. Takes good care of me, that medicine." Nitish said faithfully.

We watched the die-hard quadrilogy in the hall while Nitish kept telling me about all the novels he had read. He fell asleep in the couch at around 4 in the morning.

I went back to my room and shut the door.

I closed my eyes and couldn't really figure out the truth anymore. Sunny Lodha was a very good guy who had thrown me out in the evening. Nitish Agarwal was a drunkard who was fun to hang around.

Who was I now? Was I at all in the definitions of a good guy anymore or had I too been swept away into nothingness where the truth and the lies didn't matter.

I yawned. Maybe, sleep could tell.

✳ ✳ ✳

"Hey, bro, mind if I sit beside you?", My eyes were heavy with slumber but still I was before time at college and finding Sunny already seated on the first bench was no genuine revelation.

Sunny didn't react, as if the words were never spoken.

"I'd take that for a yes." I settled beside the to-be-topper.

"Hey, man, really sorry for what happened yesterday. Shouldn't have done that." I managed quickly.

"Why did you leave the rent behind? I asked you to collect it from the drawer." Sunny wasn't negotiating.

"No, dude, that would not be fair." I sounded corny but anything for manipulation, "We signed up together for that flat. Can't just leave you alone in the mess. "

"So, create a ruckus now?", Sunny's voice was without emotions and strict. I was sure it was the imitation of Amitabh from back in the days of "Agneepath".

"Trust me, man! I was forced into that drug thing! "

"I had told you clearly that Nitish was a spoilt good-for-nothing." Sunny said coldly.

And also, the guy with whom I had dinner yesterday and we saw movies together, too! And oh, yeah, I crashed at his place too.

"I know ... I know ... I completely agree. Never again. Just gimme one chance."

"Nopes ... not gonna ...", Sunny trailed off as the tall girl with the Gucci bag and the hidden-somewhere BMW keys approached him.

"Hey, Sunny, I needed some help with the applied science assignment. Have you by any chance completed it?", Her voice was soft like some ancient sweet-singing bird and I could see sparks flying out of Sunny Lodha!

"Ohh ... ye ... er ... yess!" Sunny took 15 seconds just to say yes, another 2 minutes in finding the assignment which seemed a rigorous and super-tense situation and then finally when the tall girl thanked him, there it was, the million dollar smile and the apparent big-blush spread right across Sunny's face like a billboard.

"Whoa! What just happened there big-guy?" I couldn't help but smirk when the girl left.

"What!! ... er ... Nothing ... I don't know what you're talking about!" Sunny sounded insecure.

"You so dig the hottie, don't you!" I burst out laughing.

"What!" Sunny faked a laugh, that sounded like a squeak, "Of course not, anything you say."

"Is that so?"

"Yeah, man!! Definitely. And anyways, she's way out of my league." Sunny conceded.

"Well, let me tell you one thing, dude." I whispered now, my words spaced out with the right precision so Sunny would be tempted, "She kind of adores you, I can tell."

Sunny looked straight into my eye and for a minute I was sure he had caught my lie.

He paused for a minute.

"Are you sure?"

I nodded confidently.

"You promise you'll help?" Sunny's voice had a pleading tone.

Oh my god ... You so like that girl! You're gone Lodha ...

"Of course, I will. That's what friends are for!" I made it sound as honest and loyal as a pet dog could!

"Okay, get back to the apartment tomorrow!"

"Tomorrow? Why not today?"

"It's your punishment for misconduct!"

Yes teacherrr!

"Hey, Aakash, don't hobnob with that Nitish again. He is not good for you." Sunny said after the last lecture. He had been helping me with the concepts throughout the lectures and I could not help but notice genuine concern in his voice.

"Will keep that in mind, bro." I packed my bag and left for Koregaon Park.

Just one last day with the drug addict /super-rich/genius.

LIE 070

The Craziest Night–1

"Did I tell you this night is gonna change the story of your life?" Nitish's lazy broken voice has a hint of malice.

"Um ... not that I remember." I said, putting my t-shirts in my bag.

"Okay then, Aakash." Nitish's voice change, into a stylish baritone, "Bong! This night is gonna change your life forever."

"I think I got you the first time. Can we change the topic?"

"We could get started with the night!" Nitish was already one step out of the door, "Let's get out, Bong! The city is ours as long as the moon looms around." He winked.

"Okay, er ... first ... you're getting creepier by the hour!" I shrugged, "I hate to break this to you, but I'm getting back at Sunny Lodha's apartment tomorrow."

Nitish went pensive for a moment.

"What?" I enquired.

"You're moving tomorrow, right!" He asked a bit lost.

I nodded.

"So, why bother with it now. Let's get going, Bong or we will miss the party."

I sighed as I followed him into the night, "I just hope it doesn't turn out like your last party!"

"Never, my friend, trust me, I have good intentions for this night!" Nitish lied.

***

Nitish drove the Avenger at breakneck pace through the crowded corners of the town.

"Where are we headed for?" I asked when he paused at a liquor shop .

"Patience, Bong."

Soon we were channelling through more twisted roads and detours.

The crowd kept getting thinner and the lanes kept getting narrow and we passed a dozen of book shops. For a minute, I had a strange feeling Nitish was planning on buying college stuff and get me books of Osho. But I never saw the bigger plan.

Budhwar Peth. I read the boards and had just started to wonder whether the city had other peths named on the days of the week when a chill drove down my spine.

Some girls stood there on the corners of the lanes scantily dressed in sparkling and exposing clothes.

A foreign teenager smoking weed and in a small top and mini skirt winked at me and my brain went fuzzy as I felt a panic attack crawling towards me.

"Where the hell have you gotten us, moron?", my voice was filled with apprehension.

Nitish sniggered, "Guess."

In a minute or two, we were inside lanes which were jammed with escorts, barring any age groups, every lady shouting prices and whistling at us. I could see old men and passers-by, negotiating with the girls, some getting slapped, some being dragged inside small compartments which fenced around the huge red-light area.

"Let's go! Drive faster" I begged Nitish.

"Hold that thought." Nitish smiled smugly and turned the ignition off. For a minute, I felt like punching him red and white and then dragging an axe through his head.

Nitish inhaled deeply, while a couple of prostitutes approached us, asking for deals.

"Twenty bucks for an hour." A thin small girl asked me.

"What? Nooo." I had gone all sweaty and a brain freeze had taken toll "Let's get out of here. Please Nitish."

"Just a minute now, Aakash." Nitish looked at me, "You know the thing about prohibited places." He smiled, "They make us free".

I was at the verge of breaking into tears as all the girls now started poking at us, offers free flowing, pleading us to have a look at them just for one strip-tease.

I was holding onto the pillion seat so tightly, I could feel the leather getting ripped.

I'm gonna burn this bike later tonight, I swore.

It was then, that what could possibly be the next worst case scenario happened.

The sirens blazed from a distance.

"Raid, filthy bastards back for money and free sex." One of the old prostitutes whispered and fled.

"Uh ... oh." Nitish's voice for the first time had a hint of nervousness, "Didn't look ahead for that now, did we?"

"No asshole."

He started the ignition. The bike revved once, then stopped.

"Not a good timing, I must say." Nitish said a bit panicky now.

I had my hands over my head.

Dad would not be pleased.

Nitish kicked the bike again and again, but it wouldn't budge.

The sirens were getting closer, and I could see the dazzling red lights, not of the area but of the police jeeps.

Finally, he gave up the bike, picked up the key and looked at me, "Bro, if you don't wanna end up in jail and get looted and beaten up, then trust me, it's high time we should go for the run."

"Don't you call me bro, jackass." I looked at him in disgust as we started galloping.

A second later we were sprinting like crazy.

"This place is like a maze or I'm really drunk!" Nitish observed as we were back at the crime scene, five minutes of jogging later.

"We are getting caught!" I gasped.

A fat cop emerged at the corner of the road. From his pocket, came along a small whistle and next thing, the alarm was set off.

"Run for your life, Bong! We have been spotted."

Two lanes of darting and scampering, and we were at a small bus stand.

"Quick, get on that Volvo." Nitish pointed at a Shivneri bus.

I climbed without protest into the empty bus and dashed for the last seat. Nitish quickly paid the conductor for two tickets and then he joined me.

"We're safe, Bong." Nitish took a sip from a can and smiled at me.

That was before I knocked him out with a punch.

He fell on the opposite seat, and instantly went to sleep, snoring heavily.

"Nitish." I made sure he was alive and then, scrolled back to my seat at the extreme end. I closed my eyes and fatigue took control.

✹ ✹ ✹

"Wake up, Bong!"

"Stop calling me that! I have a name." I opened my eyes to the dark inside of the rocketing Bus.

I looked at my watch. It was 1 am.

"We are still moving?" Another shocker was approaching me, I could tell, "Where are we headed to now?"

"Haha." Nitish was clearly drunk again, "The city that doesn't sleep."

"That's New York, for god's sake." my fist hungered for another fast punch.

"No bro, that's Bombay for you."

LIE 071

The Craziest Night 2 – Surprise Surprise!

"Was this your grand plan?" I couldn't even recognise my own voice as it strained with fury.

"Well, mine had intercourse and a black eyeless face starring in it, however this is commendable, too." Nitish walked beside the Gateway of India through the cold breeze of the harbour, as the steel waves clashed at the bay, massaging his forehead and eye where my punch had left a visible patch.

"I think you're suffering from a term called 'INSANITY!'" I shouted at Nitish, who seemed least bothered.

"Yeah yeah, you get to decide all the norms of life, Bong", Nitish mumbled as we kept walking on the empty road.

Behind us, The Taj Hotel stood proudly, its beauty and ethnicity majestic, spell binding the night.

From his pocket, Nitish took his diary out and opened a random page.

"Let me read you something, Aakash, it's one of my jokes."
"One day we'll find 'me',
Lock Him Up and Throw The Key.
Chain Him Up and Ask Him Why...
That I stopped long ago,
But he would still try ...
One day we'll Explain 'me' the Rules ...
Ask 'me' To be part Of The fools ...
And when I laugh, we'll darken the day into a demented night...

Cripple 'my' wishes, put an end to 'my' fight".

He closed the diary and looked back at me and for a second his face illuminated in the moonlight, with a strange look, of a person who was untamed, unpredictable. I couldn't place it, as if he had no limitations, no boundaries, as if the rights and the wrongs didn't matter to him.

"What is that look in your face?" I asked stupidly.

"Oh, that", he smiled, "nothingness defined."

"I think I'm imagining things." I felt a bit dazed, probably due to the running and trepidation I had gone through a while ago.

"That must be it then." Nitish supported, "Why don't we get inside and get you a drink and some time to relax your senses. We're here."

I turned my gaze to Leopold's Bar.

"I hate my life." I walked into the bar to grab a bite.

A lot of hippies sat inside, drinking vodka and beer. Random people sat there, some gossiping about football scores, some discussing drugs, some just lost like me.

I took a corner seat with Nitish and ordered a sandwich while he settled for another vodka.

The glass door opened and the cool breeze swept inside bringing her in, and my heart skipped a bit unconsciously. I was tired of even turning towards the door, so I put my head down over the table instead of noticing the familiar face.

I imagined Sunny Lodha sitting back in his apartment completing the assignments for the weekend, my dad in his study, lost in ministry of finance matters, everyone preoccupied, everyone sharing a piece to stick by in this world of nothingness.

A bout of laughter grabbed me.

"What happened, Bong?" Nitish asked merrily.

I grew silent again, utter confusion settling in, "I don't know! Tonight was crazy."

"Well, it's not over yet, is it?" Nitish smiled. He was a non-judgemental insanely weird human being.

We left the place an hour later. As I walked near the exit, I collided with a girl and her sketch book fell.

I bent down to pick it up, while Nitish was busy reading the last lines of his poem, oblivious of the present scenario, totally drunk and completely off the hook.

One day then, after those endless years ...
When I'm finally blinded, can't recognise these tears ...
We'll break the prison cell where 'me' had been locked ...
To witness The final joke that I mocked

I looked at the open parchment of sketch in the drawing book. It had a tomb stone structure. Four roads meeting at a dried up fountain, and snow settled lanes marking the square with love.

Love square.

I looked up, my eyes met hers and I was stupefied. The spell took control and I was back to the sunrise at Tiger Hill, Darjeeling.

"*Aakash ...*"

"*Hmm...*"

"*Open your eyes ...*"

Infinite sky, Orange streaks across the horizon silver lining the black sky which viscously turned yellow, and out there, right across a far peak, a small orb of pure orange, The sun ...

It was breath- taking, the serenity and the spell-binding beauty of nature that I witnessed.

The perfect sun rise.

Katie whispered in my ear, "See, I kept my promise. "

I could smell her lavender perfumed hair, I could sense her breath, her glowing eyes burnt into my heart.

Katie ...
That day, In that dark cell, we won't find "me'
Cos, somewhere down the road, I let loose ...
I was free.

LIE 072

The craziest night ended: shock shock!

Nitish had passed out again in the bus, maybe, for the best. I could not handle a distraction at the moment. I was busy beholding my dream.

Katie Thomas was seated right next to me, the angel I had fallen for long ago even before I knew the meaning of love. And, the serendipities of the universe, after losing her twice, there she was once again, handing me my last chance to make things right. The last thing she had said at Leopold's before losing consciousness was, 'pune'. So, here she was, in a Volvo with us, back to where the night had started.

I still remembered the last time that I had seen her, back at the hospital, right after getting out of a stupid coma, I still remember confessing my love for her. That was the last day of my stay at Darjeeling. The place that broke my heart, over and over again. I closed my eyes and the memory of love square flashes back, Deb and Katie.

She swayed along, her eyes half-closed, as she held on to me for support.

"Hey, Katie?"

"Hmm," she mumbled, her arms over me, her head on my shoulder.

"How come you are here?"

"Hmm," she mumbled again.

All drunks in the world!

"I love you," she whispered in my ears.

"What?" I'm wide awake.

"I love you Deb", she said as she went back to sleep.
dire sigh

✳ ✳ ✳

We reached Pune at five in the morning after an eventful, startling and full of epiphanies night.

Nitish was awake again and he was eyeing Katie.

"She's a friend. Stay away.", I warned him viciously.

"No feelings." Nitish raised his arms in humble declaration, "By the way, do you mind me asking, what you intend to do with that sleeping beauty of yours?"

Now that's a bummer.

"You could get her to my place until she wakes up and tells us her story." Nitish suggested after my two-minute-blankness.

"I've got to get back to Sunny's apartment, too. He called me around fifteen times in the night." I checked my cell for missed calls.

"Better off." Nitish thought out loud, "Let's take her to your old apartment. I don't think Sunny would have a problem with that."

"I'm breaking all his rules." I sighed.

"Your choice." Nitish said casually.

"I don't trust you with a girl", I looked at Nitish loathingly.

"Completely understandable." Nitish looked smug.

"Alright then, let's take her to Sunny's place."

We hired an auto, cramped the inebriated Katie inside and reached Sunny's flat.

"Wait here." I instructed Nitish, "Let me explain the situation to Sunny and then I'll come back for Katie."

"Aye, captain", Nitish nodded, yawning.

I climbed two stairs at a time. My excitement knew no bounds. One part of me was really confused and trying to still figure out the order of things that had just happened to me in the last few hours and how Katie had turned up while the other me was elated with the prospect of bringing Katie to my place, watching her sleep for the rest of the morning and to talk to her again.

I rang the bell twice and waited impatiently thinking of excuses to explain the situation to Sunny Lodha.

The door sprang open.

"Okay, here's the thing." I started and then my voice trailed off.

She hugged me even before I could comprehend her action. Her hair spread over my face and her warmth made me take a step back.

"Kat ... Katherine", I was as if tongue tied.

"Surprise surprise," she hugged me again, "I missed you so much, Aakash Roy. See, I kept my promise."

Two promises kept in the last few hours! What happened to the 'promises are meant to be broken' clause!!

"Tell me about it." Sunny Lodha grumbled from behind."She stayed up the entire night since she got here in Pune yesterday. Found out information about you in the college office, the name of your room-mate, then got hold of the address and stalked me right up to here. Since then, even after my constant pleadings she has refused to put even one foot out of your cot. That adamant girl I tell you!"

"How come you're in Pune?" was the first thing I asked my best friend.

"For you." He said softly.

I swallowed nervously. Katie and Nitish must be waiting downstairs. He might come upstairs any minute now.

"Stupid," she slapped me on the arm, "I came here because I got admission into M.I.T. Now, isn't that ... "

"Miraculous, serendipity,*" I knowwww! Isn't that a common thing now!*

"Exactly." She was so happy she was hopping up and down.

"Hey, Katie, you've been up all night?" I asked.

"Yup. You wouldn't pick up your calls no matter how many times Sunny would call. You didn't leave me much of an option and frankly, he's a strict guy." Katherine Andrews said with a slight hint of anger but her joy was boundless, anyways.

"Why don't I drop you off to your place wherever that is and you can have some sleep and I will meet you whenever you are awake. Just call me."

Katie pondered for a moment, then she made a face, gradually smiled and two minutes later she was packing her bag.

"Hey Sunny, listen I need a big favour." I whispered to Sunny taking him to the other corner of the room.

"Fire away. My role's all about that after all." Sunny grimaced sadly.

"Listen, while I'm off dropping Katie to her PG or wherever she stays, Nitish will come to the flat with Katie. She is a bit hung over and needs a place to sleep for a few hours. So, let her in. Okay bro?"

"What the fuck did you just say?" Sunny scratched his head, "Katie going with you, Katie coming back with Nitish and hung over?"

"Arghh", I hit the wall in frustration, "You'll figure it out. Just let them in."

"Kill me." Sunny jabbered.

"Kill me twice." I mused.

✳✳✳

"Hey, Aakash, stop." Nitish intercepted me while I tried to sneak out with the constantly chattering Katherine.

"Who's she?" Nitish asked, curious.

"Katie." I sighed.

"Katie ... the sleeping beauty?"

Katherine was confused, sharing the sentiments of Nitish.

"When did you watch me sleep? And, who are you?", she retorted sharply.

"I'm Nitish. And, I saw Katie sleep."

"Hey, are you stupid?" Katherine now shouted, "I'm Katie, and you saw me sleep?"

I have my hands over my head. This is unstoppable.

"You're Katie?", Nitish had gone haywire, "Then, who is the sleeping beauty?"

"How'd we know, duffer!" Katherine shouted deafening both of us, "Aakash, who is this doofus?"

"Katie ... er ... Nitish." I made one last attempt, "Hey, Nitish, clearly you're drunk. Go upstairs and do what I had said earlier. Sunny will understand."

"He will?", Nitish asked doubtfully.

***

I dropped Katherine off at the girl's hostel.

We had a cup of tea at a small stall.

"I never thought I'd see you again, Katherine. The way you left me there when I needed my friend the most."

"I'm really sorry, Aakash. There has not been a day that I didn't think about you. The last two years have been a nightmare for me and when I got back to Calcutta, your dad told me you had left for M.I.T. Imagine the shock." She said sipping the tea.

"I had to escape Kates, couldn't take that city anymore. The city of joy sounds like an irony sometimes."

Katherine brushed my hair gently "Enough now. No more senty lines. Let's have some fun now. What say Aakash Roy? Remember the good old days."

I nodded, as I felt all my insecurities and fears melting away. Katherine hugged me one last time before she departed.

"Catchya later." She strolled off.

"Hey, Katherine", I called her from behind.

She turned, her face glowing in the sunshine strengthening me.

"I missed you, too."

LIE 073

The changed Katie..

"So, you two-timing now?" Sunny said viciously.

"What?", I was stunned, "No ... of course not."

"Then, who is that girl Nitish dropped off on your cot an hour ago?" Sunny challenged.

"Katie."

"Huh? I thought the other girl who stayed up all night telling me boring stories of your life is Katie."

"Yeah, that's her nickname. She's Katherine Andrews."

"And, this?" Sunny pointed to the sleeping Katie in my cot.

"That's Katie Thomas. She's a friend."

Sunny scratched his forehead, "Are these two Katies sisters or something? "

"No ... no", I was getting tired of the rapid fire round, "They don't even know each other, so it was sort of weird today morning."

"Ohh ... I see." Sunny laughed sarcastically, "Since you're having flings with two random Katies, it must be a bit weird. The upside is you won't mix up the names."

"For the one-hundredth time, I'm not the lucky guy here!" I said through clenched teeth.

***

Katie Thomas woke up at around eleven. She didn't start off with the usual clichés and directly stressed the surprise, "Aakash!"

My face sparkled up just with the small fact that she remembered my name.

"Hey, how're you now?"

"Just a headache. I'm new to vodka, you know." she sat up on my bed as she massaged her scalp.

"How come you're here, Katie?" I asked the same question that I've been using lately.

"You tell me. I've never seen this room in my life before," she replied, a bit dazed.

"Oh ... this is my room." I explained, "You remember last night?"

"Not really, it's all foggy, bits and pieces." She strained, "I remember getting thrown out of Taj. They said my dad's credit card had expired. Stupid me. Of all the cards, I had to choose the wrong one!"

"What were you doing there? I found you at Leopold's. You had passed out, so I brought you to my place."

"Hmm." She nodded, "Thanks. You're a good friend. I should get going. My friends must be anxious."

She stood up.

And, my heartbeat stopped. *Already!*

"But!" I couldn't think what to say, "Um ... er ... where are you headed to? I could drop you."

"Juhu ...", she looked at me.

"Juhu, as in Bombay?" I asked her, nervous now.

"Where else would it be? We're in Bombay after all." She looked at me in utter confusion, "Wait a minute, aren't we?"

One minute of awkward silence.

I shrugged.

"Where are we?" She looked out of the window, trepidation creeping in.

"Um ... back at Leopold's, you said something about 'Pune', so ... "

"What!", she literally screamed at me, "So, you brought me to Pune, Aakash!"

"It's not that far." I was out of my breath.

"No no no, I need to get out of here now!" Her voice grew wary.

"Hey, don't worry. I will come with you. We'll be in Bombay in no time.", I tried to calm her.

"You don't understand." she scolded, "Where's my cell?" She rifled through her bag, took her cell out, and dialled.

Moments later she was talking to some 'sweetu' or somebody and they were both super-serious over some 'chances of getting caught' issue.

What had Katie turned into at 19? Arms dealer!

"Drop me to the nearest Volvo bus stand. Where am I right now?"

"Um ... Kothrud."

"Damn it!!" She could cut me into half.

✶✶✶

I took the blanched and anxious Katie to the Volvo stand near Durga Café and got her the first bus to Mumbai.

We were waiting for the bus. I was afraid that Katie would slap me any moment now, while she looked at the time every ten seconds.

Finally, the blue bus arrived and I could already feel a lump building in my throat.

Met Katie after two years and didn't even catch up, not even a proper 'hello'. Heart, breaking!

"Let's get you to your seat." I said, but Katie didn't move.

"I'm sorry." she said slowly.

"For what", I said, sitting back beside her.

"For getting all angry with you." Her voice trembled a bit, "It was sweet. What you did there for me." A tear formed in her eye.

"Hey, that's alright. No issues, Katie." I tried to cheer her up, " Anyways, I would be pissed too, if I went to sleep in my house, and woke up in some field."

"Huh?" she looked at me confused.

"I'm confusing my examples." I concluded. She giggled.

"You're still the same. I wish I could stay that way, too."

"Hey, if it's any relief, you're still as beautiful." I smiled at her.

She giggled again.

"I'm all messed up, Aakash."

"I could help you. Tell me." I said in earnest and realised how much I wanted her.

She looked into my eyes and then smiled, "You'd call me?"

"*******209?" I asked.

"No." she chuckled, "It's changed. But am glad you still remember."

"I was kind of planning to call on that soon." I winked.

"Yeah, right!", Her old sarcastic voice was back for an instant.

Thank God!

"Gimme your number, I'll do the honours this time." Katie saved my number.

The bus left five minutes later.

"Hey, Katie, why were you so panicked at first? Something super-wrong with Pune?"

"Oh, that … er … Nothing, Aakash. Just the shock of being away. Never been to Pune before."

The bus left me lost in a small wind of smoke and questions.

Did she just lie?

I kind of knew it was her that I had seen the first day, that I had landed in Pune. The ghost passing by in the vehicle near Garware square. That was Katie Thomas. Then what was she hiding from me? What was Katie's secret?

✳ ✳ ✳

I met Katherine an hour later and we had a sumptuous lunch at Chaitanya, thanks to the suggestions of Nitish Agarwal. We went to Catch a movie, "No smoking", later the day. Katie was snoring half-way through the movie, but I ended up loving it. Maybe, because of its weird storytelling or maybe it was Katherine who was rubbing off on me. I was optimistic and starting afresh and I didn't even know it yet.

LIE 074

Galore of glory …

If Katherine Andrews was in town, so must be her alienated brother, the super-genius eccentric and kind hearted Robbie Andrews.

Katherine was there in the class on Monday. And, to no surprise, she sat beside me. It was kind of cool after all, as everyone eyed me with envy. I was just in my first year, and already had a girlfriend (friend, whatever!) to flaunt. And soon enough, I had grown tired of explaining to the class that she was not, in fact, my beloved or something, but my best friend from Calcutta, I was overexcited with Katie, back to attending classes, back to telling super stories of my adventures. Katie and I had a lot to catch up. She knew nothing about Darjeeling, nor about the two morose years in between, my sudden decision to study at Pune and my expeditions with Nitish. I could see that she loathed Nitish already.

But Robbie was nowhere, and I could not ask Katie, all thanks to an old promise to Robbie to never discuss him with Katherine or any member of his family.

So, it was kind of a surprise to finally find him.

Robbie looked unchanged; two years had not modified a single feature in the geek. He still had his untidy, piled up hair streaks, his unshaven face intact, his eyes still tired, and the smile, in place.

I met him on the steps of Dyaneshwara Auditorium of MIT. Students from all streams would gather around the place most of the evenings, either to gossip or for group study sessions. Robbie sat alone, near the small fountains, his eyes focused on a thick book, earphones plugged into his ears, drowned in his own world.

I placed him in an instant. It was as if I was looking out for my old geek friend ever since I had met Katherine.

"Avoiding me." I tried to provoke him.

"Oh, look who it is! Aakash Roy, the old friend who once dared to kiss my sister." He hugged me with profound happiness, "Missed you, brother."

"Me too man! Ain't no intelligence in the world save you!" I winked.

"That's generous and can be clearly falsified", he smiled, "So, met Katherine?"

"Yup, I did. She never mentions you!" I always found the brother–sister relationship super-discrete and hush-hush.

"Yeah … We are a strange family. However, you remember the old oath, right?" He looked at me seriously.

"Yes, of course. To never raise your topic in front of anyone of your family. As crazy as that sounds, I'll still obey that. What's this by the way?", I picked up some papers which looked like some newspaper articles.

"Ohh … This is e-commerce, dear friend. The medium of business at the moment. These are some international conference papers I'm going through." He showed me his entire collection of research papers. Remember the thick book, it was a compendium of all these journals.

"How come you into economics and money making?"

"Oh no, Aakash." Robbie smiled, making me as if conscious of my ignorance, " I'm the open source guy. Just trying to help make the business simple. Save every common man from making mistakes. I've the best interests for the world. "

"So, what is your plan here? I mean, if it's coding I can help." I beamed, "Have been doing some programming for the last two years. You can count on me if it's C or C++."

Robbie beamed, "That is wonderful. Having a partner on this like you, is a miracle indeed."

"Now now, big guy, easy with the mockery." I smiled.

"No, seriously Aakash. You'd be a great help."

"Cool. Book me for every Sunday. I'm free on that cursed day."

"Alright, I'll meet you here at the college auditorium and let's make this project happen." Robbie's voice was filled with enthusiasm.

That was the great thing about Robbie. Five minutes of a friendly chat and you're already a part of something ambitious. I had no idea what I had delved into, but I knew it must be something out of the box, for Robbie's plans had always been that.

"So, I hope we will change the world soon," Robbie smiled.

"We will, bro." I said walking down the steps to meet Katherine at CCD, "Together."

I didn't even know the lie then.

P.S. *Together was never an option.*

LIE 075

A month had passed since Katherine had taken up my entire life by magic, created a fortress out of it and I was a completely changed man even before I had felt it myself. We would watch movies together at E-Square, attend classes together, at times, bunk them. We would solve the programs in pracs together and everywhere it was just the two of us as if an inseparable pair.

Sunny was happy with his changed roommate, who'd complete all his home assignments on time, who would be at home every night at ten sharp, no drinks, no addictions, just a supervibrant smile and a cell with enough balance to spend half the night talking to Katherine. Life had changed. And, I even ended up calling my father by myself one weekend ...

"Hey, Aakash." dad's voice sounded a bit broken, as if an evidence of the betrayal that I had caused him by not complying with his wishes and then by initiating the growing distance.

"Hey, dad, how're you?"

"I'm fine. How're you coping up with engineering life? Met Katie?"

"I did. How do you know about Katherine being here?"

"She didn't tell you? She came here a week after you were gone. She had taken admission in some college at Calcutta."

"What? No. She said she got admission here, at MIT."

"As far as I know, she had got admission in some NIT college here in Calcutta. You should see that girl's AIEEE marks."

"But then, how come?" I felt disoriented.

"Well, she came to me asking about your admission and I told her. She said she had promised you something."

She'll come back for me.

"So I guess." dad continued, "I am really confused how she might've persuaded her parents. All the troubles she must have had to go through. She's a good friend, Aakash, that girl." Dad stopped as if asking me for something that left me totally awestruck.

When I hung up, I was speechless. Katherine had lied to me about getting into MIT for studies. She was here for me.

✳ ✳ ✳

Submissions are the definition of pain in the ass! They are as if a constant medium of vehement torture over young hands and minds, gift wrapped with a deadline that looms over like a serpentine curse. Tens of files, hundreds of assignments and also the preparation for mock vivas and tests that constitute the term-work, it's like a herculean task every sadistic university bestows as a punishment on every human who dares to take up engineering as a career option.

We spent sleepless nights, engrossed in writing the same assignments, mostly copying the same contents from Sunny who had done it during the weekends, already!

Katie would come to our flat and we would stay up late, completing the assignments, gossiping or singing out loud in the meanwhile. We would get bottles of coke and wafers and watch episodes of 'friends' when we got bored.

It was on the last day before submissions that Sunny Lodha had to stay at another friend's place for some notes, when I felt completely new feelings growing for Katherine.

She was sitting there, right in front of me, eating wafers and humming to "ten things" by Miley Cyrus. Her beautiful blue top and pink skirt gave her a marvellous look, even though I had seen her in the same pair of clothes for tens of times now. She had grown up so much, I noticed, she looked beautiful and so innocent. Suddenly, I felt my heart skip random beats! She was completely kissable and I couldn't take my eyes off her lips.

There was this magnetic pull today about her, something that was making me conscious of her presence, something that made my brain go all haywire, think of all crazy stuff that were possible under the current circumstances! My eyes moved on to her legs and I felt dizzy now!

I gulped.

Aakash! Control buddy!

"Hey, why don't you complete that last assignment of B.M.E., I'll get some fresh air." I left the room, unable to contain the feelings anymore.

I started jogging through the deserted road on the full moon night.

And, the slide show began. I remembered Katherine right from the first day I had met her, the first time I saw her in her house when I went for tuitions, when I fought with Deb and his gang at the fete just because they had made her cry, when I had kissed her.

I stopped ...

A cold wind relaxed my senses and every thing fell into place.

Katie came here for me. To keep a promise.

So, was it vaguely possible that she had feelings for me?

I remembered the depression that had engulfed me bereft of Katherine and her laughter, I tried to imagine days without her, and the world seemed to crumble away.

I needed her.

I started sprinting towards the apartment, climbed two stairs at a time, reached the room, out of breath.

"What happened?", Katherine looked at me, her round eyes piercing into mine, her face glowing as if reflecting the full moon.

It was instantaneous.

"I think I love you."

"What?" Katherine looked at me, aghast.

I approached her.

I could feel her heartbeats growing stronger too, as her face turned more attractive by the minute.

"Do you love me too, Kates?" I felt the question come out spontaneously, as if my soul was in charge of the enquiry.

I cupped her face in my hands, my eyes reflecting in hers now, my lips just an inch away from hers. I knew I could not stop myself even if I wanted to now.

"Yes." She closed her eyes as she let me kiss her.

★★★

My cell phone rang a time or twice. But I couldn't care less.
Two missed calls – Katie Thomas.

LIE 076

I didn't call Katie Thomas back.

Sunny Lodha was apparently sad.

"What happened, big guy?" I sat opposite to him, at Pallavi Restaurant as he sat there, his mind miles away.

"Oh … Nothing … er … classes kind of finished, you know so, it's sort of boring."

"Yeah of course, those enlightening classes I always tried to bunk." I chuckled.

We sat quietly.

"You have Katherine. She's a good girl, Aakash. Hold on to her." Sunny said after a while.

"Will do." I looked back at my cell.

Why did Katie Thomas call me?

"Hey, is that what's eating you? Me and Katherine. Wait a minute, what about that tall girl, Gucci bag? Did you talk to her?" I asked, the old story flashing back in.

Sunny Lodha sighed and shrugged, "You never helped now, did you?"

"Hey, I'm really sorry, man!" It felt bad, breaking his trust again, "But you know what, that girl Sunny, she's a big shot, you know the party-typos."

Sunny was listening intently.

"So, I think, you'll have to show some super-attitude. Be a changed man! You know, impress her a bit. Break some rules, bunk classes, help her with proxy's, show her your other side, you know."

He grimaced.

"What?"

"I have," he cleared his voice, "no other side."

"Then fake one, Sunny." I was guiding someone towards the path of lies and treachery and I felt proud for an instant.

"No, it's okay." Sunny appeared bored.

"What, don't you like my idea?" I felt a bit offended now. I used to be a good manipulator back in school days.

"No ... it's just that." Sunny looked at me, "That's not how I live my life, Aakash and no matter what you say and how efficient it sounds, something wrong." He took a bite of the pastry.

Will stay wrong, I know!!

***

I called up Katie Thomas.

"Hey, you never picked up my calls yesterday?" Her voice was a bit heavy on the other side.

"Yeah ... er...," I looked at my watch.

1:30 pm. I had to pick up Katherine in fifteen minutes. We had plans for Wonder Funkey, an amusement park.

"Anyways," Katie interrupted, "I have to meet you, Aakash."

"When ... where?" I was astonished!

"Pune ... your city", She smiled, "Koregaon Park. Theres a big Natural's ice-cream store here. Meet me there today at 5:30 pm."

"Yeah, about that," My phone flashed with Katherine's call waiting behind.

I panicked, "Okay, I'll catch you later." I took Katherine's call.

"Hey, Aakash, miss me." Katherine's voice was filled with immense happiness.

***

"You asked Nitish to come to Wonder Funkey with us!", Katherine hit me hard on my arm as she whispered between clenched teeth.

"I thought it'd be good if he tagged along." I tried, handing her the bowl in the bowling arena.

"And, you couldn't have called Sunny?"

"I figured we always have him around, you know."

"Hey, already fighting like hubby and wify." Nitish cut in from behind, with his evil grin.

Katherine cursed under her breath and then almost threw the ball, which soared in the air for a good three seconds before clashing against the wooden pavement and then going off track.

"Whoa!! Lot of energy," Nitish chuckled.

Katherine could have shot us in the head if she had a gun.

Two hours of relentless anger and frustration later, Katherine finally went to make some calls to her parents.

"You know." Nitish sipped a Red Bull, "judging by the ambience here, doesn't look like my invitation was a joint venture."

"Nothing like that, man. We both thought it'd be good." But Nitish dismissed me again with his lordly air,

"It's okay, liar." He smirked, "Good girls hate me. That's my USP." he winked, "I'm tailor made for bad biatches."

I rolled my eyes. "Yeah, okay, I made the judgement call." I sighed.

"Then, come to the point. Why the last minute invitation?" Nitish took another big gulp, "need help from your role model?" He smirked again.

"This was a bad idea." I shrugged, "But you're my last resort, you remember Katie Thomas. My friend that.."

"Yeah, of course, sleeping beauty." Nitish said.

"Yes, about her." I continued, "You know, she called me up today and she is here in Pune. Wants to meet me."

"And?" Nitish raised his eye brows.

"And, what?" I asked, "That's it. I am not sure if I should meet her. I mean, I have Katherine now and we're kind of seeing each other you know."

"So, what's the big deal meeting an old friend. Katherine won't have a problem I guess, but of course, if she is not the old generation types." He snorted.

"No ... It's just that." I couldn't phrase it, "I kind of had feelings for Katie too, once."

Nitish trashed the can and looked at me, "Do you still have feelings for Katie Thomas?"

"No." I responded.

"You definite?"

I paused.

"Don't meet her, Aakash." Nitish said, seriousness in his voice, "You're happy here. I can tell."

Katherine joined us, still a bit upset by the presence of Nitish.

"Hey, guys," Nitish grimaced, "Really sorry to inform you, but looks like I just got a date." He flashed some random message in his phone, tiptoeing away, "You never know where I might take this down to."

Katherine rolled her eyes while I could easily read his deception.

"Catchya folks later."

"Bbye," Katherine was kind of relieved.

"See yah ,Kates", he winked, "and Aakash, DON'T ... okay?"

I nodded in understanding.

"What 'don't'?" Katherine asked me curious.

"Um ... err..."

"No wait, I don't wanna know." she discarded her question, clearly uninterested.

✳✳✳

"Hey, Kates, I got to finish up some bank related work. So, I'll be busy the evening."

"Oh," Katherine looked a bit sad.

"But I promise I'll take you out to that amazing old place, Good Luck Café in the night."

"Alright", she hugged me, her warmth lightening me up a bit.

She turned and left.

P.S. *And, I realized the only person I felt hurt to lie to was Katherine ...*

LIE 077

Katie's secret

It was a Sunday afternoon and I sat with Robbie Andrews trying to design the negotiation engine we had been working on for the last two months.

"So, this will have an alliance engine you know, that would help to integrate a lot of parties, for example, a lot of sellers or buyers together into a group and hence help negotiate for better deals at lower prices, but they should have intersecting demands." Robbie went on enthusiastically while I zoomed back and forth, shifting through the incidents that happened yesterday.

****

At 5:30 pm I met Katie Thomas at Natural ice-cream shop at K.p.

"Hey there, Aakash." Katie beamed and waved at me.

"Hey, real happy to see you again. So, how come you're here?" I couldn't help but get to the point.

"Looks like it's your perfunctory question." Katie said, "Let's order some ice-creams first."

I nodded and took the seat beside her.

She was looking graceful and I appreciated the highlights in her hair and that constant fragrance lavender. It was intoxicating.

"So ... you know why am here, Aakash?"

I shook my head, a bit tense if she would also go corny and take my name or something.

"The heart is where the home is." Katie double-quoted the phrase satirically.

"You ... live here?" I really needed something stronger than ice-cream now.

Katie nodded. "You could say that, too. This is my prison cell. That would suit the situation better".

"What do you mean?" I asked as the two sundaes arrived. Katie had ordered for the both of us. She was back to her callous self, it relaxed me.

"Just that when the explorer in me attained limitlessness, my wings were cut short, and bamm, I crashed right into Pune."

***

It was 10:45 pm. Katherine and I strolled through the nearly empty F.C. Road, as we walked towards the Deccan Gymkhana bus stand.

"That was a lot of butter!", Katherine giggled, "And that thick shake from that stall! It was so awesome. And then, to top it off, the hookah!!"

I could not smile much.

I had to tell her the truth today. And I didn't know how.

"Imagine how great it would be, if life were as simple as this. Studying, killing time, bunking, eating junk food and just loving each other." She came and pecked me.

I shrugged. Truth had always been the hardest part with me and I had to tell some today.

***

I stopped the drawing as I looked at Robbie.

"Hey, Robbie, have you ever lied to a person who trusts you with life?"

Robbie was still explaining the concept of ad-hoc alliances to me when I stopped him abruptly.

He brushed his unkempt hair lightly.

"No, man," he smiled, "I trust the reality more. Truth is always the best way, you know, it always helps in the longer run. "

"But how are you so sure of the truth?" I retorted, "You must've heard a lot of facts from someone else. All those moral lessons taught by your parents. How do you know they didn't lie to you? How do you know the truth is not adulterated?"

Robbie's eyes pondered a bit, "You know, Aakash. The thing with you is you always process everything through that brain of yours. Never use your heart. You know how I believe in truth?" he continued, "It makes me feel right, Aakash. The truth sounds right. Every single time."

I stopped and thought for a moment.

Then, why didn't my feelings feel right?

✶ ✶ ✶

"It all started when your old buddy Deb ditched me big time."

"What?", I nearly choked, the ice-cream melting in my throat.

"Not like the contemporary ditching. He just kinda abandoned me, another small insignificant chunk of his super-expensive life. Kept forgetting to call back, messages stopped and then, he was out all the time."

"So, what did you do?" I asked, strangely interested in the story now.

"I freaked out, Aakash. For the first time in my life I couldn't just ignore it. I mean, I'm used to rejection. Close ones have always been inconsistent with poor me. But Deb, I would die without him. I loved him more than I could contemplate."

I looked at the saddened expression of Katie as she continued with her secret.

"So, I fled to Calcutta," she put in normally, "to meet him once. To clear the air, you know."

I nodded in vague agreement.

"And then, the families intercepted us. Ruined the little bit of chance I had. The old family rivalry came between us and I could never make him understand my worries, my insecurities. Instead, he got pissed at me for making such a fuss and distanced himself further." Katie shrugged and made a puppy face.

I sighed.

"Yeah, I know. Same old rhetoric." She look out, "My parents are ashamed of me. Like they care." "I'm here, Katie, don't worry. We'll get you out of this mess." I tried to make her smile.

"'This mess' is my life, Aakash." Katie smiles.

***

"Something's bugging you, liar boy." Katherine proved.

"Hey it needs gut, to lie." I replied, a bit conscious at getting caught. Yeah, I still could not decide how to tell her the truth about the other Katie, the one I still cared for 'more than I could contemplate'.

"Naa, the tougher deal is truth. Lying is child's play." Katherine stuck her tongue out.

"You can never lie, Katie ... You don't have the guts. I teased Katherine as she grinds her teeth.

"Ohh really, Mr smarty pants ... you think I have never done it, huh!!"

"I bet ... never in front of me, at least! You can't fool me, lady Katherine!" I smirked though a bit sad.

"Misconceptions and that ego of yours would never make you see the light, I assume, Aakash, so let me just recall an event!!"

"Fire away." I smiled.

"Remember, the night we kissed by the pond." She whispered.

"Ohh that ... yeah, your first kiss, haha." I grinned.

"Yours too, doofus." she retorted back.

"Whatever, so what about it?" I yawned as I looked at the watch, acting casual. Pune was boring at nights! She will kill me and might turn it interesting when I told her my secret.

"Yeah, so do you really think that I got all stuck at that pond that night?" Katie's eyes glinted maliciously.

"What do you mean ... of course, you were stuck, your legs had got tangled in the weeds."

"Or, could it just be one small attempt Aakash, to make you realise that you were more than your fears.. that the stupid hydrophobia thing was all in your mind!!"

"You're not making sense, weirdo!" I said half-serious now as that entire night played back in my mind.

"C'mon, Aakash, think of it this way. You were not gonna meet your mom, you were not ready to face your worst nightmares ... someone had to do something for poor you!! " She smiled.

I was all silent. Man, the hookah must've gotten to my nerves something! Could she be telling me the truth and could it be that deceptive?

"And, holding your breath for someone like me, ain't that difficult after all" she winked as the last bus arrived at the stand.

"Catchya later, Aakash." She got into the bus to her hostel.

I was all grim, unable to speak.

"Have a haircut, by the way, Smarty, you look all messed up." She stuck her tongue out as the bus started to move away,

"For me, Aakash ... "

I sat at the bus stand alone, the truth still untold. The lie still intact. A lie that could keep things sorted and life good ... was it worth living that lie?

✳ ✳ ✳

"You're wrong, Robbie." I smiled, "the concept of truth is flawed. It's objective reality. Everyone has a different understanding of every single thing in the universe." I as if spoke to myself, "They all made up lies out of it to believe in. Truth doesn't exist. All lies, all modified versions, the same story spiced up, cocktailed and served in different bottles, old and new."

"I agree to disagree." Robbie protested.

"Agree to disagree, what's that shit now?", I broke into fits of laughter.

"Just another line." He joined in, too.

"You know what my line is" I said amidst the giggles, "Lies ... are my objective reality."

LIE 078

Two-timing …

The second semester had started and with ongoing classes, spending time with Katherine and working for Robbie's ambitious project, I sure had developed an incremental need for some more hours to the day.

Though at times I wanted to, but I couldn't let go off, the negotiation model that Robbie and I had been working on. It was a unique and stunning breakthrough made possible with Robbie's intelligence and my mediocre programming skills I sure had some long-term goals. The plan was to make a "Multi-Party Multi-Issue Negotiation model", the very first of its kind, which had some features that could actually question the credibility of the current markets present all over the internet, such as the Amazon and e-bay. We were looking at a better, more advanced and more viable platform for bargaining, negotiating and most essentially making successful deals that would be optimal for even the common man.

So, when Katie and her messages popped back into my life, it was really difficult to hide her from the world. I knew I was going to run out of excuses soon.

Katie and I started meeting at a club, 'The Elbow Room' every second night, after dinner, as we'd sit back and kill some time. Talk about her problems, try to catch up and also tell her about my un-happening life-expeditions, somehow everything except my budding love story with Katherine. I kind of kept it under wraps, for all Katie knew, she was the only owner of that name. Katherine didn't exist. They would show the Fifa World Cup matches on the wall mounted plasma TV and we soon discovered a common ground there as well. Katie had grown into quite a drunkard. Every night, she'd topple over after a few drinks and I had to drop her home, lucky for me, her parents were always out of town, on their business trips. It was not some addiction thing for Katie Thomas, she was actually turning self-destructive. She would tell me about how her parents were never home for her, busy in their schedules and estates, how it was only hotel-take-aways that she had subsisted for so many years now. She would try to get back with Deb at times, talk things out, at times they would actually get along too, while I would sit staring at the muted television sipping cocktails waiting for another small feud to happen, and eventually Katie would return home disappointed every night. An ego clash was always the outcome of every Deb–Katie call. As days passed on to weeks and then two months blinked by, I could not settle the soup I had gotten into.

Katherine and I have always been simple, uncomplicated. We would be contented with just a coffee and some optimistic chit chats. Nitish would catch up on us at times over dinner i.e. whenever Sunny Lodha was way to his native place or was somewhere far from our vicinity. Nitish and Sunny hated each other. The only point of intersection was Katherine and I. Nitish sort of liked me and Katherine. He would never miss an opportunity to meet us.

When asked once, after we dropped Katie at her PG, Nitish blurted out, " You and Katherine are like bread and butter, you know…"

"Er … say again?" I was confused.

"Its like you guys are made for each other, you know, no matter how much or how less butter it is, it always tastes good with bread." Nitish looked at me trying to convince me.

"You should get some sleep." I tried to ignore him.

"And, you should not make the mistake." Nitish's voice went a bit grave.

We stopped.

"What do you mean?" I faced Nitish.

"I know you meet Katie Thomas." Nitish looked me straight in the eye, "What's that café … um … yeah … Elbow Room."

I stared at Nitish. *How does he know* … "you're two-timing, Aakash."

"Katie Thomas is just a friend."

"Convince yourself first." Nitish sat on his avenger and started the ignition, "I like you guys, I look up to this special thing you got Aakash, with Katherine."

I sighed and so did Nitish ..."Don't ruin it, buddy."

***

The indecisive me tried to escape in "MINDMAP", the negotiation model that Robbie and I kept developing. I started avoiding both the Katies soon. I had made up my mind to close the book of Katie Thomas forever. Maybe, Nitish was right. I was sure, Sunny would've advised me the same if I had told him my secrets. He might've even slapped me.

So, I stopped answering Katie Thomas's calls. I had to focus and get back the feelings I had for Katherine.

Katherine was fine with just lunch and ten minutes of small talk but it was my loyalty in question that strangled me. She trusted me and I think I could fake love, too, perfectly. She never had a shred of doubt of this storm that had enraged inside me.

I kept consoling myself that I would get over my demonic side, but as days passed, it started dawning that I had misjudged my heart, too.

***

The next two months, I kept working day and night for the project and my interest grew on the concept that the genius Robbie had spawned. We started writing international papers on our concepts, we cited several international journals and submitted our idea to the IEEE transaction and ACM and some other conferences. A month later all our papers were accepted. In fact, the small startup telekines that helped us with our project by supplying us with guidance in the knowledge of the markets that existed today also showed immense interest in buying our market model once it was tested and deployed.

As two students in their sophomore year, it was more than we had bargained for.

So, when I would comply with Robbie's wishes in making our project open source, free to the world once it really worked out, I knew I was lying somewhere.

LIE 079

Indefinite termination

I would lose track of Katherine sometimes whenever Katie's message would drop by and I would not reply anything against my heart's wishes. Katie Thomas was what you call in Hollywood, a damsel in distress, and I was the love-struck nut case whose heart always beat for her though it had settled for the best friend, Katherine. I could feel Katherine eyeing me with suspicion and getting a bit upset at times and I would always fake attention and interest to hide my emotions. But something was breaking apart and I knew the realization was mutual. I had actually started bunking lectures and coding for the amazing model that we were simulating.

We had applied game theory and heuristic techniques to apply to the current stock market scenario to get a quick picture of the best deals and then shape our logic in the best interest of our customers. We were designing both an optimal and a best deal logic for the customer, but Robbie's idea was to finally adapt the pareto optimal solution, i.e. the solution which would benefit one agent while keeping other agents or customers at least as happy, i.e. the most transparent and honest market scenario ever made. It was a completely automated scenario and hence, an attempt at the most ideal e-market.

Nitish remained absent for the entire third semester. He could only be traced at smokeys or Miami. His life had lost control and the rebel finally got expelled for a year that semester.

I met him two weeks before our semester-end exams when our preparatory leave had just started.

He looked his old self and not prepared to discuss his troubles with me. He had his vodka to sort out his issues. All that constantly bugged him was my reluctance at bringing up my ongoing status with Katherine. "You know you're making a terrible mistake, Aakash, don't you?"

"Yeah, says the guy who bunked so much that he has to skip a year." I sipped my cold drink.

"Yeah, dude, and you know what, I'm the best guy to tell you this."

"Huh? I think Sunny would be preferable, accept it!"

"Oh, c'mon." Nitish waved me down with his hand, "Sunny would slap you red and white and tell things straight to Katherine and the next thing ... break up."

My heart hammered just at the thought of it.

"So," Nitish broke my train of thoughts, "As I was saying I'm the best person for this suggestion you know, cos I make mistakes and so I know the type," he went quiet for a second, "and", he resumed, "I know you're just steps away from one."

"It won't happen", I got up, "I have a project to make, exams to give, I don't have time for a messed up love life now."

"You know the problem with love?" Nitish took his last sip of vodka. I didn't know then that this was the last time I would be talking to Nitish.

"You can't postpone love, Aakash." he looked up at me and smiled, his mischievous, yet insightful grin.

"I'm gonna work it out." I said, And, I left him there to move forward, another wheel detached, a great guy who might have had the most twisted brain of this century, but had his heart at the right place. Surprisingly, I lied to my friend even in my parting words. I was gonna screw things up, settling for a peaceful end wasn't an option anymore.

***

That night I got a mail from e-Bay's marketing chief. It shocked me to the core. A month earlier, I had mailed him our international papers and teacher's recommendations and had asked for his opinion.

I had done it in secret, I knew Robbie would never agree. He hated money-making institutions and my brain always went for the big coup-de-grace. And somewhere, I was getting accustomed to accept the fact that unknowingly I had hit gold. The project was great, in fact revolutionary, something that had the potential to change our lives. So, when I read his reply, much to my elation and adrenaline rush, I kinda got near an alternative to my life.

$$\star\,\star\,\star$$

I was finally settling back to my old life routines without the love issues when Katie's message came that Saturday evening that provided the final twist to the story.

"Hey, Aakash, I know you're not going to reply, but I am not complaining. I just want you to listen to me. Nobody has ever done that to me, except you and so I've expressed in my last wishes to have you as my bestest friend in all my next-lives. This one just plain away sucked. I hope in next life, you and I meet at love square. I hope next time, our story doesn't have a sad ending. Take care."

Katherine looked at me from her discrete structures book.

I looked at her silently as my brain froze. I sat there for almost an eternity petrified, before I left the room and ran for her ... for Katie Thomas.

LIE 080

Traffic, the blurred crowd, lives entwined, strings loose. I await the final pull that upsets the equilibrium and lets out howls of chaos. My mind keeps zooming back and forth amidst her memories and there's a small shred of absurdity in me that realises that I might not actually exist without her presence, as if the decoupling effect would take away my life as a toll. Katie Thomas was the one.

I run to her house. There's nobody in the bungalow. There's a fear growing in constant intensity. I search for her. I totally avoid the friend who's looking out for me just on the next street.

There's an old peepal tree just behind the huge lawns of Katie's bungalow. It's then that I see the flames. Poetry and paintings, ashes and the torn papers, the smoke and the crackling fires is where she sways, her hands clutching on to a torn sketch book.

"Katie." I pulled her out of the mess that she had made of her creations, "Katie", I shook her to bring her back to senses. But she trembled; her eyes just wouldn't meet mine. Fresh tears and red eyes, she was losing her soul with every bit of the demented fire. She wouldn't untangle her hand forcefully from mine and then stumbled to the ground weeping. I looked at her and the shock was unnerving, the spark had faded today. The brilliance and the callousness, the ambitions and the pride, Katie had lost it alright before my eyes and it had turned the night ominous. She wept and I couldn't help it. Maybe, it was the inability to change the facts, to lie to the universe and change its rules that brought forth unfathomable anger in me. Deb was all I could blame and it was intolerable. "It's okay, Katie." I hugged Katie and pleaded her to stop. I couldn't let her go like this. I took her back to her room as she clung to my chest, sobbing uncontrollably.

"Go to sleep," I wiped her face with a wet towel, then lay her on the bed and put the sheets over her. I could still see the flames through the open window far ahead. Katie looked at me and then her lips moved up to mine. "Thanks," she whispered.

I walked down the staircase to Katie's study. All her paintings and diaries were missing, stacks of catalysts in the ever burning anger. The bonfire had snapped her dreams.

Tear, come to my eyes as I switched on her cell lying on the desk and read the last message she had sent me. I moved to the inbox next and started rifling with her received messages. Deb's messages had flooded it and messages of hatred and unforgiveness were all I could find.

"Don't talk to me ever again." "We're done here, Katie. I have nothing to say to you except the fact that my heart has no space for you anymore." "There's no love now here, Katie. It's just pure resentment."

I am shocked at Deb's apathy and the anger burned me like the flames outside. The phone suddenly vibrated and Deb's number flashed on the screen. I picked it up instantaneously. "You, ruthless moron."

"Who's it?" Deb asked. "How could you do this, Deb? How could you break her heart of all people? That one heart I would've died to just etch my name on."

"Aakash." Deb's voice was alarmed as the smoke cleared We were talking after two years and if anything, my hatred had just increased tenfold, "It can't be you?" Deb was stunned.

"Yes, it's me Deb. And, this time I'm here to stay." Deb processed the words for a moment, then he almost shouted, "Give the phone to Katie. I need to talk to her."

"Why?" I snarled, "You want to kill her now. Do you?"

"What do you mean?" His voice lost a bit of sharpness.

"You nearly killed her today, Deb. I can't believe she was going to burn herself because of a priceless speck of dust like you. "

"No … You're lying. I need to talk to her. I need to apologize."

"No apologies." I almost spat venom, "Not, you Deb. No more of your hatred and no more of your love square. "

"I don't understand you?" Deb's voice trembled.

"It's plain English. I love Katie and she loves me now. You just have to let her have her peace with that." I couldn't believe what I said as I continued my lie, "We're together now, Deb and you're the only one who can ruin it all. Who can turn her back into the suicidal girl that I'm trying so hard to change."

Deb was quiet as he could not mistake the resolution and strong determination in my voice. He believed me.

"But I ...", he stuttered, "I love her, Aakash." "I love her ... more."

Deb's voice was sandpapery when he put down the receiver finally, "Take care of her."

✳ ✳ ✳

It was dawn when I left for home. The streets were empty.

A girl in a black jacket sat on the bench on the street opposite Katie's bungalow, her head in her lap as she slept.

"Katherine." my voice woke her up as she looked at me. Fresh tears formed in her eye.

"We're over, Aakash."

She said it even before I could walk up to her.

I stood there on the road, midway, trying to say something, anything ... make up another lie, turn all of this into a story without any deception or betrayal, win her back but I knew she had finally caught me red handed.

She walked away and I stayed there.

Traffic, the blurred crowd, lives entwined, strings loose ... I was lost here, with a thousand choices that I didn't choose.

LIE 081

Robbie and I were at our last stage of creating a unique and brilliant product and all we could do was argue.

Points of conflict and disagreements had increased after my break up with his sister. He wouldn't reveal it, but Robbie hated me. I disgusted him, in fact, for my constant pleas on selling our product. He had his prospects clear, his priorities straight, he was creating it for the betterment of the rich and the poor, to help a developing country like ours; while all I wanted was to make the full use of the potential of this small home-made dynamite. I didn't want this flame to die out. I wanted it to be the grapevine fires, spreading through the world, bringing on a change. A multi issue multi-party negotiation model was a first of its kind experiment and it had a cent percent chance of striking it, I kind of was assured after the set of mails that I had been receiving bereft of Robbie's knowledge.

So, I initiated my plan at last. It took me three weeks to finalise things but if truth be told I had started my preparations the minute Robbie had stood in front of Dyaneshwara Hall and told me his idea of creating this project. I just didn't know that this would be so life changing.

But I was ready for it. And, I knew it every time I looked at Katherine's empty bench in class. She had gone back to Calcutta for a few days. She had taken medical leave but I knew she was avoiding me forever. She would show up eventually, maybe, a month later, and if I was still here, she would ignore me, but there it was, a certain end to a great friendship. I knew there was nothing for me here, anymore.

Katie Thomas' parents had come visiting and they were consulting doctors. I didn't visit them. All I could do was SMS her and know that she was still recuperating from her sadness.

I didn't know how I would explain my actions to her over the next few days but if I had got it right, I knew this. The last 20 years of my life had just turned me into an escapist and I was good at it.

✸ ✸ ✸

Eventually, the project was successfully completed. It implemented the optimal solutions for better negotiation while I kept a secondary CD of all the equations for incorporating the logic of the best decisions for a biased decision which'd be beneficial to only one customer.

Robbie was more than excited and he kind of forgave me once the project got completed. He couldn't thank me enough for trusting his instincts and helping him throughout.

At times, I wanted him to hate me. I knew it would be the final outcome and so I wanted him to start early.

And then, one fine day, the time came for my greatest betrayal.

✸ ✸ ✸

We got drunk that night, as we had decided. It was the night that our project was finally completed, the user interface prepared, the killer ready to win every competition it was submitted to. "This changes everything." Robbie couldn't stop smiling.

I nodded, trying my best to fake a smile.

"Aakash, boy", Robbie actually broke into a nerd-dance, "We're gonna be famous, bro."

I raised my glass to him.

Then, I took another sip of the poison.

I need a lot of alcohol to do this.

"You know," Robbie too took a swig, "I never thought we could achieve this. And, you always did, man!! I respect you, friend. You are the best thing."

And then, he came and hugged me.

It caught me off guard, and I tried to cut myself loose, but he was too drunk to notice.

He wept on my shoulder.

"You made me realise my dream, Aakash. God bless you, yaar." He said with such honesty that it stung me.

"Naah," I made another glass of the strong vodka for him, and then slipped the small capsule in it as I handed it over to him.

"No blessings here, Robbie." I laughed at my own self, "I'm too rotten for anything as optimistic as a blithe."

"No, man!!" Robbie was not convinced as he sipped the drink, "You know what!! I agree to disagree."

We broke into fits of laughter.

"Your suckiest line ever." I made him take another sip.

"We'll be famous, man!! We'll change the world.", Robbie whispered as he fell flat on the floor, unconscious, the adulterated vodka spilled over the ground.

"Yeah, bro, that we will.", I lied to him one last time.

I looked at my watch. I don't have much time.

I tiptoed to his desk, his laptop screen was on, unlocked. He was just using it, minutes ago.

I wrote the commands.

The last file got deleted ten seconds later.

Then, I opened the bottom shelf of his drawer.

The last CD titled, "MINDMAP", lay there in the cabinet, with all those thousand mathematical equations and logic diagrams.

I picked them up and out came the cigarette lighter.

I set it all ablaze, as Robbie's dreams faded into dust.

I looked at Robbie for the last time as he lay snoring on the floor, beside the ashes of his hard work.

"So long, my friend."

✱ ✱ ✱

I left Robbie lying unconscious in his room. He was gone for the next twelve hours. The drug confirmed it.

My heart throbbed. I had just committed a heinous crime. I couldn't believe I had actually the guts to pull this off, but here I was, taking those extreme measures.

Calm and composed, I went into my room. My luggage was packed, my ticket that I had received six days ago was right there in my backpack. Sunny Lodha sat there finishing "Five Point someone", as he looked up at me.

"Hey, Aakash," he beamed, "When will you be back from Calcutta?"

"In a week." I lied.

"Cool." He smiled, "Hey, remind me when you get back, I owe you a treat."

"For what." I said grabbing my bags.

"For the girl with the Gucci bag." He winked at me, standing up, "I asked her out today and she said yes."

As much as I was afraid thinking of my present situation, I couldn't miss out on my last conversation with Sunny Lodha. He was like a brother to me and was happy today. Couldn't miss on that.

"That is the most awesome news I've heard in this entire year!!" I went and hugged him.

"Thanks man!" He almost jumped in joy.

"So...," I said, "What worked for you?"

"Truth, liar boy," Sunny Lodha, "Seems she likes the real me. Says I'm the most honest guy she has met." He blushed.

"Hmmm." I managed to smile, "Looks like you were right all this while, after all."

"Told ya." he squeaked.

"Anyways, you should be going now. Don't wanna miss your flight." The sweetest guy in the planet bid me goodbye.

My eyes moistened a bit as I took one final look at him and left.

✶✶✶

LIE 082

I rechecked my ticket.

Santa Cruz to Lax. Mumbai to Los Angeles.

Three more hours to go.

I closed my eyes as I recounted this crazy journey life had been and all I could find were my lies.

It frustrated me. My betrayals. I just stole the dream of my best friend Cos I wanted the money and he wanted what was right. I broke the heart of my best friend just because she made one mistake, loved me endlessly. I ended another relationship of a girl, who was the love of my life, because I couldn't stand her boyfriend, who also surprisingly happened to be a guy who respected me. I couldn't even come to think of what they would all say tomorrow, Robbie, Nitish, Sunny, Katie, Katherine.

I sighed and closed my eyes.

***

"Hey, Aakash".

I opened my eyes and she sat there, right beside me ... Katherine Andrews, my sweetest best friend Kates ...

She smiled at me as it soothened my heartbeats, balming me with a love that made me resistant to all the insecurities of the world.

"How did you find me?" I asked her, knowing the answer.

"I never lost you." she smiled like a princess, tufts of her hair flying to her eyes, her beautiful fragrance looming all over me.

"I lost you, Kates." I hugged her so tight, I couldn't let go, "I am such a bad friend, am I not, Katie, all I ever gave you was pain and lies."

"No, you're not, Aakash. You gave me something much more than that." She held me, brushing my hair, "You gave me faith, in all those indecisions and all those betrayals, there was this one constant thing, this connection that never broke." She came close to my ears, "You have always loved me, Aakash."

"Don't you see what I've done to you, Katherine? I have made you believe in this fairy tale." I stood up and started walking away.

"You know, the first time you came to my house, my dad sang all evening. He was really happy." Katie said suddenly.

I laughed amidst tears, "Military uncle smiled at me once! That's so strange to believe."

I remembered Dennis Andrews and his horrible mathematics classes.

"You know why? It's because you were the first guy who ever knocked at my house searching for me. You were the first guy I talked to and you came unannounced, like you always do."

"It's all make believe, Katie. It's a fairy tale ... a dream."

"This fairy tale, Aakash," Katherine stood up and came closer, "is your life."

She kissed me and my fears were gone, my guilt had melted away and my brain was clear of all thoughts.

She came close and her lips touched mine and she whispered, "I am your dream, Aakash and I know you don't want to wake up."

✳ ✳ ✳

I opened my eyes and the lights zoomed back. I had been dreaming and I had tears in my eyes. I didn't meet Katie that night. I wanted to say goodbye, fall back to sleep, just to find her there, waiting for me.

I started blogging instead.

I wrote about Katherine, my best friend, her beauty, her jokes, her favourite songs and her pranks.

It was then that I met Kabir (remember Lie 004)!

101 lies started that night at the airport and the next 19 chapters talk about how it all ends.

***

Prologue to the last part: That night, in another part of the world, in a pink and blue house at 24 Parganas, a girl wakes up with the same dream that I had. She coughs and spits blood. Terminal leukemia is taking its toll and she knows the end is near…

VOLUME 5

U.S. Diaries

LIE 083

One for the money

The flight landed at Los Angeles, morning 7:30 am.

I had never been outside India, and although the sights were breathtaking, the constant reminders of my past and uncertain future filled my mind with frivolous worries.

All I knew was that a person named Mr Chris Adams would be at the south terminal to collect me. Let me tell you from the beginning, i.e. the first mail from the chief marketing executive of eBay that I had received three months ago. It had in it, all the reviews of market developers of e bay and how much they appreciated this idea of the multi-party multi-issue negotiation model that Robbie and I had designed. They wanted to discuss further about its implementations and had sent us the invites to their annual conference at Los Angeles. I had replied with an entire demo of our model and asking them to arrange for my ticket because it was unaffordable for me to attend their conference.

I had very thin hopes for a response, but they did reply and this time, it was the ticket.

They in fact threw an offer, to work with them, if all went well, for our design. I knew it would be hard to manage things in Robbie's absence at the conference but I knew I could still make it.

Now, all I needed was to persuade Robbie.

But he wouldn't agree. His intentions were that of selling this model for free. I, on the contrary, knew the rising demand, and I couldn't resist the temptation. The greed had played into my mind and I knew I could sell it for a lot of bucks.

So, that day at Los Angeles, as I got down from the plane, I had no alternatives. Either Mr Chris Adams would be there waiting for me at the south terminal or I was gonna be lost out here. I didn't have a plan B for the first time in my life.

With the backed up CDs of "MINDMAP – Multi-Issue Negotiation Development using Multi Agents project" in my backpack, I trodded towards my pick up point. The crowd was thin there, only a few bystanders and among them, a thin middle-aged chauffeur in a black suit and with a placard that displayed my name in capitals.

"Hello, that would be me." I introduced myself.

"Ohh, a hearty welcome, monsieur." The man spoke in a lucid but heavily accented English, " I am Tom Martin, your chauffeur and Mr Chris Adams has asked me to drive you to the north software park, where the conference is being held. May I carry your lugguage to the car, Sir?"

"No, thank you, it's just one bag." I politely refused his help with my sack that had just two pairs of shirts, a bunch of undies one pair of jeans and an aweful lot of files and documents.

I walked half a mile with him to the parking arena and when he pointed at my pick up cab, I was mindblown.

A limo. I gaped just at the sight of the divine beast. It was out of this world.

Nice start bro, I mused as I sat inside the car that had sushi inside it for lunch and a lot of drinks in a mini bar all easily spaced inside it.

Soon, I was rocketing off through the highways of the city towards the conference venue that was actually going to decide my fate.

There was a partition between the driver's chamber and my sitting space inside the car but I insisted on keeping it open so that Mr Tom Martin could give me a quick tour of the city on the way.

"So, you are from London?", I asked him curiously as he explained his British accent, "How's it like now there?"

"It snows at this time of the year, Sir. My house is always covered in thick snow", Tom chuckled lightly as he steered through the light traffic.

"And this car? Is it yours, Tom?"

"No, Mr Aakash." Tom laughed a bit, "Well for once, if I had that sort of asset Sir, I would right now be listening to Beethoven beside the fireplace at my home."

"Hmmm, I bet this one costs ten million or something." I said it more to myself than to him.

✶ ✶ ✶

We reached the conference venue an hour later. A gigantic structure, it looked like a stadium from the outside.

"Well, here's my card, Sir." Tom handed me his card, "Whenever you require the cab, call me an hour or two before. And, Mr Chris has also asked me to give this cell phone to you. It has me and him listed in contacts."

He handed me an iphone.

"Whoa!", I looked at the gadget with pleasure and optimism. Somehow I had a feeling luck had this dice going for me.

I met Mr Chris Adams and a bunch of other middle-aged guys who eyed me skeptically as Mr. Adams walked me to the side of the auditorium for a private word.

"So, you're the kid who developed that incredible model." He smiled at me.

I nodded, nervousness hitting my neurons.

"Alright, so here's the drill." Mr Chris got straight down to business, "We're going to discuss around 130 potential project ideas for our research and development field today. Around thirty more commerce companies are part of this entire conference and they would also show interest in spending and sponsoring new and genuine ideas. And, yours is quite a good one for that matter. It has already been ventured on before in the last three international conferences but the project has not gotten anywhere till date. Yours is however, a fresh start with a very precise and unique idea."

My mind went back to all the conference papers I had seen on Robbie the first time he was discussing the inception of the idea with me. The guy knew this could be a breakthrough and he outdid every competition.

"So, Aakash, to boost a bit of your moral, I think it is safe for me to say that we at our r&d department considered your demo and put in your equations and logical solutions to test and I have to say, we are quite impressed by your efforts. If all goes well and we have a good presentation by the evening, I think your project would be sponsored by E-Bay" He winked.

"Thank you, Sir", was all I managed to say, overwhelmed.

The conference started at 10:30 in the morning and went for its first break at noon. The first session discussed all the current developments and the changing prospect of the e-market. It had introductory speeches from the CEOs of the companies present and a brief discussion of analytics and sensex by two business analysts from Wall Street. One of them went by the name of Mr Karl Henrick. The guy had a French beard, brown hair, green eyes and looked like a Hollywood superstar with his cool demeanor.

I kept on rehearsing the presentation in my head. The lunch felt amazing as I browsed through a hundred different dishes and listened to discussions of a billion crore deal alliance amongst e-trade and another firm.

"Hey, aren't you Aakash Roy?" Karl Henrick, the business analyst enquired to my utmost amazement.

I nodded, speechless.

"Well, nice to meet you, boy." He shook hands with me and took the seat next to mine, his plate filled with pasta and French fries.

"So, you might be wondering how I know your name out of the blue!"

I nodded again, a dollop of Belgium ice-cream still melting in my mouth.

"Well, you see, I take care of a lot of shares for e-Bay. I'm an external advisor for them and just yesterday, I happened to read your file. One of the aspirants for the annual funding project of e-Bay, aren't you?"

"Yes, my project is called MINDMAP." I tried to bring something to the table.

"Well yeah, I know, nice name, I must say." He said encouragingly.

"So, Aakash," he continued, "Well, while I looked into your project I have to tell you, I found enormous potential. It was a full-fledged market and if you know what e-Bay will do to it," his voice went down a decebel, "this I have to specify is confidential stuff, but what they are going to do is only implement a few ideas from that entire model of yours, incorporate one or two of its features into their extensive e-market scenario and that would be the end of it. Next thing you know, you'd be on a flight back to India and you'd have to scroll down hundreds of names just to find your credit somewhere down the list. Your project will not be yours in another year, its best features inherited and the rest of it, useless."

He paused and looked at me for a response.

"Why are you telling me this?" I was blank with the news.

"I am telling you this" Karl bent forward and whispered, "because I know there were two of you who made this project but only one thought of a lucrative business idea out of it. The project had been designed to implement an optimal solution but you have plugged in the concept of a biased result so as to filter out any downsides or mutual settlements and thirdly, Aakash, because I know you came here for the money. You want to sell your thing and you want it all, for your own."

I was thunderstruck.

How could a man from Wall Street, being a super-rich business analyst, has managed to find out, not only about this small concept of mine, but also figure out my entire freaking strategy.

"How?" was all I could mouth.

Karl Henrick chortled and had a few more fries before he answered.

"Let's just say, I have an eye for raw quality and I like your work."

"So, what're you trying to put up here?" I didn't have any more assumptions to make here. This man was either a potential threat or a boon, and the prospect was hazy at the moment.

"All I'm trying to tell you here, Aakash, is that the moment you're done with your presentation here in this conference, you're done with your authenticity and your idea is just another test experiment for a million dollar enterprise."

"And, what's the alternative?"

"Take a risk. Don't present this idea today at the conference. Don't submit it."

"And then, what?"

"Then me Aakash."

Karl then gave me a card.

Karl Henrick, CEO, TesttubeTechnologies Incl., Silicon Valley, California.

"You own a company?" I was stupefied.

"It's a startup. I've all the other support facilities, Aakash, the perfect security enhancements, the artificial learning techniques based on the present market scenario and an experience. All I need is a new idea." Then he looked at me and this time, those green eyes had a revelation, "I see that in you."

It was 1 pm and the lunch break was over.

Karl left me in dilemma and joined the rest of the I.T. guys to the auditorium. I sat there till the entire café emptied, I sat there wondering and with indecision, and I sat there for another hour weighing all my options until I took the judgement call.

The only bits and pieces that I had not known then was that Karl Henrick had been studying my file for over three months now. He had also been a business analyst for e-Bay purposely for the last three years, he was studying all their future endeavours so that when he entered the market he could overthrow his primary rival in terms of future innovation. His team was forged out of the few freshmen that he had gathered from these submissions at e-Bay for project fundings. He talked Mr Chris Adams into fetching me to this conference, because he knew this was the only way I could be brought in here and he also did not pass the entire demo that I had submitted. He cancelled a module of the entire design in his revaluation intentionally while finally submitting it for the fund project of e-Bay to reconsider. He had cut out a chunk of my project that he was going to use in his startup even if I didn't agree to his proposal.

Karl Henrick was probably the most manipulative person in the history of the electronic market industry but he was witty enough to keep it all under wraps, live his life like a lie.

LIE 084

What might have been…

The presentations started after three in the afternoon.

I had another chance of talking to Mr Chris Adams and enquired of him as to what was going to happen to my project once it got selected. He told me it was a very prestigious thing to get selections in this conference, showed me another bunch of thirty to forty students who were in the queue with their projects from across the globe and informed me that every year, they sponsored around seven projects that helped them to enhance their market model. I told him how much honoured I was to be there, then went back to my seat, called up Karl Henrick from his number in his card one last time to clear certain things. He was sitting on the other side of the auditorium and after the call ended, he left the premises in the next ten minutes.

I was to present at 5 pm. When my turn came, they could not find me in my seat.

All I knew was my name must have been announced three times, the judges must have awaited my presentation, after a while they must've forgotten my name and called the next participant, and then a very disappointed Mr Chris Adams might have called me up at the cell he gave me only to find that I have left it with my chauffeur Tom Martin and apologised for my behaviour and my lie. But I had no time to spare to find out whether everything went as planned.

All I knew was that I was on another flight to California at 5 pm with Karl Henrick.

I signed the papers at 7:30 that night and Karl Henrick gave me my first cheque of a thousand dollar, to get a new phone and also accommodated me at one of the rest houses allotted for the TestTubeTechnolegies international staff members.

My life had gone for a 360% spin, I had signed up for working at a start up with a complete stranger and a shrewd manipulator for a boss. I couldn't believe that MindMap was the innovative idea on which this entire new firm Tcube (Testtubetechnologies) set up only a month ago would invest upon all its resources.

I knew that Robbie would have been very proud if he could witness the radical change he had envisaged for the world was being accepted but then, Robbie might have always known it. Maybe, that's why he had decided to make it priceless.

I called up dad the next day from the ISD booth, told him to his surprise, rather shock, that I was in the States, I had joined a firm in the Silicon Valley and that I had decided to drop out of college. He was utterly bewildered and panicked but I knew I had to stick to my plan, even if it were against my dad's wishes. The bigger picture was this and this was my only shortcut to success.

Next, I called up Sunny and revealed him the truth. His reactions seemed like a rip off from my dad's call and I was already net practised with my set of answers. Only this time he cursed me too, at the end because my being here meant I was breaking up with Katherine. The break up however, had already happened. Maybe, it was one of the catalysts that led to all these extreme measures. However, the past was a mess up to delve into and I couldn't dare to do it.

I neither called Katherine nor Katie Thomas.

I later mustered all my courage and called up Katie's parents to give them a heads up as to how their daughter had just a few days ago turned suicidal and had made a bonfire of her stash of drawings and how important it was for them to be there for her now, with me gone.

They refused to accept my random news and tagged me as a lunatic, but I was certain later that day, they must have summoned Katie, asked her about the fidelity of the entire episode and her responses must have ascertained the truth behind my story.

I sat and watched the sunset in the bay area at San Jose while having a hot dog and cappuchino, all alone, without a person to talk to, without one friendly face in the vicinity and without much awareness of my directions back home.

The old me was no more to be found in this alien land and I felt satisfied even in this moment of solitude. I was happy because I was starting over and I knew this might be it. The end of all my lies and all my short cuts. My destiny. Maybe, my story had come to the point where I could start it afresh, new pages and a new diary.

✶ ✶ ✶

But maybe, the universe was just lying to me like I lied to Chris Adams or Robbie or Katherine. Maybe, I was just nearing payback time. My reckoning.

LIE 085

I was the youngest guy in the team and although the basic foundation came from my e-market model, it kept on getting comprehensive and more complex with the involvement of twenty new guys into the redesign and technical specifications. We put in new test cases, tested the project for boundary conditions, errors were brought into the limelight. The algorithms were put into the extreme case scenarios, the worst and the best, and flaws were redundant.

Soon, I would find myself staying up all night rejecting out equations that I was once proud of. Even then, I was lagging behind, falling back and I could feel the sense of defeat drawing closer. Karl had never told me how advanced his techniques would be, how far I was from these new technologies and how much expertise I actually needed to master them to stay important to the group. He just kept on pushing me to the limits waiting patiently for my shell to break. I soon realised that he was craftily making me incompatible for the model that I myself had envisioned once. He would often send me as the presentation guy to other companies to endorse our market model. His prospect was that because MindMap was going to be a new cult in the e-market sector so the company needed fresh youth as the face of the company. TestTubetechnologies should look cool and trendy to the world, the output of young minds and a paradigm shift and hence they wanted a young guy to present the project to the world. Secondly, I was also the least experienced and amateur engineer in the group and hence I became an obvious choice for presentations and peoplesoft stuff.

Karl was like me, he wanted it all for himself. The problem was, he was way too efficient and had a fortune of experience.

Three months down the lane, I took my first break, attended a show of Coldplay at the Hp stadium. It was the premiere of their brand new album Mylo Xyloto, and the kaleidoscopic colours could spellbind any eyes, but my mind kept wavering back to the codes I was developing, Java persistence and the set of equations at my cubicle downtown. I could feel the restlessness as they would play one after another, all my favourite tracks, "Yellow", "speed of sound", "up in flames", "paradise". I couldn't enjoy the sweetness yet, the melody, the vibe of the moment. I was stuck with my self-demons.

I bailed out on the show half an hour later. Tom Martin picked me up in the limo that I always liked to call up whenever I needed transport facilities and had just got my salary cheque for the month.

"Where to, Aakash?" He said in his heavy and professional voice.

"Back to my office Tom, I've to work tonight."

"Isn't it getting very strenuous these days for you, Aakash?" He said turning on the ignition.

"Tell me about it!" I sighed, "But it's okay you know, I kind of like the work. I have nothing else to do here. No other errands to run, no family to visit."

"I hope you'd be visiting your parents soon in India, right?" Tom must've recognised my monotonous tone, so the question.

"I have nobody there, Tom." I mused, "Just my dad and he really doesn't love me that much."

Dad's calls had become infrequent in the last two months. He had finally started to estimate the growing estrangement between us and the distance kept on increasing.

"I beg your pardon, I might speak a bit out of line here, but you are too young to be working for so much money and such a complicated industry."

"Well, you know what Tom, I chose this and I'm going to win it. Going to make my way through. Testtubetechnologies was my choice over eBay. eBay would've known my limits, it'd been probably easier back in there, but I preferred a startup over that life. I've to make my choice count, Tom."

I reached the office an hour later. Most of the staff had left and gone out to enjoy the weekend. I sat back in my cubicle that entire night, figuring out all the fields of my incompetencies. I made a plan that night, chalked out an excel sheet of all the do's for that weekend and for the rest of the thirty weekends before this project got live to the world.

I was going to be there when my dream came true. MindMap was my brainchild; I couldn't let them steal it from me.

Every Tuesday there would be a weekly review meeting held in the office premises and everybody would put their task-accomplished sheets up for appraisals.

I would sit there, listen to them blurt out all their current work scenarios and their agendas and every single meeting since that first weekend of exhaustive studies, I was ahead of them all. I didn't reveal it to Karl Henrick or any other colleague. My extra efforts were going to be my secret.

What I assured instead was just a month before the project was to be launched; I came back in full swing, with all my last minute suggestions, which had months of weekend efforts put behind them.

The entire team of nearly sixty people was now in for a surprise.

I lied to them all along since the very end and for Karl, it became difficult to put me aside now.

In other words, I had nailed my way through the team into our virtual e-market.

MindMap was changed to MindMark(et) with a last minute suggestion for a catchy name, and it released on 21st August 2009.

My name was in the newspapers as one of the fourteen chief designers of the new e-market.

We managed to rope in great deals from product supplying companies such as acer and Phillips and Sony in the first month.

Six months later, our catalogue had a list of market items that ranged a total of 348 companies.

MindMark had a database that changed from gigabytes to terabytes in an year, with all kinds of ads and alliances pouring in and the success story continued.

LIE 086

The second craziest night!

TestTubeTechnologies became an iconic industry which was nominated as the top ten best startups of the year 2010. MindMark was called a trendsetter and its graphical user interface became critically acclaimed.

Our turnover increased, so did the team members. In one and a half years, MindMark had from 183 employees from the 60 they had started with.

I was famous in the premises. They called me neo, the guy who dreamt of changing the system and succeeded. It was also because I used to quote the line of the movie matrix, "Don't think you are, know you are" as a tag line in almost all my presentations. My face had already been displayed in *New York Times* and I gave a BBC interview too on behalf of Tcube.

I also owned a considerable amount of the company's shares and could see myself replacing Karl Henrick in another year or two. I had the chance of becoming the youngest CEO from India to own a multi-million dollar firm.

The problem, however, was that Karl Henrick could see through my lies and strategies. He just yet didn't figure out the pace which I was trying to adapt towards my rise.

That new year, Karl Henrick and the rest of my team members, around 25 of us from TestTubeTechnologies went to a famous club "Greystone Manor" at Cienega Blvd, Los Angeles to celebrate our recent success.

The place was what you would see in movies and fantasise about. It was orgasmic, the music, the DJ, the girls and the party. Champagne and booze and strippers, the place was wild and exotically mindblowing.

Karl was around 35, he was what you could call a doppelganger of Brad Pitt in certain aspects and he was a billionaire. The guy charmed his way to a table of some infinitely hot girls in a matter of minutes and introduced me to one of them. I was awestruck at first and stammered even while saying "Hi," but soon enough I realised she was actually "high".

"So, Aksh," the drunk chick mispronounced my name, put my arms around her exposed hot waist and asked over the music, "Wat do you do??"

"Oh, I," I stammered as my hands went hot just touching her athletically seductive body, "I ... er ... I work as a senior software developer at Tcube, you know the new MindMark thing."

"Oh, hey, aren't you that guy who spoke in an eerie accent at that BBC interview last Friday night?"

"Yeah, well, I'm an Indian and it was proper English." I felt quite proud of myself.

We danced into the wild party and she kept on taking tequila shots while I settled for a can of beer. Soon enough, she was kissing me and I had a crazy feeling I might get lucky tonight after all. It was after midnight, that the music got so loud, she finally threw up all over my new leather jacket. Next thing, the hot chick fainted in my arms.

"Karl!!", I shouted at the top of my voice but the music beats were way too louder.

I dragged the girl whose name was either candy or brandy to the nearest lounge and then rested her over the soft cushions.

"Aakash", I suddenly heard Katherine's voice through the crowd and turned around, adrenaline rushing through me.

All I could see were crazy dance steps and drunk teenagers. I walked back to the dancing maniacs, disappointed. It played back in my mind, Katherine's voice and a bout of restlessness took over.

Karl came back dancing and laughing with a blonde and then asked me, "Where's that chick I hooked you up with?"

"Nice try wingman, but she is fast asleep and I feel tired." I felt my head heavy with the two cans of beer that I had had earlier and Katherine's thoughts were suddenly pinning my bubble of complacency.

"Oh, c'mon man! The night's young. Here take one of these", Karl put a white tablet in my hand, "this will calm you down."

"No ... I'm sorry, but I don't take pills."

"oh don't be a baby Aakash. Remember you're the guy who never says "no". Now, take it and forget your worries, dude. Enjoy this night." Karl almost put the pill in my mouth.

"But what is it?" I asked a bit wary.

"Aah, it's just a stress buster Aakash, relieves your nerves." Karl lied swiftly.

The drug took me instantaneously. It was 'ecstasy' as I later found out and I lost my grip in a fraction of seconds. Everything blurred from that moment on. I was dancing and swaying, and my thoughts were random and eccentric. I was kissing random girls and I was drinking beyond control. I revolved out of sanity and even then, she was there, Katherine, looking right into my mind.

"Here Aakash, take a seat", Karl made me sit in a secluded counter. The music rang in my ear and nausea drifted in but Katherine was becoming clearer by the minute. I watched her as she danced in a white gown right in front of me, her beauty entrapping me, disarming my defenses.

"Okay now Aakash." Karl's voice became serious and he lit a cigar as he looked at me with loathing, "You are going to tell me everything from the beginning."

LIE 087

I remember that evening Katherine and I broke up.
She found me at Katie's place that morning, left me there and ran away crying. For the first time she could see things as they were, without the lies and the discrepancies.

"Why did you call me here, Aakash? I don't think we have anything to talk about." Katherine's eyes are puffy. She had been crying all day. Her face was swollen and she looked ill.

"Katherine are you alright?" I couldn't even start to describe how terrible I felt as I looked at my best friend, "I am sorry, Kates, but I need to clear it all up."

"Go on then, Aakash. Talk."

"Okay, Katie, that friend of mine at whose place I spent the night, would have killed herself tonite if I had not been there." I presented the fact without a single modification. Katherine had the right to know the truth this time.

"Don't you feel any shame, Aakash?" Katherine sneered.

"I don't understand, Katherine." I was confused.

"Do you even think what you say?" Katherine said outbursting with tears, "You have to get stuff done at the bank on Sundays. You delete all those messages from that girl and you think I never read them? You are telling me that girl would've killed herself if you had not been there? Why do you make up such lies, Aakash? Why can't you just tell the goddamn truth!" She was shouting now and the entire CCD crowd had their eyes on us.

I was unnerved. Katie stopped talking while sobbing hysterically.

I didn't know what to say anymore.

"I trusted, you Aakash. Of all the people in the world, I came back for

408

you. I thought you'd make me live, Aakash. You killed me." Katherine cried in earnest.

People were standing all around us. Random noise everywhere. I could tell that half of them wanted to beat me to death at the very moment while the other half were considering whether Katie would make it without a relapse.

✱✱✱

"Tell me, Aakash." Karl prodded me, "What happened to the other guy who made that project with you? Why don't you ever mention him? "

"Robbie." I stammered as my mind was zooming uncontrollably, the pill taking away my senses every second. I felt dizzy and my legs couldn't support me anymore.

"What about him?", Karl keeps asking incessantly, "What did you do to him, Aakash?"

"I …," I saw Katherine jumping with joy all around me, her smile as radiant as the sunrise, her lips resplendent with songs, her eyes lost in dreams and hopes.

"Talk to me, goddamit!" Karl slapped me. He wanted the truth tonite. He had drugged me into this. Everybody wanted the truth.

✱✱✱

"Just hear me out Katherine." I paused, "You know, you don't have to. Just don't cry Katherine. Please don't. I'm not worth it."

"That's the problem Aakash." Katherine looked at me between tears, "You were my treasure. Why did you deceive me like that? You know I will be lost out here without you.."

"I wouldn't let that happen. I could still make things right Kates. Please, let me explain."

"No…," Katherine suddenly went quiet. She picked up her bag, "It's too late for that now. You've lost me Aakash. ".

She stormed out.

I ran behind her, "Kates, stop."

✱✱✱

"I stole Robbie's idea. "

Karl was petrified. He was thunderstruck as he tried to process what I had just said.

"How exactly?"

"I drugged him. Burnt his papers. Made a back up CD and came here. I stole his dream and I ruined it for him." My head fell to the table and I passed out.

Karl left me and celebrated some more of the night. He knew I would forget it all when I woke up next morning in my hotel suite with Candy by my side. It would be stored in a drugged memory of my mind and I'd never know the biggest secret of my life had now been revealed to my greatest enemy.

Karl Henrick never valued me. He always knew I had a darker shade. He always knew I had secrets and he knew they were what would ruin me.

✳ ✳ ✳

"Don't Kates." I stopped her midway, "Don't leave me like that." I fell on my knees, "You're my best friend. I love you."

"Don't." Katherine squeaked, "Don't lie, Aakash. The only thing you ever loved is you."

I knelt down there and my eyes were misty. I couldn't believe my heart would ache so much.

Was Katherine more than my friend? Or, was I lying unconsciously again? Was this more than a bond of friendship? Did I really love Katherine Andrews?

"I pray to god that one day you suffer the ache of a broken heart, Aakash. That day you will plead for that one person who cared for you the most and all you will find is a mirror and yourself... I hate you, Aakash Roy."

LIE 088

"Hey dude! Guess what just happened." Ricky Patel, a colleague called me up at 3:30 am in the night february 2011, more than one year after that night at the club.

"You woke me up from a great dream! That happened!" I tried to open up my eyes and get some water.

"Dude, T³ is now officially in the latest fortune 500 companies in the world."

"What !!" I nearly choked, "You're kidding me!"

"No neo ... it's your day today!! Gear up boy! You're famous!!"

✳ ✳ ✳

Mercedes Clk – 350, an Armani suit, a Rolex Daytona, I drove to my office. I Aakash Roy, was a success story.

I took the elevator, 22ⁿᵈ floor.

As I entered the premises, there was applause, astounding applause. Colleagues howled, hugged, shook my hand, patted, congratulated me as I prepared for another interview by CNN up in another 4 hours.

I celebrated, had a sip of champagne to start my day excused myself for a moment, went to the washroom, tucked in my shirt properly, combed my hair and appreciated myself again.

Then, I walked back, arranged my files and I was summoned by the boss, Mr Karl Henrick.

I wore my tie, cleared my voice and walked towards his cabin.

"I bet it's another raise." Julie Mcarthy chimed from beside.

"He's gonna be gifted a house at Beverly Hills this time." Robin said, winking at me.

"Yeah, right." I stuck my tongue out before I entered Karl's cabin.

"Hey, Karl, Congrats buddy." I closed the door.

Karl stayed quiet. He was looking at the view outside his gigantic cabin through the glass pane. I could see a chopper circulate far off under the California sun.

"So, where's the party tonight?" I smiled and picked up the issue of *New York Times* from the table.

"There will be no party tonight, Aakash." Karl Henrick's voice was grave and it caught me off guard.

"Whoa! What happened, man! Don't tell me you're having a bad day, Karl! I mean, you know the news, right?"

"It's not me, Aakash. It's your turn today." Karl now looked at me and his face had no signs of a joke-on-its-way expression.

"What do you mean?" I said slowly trying to anticipate the situation.

"I mean, there's a blank cheque there on the table. Make it your last paycheque there. Pick any number, Aakash. But once you're done with it, leave and never come back here again."

"What ?" I looked at the blank cheque, "Is this some stupid prank? Where are the cameras, Karl?"

"This ain't a joke and I'm not firing you, Aakash. It's a simple request. I'm asking you to quit. Resign."

"And, why'd I do that?" My throat had gone dry and my chest is lead.

"Because I don't think I need you as the face of this company anymore. You're not worth the acclaim. This TestTubeTech, Tcube is not your company, Aakash, I own it. It's mine."

"I have one third of this company's share, Karl. You can't just make me go away like this." My voice was shaky, "And, what do you mean I have to resign? MindMark is my model, I resign, the company stops. I'm not just the face here, Karl, I am the body of this very firm, Karl, you can't make me leave it, because without me, there's nothing to keep."

"Oh, is it, Aakash? I am the CEO here. I do what I want. I fire whom I wish to and right now you're the one I don't trust."

"Are you vindicating me or are you just afraid I might take over this company?" I said spontaneously.

"Fuck off, Aakash. You can never own this firm. I'll sue you and ruin your career. I'm a forty-year-old guy Aakash and you're half my age. I have been in this profession even before the day you were fucking born."

"Well, you can flush those stats down the toilet because we both know here that you are nothing but a manipulative fraud who stole the best future innovations of eBay three years ago and now are hellbent on defeating that very same company. And, you know that I'm the cover story of every article which had Tcube in it, you know the other share holders appreciate my genius over yours and you know the entire staff of Tcube wants me to be the one who gets the fame and take this firm to new levels. You're just jealous, Karl, so wash your face, get over your ego and lets, start over again, like this never happened."

"You're fired." Karl said even before I could finish my sentence.

"I will sue you, Karl."

"Then I'll see you in court."

"What!" I was shocked and I almost pleaded though I knew Karl was a lost cause here, "have you lost it completely, Karl, how will you win the case? I will get your firm. Do you want that to happen?"

Karl walked to me, dragged me outside, as all the employees watched with utter confusion, "Ladies and gentleman! You want to know the big news today. Mr Aakash Roy here, your dear colleague is hereby fired. Charges—fraud!"

People gasped and gaped.

I was quiet, numb. The shock was taking time to settle in.

I picked up my file, my cell phone and walked out ready to call my lawyer in ten minutes.

I knew Karl was lying. I just didn't know his master plan yet.

LIE 089

I sat alone in my room. Seven days in a row and I was out of work for no reason, none I was aware of except a jealous and cranky boss.

It felt suffocating, a solitary confinement. All I did was talk to my lawyers, clear things out, call up the share holders of Tcube and discuss the options that I had for the time being.

The court had assigned the trial in a month and half. I had 35 more days of monotonous frustration and I had nothing to look forward to. I knew it was going to be rough, fighting with a billionaire tycoon, Karl Henrick. He was not going to give it up easily and I couldn't let go of MindMark and Tcube. It's all I had, it's all I ever wanted.

I closed my eyes, and she walked right back.

Katherine Andrews.

Ever since the day I got sacked, Katherine had been waking me up, she had become the nightmare that I walked into unaware, in my subconscience and she was always there, smiling at me, haunting me, the only reminder of my past.

I did not know what it meant, this sign. Was I overstressed, was I mentally exhausted or was this nightmare an indication of certain aspects of my life that were left unfinished? Did I keep running back those memories because that's where I belonged?

I called up Tom every time I was upset. He was my only resort for a normal lunch or breakfast.

He had over the years become a great friend, rather a supporting guardian. Tom Martin was actually someone whom I looked up to for advices and suggestions and I knew it would be better consulting him than a therapist.

"So, don't you realise what your priority here is?"

"My job, obviously." I said confidently to him as we savoured Indian food at the restaurant just two blocks from my apartment.

"No Aakash. The priority is that girl of yours who keeps waking you up." Tom said sipping a latte.

"You are kidding me, Tom. Look at me. I just got fired for no reason but politics from a firm that had me as its foundation. I'm currently spending all my income on my lawyers and I spend five hours of the day just sitting with those boring money-minded morons trying my level best to build up a strong case. This is my life, Tom."

"And, even then, with such a preoccupied routine, such torments, your mind keeps moving back to, a girl you dated for a few months, three years ago. Don't you see it, Aakash? She is becoming the breath you need for a life. There is something there Aakash, and you have to face her, you have to find it out for yourself."

"Well then, Tom, I guess it will have to wait." I ended the discussion and was resolute though I knew that Tom Martin was talking sense again.

✳ ✳ ✳

A reporter from CNN called me up that night.

"I don't work at Tcube anymore. So, no more interviews." I was going to hang up when she interrupted me.

"No Aakash, it's not for Tcube."

"Sorry?"

"Aakash, I am Anna Keith and I want you to feature in CitiBlitz for this month end episode."

"Whoa! Citiblitz!?" I was astounded.

CitiBlitz has been a star-studded prime time talk show for over a year now. Its first episode had featured Steve Jobs, the second George Clooney. It had won rave reviews and was one of the most discussed show. They called in sport stars and business tycoons and often controversial matters were the topic of discussion. I realised why I was being summoned.

Controversies and lawyers, MindMark and my getting sacked might have been my reason for a place in the talk show.

"What am I gonna say over there?"

"Every secret that Tcube might have. Every reason behind the growing rivalry between you and Karl Henrick."

"And, whose side will you be in the show? Tell me now whether I might have to regret this decision."

"Trust me, Aakash." Anna Keith smiled, "If you have nothing to hide, you have nothing to fear. We are an unbiased panel of hosts here at CitiBlitz and we do it only for TRP and the spice."

"Somehow, unbiased and TRP doesn't go hand in hand."

"Trust me, Aakash. No controversies or vindications for you." Anna Keith lied, "If anything CitiBlitz will help your cause and we have the best interests for you in our hearts."

"I get that" I smirked.

I knew the media and the rules for hype and publicity. It was always an alteration of the truth and I being a liar, kind of liked it all.

"So? What do you say? A shot at being famous?"

"Count me in." I hung up.

Anna Keith hung up, then she dialled another number, "Hey Karl, your boy has accepted the offer. Start gathering your digs to ruin him."

Karl Henrick smiled on the other side. He had promised Anna he'd get her the best episode of CitiBlitz. The only thing he needed now was to go to India and bring in the special appearance, Robbie Andrews.

LIE 090

"Hey, Aakash." Her soft voice echoed in my ears.

I ran through the field of snow and the dense clouds trying to find her.

"Where are you, Katherine?" I said.

"Here, right here." She said from behind.

I turned back and am again lost in dense clouds.

"Come back here, Katie!" I pleaded.

"I'm here, Aakash. Don't you see me?" she giggled.

I felt suffocated by the fog.

"Oh, they are calling me Aakash."

"Wait. Stop. Please, don't go away." I cried, "Don't leave me alone."

"I have to go now Aakash, promise me you'll always love me."

"I promise you. Just stay on, Katherine."

"Goodbye Aakash. And yeah, wake up." she whispered.

The ringing of the phone shattered my dream and I woke up in a pile of sweat and sudden hollow.

I looked at the screen. It was my dad.

He had called me after three months, today.

"What is it dad?" I spoke softly.

"She's dying, Aakash."

I sat there, cold and numb, my hands trembling, my head in a daze.

"Who is dying, dad?" My heart beat and when dad answered, I dropped the phone. It happened spontaneously, as if my body had lost all its energy, I sat there shaking, all alone.

It ain't possible!! It's just a nightmare.

Wake up, Aakash, I shouted at myself. But it didn't help.

I called Katie an hour later, my packing done, my ticket booked.

I was leaving for India in three hours, the first flight.

Dennis uncle picked it up, "Yeah?"

"Uncle, it's me, Aakash."

He started sobbing. "Oh, Aakash beta, look what happened to Katherine." His voice broke completely and I didn't know what to say.

"I … want to … talk to her." My hands went cold and my mind kept on imagining my sweetest friend Katherine lying there, in a hospital bed, dying...

I heard her voice five minutes later. She coughed.

"Hello, Katie …", I repeated twice. No reply. Only heavy breathing, "It's me, Aakash."

She replied this time, "I knew you'd call."

Her voice was heavy and broken and it was unlike her, so much so, that I punched on the wall with helplessness.

"Nothing will happen to you, Kates, I promise you, nothing will happen to you."

"Don't come for me, Aakash." She said after another minute. I could feel her struggling even to form the words.

"I will, Katherine." I repeated as many times I could, "I will come for you. You just hold on, sweetheart, I will come get you."

She coughed and I think she tried to giggle, "You promise, Aakash Roy? I don't love you, you know. I hate you."

"I do. I promise you with my life."

It ended in a lie.

LIE 091

Katherine's story ...

Katherine was born in Kerala. They said she never cried as a baby. There would always be this ever glowing smile on her face like she was sent here to cheer the world up. Her mother was playful, a very humorous lady and a great parent. Katherine had the world in her arms and her wish was to be that happy, throughout life. Her dad Dennis Andrews was a professor and an author of mathematics books. He divorced his wife when Katherine was 8. He then moved to Calcutta and he also got the custody of her because Katherine's mother didn't have that kind of money to raise her like Dennis did. She was poor and illiterate and she was helpless when Dennis announced his decision. Her choices were in the best interests of Katherine and hence even against Katherine's constant pleadings, she had to come to Calcutta. And, right from the day she came to Calcutta, her life changed completely. It followed a strict regime. She was brought up in a conservative environment, there were no jokes, no laughter, life was all about education and sincerity.

Katherine changed, too. She turned short tempered and killjoy every passing moment. She turned compulsive, cleaning her room, making sure every non-materialistic thing in her life stayed perfect, the way she wanted her materialistic life to turn into. Students in school hated her. Nobody sat with her. She argued even with teachers and although she was a bright kid who always completed her homework in time, teachers always found an excuse to drop a complaint against her. The conclusion would always be scoldings at home and a dad who would ground her for months in a row.

419

And then, one sudden day, September 2001, two fateful things happened.

Katherine fell down the stairs that night as she felt dizzy for the first time. This had never happened before. Her dad rushed her to the emergency at four in the morning. There were no injuries and the doctors said it might just have been weakness or maybe she sleepwalked.

Dennis wanted Katie to stay at home that day, take rest, but Katherine hated the entire concept of a home without her mother.

She figured out anything in the school would be better for her health than the general sulking at her room.

That was also the day the strange boy came to class. Torn trousers, no tie, profusely sweating and with a retarded look he stared at the entire class.

They punished him by the second lecture for misbehaviour and kneeling down, his eyes were on her legs.

Katie felt insecure just by his nasty look. Somehow, the boy had targeted her legs in the entire world to kill his time while getting punished and all Katherine wanted to do was punch him in the face. But as luck would have it, the new boy was made to sit with her in the next lecture.

Katherine was more than disgusted as the new boy eyed her with a very alien expression of shock or regret, she could not place it! Then, he introduced himself, "Hi , I'm Aakash." He said.

Katherine insulted him, acted sarcastic and was bowled over when even after all these hurdles, he sat with her the next day. After such a long time, Katherine had been valued and it shocked her. She avoided him completely. What was to follow was hostility from both parties for a long time that assured Katherine that Aakash was just another unimportant guy in the crowd that the world was.

In the meantime, Katherine kept on having bad days, when she would feel dizzy, her body would ache, and she would end up with high temperature. After two months of various treatments and blood tests, the doctors established the fact that Katherine had leukemia. She had never heard of the disease before, but she figured pretty soon that there was enough reason to worry with the changed mood of her dad. Dennis consoled her daughter it was a minor disease and would go away like any other, but clearly he lied. He started going easy on her, never scolding her, asking her to have a time out from studies. The daily regimes suddenly came to a halt, and Katherine felt free while Dennis would spend more time pensive, locked in his study.

She did not want it to change, but had no one to share the feeling of happiness with. That was when the strange boy came back.

Like an angel he knocked on her door, and ten minutes later he was in her room, pleading with her to lie for him. Katherine had never done that before, never broken the rules, her compulsive life never had a wind of change, but yet here he was and there she was, committing it all for him. She thought she could understand it, Aakash was just a breath of fresh air in her solitary life, and that must be it. But it turned out that Katie's heart suddenly had feelings for that change, as if all Katie wanted to do was to hold on to it and never let it go.

And, in months, she had forgotten her sickness; Katherine was in fact in seventh heaven with Aakash, her best friend.

She liked him for everything, his silly mistakes, for his innocence, his smile and his attention to her. She would often watch him, from the corner of her eye, looking at her, and it would quicken her heartbeats. Katherine had fallen for Aakash head over wheels. It changed her, she was ecstatic, in fact, she laughed and joked. It was a fairy tale story, she would go out to fetes and places with him, where he would fight for her, winning her over, every single time.

And then, one night, they kissed and Katherine knew instantly, right at that precise moment of intimacy, that it all made sense. It was all perfect. She knew she would stand by Aakash for the rest of her life, she would help him find his mother, the only thing she lacked so much in her life, she knew she would encourage him to fulfil his dreams, record his songs, make him achieve stuff that he had always dreamt of.

Aakash left later that month, for a show "Rockstars" which was held at Darjeeling. Katherine fell ill the next day. She was very sick and was admitted to ILS at Calcutta. They confirmed it there, that Katherine, in fact, had Terminal leukemia. Dennis decided right then, that he would not let it all end like this. He was adamant on taking Katherine to Appollo, Chennai and getting her the best treatment in the country. He also decided to then move back to Kerala. He wanted Katherine's happiness and thus, he wanted her to spend more time with her mother.

They were to leave in a week.

Just a day before her departure, Aakash came back to Calcutta and that afternoon he met Katie, all he did was hug her and cry. Aakash's mother had just died. Katherine could not tell him the truth yet, tell him how she was diagnosed with a fatal disease too, could not tell him how she would have to leave the city the next day and how she would never come back here. So, all she did instead, was promise him that she would find him and come back to him.

The rest of her little life was all about that promise.

Katherine's life in Kerala was never the same again. She became depressed, grieved. The thought of an eventual end kept keeping her awake at night, haunting her life with sadness and making her considerably weaker. But mostly, Katherine missed Aakash. She missed his breath on her neck, his hands on her hands, his laughter in her ears and his shoulder to rest on. She was home tutored, and although she scored great marks in AIEEE, got every engineering college to pick as her option, her plans were already made.

Katherine rejected her admissions at NIT, she found out about Aakash from Mr. Anshuman Roy, and then, against her family's wishes, she went to Pune. Dennis never wanted it to happen, he wanted her to stay at home, stay well, but Katherine had resolved that if it all had to end one day, it had to be a happy ending.

The magic happened again. Katherine was swept off her feet again by Aakash. She was whimsical, flippant, merry and well. As days passed, Aakash developed the same feelings that Katie had for him over all these years and finally, he confessed his love to her. Life could not be better for Katherine.

She was so high spirited, she overlooked all Aakash's lies, trusted him with her life, and there was a belief, rather a coviction in her, that if she could fight off her disease, she could resist death, hide from it when it came knocking, because she had Aakash with her.

And then, her bubble world burst, her heart was shattered into pieces by the God she worshipped.

✳ ✳ ✳

Katherine struggled with her life for the next three years. She faced pain, torturous cruelties of life and lived on the last shred of hope. She didn't realise what that hope was until the dreams started.

Aakash walked right back in, through her aches and turmoil, and he soothed it, with love. Every night, Katie woke up in tears, but they were of a strange happiness.

The doctors put her on the vantilator and life support a week later.

She fainted, and woke every second hour. It kept on getting blurry every moment. After a certain period, everything got hazy and white, like a cloud, only one image remained consistent. Aakash was still there in her dreams, and he was calling out her name, he was lost and couldn't find her. Katherine almost giggled as she saw his anxiety in finding her. She playfully tagged by his side, no fear, no pain, only a bit of heaven.

"Hello Katie, it's me … Aakash."

"I knew you'd call", her voice broke but she tried hard to say it, "Don't come for me."

"I will, Katherine." Aakash's voice rekindled her love, "Just hold on sweetheart, I will come for you."

"You promise, Aakash Roy? You know I don't love you, I hate you."

"I do Katie … I promise you with my life."

Katie tried to laugh and fainted. Her eyes closed and two hours later, she died.

LIE 092

I stood there silently, my posture calm.

My eyes were a bit puffy though but I could blame it on my insomnia.

At moments I would feel dizzy and silently sigh but it was all so invisible, so indistinguishable from my usual personality that only my heart could register it.

So, was it really possible?

Was love so strong a feeling that it could break any person, no matter how tough he would try to be?

That it could completely ruin the definition of one's existence and prove every step of his life, an utter mistake?

Love and life were so confused that they were always infused together ... members of the same string ... you pulled one, the other came down. But hey, that was never the story of a shrewd, smart and bad ass...

Damn. How could it end up being mine?

People besides me were crying, mourning, aghast and broken ...

They would take out their handkerchiefs every now and then and wipe away their tears, they could do it.

I was stunned, as if petrified, as if all my responses had gone numb. I tried to cry, at least for the sake of my heart but my tears had frozen in the morning wind. I was helpless and for the first time felt my head waver.

"Oh, get a grip, dude." I thought to myself ... I repeated the statement for a count to infinity and then they opened the coffin.

My lips twitched and I felt my heart turning into a block of iron ...

the priest started saying the last prayers. The requiem had begun and my story had ended.

Katie lay there, silent, the light gone out of her eyes. Hail the sarcasm of life, the girl who talked the most was so silent today that it made a Sunday morning ominous. I watched Katie's mom run towards her, hug her and sob uncontroll ably, I watch general uncle fall to his knees as others hurred to hold him. And then I saw Katherine one last time.... Katie, my best friend Kates.

I started to leave ... couldn't take it anymore ... I needed some black coffee ... I needed it now!

But then something happened ... I discover, the last lie ...

***

The funeral was over an hour later, and so was the love of my life. I would never see her again. Never ever. Katherine Andrews was dead. She had left me alone. She came to my dreams, said goodbye and left without a sound.

And, you know the worst part. I could not even keep my last promise to her. I couldn't be there on time, with her, when she died. She died waiting. Katherine Andrews, the most beautiful girl in the world, died in vain, hating a liar.

There are certain events that change your life, rather questions the entire reason of your existence. Katherine's demise marked that event for me. It left me clueless, sucked my soul out, and threw me to a square I had been once before when my mother had died.

My heart ached as I staggered for any source of salvation, peace of mind.

LIE 093

A month later …

I had never been to Hollywood before. I drove my Mercedes through the thick crowd of paparazzi and spectators as the huge façade of CitiBlitz neared. Tom Martin accompanied me, he was my companion for the prestigious night. He was my only friend in the U.S. and he sat beside me, as friendly as ever.

I had the windows closed and I sat there, still without the answers, still clueless, hyperventilating.

I stopped over the red carpeted walkway to the dazzling glass building of the prime time television show. I opened the door and stepped onto the pavement. The flashes blinded me. Cameras, questions and journalists, it was chaos out there.

"This way, Sir." five suited body guards directed me inside.

Tom was by my side, his face taut and expressionless and the professional look on display.

I was taken to the elevator and then we went up to the 16th floor.

I sweat in the centrally conditioned dressing room as Anna Keith, the host of the talk show, a former television actress entered the chamber and smiled at me.

"You look nervous, Aakash."

"I look unhappy, too." I looked out of the glass windows, "The problem is I can't help it."

"Well, relax Aakash." Anna smiled, "It's all going to turn out fine."

Of course, get Katherine for me from heaven and it will be fine!

"So," Anna sensed my silence for a no comment zone and responded,

"Listen, you can relax and freshen up and prepare your questions and all, while I go and prep up the set. Meet you." She checked her watch, "An hour." She sported her million dollar smile and disappeared.

I looked at my watch, too. 8:00 pm.

In another hour, I would be live to the entire world, except for some parts of Saudi Arabia and Sri Lanka.

About five million people tuned into "CitiBlitz" every Sunday. Tonight, they would all be listening to me, watching over my accusations and my heroic story of "How I became so successful at such a young age."

Heroic ... I laughed at myself.

"You feeling okay, Aakash?" Tom said from the other side of the room.

"Huh ... oh yeah, you know. This is the max I feel nowadays."

Tom came and stood beside me, "You know what your problem is, Aakash?"

"Yeah, I've lost it." I shrugged sarcastically.

"No, you haven't. You've just closed your eyes and deny visibility. Open them, Aakash. Don't you see you've been looking at the wrong places? Don't you realise how your sitting here right now is the mistake?"

"Um ... no." I discarded his opinions as I opened a bottle of champagne and made myself a drink. I had been on a journey for redemption for the past thirty days and I just couldn't find it. I just couldn't dream of her anymore. Katie was there, no more. No matter where I went, what I did, I was hollow and it didn't change, the sting in my heart, the purposelessness of my life.

"Well, then, realise that you have a choice. All of us have." Tom pressed the elevator button, "I'm going out to take a stroll. I will be back here in half an hour."

He looked at me firmly one last time as if trying to force me to understand. Then, he walked away.

I sighed. Left alone in another room. Claustrophobic or was this just a heart attack on its way!

I opened my side bag, took out the file that the lawyers had written for me. It had documents containing the most probable questions for tonight's show with apt answers that my lawyers had diplomatically jotted down for me. They wanted me to win back my dignity, what was rightfully mine, they supported me. The question, however, is what I needed.

I flipped through the pages.

1st question: What made you so ambitious, Aakash, what's the reason that an average guy from India,

With an engineering background ended up designing a software for e-commerce and attains success?

Answer as written by the lawyers: Well, I had consistently been a motivated guy throughout my career. I grew up with interests in solving commerce problems, in other words, I wanted to change my country, India. I never worried about fame and money, my dream was a change, a rebellion, blah blah.

I guffawed, "oh, liars!"

My mind immediately went back to the moment it all started, that day, 8 years ago, near a hut at Belur. The true story for a change.

The day I had come to know of the magician Paritosh Sorkar's sad demise, from his daughter Kiran.

Paritosh, a friend of mine, rather someone I looked up to in my childhood, had killed himself facing a train, trying to pull off a magic trick so that he could get his daughter married. Maybe, the person who influenced me, messed me up with that one act.

I remembered it all, how Kiran di, Paritosh's young daughter hugged me and cried. Later that month, the day of Kiran's wedding, I was present and I heard this heated discussion.

It turned out, the groom had a bad reputation in his village at Tarakeshwar, West Bengal. He was a drunkard and he had been jailed twice earlier.

The entire marriage was based on lies from the groom's side.

I saw relatives of Kiran weeping and praying for her safety, but they all continued with the preparations of the wedding even then.

So, I ran up to Kiran's uncle and asked him why they were not calling the whole thing off.

"Kiran's life will get destroyed. Why are you not stopping it, uncle?" I asked the poor man.

"*Because Aakash,*" he retorted a bit angrily, "*I cannot. I don't have the money to organise another wedding if we cancel this one. You know how much we had to labour to make this happen. Kiran's father died for this, Aakash.*"

"*But,*" I stammered, "*Paritosh Sorkar wouldn't have wanted this for his daughter.*"

"*Well, beggars can't be choosers Aakash.*"*The old man continued with the preparations of the wedding even though I knew it was all over, the happiness sucked right out.*

She got married that day, my didi Kiran, I witnessed Paritosh Sorkar's last wish turn foul as draped in a red saree, she married a goon.

While leaving, the last words, Kiran di said to me were, "I had a bad marriage, didn't I, Aakash?"

She smiled as if mocking her own life, mocking her father's suicide, mocking the rules of the society and all I did was just watch.

That is what revolted me. My thirst for money. My craving for *success and fame was no tale of inspiration. It was a cry for help from poverty stricken human beings.*

I flipped the page over. Couldn't tell the real story though. Media would like some spice, not a reality check. Looked like I was going to lie a lot tonight.

LIE 094

Q: So, Aakash, in this crash course of an experience that you gained in a super-accelerated three years of success life, what do you have to say about people, colleagues, friends and their influence in your path? Does it help to have those friends?

Answer: Well, friends do help a lot. I mean, what you need is a good friend and a good lawyer for a rainy day. (smile) I have had some great people who helped me through this completely new phase of my career. They were like these wheels and accelerators to my ride. (name all the major share holders of Tcube as your friends, will help your case). But however important is that one right reason to fight for, to go to the extremes and succeed ... blah blah..

I massaged my head. I just wasted two minutes of my life! The lawyer's clear instructions freaked me. They stood for truth, didn't they!!

I closed my eyes and they all appeared, Katherine, Katie, Deb, Robbie, my dearest friends. I opened my eyes with shock. I had betrayed all of them at one point or the other.

So, was friendship overrated?

∗ ∗ ∗

Ten days before CitiBlitz interview

I travelled through the forests of redwood, until there was no light. I stood on the frozen sea of ice at Greenland and looked up at the vast expenses of infinite skies searching for one reason. I meditated, I prayed, I begged, but I was unanswered. God didn't answer me.

I lied all my life, I lied to escape, to make my life happier, to sort things out, to make my dreams come true, and now that I finally had money and problems and a busy life, the one I actually expected, why couldn't I let Katherine's thoughts go away?

Why did my mind loop that one thought over and over again? Why couldn't I just compromise on love? Why had my purpose changed?

I met Deb at a club in London one night. I was supposed to drive to Arizona the next day.

"Aakash? Is that you?" Deb Roy, the marvellous looking, hot shot rich brat from SMI, Calcutta, shouted over the music, came and hugged me before I could even register the event.

"Whoa! What happened to you buddy?" he inspected me carefully. "Long freaky hair, a beard, dark eyes. Looks like you've joined the hippies or something, man!"

I looked closely at my once-great-friend Deb Roy. He hadn't changed. Still handsome, still dashing and still the old charm, although I sensed the sadness within. It's like I had become a sadness scanner, I had hit such a rock bottom in my life that all I could smell in the air, was depression and joylessness.

"Yeah," I brushed my filthy uncombed hair, "Haven't gone to the hairdresser for a while."

"Man! You look depressed!" He asked for two tequila shots, "Trust me this will help."

You too!

I took the bitter poison, squinted, sucked the lemon, and let my soul drown a bit more. Deb did the same and for a moment, I saw his mind drift elsewhere.

"So, you still have the no-talk-code with me?" Deb chuckled, "I mean, common man! I don't hope we are enemies any more. You have Katie Thomas now after all."

"Katie Thomas?" my mind zoomed back to the lie I had told Deb over the phone years ago from Katie's cell. I had asked him to leave her alone, telling him she was with me.

Evidently, Deb actually did sign that agreement. He never called. Never confirmed the news. He let Katie carry on with her life.

No more lies.

"You know what. The no-talk-code is definitely over. Forget about that." I looked at Deb right in the eye now, "As for Katie Thomas. I was never with her, Deb. I lied to you that night."

Deb went pale. "You are kidding."

"No, I'm not. I haven't heard from her in three years."

"But then," Deb's eyes were transfixed on me now, "why would you do that to me, Aakash? I trusted you."

"And, she trusted you, Deb. You should have gotten over money and looked at her as more than just another girl." I yawned showing Deb my finger.

"I loved her, Dammit!" Deb took me by my collar.

"Well, your love would've killed her back then Deb."

"In that case," next thing, Deb punched me right on the face, "Nobody asked you to act God, asshole."

I fell on the floor and somehow it amused me so much, I ended up laughing.

The bouncers of the club dragged Deb out.

"Call her Deb. You can still make it up to her." I shouted as blood spurted out of my nose.

I stood up, as the bartenders came for help.

"Naah, it's okay. I deserved that" I laughed as the searing pain got Katherine out of my mind for one moment.

"Here Sir, your things" the waiter handed me my bag and put the diaries I had lying on my table inside it as I left.

✳ ✳ ✳

With a stitch and bandages over my nose, I set off for Arizona the next morning, driving off in my Mercedes CLK.

I unpacked my stuff on the way, searching for chips or cakes. That's when I saw it, Deb's Diary.

It must've been placed in my bag by mistake during yesterday's sudden scuffle.

I opened the diary and started reading.

I read the entry when Deb was probably 8 years old.

Entry 101, 1994

I saw Katie for the first time today. She's the daughter of my dad's business partner, Mr Heath Thomas. Now you people know how infrequently I updated my diary but you see, today was that special, in fact, it was amazing!!

She is very beautiful. She smells of roses and jasmines and is the prettiest girl I have ever seen in my life. I swear!! And, she has accepted my friendship too! In fact, dad got me admitted in her school here in Darjeeling. We'll go to school together from now. I will be so famous. I will have the most gorgeous girlfriend in class.

Mom gave me a basket of ferrero rochers to eat today. I have kept it hidden in my secret cabin which is my third drawer on the small cupboard. But you know, I will not eat them, I will gift one each day to Katie. I'll do it for the rest of my life. And, she spells "so" as "cho" and "sweet" as "shweet"! She really is so sweet!!

I stopped my car in the stony desert as I ended up smiling at little Deb's diary entry, his love at first 'shight shtory'. I kept on reading his entries, things he wrote about me, how much he actually valued our friendship. I read on to find, how much he suffered after letting Katie go in the past three years. How much he still missed her. And, how he realised his mistake.

I placed Deb's diary on the stone steps as I sat near the Grand Canyon. Just a one day trip from Los Angeles. Grand canyon is an amazing and a lonely place all the same.

The zephyr roared through my ears and I feel broken again as Katherine came back ...

See, our mind is one big liar! it just frames views of others on our minds and oblivious of the truth, we keep on hating those people, not even knowing how important they actually were ... if only we could read minds.

Oh, Deb, I wish I could understand you! how great a friend you were to me.

The punch served me right! I realised the joke that made me laugh yesterday now. I had been deserving that punch for the last eight years, the first time when I had broken my friendship with Deb Roy at SMI canteen.

The ink looked faded, but I can still feel his emotions, I could still hear him laugh or throw flying kisses at the crazy audience through his diary.

I plug my i-pod in my ears and play my favourite track.

Jo thi dil ki khushi— rock version.

LIE 095

Robbie's Story

"Where are you, Karl?" Anna is panicky now, "You promised me you'll get the digs, the proof against that fraud Aakash." She shouts over the phone.

Karl is silent on the other side as he tries to frame it.

***

Five days before the interview

Karl Henrick's master plan would have ruined Aakash forever, and Karl wanted the insult to be public, an international sensation. He wanted it to be the end of Aakash's career forever. Karl Henrick's plans had its inception three years earlier, in fact, around four months before Aakash even landed on Los Angeles. Karl's dream was to come up with a totally new e-market, the one which had his ideologies and strict profit-making as its innovative goals. That is when he came across MindMap. He could see the unparallel conception of the project and he knew he had finally hit gold. The demo he received had two pair of equations in it, one: an ideal solution for pareto optimality, and the second was a modified business logic for a biased decision that profited only one agent, the one the software chose.

Karl Henrick liked the biased decision system, he knew it would profit him in the long run. So, he passed the project for eBay's annual conference, so that Aakash and Robbie, the authors could be called in to Los Angeles. Although Karl always wanted these two guys to join his

435

startup Tcube, he knew they would not agree to come such a long way for a company that they had not heard of. But he did not want to give it all away to eBay too, and hence, he forwarded a modified version of the demo to the project funding committee while keeping the biased solution plugin for himself.

A few days later, Aakash replied to eBay with his request for one ticket. He announced that Robbie was no longer part of the project and that was when Karl Henrick realised that he finally, had found a match. Aakash was a true entrepreneur and he was shrewd at his profession. Just the prefect employee for his start up.

A little manipulation worked and next thing, Aakash actually quit the project fund and joined Karl Henrick's firm. Karl Henrick made Aakash the face of the company, he knew only a young voice could turn out as a trendsetter for MindMark. The world loved him. Aakash was famous and Karl appreciated it. He always knew the guy had potential.

However, the setback came the day Aakash announced his willingness to have one-third of the shares of the company. Karl Henrick's suspicions arose. He always knew, one day things would complete the circle and Aakash would realise his strong hold in the firm, but he did not anticipate it to be that fast. So, Karl initiated his back up plan and it worked fine again, infact amazing.

For Karl now knew Aakash's secret that nobody else did.

Karl knew about Robbie and how Aakash had stolen Robbie's ideas and betrayed him. The 'ecstasy' at Grey Manor had made sure of that.

Karl Henrick then waited on to build the hype for an year, so as to bust it open right at the precise moment, making it a globally catalyst for the success of his company and also the detachment of the myth named neo from his firm.

And, one fine day Aakash was fired, there was no show-cause and Aakash went public with retaliation, just what Karl wanted it to be like. Negative publicity helped quite often.

Anna Keith was an old friend of Karl, and she loved controversies. She was also the host of CitiBlitz and shams and controversies were the show's USP. The old relationship worked wonders for Karl and Anna agreed to interview Aakash on her esteemed show and to reveal his plagiarism in public.

All Karl needed now, was a written document from Robbie stating how he was betrayed by Aakash, how Aakash was a fraud, how his getting sacked was justified.

So, five days before CitiBlitz's Sunday episode, Karl visited MIT, Pune personally. He checked the records of the batch of 2008. To his utter amazement, there was no entry of Robbie Andrews. He googled Robbie, scan the school directories of SMI and visited even the family of Dennis Andrews. They refused having a son with that name.

Karl was stunned. He did not have one living proof even of Robbie's existence. The guy who could have actually ruined Aakash, revealed the sham, was himself turning out to be a mystery man.

Where was Robbie?

Robbie Andrews was a ghost to the world, no records, no friends, no witnesses.

Karl was frustrated, called up every source he had, every help he could arrange for, and even then, ten hours before the show CitiBlitz would go live on television, Karl had nothing to reveal to the world! No witness, no classmate who could confirm the existence of Robbie Andrews.

Helpless and shocked beyond anything, Karl finally visited Aakash's dad, Mr Anshuman Roy, his last resort.

The man appeared aged, rather weak and frail.

"What do you want?", he didn't even recognise Aakash's boss.

"Well, hello." Karl said warily, wondering whether Anshuman had a clue as to how Karl had fired his son without any reason a few days ago and how he was here to bust Aakash's lies, "I'm Karl, CEO, TestTubeTech, California."

"Aah!! You're my son's employer." Anshuman recognised him, "Never thought I would meet you. Why? What happened? Is Aakash okay? He was here a few days ago."

"Ohh, was he?", Karl was completely oblivious of Aakash's love life and his visit to India on Katherine's death, "Aakash is fine by the way, he is doing a television show later tonight, I hope you know."

Anshuman shook his head, "Which channel? What time?"

"CNN, CitiBlitz. 9 am IST." Karl answered a bit taken aback with the distanced relationship between Aakash and his dad, "Anyways, the reason I'm here is because of Robbie, a friend of Aakash, have you heard from him?"

"Oh, Robbie Andrews." Anshuman stroked his chin, "Of course, I have."

Karl felt relieved for the first time. So, Robbie was here somewhere after all.

"Aakash still talks of him, does he?", Anshuman said, pensively.

"Highly." Karl lied, "Where can I find this guy, Robbie?"

At this, Anshuman smiled, "Nowhere, you could however check Aakash's mind for once."

"What do you mean?", Karl was startled.

"Well, the thing is, Mr Karl," Anshuman relaxed in his easy chair, "There is no Robbie Andrews. It is an imaginary character. A lie inside Aakash's mind."

"What?", Karl is confused, "Come again?"

"Okay, let me try to explain." Anshuman drank some water, then walked over to the almirah, got a file and displayed it to Karl. It had medical reports and CT scans of someone's brain. Karl read the patient's name: Aakash Roy. He picked the prescription up.

Patient: Aakash roy.

Diagnosis: mild Schizophrenic. Hallucinations.

"What does this mean?", Karl looked up at Anshuman for answers.

"Well, it means my son has been quite a nutcase", Anshuman chuckled sadly, "He is a schizophrenic. It started back when he was just 13 and had fallen off the deck of a ship he thought to be a pirate ship. He was hospitalised and the effects scarred him for life. He became less apathetic to friendship, developed hostility even with me, turned into a liar and started hallucinating, that is imagining a virtual nonexistent friend."

Karl's heart nearly stopped. *Aakash's lies had an explanation.*

"That illusionary friend's name, was Robbie Andrews. Aakash would never discuss Robbie with anybody. Once he revealed it during his therapy sessions, it was because he had made a promise to Robbie never to ever discuss his life even to with Robbie's parents."

"But ... but ... " Karl stuttered, "Do you mean Aakash always worked alone, that there was no Robbie?"

"Well, we tried several therapies here. I never told Aakash he had this mental condition. I put in pills, in his food and drinks. And then, after a while, Aakash actually did stop talking about Robbie. "

"Then what happened?"

"Well." Anshuman Roy sighed, "Then, Aakash went to Pune and without the medicines, finally Robbie resurfaced in his thoughts again."

"No. That isn't possible, who made the entire project then? MindMap?"

"Um..", Anshuman looked perplexed, "I'm sorry to say, but I don't really know much about Aakash's current life. He doesn't talk to me anymore. He has abandoned this part of the world and I can't blame him. His mind is like that Mr Karl, he doesn't trust anybody. I am telling you all this so that next time you see him, forgive him for any rude behaviour on his part. The guy's a genius, he just doesn't know it."

Karl Henrick felt dazed, out of his wits. It was inexplicable, the explanation. He couldn't believe it as he kept on reading the prescriptions and medical bills that confirmed Aakash's condition.

"Robbie to put precisely," Anshuman says, "is just an alter ego of Aakash. His honest face. The good Aakash."

✳ ✳ ✳

"Who made the project. Tell me quickly." Anna pleaded over the phone, "I need answers!"

"It was him." Karl stammered as he realised, "All him, all Aakash."

"What? But you ..."

Karl hung up. He had finally lost his biggest business transaction.

He underestimated his greatest rival, a boy of 23 years.

Aakash Roy was Robbie, he was the genius who had created MindMarket, who created a TV jammer as a kid, who made a sun dial in his project at school. He was not fake, not a sham and though Aakash would never understand it, it might probably have been his biggest lie.

LIE 096

35 minutes before Interview

Q: We have had reports. They say you have been unhappy for the past month, that you have spent all your savings going on a trip round the world, looking for redemption? So, have you finally achieved it or is it just an early midlife crisis you're dealing with here?

Answer: I think it has to do with the sudden change that I faced when I got fired for no reason (explain the entire episode, audience like to visualise things). It's the sudden feeling of betrayal that has led me to this sudden phase in life. Blah blah …

✱✱✱

Robbie worked quietly in his small dark lab that he had turned his room into. He was oblivious of my presence.

I observed the genius at work, his passion, his honesty, his innocence and it grieved me.

How did I betray this person? Stab my friend in the back …

Robbie looked at me warily, "Aakash, is that you?" he switched on the lights.

"Hey, Robbie," I said looking down, didn't even have the guts to look him in the eye, "I am sorry for your loss."

Robbie was quiet.

"You never showed up at the funeral?" I asked my imaginary friend.

"Well," the hallucination answered, "I couldn't bear the last goodbyes to my dearest sister Katherine."

"I understand and I'm sorry," I repeated.

"So," Robbie said, "Why are you here, Aakash? I thought I'd never see you again."

"I came to apologise for stealing your dream. I know I don't deserve forgiveness. I just want you to know that I am ashamed for what I did to you."

"Is that it?", Robbie walked closer as his presence forced me to face him, "Is that why you are here?"

I shook my head.

"Then, why?" Robbie was curious, "Tell the truth, Aakash. What brings you here?"

Tears formed in my eyes, "I strive for redemption, brother."

"And, do you think you will have it if I forgave you?" Robbie asked casually, his face neutral, no signs of the resentment or the hatred I expected to see.

"I can't find it yet." I said, as helplessness took control, "I can't stop missing her, Robbie."

I broke into sobs.

Robbie hugged me as I cried.

"Katherine is killing me, Robbie," I wept, "Look, what she has done to me. I can't smile anymore Robbie. The only thing I have now is this guilty conscience and it is eating me from the inside. Guilty conscience for trying to be successful by ruining others, for winning while disappointing my own father, becoming the monster that I am. And here, I am doing whatever it takes to get back the old self but my mind keeps on lying to me, directing me pathless. Where is it, Robbie? Where is my redemption?"

Robbie patted me on the back, "It's okay, Aakash. You're close."

I looked at his undeterred friendly consoling smile trying to understand what he meant but he didn't reply.

"So, you forgive me?", I asked him, rather begged of him.

"It's not my forgiveness you seek, Aakash." Robbie smiled as he got back to his experiment and switched the lights off, "It's yours. Forgive yourself, Aakash."

LIE 097

Twenty-five minutes before the interview
Q: So, what now Aakash Roy?

I closed the file as Tom opened the door.

"It's nearly time." he checked his watch and looked at me, "Why don't you freshen up, Aakash while I get you some coffee." He walked over to the coffee machine.

I stood up, my brain racing as I flipped through all the scenarios I had considered for the last one month after Katherine died.

It started with guilt, it turned into remorse and now it was killing me. After travelling from India to Greenland to Switzerland and to Arizona and Los Angeles, I was still clueless as to why I could not laugh anymore or work anymore. What was the reason of my temporary lapse ...

I walked over to the basin.

But why did I miss Katherine so much? I remembered the time when I actually chose Katie Thomas over Katherine Andrews because I was sure Katie Thomas was my true love.

Why then, was I sure now of my love for Katherine? Why did I miss her the most, why was it that I never called Katie Thomas back and why did I keep going back to wishing to be with Katherine when I had a job to fight for, all my credentials were at risk and I was going to be live in twenty minutes.

I turned the tap, sprinkled the water over my face and looked at myself.

A normal, innocent, gloomy and weak person stared back at me.

How could this guy have been so bad and merciless? What was the one good thing he ever did?

My mind suddenly cleared as the thought hit me.

I inhaled as the spell of self-introspection bound my conscience.

In that moment of revelation, I found my last attempt at redemption, my answer.

"I loved Katherine." I whispered.

Yes, that was the only truth in my life, the only good thing that I ever did. The only real feeling I cared for. And, that is why it kept aching in my heart. That is why it never left me.

Money, Katie Thomas and success, they had all been mere lies.

I remembered Robbie sitting by my side one day and saying that truth was when it felt right.

My love for Katherine felt right.

Nothing else mattered. The acceptance suddenly lightened my burdens. So was giving it all up the answer?

The person in the mirror broke into a smile.

I laughed heartily after a month for the first time.

"Aakash, you alright?" Tom walked over to me.

"Never been better." I faced him.

"Whoa", Tom appeared surprised, "What happened? You had a chat with Jesus, did you?"

"No. In fact, for the first time I talked to the real me Tom."

Tom's face sparkled. "And, what did your soul say?"

I went quiet for a minute as I tried to figure it all out.

"It said," I was shocked as I said it out loud, "that I don't want to give this interview."

"What?" Tom Martin was flabbergasted, "Aakash, why do I think it's not your soul but stage jitters?"

"Trust me, Tom," I looked at him so firmly, I couldn't have been more honest, "I've never felt more sure in my entire life. This interview would mean a wild chase for money again. My accusations, answers, all a bunch of crap Tom. This interview is just going to be lies and I don't want to lie anymore. Not to the entire world."

A thin person in a suit entered the dressing room.

"Sir, please report to the back stage in five minutes. We're about to be live in 15."

"I will be there." I lied.

He left without another word.

Tom Martin analysed the situation for a moment and then he chuckled, "So," he said proudly, "What now, Aakash Roy?"

LIE 098

I threw my tuxedo out of the 16th floor window.

"I am leaving." I smiled at Tom Martin as I tore the documents of the file the lawyers gave me and flushed my tie down the toilet.

"Meaning?", Tom Martin was amused, "How do you propose to do that? The stage is set, you have less than three minutes to report at the back stage now and the paparazzi is waiting downstairs. How do you plan to bail out?"

"Well, I don't have a plan, I was just thinking of going for a wild sprint!" I looked at Tom, searching for better alternatives.

"There's a back alley you can take. We just have to get your car there."

"Wait a minute." I unlocked my wrist watch, the Rolex Daytona and kept it over the table.

No more of these.

My mind flashed back to the day I was leaving for Darjeeling years ago, the day my dad kept telling me how life is a vicious cycle where we had to follow certain conventional rules, study hard, get a job and earn money to retain happiness and how I denied the order of things that night. How I had pledged to change the rules. What if the joker was the strongest card in the pack.

I remembered how I had met this pick pocket Rakesh once, while travelling for the first time in a local train to Belur to meet Paritosh Sorkar. I remembered him talking about the system and changing it.

"How can we change the system, Rakesh?" I had asked him unsure what the system was all about!

445

Rakesh had smiled, "See i'll give you an example." he had said, "Suppose, you have a BMW, that's what the name is I think of that costly car."

"Yes." I had encouraged.

"Yeah, so the day Aakash, the day you're powerful enough not to keep it for showing off, but you have the strength of gifting it to an underpaid clerk, that day you'll change the system."

"What", I had laughed out loud, "That's absurd, Rakesh, why'd I do that?"

"Exactly Aakash, it's so absurd Aakash, that it's the only thing that would ever make sense.", He had patted my back.

I looked at Tom Martin who stared back scratching his head.

"You know what, Tom." I took out the keys of my Mercedes CLK, "I don't think I want this anymore."

"What do you mean?" Tom was confused.

"Look Tom, all these things, the Rolex, the car, the apartment, all of it made me live this life of false satisfaction. They encouraged my actions, they made me believe the system and supported my fake twisted venture towards success."

"So?"

"So, I don't want them anymore. They are not important. I am starting all over again, Tom, and I'm starting afresh."

Tom Martin loosened his necktie as he tried to absorb the concept, "So what do you plan to do with them, may I ask?"

"Well, don't know about the watch, but the car is yours."

I tossed the keys at Tom.

He grabbed the key, looked back at me, his face has lost its colour, "Are you insane? Have you lost it?"

"I don't have time to explain." I pressed the elevator button, "I've got a show to miss and a life to begin."

"But ... but ... what am I to do with this?"

"Sell it, man" I chortled merrily, "Go back to your family in London. Live a happy life of retirement. I still remember your dream of sitting by the fireplace and listening to Beethoven." I winked at him.

"But, Sir." Tom stuttered, "Why are you doing this?"

"Well," I entered the lift and pressed the buttons, "Because you are a great man, Tom Martin! And, you deserve all the happiness in the world. Thanks a lot, buddy."

I watch a tearful Tom Martin staring at me for the last time as the doors closed, and then I was at ground floor.

I looked at the clock. Ten minutes to nine. They must be checking the dressing room by now.

I tiptoed to the back exit, walked down to the back alley, hired a cab, and was zooming through the windy roads in no time.

"Where to, Sir?" The cabby asked.

"Take me to the airport and drive as fast as you can. I handed him two hundred dollar bills.

It was 9:20 pm, when I reached the airport. I ran to the counter, got the ticket for the first flight to India and then, waited in the lobby.

They had switched on CNN and I saw the news flashing: "CitiBlitz episode cancelled for tonight."

A tense and sweaty Anna Keith appeared next on the screen, "In a shocking turn of events, Aakash Roy, ex-employee and the chief designer of MindMark has gone missing from the CitiBlitz studio. The police is investigating further on the matter as we speak. We now talked to his friend Mr Tom Martin who was present in the dressing room of the CitiBlitz studio moments before the entire event happened."

I smirked as an ecstatic Tom Martin appeared on the screen, "Well, I think some terrorist group is behind this kidnapping", he lied. I broke into laughter.

✳ ✳ ✳

I woke up from sleep. A good sleep in almost 40 days now. I felt light headed, a feeling of relaxation over my senses. It was calm here. I looked out of the window of the British Airways 747. I saw the infinite sky and small patches of green fields down below, I saw India. I felt relieved, happy at last. It felt right, as if I was nearer to Katherine now, as if she was proud of me for all my crazy stupid acts.

I pressed the bell and thought of my excuses.

But no lies this time, remember! I was not going to fake it anymore. Life would be what it really was, nothing artificial, nothing different. Original and great, like Katherine Andrews.

Mr Anshuman Roy, my dad opened the door a good three minutes later.

"Aakash!" he gaped at me.

I stood there, out of words.

"I didn't think you would." My dad paused, we are both bad at reunions and sentimental situations, " I saw the news and I was worried ... I ..."

"I am sorry, dad, for not being here all these years, for breaking your trust."

Dad looked at me, I couldn't tell what he was thinking, the man had always been a mystery.

"I made some rice and sabzi. You wanna taste it?", he asked.

"When did you start cooking?" I laughed.

"Well, son, you and I have a lot of catching up to do."

LIE 099

The happiness they talk about ...

I heard a lot from the lawyers in the next couple of weeks but I paid no heed. I, in fact, ended up missing my court trials and receiving law suits and notices. I paid all the dues, I withdrew my complaints that I had filed against Karl Henrick and I gave up my entire career to start a new one.

I got a call from Karl Henrick the evening I withdrew my case.

"You win Karl. Keep your company, Tcube is your dream." I smiled.

"Tell me how you did it, Aakash? How did you get over your ambitions like that? Isn't that suicide?", Karl sounded frustrated rather than glad.

"And here, I thought nobody liked their asses whipped!" I mocked.

"It's not about me, Aakash. I know you made that entire model, Aakash." Karl said over the phone, "You had the full authority to sue me and you would have won all your claims if you had shown up today."

"Hey, You keep forgetting Robbie, Karl." I reminded him although he knew better, "And, I didn't want your company or your money or my claims anymore Karl. It was not part of my dream Karl."

"Who are you kidding, Aakash? You were the most enthusiastic and motivated guy I have had over in my office. And, you tell me this was not your dream. You are broke now Aakash."

"Well, you know what, call me crazy, but I am happy now. Yes, I loved coding and developing MindMark, Karl, but my reasons for the love was flawed. I wanted the wrong things. Fame, pot full of money, all that could provide me assurance and a nice car, not happiness."

Karl was silent on the other side, he knew exactly what I meant.

"So ... what now?" Karl said, admitting defeat at last.

"Well, for starters, I have yet to finish my bachelor's degree, I am a drop out remember." I eyed the readmission forms of MIT, lying at my table, "And then, yes ... Songs. I have to record an album, Karl."

"What?", Karl chuckled, "You sing, Aakash?"

"Funny story." I giggled back, " I once got to the finale of a rock show. I'm a bang-on lyricist dude."

"Well, all the best with that Aakash and you know what, I have a surprise for you. Will notify you at the earliest." Karl's voice was one of utmost sincerity, "I hope you get all you really want, Aakash. You kinda deserve it."

I opened my wallet and look at a faded photo of Katherine.

Not everything I want. I can't get that anymore.

*"*Well, then, I will catch you later, I guess.*"* Karl broke my train of thoughts.

"Yeah, will do."

"And listen, two years from now, when you're done with your degree and that album of yours. Give me a call if you want your job back. Tcube is always yours and I apologise for even considering it without you."

"Thanks Karl. I appreciate it." I hung up.

Three days later, I received a cheque of 16 million dollars.

It blew my mind off.

"How the hell" I opened the envelope that was attached with the cheque.

"Best regards from Karl Henrick. I sold what was rightfully yours. Your one-third of the company's share. Here's the selling price. Hope you make the best use of it. Do let me know when you will be back at Tcube to repay this loss."

✳ ✳ ✳

LIE 100

The lost ways ...

I drove through Darjeeling after almost a decade. It was fantastic at this time of the year. The winter vacations were on, and I had been having a gala time back home with dad, but every once in a while, I enjoyed this solitude, this momentary break from the redundant routine of life.

I drove through the winds in my convertible, the money from my shares had let me afford that. It felt comforting, the clouds, the chilly winter wind and the thin beautiful snaky lanes of Darjeeling.

I didn't feel sad anymore. That ship had sailed long ago. Of course, Katherine still woke me up on some nights, and made me miss her terribly, but it was okay. I had learnt to keep my peace with the truth.

I saw groups of small Nepali children walk back from school, I heard them hum folk songs and it was majestic. The small lit up shops on the sides of the road, the girls selling tea at corners, the massive tea gardens and the moist wet rocks, it all made me whimsical, cheered my mood. I felt free, part of this divine Universe, without a plan but travelling along, going with the flow, distinct and all the same.

There had been a landslide on the road, so I took a u-turn and from flesh memory, I drove off through a short cut through the dense woods of the hill station.

The muddy road got thinner by the distance and I ended up taking an unknown left. I drove another mile and then crossed a zigzag path filed with shrubs and leading me deeper into the forest.

I switched on my headlights to manoeuvre properly through the clumsy road, and then I entered the envelope of cloud out of the blue. I braked and my car skidded to a stop.

A bit panicked and wary, I wait for the mist to clear.

I was at a square. As the vision cleared, I recognised the place in an instant.

Four abandoned roads, meeting at a small dried up fountain, the white marble structure and the statue of Cupid over it, the arrow in his hand pointed upwards at the heavens. Love square ...

I was amazed. I was back at the place where I had once fallen in love with Katie Thomas.

I walked towards the structure and then I stopped as another sight petrified me. A girl in white stands there, beside the fountain, her eyes on me as she too realised with boundless surprise, the coincidence.

"True lovers, eh?" I smiled at Katie Thomas.

"Aakash." She had her hands over her mouth, "I can't believe it, after all this while." "We meet again", I walked over to her and then hugged her.

It felt warm, so familiar, as her arms wrapped around me, my love at first sight story.

"I have missed you, Aakash." Katie Thomas whispered, "In fact I have been waiting all these years for you. Never thought we'd meet here finally, at Love square."

"Neither did I." I smiled at her.

"So, how have you been?" I asked her as we strolled through the meadow.

"Well, I am great as a matter of fact, Aakash. I am a painter now." She looked at me with a vibrant smile.

"That is so awesome!" I congratulated her, "When will you show me your paintings?"

"I am having an exhibition here at the Central Hall on Friday. Be there at 6."

"Wow! Definitely. I'll be there."

"And, what about you, Aakash? Read about you a lot in the newspapers. Your amazing tale of being a millionaire, then those controversies and that edition on why you missed the show."

"Whoa! They even wrote an article on that?" I felt surprised.

"Oh, they did. I however, I think it was a bag full of lies in there. You must have messed it all up and fled the scene." she mocked.

"Haha!! True that." We sat at an old bench as I looked at her closely. She still looked so damn gorgeous, so pretty, it quickend my heartbeats. I realised how I still had feelings for Katie Thomas.

As if Katie sensed my feelings, she leaned in closer and put her head over my shoulder, "Oh, why did you leave me like that, Aakash? When I needed you the most, you went without even a good bye."

"I ... I am sorry, Katie", I stroked her hair, "I was blinded by so many things. I had lost it then. Took me a while to get my head straight, Katie."

"I understand." Katie rested quietly on my shoulder.

"So ...", I raised the subject finally, "Did Deb call you ever again?"

"Well, funny story." Katie faced me now, as she said, a bit anxiously, "He actually did, after almost three years now. He called me a month ago, you know, a few days before that entire scene you created at CitiBlitz."

I chuckled, "So, what did he say?" I recalled the punch and I realised why Deb had called.

"He confessed his love to me, Aakash. He wanted to get back together." Katie looked at me, eyeing my reaction.

"That is great." I kinda felt a lump in my throat, but I knew this was the right thing to say.

"I haven't accepted the proposal yet, Aakash." Katie kept looking at me, "We have been talking, but I don't know why, I have been waiting for something to happen."

"And, what is that?" I asked her curiously.

She leaned and kissed me tenderly. I kissed her back and it felt romantic, perfect. But I let go almost immediately.

She noticed my haste and said, "I think I have been waiting for you, Aakash. I know you love me."

I looked at Katie, and it all came flooding back. The first time I had seen her in Delhi, the times we had spent exploring Darjeeling, every time she hugged me, my love for her.

I was about to say yes. About to accept it that my heart had always loved two people. Katherine and Katie, at the same time. Katherine was my best friend, a piece of my soul, while Katie was my first love, innocent and unblemished by time.

It is then, that I remembered the last lie.

"Aakash, say something." She encouraged me. "Tell me you love me, and I'll forget Deb forever."

I looked at Katie's beautiful face, her big innocent eyes and everything that I loved most dearly in the world and then I lie "I don't love you, Katie."

★★★

LIE 101

I was there at Katherine's funeral. In another moment, they would lift the coffin and my life would never be the same.

Of the one hundred and one lies that shaped my life, this was the one that changed it. Reformed me.

There was no universal truth. We all had our objective realities and it changed from our own perspectives, I believed.

The world and its people were always part of the plan, I didn't grow up trusting them, I considered them only when my purposes had to be served. I disbelieved them, always ended up lying to them and as Katherine lay there, dead, I knew the monster in me would accompany me till death parted us. She was my last shot at getting to be someone else, a better me.

There was no hope, no more light, I knew my best friend had abandoned me and I had nothing to do with this reality anymore. Katherine died hating me. In the last moments of her life, she did want to talk to me, but I knew there was no love there. Only sadness. Disappointment. Loving a monster like me was impossible and I knew, this was how I would always be. A demon. There was no God and even if He was watching this circus, he had already decided my fate.

I, Aakash Roy, was headed for hell.

They lifted the coffin. My eyes looked at her for the last time. Katherine Andrews, she lay silent, lifeless, her eyes closed, her wavy hair, tied in a knot, and then, my eyes moved onto her neck.

It sparkled there, carefree and iridescent, the pendent that my mother had once given me to gift my wife.

She wore it, as she was in her death.

Katherine's last wish was to be with me.

She didn't hate me, like she kept on saying on her death bed. She kept on lying to herself.

She lied, when she said that she hated me. She lied, when she refused to take the pendent. As I saw that pendent there, safe on her neck, I realised it belonged there, as if mom always knew I was meant to love Katherine. I saw my mom looking at me.

So, was it really possible?

Was love so strong a feeling that it could break any person, no matter how tough he would try himself to be?

I couldn't stand it, I needed to get out of here. I need some black coffee, I felt dizzy. I needed it now.

I remembered my mother, her smiling face when she had left me, her last gift was that pendent. She had once asked me to end my story on a happy note. Was she asking me to find that end? I didn't believe in epiphanies and angels, but there the pendent was, and there lay Katherine, falsifying both my disbeliefs.

That day, when Katherine died, when I realised that the rest of my life could be wasted away living in this same old bubble world of fame and money and desperation, my journey began.

Those 40 days that followed, my search for happiness, was all because of her, Katie's last lie that I caught.

She loved me, I could have had a happy life just being there for her. But I missed on it.

What was my redemption? The day Katherine died, was the day I gave it all up, all my lies for all those wrong reasons.

*** *** ***

I looked at Katie Thomas now. She had tears in her eyes.

"I don't love you, Katie. Go back to Deb."

She nodded, and then, like everyone close to me, she left too.

Today, I lost both the persons I loved, I lost them because of my own wrong decisions.

Katherine's death had killed me from within, but this one felt right somewhere. I had to let Katie go.

I was confused … Why did it feel right when it should ache, should make me sad and break my heart? Was this truth … was this how it feels when you chose the greater good …

I started the ignition, and drove away, Katie in my rear view mirror and the endless roads in my eyes.

★★★

www.ingramcontent.com/pod-product-compliance
Lightning Source LLC
Chambersburg PA
CBHW070542030726
47505CB00001B/127